The Missing Girl

Kerry McGinnis was born in Adelaide and at the age of twelve took up a life of droving with her father and four siblings. The family travelled extensively across the Northern Territory and Queensland before settling on a station in the Gulf Country.

Kerry has worked as a shepherd, droving hand, gardener and stock-camp and station cook on the family property, Bowthorn, north-west of Mount Isa. She is the author of two volumes of memoir, *Pieces of Blue* and *Heart Country*, and the bestselling novels *The Waddi Tree*, *Wildhorse Creek*, *Mallee Sky*, *Tracking North*, *Out of Alice*, *Secrets of the Springs*, *The Heartwood Hotel*, *The Roadhouse* and *Croc Country*. Kerry now lives in Bundaberg.

Also by the author

Pieces of Blue

Heart Country

The Waddi Tree

Wildhorse Creek

Mallee Sky

Tracking North

Out of Alice

Secrets of the Springs

The Heartwood Hotel

The Roadhouse

Croc Country

KERRY McGINNIS

The Missing Girl

MICHAEL JOSEPH
an imprint of
PENGUIN BOOKS

MICHAEL JOSEPH

UK | USA | Canada | Ireland | Australia
India | New Zealand | South Africa | China

Michael Joseph is part of the Penguin Random House group of companies
whose addresses can be found at global.penguinrandomhouse.com.

First published by Michael Joseph, 2021

Cover photography: field and sky © Drunaa/Trevillion Images;
house by Walter Bibikow/Alamy; birds by Stepan Chour/Shutterstock
Cover design by Louisa Maggio © Penguin Random House Australia Pty Ltd
Typeset in 12/18 pt Sabon by Midland Typesetters, Australia

Printed and bound in Australia by Griffin Press, part of Ovato, an accredited
ISO AS/NZS 14001 Environmental Management Systems printer

A catalogue record for this
book is available from the
National Library of Australia

ISBN 978 1 76104 063 4

penguin.com.au

For Jenny, who is my BF (biggest fan), and Gordon, who told me about writing with light. Love you both.

Chapter One

Nineteen-ninety, I reflected, was not turning out to be the best of years for me. It was only the fifteenth of January and already I had lost my job, and my partner, Phillip, who was a photo-journalist, had taken a posting overseas – just a temporary thing, he'd said. But that depended on the nature of the current emergency, in this case an earthquake and tribal fighting in New Guinea. And now this.

I glared at the phone. If the call had come a week earlier I could truthfully have claimed to be unable to leave Hahndorf. Jobs didn't grow on trees and mine was vital to the business. Or so I had believed until two days ago when my boss, Gwen Parfell, told me we were closing our doors.

'It's over, Meg. We gave it our best shot but I'm skint. Another week and I won't be able to manage the rent, never mind your wages.' She had pushed a hand through her coarse, bouffant hair and then pinched tiredly at the bridge of her nose. 'It's no good flogging a dead horse. The owners will have to take their stock back and any I've been mad enough to buy outright I'll have to try selling at the markets.'

It had been a shock, though, if I was honest, not totally unexpected. The Christmas crowds hadn't spent up as much as they normally did but I'd still thought we might hang on and make it through. We'd had slow patches before, after all. 'What will you do?' she had asked when I'd stopped protesting. I'd shrugged, for I was fond of her and didn't wish to add to her worries.

'Oh, something will turn up, I'm sure. I'm sorry, Gwen, truly. If there were more tourists . . .'

She'd grinned then without mirth, a stocky, fortyish figure with shrewd eyes and unconvincingly blonde hair framing a square-jawed face. 'Yeah, or if I'd gone in for kitchenware or something else practical rather than arty stuff. It's something the town's already got too much of.'

I couldn't deny it. Hahndorf, with its arts and crafts, little boutiques and expensive cafes, lived off the tourists. Weekenders from Adelaide flocked to the picturesque old German town for the wine and cuisine and its overpriced lodgings in quaint old stone buildings with their history of hardworking German forebears. It was an expensive place to live and I had a moment's panic at the thought of being jobless there.

Gwen must have seen it for she patted my hand where it lay on the counter. 'You'll find something, sweetie. I'll write you the best reference. Every business in town'll be fighting for you.'

'Well, thanks.' I had forced a smile but reflected now that it made no difference: regardless of prospective employers queuing in the wings, and as little as I wanted to, I knew I'd have to answer the summons I'd had. Phillip's absence helped in a skewed sort of way because now I truly had nothing to stay for. Of course, his job often took him from me; he was always jetting off to strange places, to document uprisings and famines and refugee camps and natural disasters. He had won prizes and acclamation for his work, but a stranger looking at his rangy form, with its big feet and long sun-bleached locks gathered into a careless pigtail at his nape, would never guess that his rough exterior held the soul of a sensitive artist.

His camera had captured everything from African elephants to Antarctic glaciers calving into an ocean of frigid blue, but his best work, he said, dealt with portraits, and of all those he had taken he most liked the one of me that he'd framed above the fireplace in our living room. I walked across to stare at it now. It had never been a favourite of mine, possibly because I believed it revealed too much of me. It had been taken without my knowledge even though it was a full-face shot, for Phillip was always messing about with his camera.

'Elf,' he had said, which was his name for me – vastly preferable to the 'Midget' and 'Shortstuff' that I had suffered through my school years – 'when you look like that you make me want to cry.' He had wrapped his arms around me then and held me close, kissing my hair. 'If I could take that look away . . . It breaks my heart. It's a wonderful pic. My best. And I wish it wasn't so, because your soul is sad, my love, and when I caught you unaware like that, it showed.'

I didn't know about my soul, I thought, as I studied the likeness I saw every day in the mirror. Short fair hair in a feathery cut about an average-looking face with a straight nose, a small pointed chin and green eyes. My mother's sullen eyes, I'd been told. My ears were small, but then I was small all over – I barely came to Phillip's armpit – and the tips of my ears were slightly pointed, which made his sobriquet the more fitting. I wasn't smiling and my expression in repose looked . . . vulnerable, I decided, perhaps a little lost. Which was quite ridiculous and probably just a trick of the light.

Impatiently I shook myself from introspection; artists had their fancies. I often couldn't tell why Phillip would choose one image over another when both looked identical to me, but I had no time to worry about it now. The nursing home, or at least Grandmother Chapman was waiting for my answer. I had not heard a word from her for years – at least nine – but she had plainly kept tabs on me. The phone was in Phillip's name, the house was his rental not mine, but the receptionist at the nursing home had still addressed me by name.

'Good morning. I'm calling from Woodfell House. Is that Margaret Morrisey?'

'Who? Oh, yes, speaking.' Nobody called me Margaret these days, and hearing it had momentarily thrown me.

'Ah, good. It's about your grandmother, Ms Morrisey. She wishes to see you. As soon as possible please. Could you manage tomorrow? I'm afraid she's not accustomed to waiting, but I expect you know that.'

I had goggled at the handpiece in disbelief. 'Look, what is this about? Who are you? And why are you calling? My grandmother and I haven't spoken since . . . You *are* talking about Ellie Chapman, I take it? Mrs Ellie Chapman?'

'Yes, indeed. I'm sorry. I didn't introduce myself.' She sounded flustered all at once, a condition my grandmother often inspired. 'I'm Susan Pickering, the manager at Woodfell, Ms Morrisey. We're a nursing home in Glenfield. I'm sorry,

I thought you would've known that. Anyway, your grandmother was admitted here straight from the hospital. She's had her name down with us for years – a good thing under the circumstances, because the doctors weren't going to let her go home, you see.'

Struggling to keep up with the torrent of information, I said baldly, 'What's wrong with her? Is she dying?'

'Oh, no, don't worry – nothing like that, but she *is* rather frail. She broke her hip, you see. She's been operated on and had it pinned, and had physio, all that. But there's no denying that it has knocked her about. She can no longer live all alone in that big place of hers, which is why she's settled in with us. And she needs to see you.'

I interrupted her. 'Why? We don't get on. If she's settled as you say, I don't see the need. She can hardly claim she's fond of me!'

My spurt of indignation was tactfully ignored. 'She *is* rather an autocrat,' the woman agreed. 'But she's old, Margaret – may I call you Margaret?' Her voice had softened; she was probably used to coaxing the unwilling, both patients and their relatives, I thought uncharitably, as she carried on her argument. 'I gather that her need is more for a factotum than anything to do with affection. She's using a wheelchair, you see. Well,' she added candidly, 'she's refusing the use of the walker. And whilst she's not dying at present, she's not immortal either. I have her down as being eighty-eight, and she needs a "younger pair of legs" was how she put it, to see to her affairs. I fancy she means her property, Hunters Reach.'

'Surely she has a solicitor if she's thinking of selling up?' I protested weakly. Already I could see how this would end, and I damned my own weak nature. Why couldn't I be as ruthless as the old woman was? *She* had never had any problem ignoring duties she considered tiresome.

'Apparently she feels it's more of a family matter. Which is why she's asked for you. So I can tell her you'll come?' Susan Pickering asked hopefully.

'I don't know. I'll think about it,' I replied with a last attempt at defiance. And now, two days later, everything had conspired against me to make it possible. Really there was no choice. I would have to go.

To make matters worse, there weren't even many physical tasks to give me an excuse to put it off. Phillip paid the rent and the utilities, the bank collecting them automatically from his account each month. The small garden was really a patio of large pots, each on a timed dripper system, and we had no pets. I informed the neighbour that the house would be empty for the next week – surely whatever the old woman wanted, it wouldn't take any longer than that – packed my bag, told Gwen what was happening, filled up the little red runabout I drove and was ready to leave. Phillip was probably beyond reach but I contacted his editor with a message, which he promised to forward the moment Phillip got back in touch with the office. And that was everything. Standing next to the carport I took a last look around and sighed. *The sooner you start, the sooner it's over.* It wasn't exactly inspirational but the truth of the maxim had served me often before. Best just get on with it then.

I drove east out of Hahndorf to Nairne, turning north next to find Lobethal and later the little township of Mt Pleasant, where I stopped for a coffee at a bakery-cum-cafe. The prices were far more reasonable than Hahndorf's and I indulged in a pastie that would do for my lunch. I had driven slowly, chewing over the cud of bitterness that was my past dealings with my grandmother.

Susan Pickering had called her autocratic, which she certainly was, accustomed to instant obedience in those around her, and to having her own way in everything. A thoroughly nasty old woman. She had made a misery of my childhood once I was left in her care and had lost no opportunity to inform me that I was an encumbrance in her life, an unwanted burden. And this despite the fact that her first action after the double funeral of my parents had been to thrust me into a city boarding school, which meant that I only returned to Glenfield for the holidays anyway.

I loitered along half remembered roads, past paddocks of black-faced sheep and chunky black cattle, and still reached the outskirts of Glenfield before dark. It was a large, old country town with solid red-brick municipal buildings: columns on the public library, fancy stone facades on the two large banks and a flight of grandiose steps leading up to the courthouse entrance. There was a school of arts, as well as a quite well-known gallery in the town, a long-established grammar school and an elaborate cenotaph with reams of inscribed names of the fallen guarded by the bronze soldier. A Morrisey was there for the first world war and two more for the second. My father hadn't gone to war. He'd been the youngest of the brothers by some ten years and even if he'd been older, considering his brothers' sacrifice and as the only remaining son of a farmer, he would probably have been granted exemption anyway.

But not from death, for in his early thirties he and my mother had died in a light plane crash on one of their frequent flying trips.

Just God's mercy, everyone said, that I hadn't been with them in the plane. But then I never was. It had puzzled me for years that they had ever bothered having me; neither had space nor time for anyone but each other, and they should surely have shared that knowledge beforehand and remained childless. Their mutual infatuation, bordering almost on obsession, was all consuming. It was obvious, even to the child I had been, that each one's presence somehow completed the other, and that neither had the emotional room, nor felt the need, for anyone else. They had neither use nor time for friends; each was the other's best mate. My most excoriating memory of childhood was made on the day when I realised just how little I mattered to them.

We had been on one of our infrequent visits to Hunters Reach and they had been sitting in the garden in the summerhouse where we sometimes ate a picnic lunch. I, a nine-year-old, had come tearing up to them, bursting with excitement over some discovery I wished to share. 'Mum, Dad!' I had yelled, beaming with delight and no doubt red-faced from my run. And as I came to a stop with my current treasure held out for inspection, their heads had turned my way and I had seen the identical expression of suppressed annoyance on both faces.

'Margaret, why must you always interrupt?' my mother demanded. 'Run along. Can't you see we're busy?'

It wasn't the first time, just the occasion on which the message had finally sunk in, for the years had been littered with similar incidents. 'Not now!' 'Go away, Margaret.' 'Later.

Your father and I are talking.' But that day it had all coalesced in my understanding and I had seen that I was nothing but a nuisance to them. A tiresome duty arising from a decision not properly thought through in the first place.

The sickening wave of humiliation came back to me again, like an echo. I saw my childish self turning away, heated with shame and confusion at my blunder, my heart squeezing with a pain that I couldn't ease. And a knowledge I was never able to forget.

But that was old news, done and dusted, I told myself, coming back to the present, to the wide traffic-filled streets and colourful shopfronts. I had returned to the place I had escaped from nine years before and now I needed somewhere to stay the night. Cruising slowly down the main street, I tried to remember which turn led directly to the suburb of Burnside. That was where I would find Rose Avenue (named for the town's founder, not the flower), which had clustered along its length half-a-dozen motels and B&Bs. They couldn't all have gone out of business since my departure. I would find the cheapest (after all, I was no longer employed) and tomorrow would be soon enough to front my formidable grandmother.

Chapter Two

Woodfell House was set on a wooded and lawned block on a side street adjacent to a postbox and a corner shop. There was a bus stop too – handy, I thought, for those residents who had given up driving. It was a large establishment even before counting the row of duplexes, each with its own little garden, where I assumed the more independent residents lived. I headed for the main entrance to find Reception, from where I was immediately directed to Ms Pickering's office.

The receptionist had been young but the manager wasn't. The odd glint of grey showed in Susan Pickering's hair, and the careful make-up couldn't conceal the fine lines about her eyes. She had glossy blood-red nails and wore heels that clacked against the tiles as she came around her desk to shake my hand.

'Ms Morrisey. So good to see you. Your grandmother was getting rather impatient, I'm afraid.'

'If she knew where I lived then she must know it's a day's drive to here,' I said firmly. 'Besides, I do have a life. I couldn't just drop everything and come.'

'Yes, of course I realise that. But the elderly . . .'

'Her age has nothing to do with her understanding. She was exactly the same when I was a child. If it affected her, it had to be done yesterday.'

'Well.' She gave a weak smile. 'I'm sure you'll know how best to handle her. I'm afraid she's a little unpopular with the staff, but . . .'

I laughed without mirth. 'Don't expect that to improve any time soon. Well, I'm here. I suppose I had better get it over with. Where is she?'

She patted absently at the name tag on its lanyard around her neck and, rising, gestured at the door. 'Come. It's just along here.'

My grandmother had a corner room, its closed door bearing a small blackboard on which somebody had written *Eleanor Chapman* in a careful hand and ornamented it with chalked flowers. She would hate that, I thought. Too twee for words. Susan knocked, and immediately opened the door, saying brightly, 'Here is your granddaughter come to see you, Mrs Chapman,' then left me standing there while sharply whisking herself off.

'What is the use of knocking if you intend to barge in without waiting for permission?' my grandmother demanded, eyeing her retreating back. 'Well, don't just stand there, girl. Get over here where I can see you.'

'Grandmother.' I made no effort to approach the short, upright form seated in a wheelchair. Her hair was iron grey, her eyes grey gimlets in the stern lines of her face with its thin, compressed lips. I couldn't remember ever receiving a hug, much less a kiss from her, even when I was little. She was nobody's favourite nanna, not that she had any other grandchildren. I had never met the girl who would have been my aunt, her second daughter who had died young from some illness – polio perhaps? – and I couldn't remember ever hearing the details of it. Conversation with my grandmother had consisted of a stream of either orders or criticism, to be obeyed or accepted without rebuttal.

Her eyes raked over me, apparently finding nothing to please, for she sniffed, saying, 'You took your time getting here, miss. It's a week since I got that woman to phone.'

'It's four days,' I corrected, 'and I might have had a job at the time, you know. You can't just up and leave. I'm here now, so what did you want, Grandmother? You're looking well, considering.' She was a little worn around the edges, I thought, thinner than I remembered, and perhaps her hair, which she had cut short, as so many older women did, was sparser, but the broad brow, rat-trap mouth and high-bridged autocratic nose remained unchanged. Standing she would have been of medium height, with erect shoulders (no stooping or dowager's hump for her) and cold grey eyes.

'I'm well enough but this wretched leg stops me getting about. Besides, I'm tired of coping alone. What is the sense of owning a care institution if you don't make use of it?'

I gaped at her. The Chapmans had always had money but I'd had no idea about this. 'You *own* Woodfell?'

'I'm a major shareholder. Which is beside the point. And,' she snapped, turning my words back on me as she had always been able to, 'I thought you'd have been better taught than to ask personal questions about such things. Money is a vulgar topic for a young girl. You can sit down. You said you might have had a job – does that mean you're no longer employed?'

I sat on the cane-backed visitor's chair she had indicated and glanced around the room. It was light and airy looking, with windows in both outer walls, floral print curtains that complemented the carpet, bedspread and armchair, a rather nice little side table with turned legs that I recognised, holding knick-knacks and a framed photo of my parents, a built-in wardrobe, a wall-mounted television, and a closed door, presumably hiding the ensuite.

'Very nice'—I spoke without looking at her—'and as it happens, no, I'm not. The business folded so I'm afraid my spare time is limited. I'll need to find something else ASAP.'

'Don't use those ridiculous expressions,' she snapped. 'Who's this man you're living with? And why isn't he here with you now? I'm the only family you've got. Doesn't he want to meet me?' Nastily she added, 'I'm worth something after all, or isn't he aware of that?'

'Phillip's overseas.' I gritted my teeth. She was impossible! 'Not that my relationships are any of your business, Grandmother. I'm a grown woman. And no, I shouldn't think he would want to meet you.'

'You're living in sin, like some disgraceful slut lacking all morals. In my day—'

'It's nineteen-ninety, Grandmother, not nineteen-twenty, for heaven's sake!' I took a calming breath, quailing a little at my temerity, then tried for a gentler tone. 'Look, what was it you wanted? How can I help?'

'By moving into Hunters Reach,' she said promptly. 'I need the house sorted and packed, and someone to manage the garden. I won't have strangers pawing over my things and helping themselves. And the garden needs keeping up. It'll add to the value of the property, but not if it's a jungle of weeds and neglect.'

'You're selling the Reach?' It was the sensible – the only – solution, really, given her present circumstances, but I was still taken aback to hear the words. But what need had she now for a rambling old farmstead? It must have been a burden to her at her age even before the fall that broke her hip. As for the huge garden . . . 'Don't you have someone for the lawns and pruning and stuff?' I asked.

'A garden needs more than that.' She withered me with a look. 'It needs care, a daily eye on it. You'll live there until the place is sold, keep it running, and look after Claude – he'll be missing me and he needs attention.'

'Who's Claude?' In vain I tried to stem the battering flow of words but she just carried on.

'My cat, of course. It might take a week or two to sell, or a couple of months, or even longer, so you'll be gainfully employed, miss. I'll arrange a real estate agent to come and list the place once I know what the market's like. Then we'll see. He might advise waiting.' She must have sensed my refusal coming for she cut me off before I could speak. 'You're out of a job you said, so you've nothing better to do, Margaret.'

'Except finding another one. I need to work, Grandmother. At the risk of sounding vulgar,' I added, 'I need the money. You can hire somebody else to do it.'

'I'm hiring you, Margaret. Of course I intend to pay you. Just see that you're worth it. I've already arranged it with Cabot. Go and see him in his office when you leave here.'

'Cabot?'

'Cabot and Hawley, my solicitors,' she said impatiently. 'They're in the main street. Run along now. Buy yourself some food too, there won't be anything in the house. And I expect you to phone me with regular reports on the garden and Claude's health, mind. He's not a young cat, and he'll have been pining since I left. One of the neighbours has been putting food out on the verandah for him. Some dried rubbish, I expect. See he gets the proper tinned meals. And treats. He likes his treats.'

She settled back in her chair, the flinty gaze behind her spectacles daring me to object. I think I might have plucked up courage enough to do so had I not glimpsed the way her knuckles whitened as she gripped the arm rest. A rush of inconvenient compassion filled me then. She was afraid, not nearly as certain of me as she made out. She was old and frail and I was all the family she had. And much as she would deplore me having the run of her home and belongings, I was of her blood and thus a better bet than any hired stranger.

I sighed, seeing that I couldn't refuse. 'Very well. I'll sort and pack, get the place ready for sale, but I'm not staying. I'll give you two weeks. If it hasn't sold in that time you'll have to get a caretaker in.'

She glared at me over the top of her glasses. 'Don't tell me what to do. I get enough of that here. Run along.' She pressed the red call button on the wall, then as I rose obediently, stabbed at it again. 'Find somebody on your way out. Tell them I'm waiting for my tea.'

I found a nurse helping an elderly man transfer from his stick to the handrail along the corridor and passed Grandmother's message on, adding, 'I'm sorry, she's never learned to wait.'

The nurse rolled her eyes, patted her patient's hand and said loudly, 'There you go, Mr Lawson. Carefully does it now.' And to me, 'Right, I'd best fetch it then. She could always come down to the dining room; in fact she's supposed to. Her chair is motorised.'

'I think she's finding it hard, being here,' I said apologetically. 'She's used to having things her way. I'm sorry she's a trial to you all.'

'Not your fault, love. Old age sorts everybody out.'

Except that Ellie Chapman wasn't one whit different now to how she'd ever been – but it seemed best not to say so. I escaped into the sunshine and drove off to buy supplies and track down the solicitor who, presumably, also held the keys to Hunters Reach.

When I was a child, and even as little as nine years ago, the farmhouse had been quite a distance from town. One approached it along a stretch of gravel road and then a long, eucalypt-lined drive up to the gates of the house. It was set in an acre and a half of garden that had once been the show place of the district. Now, I discovered, the approach road had been widened and bituminised, which meant the road makers had done away with the trees save for a particular one I had always loved, a lone old red gum near the gates that stood further back in the paddock.

Many of those same paddocks that had once grown crops or held grazing stock had, I saw, been sectioned off from what had been the original Chapman holdings into acreage for hobby farms or plantations. I saw rugged horses and little training areas set up with jumps, and once a paddock of alpacas, and fancified gates hung with bells and other whimsy.

But what had been the neighbouring Robertses' property still seemed intact, though, I assumed, now under different ownership. Behind it, on Forestry land, a plantation of young blue gums shadowed the last three kilometres of the road, their leaves gleaming in the early sunlight.

Glenfield was plainly on the march, but then Hunters Reach had shrunk too. I didn't know how much of my grandfather's land had been leased out, or even if any of it still remained in my grandmother's hands. It was unlikely. Neither of my grandparents had been hands-on farmers. They had always employed a farm manager but before my grandfather's death, back when I was very young, he had already diversified into real estate. During my primary school years, playground rumour had it that my family owned half of Glenfield, so Grandmother's claim to have a stake in Woodfell shouldn't really have been that surprising.

The eucalypts had ended in a pair of stone pillars with a set of closed wrought-iron gates, presently holding in – for that, I was dismayed to see, was the impression they now gave – a jungle of growth. I had to put my shoulder to one of them to force it back against the tangle of hedge impeding its movement. It had been quite a while, I thought, since anyone had pruned, or done anything really, in the garden, at least in the bit of it I could see. It would have made an impressive park with its lawns and paths and flowerbeds, its multitude of shrubs, and its massive shade trees. There was a pool and fountain, a latticed summerhouse, a rose garden and a wishing well, a pergola that I remembered as being covered in wisteria, and at the back of it all a tennis court. All of which presumably still existed somewhere under the present Amazonian growth.

I drove into the grounds, pausing to drag the gates shut behind me, and followed the gravelled drive (now sprouting weeds) along to the front of the big old stone farmhouse with its multiple chimneys, balustraded verandah supported by latticework, and the two huge glazed urns at the foot of the shallow steps. The petunias that had customarily bloomed in them were dead, their dried brown skeletons adding to the general air of neglect of what had once been a beautiful garden.

I got out of the car, fished in my bag for the keys obtained from Cabot and, taking a deep breath, trod up the low steps to cross the faded verandah floor of red oxided concrete and open the front door. It was a big, old-fashioned one, solid timber with glass insets each featuring a stylised rose. Everything about the building was oversized. My grandparents had seemingly built for a large family but had only ever produced the two girls – my mother and her sister who had died.

The cold hit me first. It had always been a cold house; the stone I supposed, and the trees, all planted at the time the place was built. Even on a hot day like today the moment of crossing the threshold had one's skin tightening in response to the drop in temperature. For an instant I was tempted to flee both the sudden chill and the unhappy memories the house contained, but the visit to Cabot had provided more than the key. I was being paid, handsomely – which I had not expected – and would live rent free, with power and phone provided. That was no small consideration. I could stick it out for a week or two, or at least until Phillip returned. And I was no longer a child. It was more than time that my unfortunate past was put behind me once and for all. There must be hundreds, if not thousands, of people in the population who had suffered a far worse childhood than mine without letting it rule their lives.

'Get a grip, Meg,' I muttered, then nearly died as a streak of grey launched itself past me, getting in a good swipe at my bare leg as it shot by. 'Dear God!' Hyperventilating, I clutched at my heart, staring stupidly down at my bloodied shin.

'Claude, you rat!' But the cat had vanished into the garden and my blood was heading inexorably for the (no doubt expensive) rug upon which I stood. Swearing, I fished for a tissue. 'You've just done yourself out of treats, you murderous feline,' I yelled. 'Probably for as long as I'm here.' What, I wondered, would Grandmother do about him when the place was sold? If pets were permitted there, he'd already be at Woodfell.

Shelving the thought, my leg smarting, I continued on through the house, opening curtains and windows as I went. There were five bedrooms in the back but I only visited the one I had used as an unwilling young guest. Nothing had changed there – not the dark, gloomy closet that reared in the corner, the faded duvet on the bed or the screened fireplace where, on stormy nights as I huddled in fear beneath the covers, the wind had moaned and threatened in the chimney.

There were two bathrooms. One, still holding an old claw-footed bath with a step up into it and a frieze of painted tiles depicting pomegranates and pears around the wall, opened off a corridor, with a separate toilet that had the cistern at ceiling height and a metal chain that ended in a ceramic knob with which to flush it. The second bathroom had been modernised to the extent that it had a shower sans cubicle, and grab rails on the tiled walls. Grandmother's concession to increasing age, perhaps?

The small room known as 'Grandfather's office' was next, discouragingly full of filing cases and boxes and a large wooden trunk. I sighed, imagining the work entailed in sorting decades of paperwork. The kitchen hadn't changed: a sturdily furnished workplace with a slow combustion stove cheek by jowl with a four-burner gas one, a sink deep enough to drown a toddler in and a long wooden work table scrubbed white over the years by sandsoap and elbow grease. Cabinets and cupboards filled in the wall space, and even the hook behind the door where Mrs Roberts, one-time neighbour and occasional cook to the Chapmans, had hung her pinny – ''Cause you pin it on, pet, and get to work,' she'd said when I'd asked why it wasn't called an apron – was still there.

The place was a time warp. I found the kettle and lit the gas, then carried on through the dining room with its elegant sideboard and beautiful polished table. It had brass-handled drawers down its sides and a leaf to extend it – a piece of magic that had fascinated me as a child. There was a snug with cosy armchairs and a broad fireplace for winter evenings, and a formal lounge with a chandelier and a piano, shrouded in a cover of dusty crimson that matched the tasselled window drapes. As a child I had seldom been allowed in this room – unsurprising, I thought now, clocking the delicate figurines and the pair of tall, almost translucent vases on the mantel above the fireplace.

A large cobweb hung from the painting immediately above them and dust motes danced in the single beam of sunlight that had penetrated the not-quite-closed drapes. If it was to go on the market, the whole place needed a good clean. I ran my finger along the mantelpiece and grimaced. I would be earning my handsome wage. I hoped there was a vacuum cleaner. I had vague memories of a carpet sweeper and a copper in the laundry, and sighed dolefully just as the kettle shrilled. Well, tea always helped. And I'd bought a packet of chocolate biscuits, still in the car with the rest of my shopping. Perhaps I should have picked up a second one, I thought as I went back outside to bring in the food.

Chapter Three

I spent the following day settling in, touring the property and sorting out the tasks that lay ahead of me.

The garden presented the biggest problem. Grandmother couldn't have been absent from the place for much more than four or five weeks, allowing for recovery time from the hip operation, physio and the move into Woodfell, so the neglect must have run back further than that. The lawns were in serious need of mowing, most of the beds, where the perennial and annual plantings were, cried out for water, and it had been a long time since anything was pruned. Weeds flourished everywhere. They choked the flowerbeds and spotted the gravel, growing wherever space offered. The leaves of the lemon tree were being distorted by some sort of disease, and wasps buzzed drunkenly over the fallen apricots and plums from the trees espaliered against the western wall. Where the kitchen garden had been years before the thistles and clover were knee high. It was a far cry from the ordered beauty I remembered as a child.

She would have to decide, I thought, whether she wanted me to pack up the house or do the garden. I certainly couldn't manage both, not to mention lacking the tools and experience for the latter. In Hahndorf I had grown a window box of pansies and a pot full of parsley on the kitchen windowsill, and that was it. Phillip had bought and planted the larger pots on the patio and installed the watering system there. Still, I thought, I could at least water while the matter was sorted out, so I turned on all the hoses I could find, and sat down to make a list of tasks and matters to raise with Grandmother.

Being asked to pack up was all very well, but shouldn't the more expensive figurines and china, not to mention the Venetian glassware, be valued first? And what about the truly magnificent dining table and sideboard? Surely she didn't intend them to end up in some seedy secondhand furniture place? They should go to an auction house along with the paintings and the heavy silver-plated cutlery stored in its own velvet-lined box.

I wondered when would be the best time to ring and, because Claude hadn't yet returned, settled cravenly on the early evening. In the meantime, I thought, carrying the tea things to the sink, I could make a start on the paperwork in the office. That didn't need boxing; the incinerator next to the garden shed would be its likely destination but I supposed I'd need to check it first. It wouldn't do to, for instance, destroy the deeds of the house. Then the chimes on the front door rang. Wondering who on earth it could be, I went to answer the summons.

It was a woman, small and round with a soft white halo of hair, carrying what looked like a dish of brown pellets. Despite my surprise and the years since we'd parted, I recognised her at once. 'Mrs Roberts!' My astonishment must have been plain. 'Grandmother said a neighbour was feeding the cat, but I never thought—'

'Meg, dear.' She beamed at me. 'I wondered whose car it was, and when I saw the opened windows . . . Where did you spring from?'

'Come in. Oh, never mind that.' I took the dish from her, dumped it on the nearest side table and hugged her. 'The monster's not home. He shot out the door as I came in. It's so good to see you! Come through to the kitchen. Would you like a cuppa? As to why I'm here, Grandmother called me. But what about you? I never imagined you still being here – I thought you and Ted sold up years ago. You said you were going to.'

'Ted died,' she said quietly, moving before me into the room and taking a seat at the table I had not long quitted. 'And by the time everything was settled I just didn't have the heart for the move. It just seemed too hard then – finding somewhere, shifting my whole life to another place . . . So I stayed. I still have the farm. It's leased to a man called Cox. He and his family live in the house and I've moved into the workers' cottage. I don't need much space now I'm alone.'

'Oh, God, Ted.' I touched her hand. 'I'm so sorry! I had no idea; Grandmother didn't say anything.'

'She mightn't have known, and if she had she wouldn't have cared.' There was a wryness to her tone. 'We were hardly friends.'

'No. So, how long now, since . . .?'

'Soon after you left. It was his heart; it just gave out.'

'I'm so sorry,' I repeated. 'He was a dear man. If I'd known, I'd have come back for the funeral, or at least sent flowers . . .'

'That's okay. The main thing is you got away from here.

From her. So how is life, Meg? Do you know, I think a cuppa and a good catch-up is what's called for. Or are you busy?'

'Not yet.' I made tea, brought out the diminished packet of chocolate biscuits, and told her about Hahndorf, the little art shop where I'd worked, and about Phillip.

Her kind eyes radiated sympathy and satisfaction at me as she listened, nodding wisely. She had always made time to listen to me as a child, probably because she saw that nobody else did. Her eyes were brown and twinkly, just as I had remembered, the sort of eyes I had once wished my grandmother had. 'So you've found someone to love you. I'm so glad, Meg. What's he like?'

'Phillip's a lovely man, Mrs Roberts. Very gentle, very talented too. Tall and thin.' I laughed. 'A regular yard of pump water, your Ted would've said. But he's very good at his job. He takes photographs. He's won all sorts of awards. He's overseas just now.' I sighed. 'His work does take him away a lot.'

'And what does Ellie think of him?'

'They haven't met and they won't if I have any say in it. She told me I was a disgraceful slut, living in sin, and as good as accused him of being after her money. Miserable old cow.'

'Don't you mind her.' She patted my hand. 'So what are you back for?'

I grimaced. 'She's given me a job. Hunters Reach is going on the market and my part consists of packing it up and looking after the garden. Which,' I added candidly, 'is in a real mess. Doesn't she have anyone coming in to do the lawns and pruning? She can't have been doing it herself at her age.'

'Oh, there is someone, or at least there's been a succession of them. You know how hard she is to please.' Mrs Roberts took a thoughtful sip of tea and crunched a biscuit. Ted mowed for her for a while once he started taking things easier on the farm, but there's been a score or so since him. The last one – Jacko, I think his name was – hurt his back, he said. Maybe he did and maybe he didn't, but he's not been back in months. And then she had the fall. At her age she should have had a live-in caretaker and housekeeper, Lord knows she can afford it! But you know, she's always liked her own company. She didn't mind others doing the work, as long as they went home afterwards.' She gave me a considering look. 'Don't you dare let her bully you into becoming her permanent carer. It'd be just like her to quit Woodfell now she's got you here, and come back.'

'No way! I'd be out that door faster even than Claude.' I raised my leg to show her the long livid scratch. 'That was his greeting to me as he shot by. I think Grandmother cares more for that wretched cat than anything else alive. I'm to give her regular reports on him – and the house clearing, of course.' I heaved a sigh and gestured at the room around me. 'There's just so much *stuff*. And I think quite a bit of it could be valuable too. Honestly, I don't know where to start. Well, finding a new gardener ought to take priority but how can I do that when I'm not authorised to agree wages for anyone?'

'She must have somebody who is. I'd try her solicitor. If she's putting the Reach up for sale, she won't be organising that herself. Or paying the bills here – the power and phone, for instance.'

'Yes, of course.' I had forgotten that Betty Roberts was a farmer's wife. She might have worked as Grandmother's cook years ago, but she and her husband had run a business too and that involved far more than planning and producing meals. 'You're right. I'll ring Mr Cabot. He had the keys to the house, so he'll likely be handling all her affairs, poor man.'

'And if you want,' my companion said, 'I could come and give you a hand to clear the place out.'

'Oh, but I couldn't ask that. I mean it'll take weeks but I am being paid, while you—'

She was shaking her head. 'I don't want paying, Meg. I'd enjoy helping. Time hangs a bit heavy when you're alone. Only I wouldn't mention it to Ellie. We didn't part on the best of terms.'

'But you still traipse over every day to feed her cat? What happened to the ginger one – Walrus?'

She shrugged. 'He died four, five years back. I'm being neighbourly, that's all. It's not the animal's fault she's a cross-grained old biddy. And'—her eyes snapped fiercely—'I'm going to make damn certain you get away after it's done. Being on the spot is the best way to manage that.'

'You're a dear.' I reached over to give her an awkward one-armed hug. 'But you needn't worry. If I was so weak-minded Phillip would rescue me. Besides, I'm an adult now and she has no power over me.'

'Only what your soft heart gives her,' Betty said bluntly. 'You wouldn't have come back else. Well'—she rose to go just as Claude, tail erect, stalked into the kitchen—'look who's here. I'll be away. Thanks for the cuppa, pet. Shall we say about nine tomorrow? We could start on the easy stuff – clothing, linen – get it ready for the op shops.'

'Thank you,' I said gratefully, one wary eye on the cat. 'I'll ring Cabot and Hawley, tell them I need fuller instructions about what's to go where. *They* can deal with Grandmother. They'll need to organise something we can pack stuff into, too. It's no good wrapping up china if there isn't a box to put it in.' I paused, struck by a sudden thought. 'How did you get here?'

Her eyes twinkled. 'I've a trike. Three wheels, like a kid. It's only a couple of kilometres, and I don't drive much now. Till tomorrow then, Meg.'

'Yes. And thanks again.' I walked her out and watched her sturdy frame straddle the tricycle and pedal away down the drive. She had to be in her late sixties, I thought, sixty-eight or sixty-nine. She had always been my ally and friend, the only person to make those deadly school holidays bearable, her unflagging cheerfulness a foil to my grandmother's constant disapproval. I had not been particularly happy at school, but it was preferable to the lonely holidays in my grandmother's house.

Claude meowed commandingly behind me. I shut the door and gave him the evil eye. 'Into the kitchen then and I'll open a tin. But one more attack on my person, buster, and you'll be living on dried food or catching your own.'

I fed the cat, shifted the hoses about and finished unpacking the small bag I'd brought, having first swept and dusted the room – tasks I'd been too tired to undertake the previous evening. All I had done then was to make up my bed from the linen in the big old chest, and find the spare pillows in the top of the wardrobe, which otherwise contained only empty hangers. The one in Grandmother's room, I now found, was full of her stuff while those in the other bedrooms were serving as storage space for items like luggage, pedestal fans and winter clothing. There was a pervasive smell of camphor and,

I was relieved to find in a cupboard tucked into the hallway, a modern vacuum cleaner.

I wandered, unable to settle to anything, and, eventually feeling the need to start, began making a list of the furniture. The phone, which sat on a side table in the hall, rang just as I got that far.

'Hunters Reach. I'm afraid Mrs Chapman isn't here.' The longcase clock rattled into a chime just then, almost obliterating the caller's voice

'Ah, Ms Morrisey?' It was Cabot; I recognised his slightly husky voice. 'Just a couple of developments. I realised you'd need packing boxes. There'll be some delivered before close of business today, and somebody from Sellright will be out this afternoon. Will that be convenient for you?'

'Sellright – who?'

'Sellright Real Estate. An agency, Ms Morrisey. I have his name, here, somewhere . . . Ah, here it is, a Josh Latten. An acquaintance of Mrs Chapman apparently. He suggested that I get a valuer out from the auction house to look over the contents of the house. If I can arrange it, would this afternoon suit you?'

'I – yes, why not? Look, while I have you, Mr Cabot, something needs doing with the garden. It's a jungle and, quite frankly, beyond my skill. I don't think Grandmother realises how much it's been let go, so if you could find somebody willing to prune and mow and water for at least a week . . .?'

'I'll see what I can do.' He coughed delicately. 'When I spoke to her, Mrs Chapman wished me to remind you to call her this evening.'

'I will,' I said on a sigh that he must have heard.

'Quite so. Call me if there's any problems, won't you?'

'Yes. Thank you. Goodbye.' I hung up, wrote *boxes*, *agent*, *valuer* on my list and, fetching a bin liner from the kitchen, took myself to the office to start sorting and discarding the years' worth of paperwork in the filing cabinet.

The cardboard boxes came, a van full of flatpacks that the driver, a cheerful young man, unloaded into the hallway for me, shoving each stack hard against the wall.

'Moving out? Don't blame you, stuck way out here miles from anywhere. Must be lonely. You can't see much life.' He grinned at me. 'I'm Ash, by the way.' I saw him glance at my ringless hand. 'You been here long?'

'No. I'm packing up the house. Just a temporary job. I'm Meg.' He had an engaging manner and nice smile, and was, I thought, a year or two younger than me.

'I see. You don't know any locals then? Hey, what do you do with your evenings? You fancy coming out for a drink tonight?'

'Sorry, I've got other plans. But thanks anyway. Was there some sticky tape with the order?'

'Nearly forgot.' He fetched a box from the cab. 'There you go. You sure about that drink? There's a pub I know does decent bar food – I could pick you up, sevenish? Life's short, and a fellow doesn't meet a pretty thing like you every day.'

'Sorry,' I repeated firmly, 'but I really can't. As I said, I've plans and anyway Claude would miss me.' His face fell as he heard the name.

'Ah, too bad. I always see 'em too late.' He hopped into the van and I waved him off, shut the door and took the half-dozen generous rolls of tape in with me. 'All set to go,' I told the cat, who had come to sniff around the boxes. 'Good Lord, what now? Did he forget . . .?'

But it was the Sellright agent's car I'd heard arriving, a little too fast, in a spray of gravel.

Its driver bounced out of the vehicle, a tubby, fortyish man with a glad-handing style that I assumed went with his profession. 'Josh Latten. And you must be Ellie's granddaughter?'

'Meg Morrisey.' We shook hands and he turned, fists on hips, to stare at the house. 'Grand old place, eh? We won't have a problem shifting it. Sellright holds the record for property sales round these parts. So, what say we take a walk-through and I'll make a few notes? I'll get a photographer out, print off some brochures and we'll talk about an auction date. Your grandmother stipulated a private sale, but we'll do better at auction. Just a matter of talking the old lady round.'

I privately wished him luck in that endeavour. But I hadn't given photography a thought. 'Well, I think we'd best delay things a little, Mr Latten, because—'

'Oh, Josh, please.' Airily, he added, 'I've known Ellie for years.'

I seriously doubted that. I had never heard any acquaintance speak of, much less address, her by her Christian name. 'Josh then. I've just arrived and the house in is no state to be shown, much less photographed. It'll need a thorough clean and half the rooms are under dust covers. I can have it ready in a couple of days but the garden is a mess and will take a little longer. I'm hoping to have somebody come and work on it in a day or two, so maybe we should put off taking pics for a while, at least until everything's neat and greened up again.'

He frowned. 'Mmm. The thing is, your grandmother wants it over and done with. She seems to be thinking a week is sufficient, which to be frank is a bit unrealistic. Doesn't give me much time to get the word out. But that's what she wants.'

'Well,' I said, shrugging, 'it's your decision and hers. But have a look at the place first and you'll see what I mean. Maybe you'll be able to change her mind. I assume that Grandmother means to sell off the furniture separately? Her solicitor had organised someone to value it, so we'd also have to have that done before any sale goes through.'

'Ah.' He looked thoughtful, then clapped his hands together. 'Well, onwards and upwards, I say. Let's take that look, shall we?'

However much acquaintance he claimed with my grandmother, he obviously wasn't familiar with the house, whose large rooms and high ceilings drew appreciative comments. 'Wonderful,' he kept murmuring. 'You don't see that sort of workmanship in modern places. Very gracious proportions. Great for conventions, wedding receptions . . . And the garden would certainly add that extra something. Shame, really, to waste a place like this on family living. I can see it as a restaurant – modernise the kitchen a bit, tables on the verandah in summer, and you could knock a wall through from dining room to lounge . . . Plenty of scope there.'

The garden had him shaking his head. 'You're right,' he decided. 'I'll have a word with Ellie, convince her the sale must be put back until this is sorted. You've somebody coming, you said?'

'Not quite. Mr Cabot's trying to find someone.'

'Let's hope he does then.' He handed me a card. 'Here's my

number. Give me a ring when the house is ready to be photographed. Ideally the garden too – but we'll hold off there at least until the lawns are mown, and some of the shrubbery cut back. A few pics of the rose garden, perhaps, and the gates – if those hedges have been trimmed. Yes, that might do it . . . I'll go call on Ellie now.'

Once more, I mentally wished him luck with that, wondering again as he drove off on his mission if he actually addressed her that way. He'd be a bold man if he did. She had been Mrs Chapman as far back as I could remember, and occasionally Lady Muck behind her back. I doubted anything had changed in my absence.

Chapter Four

The day ended without any sign of the valuer. I turned off the hoses as the sun sank and, steeling myself, carried a chair out past the flat stacks of the boxes to the phone on the side table in the broad hallway, and looked up the number for Woodfell. No sense waiting till later. Nursing homes would have fed their residents by now and they probably kept early nights. Grandmother might even, I thought hopefully, already be sleeping.

If she had been, she must have snapped awake again for only moments after an anonymous voice announced, 'Just putting you through now,' the phone was picked up and I heard her speak.

'Is that you, Margaret?'

'Yes. Good evening, Grandmother. Claude is fine. I fed him some tuna and I found the cat treats in the kitchen cupboard. And I've made a start sorting out the papers in the office. Are there any that you wish to keep?'

'No. That stuff's all years old. Lyle tells me you want a gardener engaged now, miss?'

'Lyle? Oh, is that Mr Cabot? Yes, the garden needs a lot of work. The real estate man agrees with me on that. I've been watering all day. It's going to take a bit of time to knock it into shape; you could lose a small dog in the lawn.'

'There's no need to exaggerate, Margaret.'

I ignored that to ask, 'Is there anything – once I start packing, I mean – that you want me to keep back for you? Any of the pictures, or crystal, a favourite chair maybe? There's such a lot . . .' I trailed off.

'No. What I need I've already had delivered.' The long-suffering Mr Cabot had organised that, I assumed.

'Okay then, only it seems – well, your whole life is here, Grandmother, and it seems wrong just to bundle it all up . . .'

'And if I were to fill my room with it, Margaret, how much do you think will fit into my coffin?' she asked dryly. 'I've done with it. Let it be sold. I believe you've had the boxes delivered, so when are you actually going to begin on the task you're being paid for?'

Swallowing a tart answer, I said patiently, 'When I've cleaned the house. The agent wants to advertise the sale, so he's sending a photographer out. He means to print a brochure with pictures. So the place has to look presentable – dust free *and* furnished if it's to tempt buyers. When he's been and gone, then I'll start. If that's all right with you?'

'Pertness doesn't become you, miss,' she snapped. 'Leave the kitchen window open tonight so that Claude can come and go. And ring me tomorrow evening.' She hung up without a goodbye and I was left listening to the dial tone.

'Yes, your ladyship,' I muttered, replacing the receiver. That was that then. I repaired to the kitchen to make myself an omelette and a toasted cheese sandwich for my evening meal. Afterwards I phoned Kevin Knott, Phillip's editor, at his home but he still couldn't give me a contact number to ring. Not that there would be that many phones, anyhow, in the wilds of New Guinea.

'It's a primitive village, what's left of it,' Knott told me. 'I don't even know how Phil managed to get there – if he has. Reports coming in from Moresby say the roads have been swallowed up. There's a mining company somewhere in the region, so I suppose he might've got a lift in one of their choppers. He's a resourceful bugger, Finchman, so he'll find himself a landline somewhere, love, don't you worry.'

He would, I knew. Phillip had rung me from obscure places in Africa where the streets were red dirt alleys between humpies of tin, and from aboard an Antarctic icebreaker – but it didn't make the waiting any easier. I locked the front and back doors and settled down with the TV. After a while Claude stalked in, tail still erect, and jumped up into the armchair opposite mine from where, paws tucked beneath his chest, he regarded me balefully through slitted eyes.

The sun was well up the following day when Betty arrived. I had the vacuum cleaner out and the windows open so I didn't hear the door chimes or her call, and looked up from my work only when I felt her presence in the doorway behind me.

'Oh, good morning, Be— Mrs Roberts.' I switched off the vacuum cleaner. 'I didn't hear you come in.'

'That's all right, Meg, and do please call me Betty.' She smiled, lifting the plastic bag she carried. 'I've fetched along a bit of cake for our morning tea. So what's all this?' She nodded at the misplaced chairs.

'Change of plan. The agent's sending a photographer around, which calls for a spot of spring cleaning. We can't start packing until the pics are taken. I checked with Grandmother last night and she doesn't want to keep anything – there'll be no room for it in the coffin was how she put it.'

'So when is this photographer coming?'

I shrugged. 'I asked for a couple of days. The rooms are really quite dingy when you look at them. I don't suppose Grandmother was able to do much, or maybe she can't see too clearly – there are spiderwebs in the corners, mould on the window ledges and the curtains are pretty grotty too.'

'Well, there's a starting point,' Betty said cheerfully. 'Just let me put this in the kitchen and I'll get them down. Not the drapes – you should be able to vacuum them – but the rest can go through the wash.'

'Oh, but are you sure you want to? It's such a big house, it'll be hard work,' I protested.

'Don't be silly, Meg. I'm glad to help – it'll give me something to do,' she said firmly. 'I'll enjoy it.' With a twinkle she added, 'I've brought my pinny along. It'll be just like when you came home from school.'

'Okay, if you're sure.' I was selfishly glad, not just for the extra pair of hands and the difference they would make but for her company too. I was missing Phillip in a different way to the other times he had been away. The Reach felt as isolated as a desert island. I didn't know the new neighbour, if a farmstead two kilometres away fitted that description and, however fanciful it was, I felt as if the misery I had experienced here as a child had seeped into the very fabric of the house, where it lurked like a vengeful ghost, waiting its opportunity to overwhelm me with memories I would sooner forget.

By lunchtime we had finished three of the main rooms, and the curtains for the rest were flapping in the sunshine. A light wind had sprung up, causing the spray I had started on the lawn to drift sideways, speckling the front verandah with damp spots.

'Time for a break, I think,' Betty said. 'I'll see what you've got to eat, shall I?'

Balanced on a chair with the broom to bring down a spiderweb festooning the lounge room cornice, I called, 'I bought tomatoes and cheese. And there's a fresh loaf in the bread bin.'

'Lovely. I'll put the kettle on.' She vanished into the kitchen.

We carried a tray out onto the verandah to a cluster of chairs around a cane table there and ate cheese and tomato sandwiches, watching the birds under the spray.

'There used to be a bird bath,' I remembered. 'Near the pergola. I daresay it's dry though. When did you start working for my grandmother, Betty?'

'Goodness.' She picked a crumb off her lap and lifted her teacup to take a sip, her weathered face thoughtful. 'Twenty-some years ago, maybe? Not regular work, just helping out as needed, and all the school holidays, of course, after your parents were killed. The extra cash was always welcome. That's small farming, Meg. Ted and I often struggled to make ends meet.'

'Was she always so . . . so hard? Was there a reason? Did something happen in her life to make her the way she is?'

Betty sighed. 'I don't know, pet. Your grandfather was very chauvinistic – women in their place, children to be seen and not heard – but that's how things were back then. It made bullheaded bigots out of men of a certain type, and he was certainly that. Maybe it rubbed off on her? But she was never kind, not that I saw. It used to fair make my blood boil the way she treated you.'

'I grew up thinking she hated me,' I confessed, 'and then I finally saw she was just indifferent. I was nothing more than a tiresome duty to her. And now,' I added sourly, 'I'm a convenience.' Thinking over what she had said, I continued. 'Twenty years – so did you know my mother?'

'As a kid just in passing, like any neighbour. After she married I saw her when she visited, but that wasn't often. I don't think she and Ellie got on that well. They went their own way, your parents. I never saw a closer couple.'

'Yes.' Long before I was ten and lost them both, I had known that Stephen and Fleur Morrisey had no room in their lives for anyone but each other. When I was older and knew about such things I sometimes wondered whether my conception had been an accident or a failed experiment, for never had two people been less in need of another to complete their lives.

'What happened to him in the end – my grandfather? Because you know,' I said wonderingly, 'I have no idea. Grandmother can't ever have said.'

'Heart attack – well, I'm pretty sure it was that. He was only in his sixties but he was given to yelling and doing his block.' Betty shrugged. 'Could've been stress-related. Ted and I went to the funeral, only because we were neighbours – neither of us liked him – but we weren't invited back to the house. Besides, I had you to look after. You were just a bit of a toddler. Your mum came up to me after the service and asked me to take you for the afternoon. You lifted your little arms and came to me straight off. Such a little poppet you were. The two of us got on like a house on fire.' She smiled at the memory, then drained her cup. 'Well, I suppose I'd better get those curtains in. They'll be dry by now.'

'Yes. And I'd best change the spray's position. I don't see many candidates turning up for the gardener's job. I do hope Cabot hasn't forgotten.'

He hadn't, for an hour later a man in a battered-looking ute drove in, parked on the gravel, and came to the front steps to yell, 'Hello, the house!'

I went out, shading my eyes against the glare. 'Yes? Can I help you?'

'You the one wanting a gardener? Jake Lynch. I've got my tools with me.' He looked assessingly over what he could see of the place. 'Gotta say, it looks to be proper run-down and in need of work. You the boss here?'

'No – well, it's my grandmother's property, so in a sense I am. But Mr Cabot pays the wages – yours and mine. I'm Meg Morrisey. When can you start?'

'Now?' he suggested. 'Gotta look the joint over first, see just how bad it is. The solicitor bloke said I'd get my meals here. That right?'

'Well, yes. I can arrange that.' I was a little taken aback by his directness. He was almost as tall as Phillip, with a pinched sort of face on which the two-day stubble didn't hide the deep grooves running from his nose to the corners of his mouth.

'Not breakfast,' he said curtly, 'and I'll be off before dark, so it's my crib only.'

'Crib?'

'Lunch and smokos – morning and afternoon tea,' he explained, impatient at my frowned incomprehension.

'Oh, I see. Yes, that'll be fine.'

'Good. I'll get started then.' He wheeled about and that was when I saw he was lurching unevenly with each step he took back to the vehicle. Lyle Cabot, I assumed, would know of his disability, and must've satisfied himself that Jake could handle the job. Besides, it wasn't my business. I returned to my cleaning and heard the vehicle start up and move slowly around the sweep of gravel to the back.

'We've got a gardener,' I informed Betty. 'None too friendly looking. Apparently we're feeding him lunch and smokos. Are you sure you aren't letting yourself in for more than you expected?'

'It's fine, Meg. If he's like farm workers, he'll need lots of cake. I'll bake tonight. Shall we say, ten and three for the smokos, and half noon for lunch? Working men like regular hours, you see.'

'Oh, but I could run into town this evening and pick up some buns or something. You don't have to cook as well!' I said, dismayed.

She shook her head, double chin wobbling. 'Don't be silly, dear – I shall enjoy it. I've had no one to cook for since Ted died. Does he look like a good eater?'

'What? Oh, not really. He's tall but not exactly fat.'

She nodded happily. 'Then he needs feeding up. How old is he?'

'You'll have to ask him – though he might bite your head off. He didn't seem too friendly.'

'Well, he has to get to know us,' she said comfortably. She glanced at her watch. 'It's not far off three now. I'll go and make some sandwiches to go with the cake. You want him to stay, don't you?' she asked as I protested it wasn't necessary. I nodded. 'Then we'd best show him he'll be well fed.' She smiled conspiratorially. 'It works, trust me. It's how I kept Ted's men happy all those years on the farm.'

'I hope he appreciates it, then. Thanks, Betty. Your Ted was a lucky man.'

Chapter Five

By five that afternoon the house fairly sparkled, with only the windows left to clean. Betty's help had halved the time I had budgeted for the task, which had also given me an overview of the stuff to be packed. There were cupboards and cupboards of it – fine china and linen and knick-knacks and books, pictures and clocks, and cushions and rugs. In the pantry beside the kitchen, one cupboard held nothing but vases, everything from crystal rose bowls to slender-stemmed bud holders, and flat containers for pansies. Vases shaped like swans, like baskets, like urns. My grandmother must have loved her garden – perhaps the only thing she did love, apart from her cats – and, looking back, I remembered that there had always been flowers in the house. Lilies in tall urns, shasta daisies garlanded with asparagus fern, roses in all their shapes and shades, violets scenting the air from small ceramic jugs . . . None of these holders were of great value, I imagined, but a secondhand dealer might take them.

Which reminded me of the still-absent valuer. Well, perhaps he would turn up tomorrow. Meanwhile, the clomp of boots in the kitchen alerted me to Jake's presence.

'Yes?' I went in to find him leaning against the sink.

'Just letting you know I'm off,' he said unsmilingly. 'Be back about seven in the morning.'

'Okay. I'll be here.' It was a pointless thing to say – of course I would be – but his curt manner and unfriendly glance unsettled me.

Once he'd left, I sent Betty home as well. 'You've done enough,' I said. 'Especially as you're not getting paid. Go home, put your feet up. If you're not tired you ought to be. I know I am.'

'And what will you be doing?' she asked.

'Nothing. Well, I might take a walk around the garden, see how much work Jake's actually done. I was thinking the photographer could come once the windows are clean, but it would be better to wait until the lawn's mown at least.'

'Make something nice for your tea then,' she suggested. 'I know you young girls – toast and a boiled egg. That's not a meal.'

'I will,' I promised. 'Chops and veg tonight. See you tomorrow then. And thanks again, Betty.'

Once she had gone I strolled around the back, surprising Claude, whom I came upon sneaking through the shrubbery, plainly on the hunt. I clapped my hands to alert his prey to the danger, and he jumped and hissed at me. 'Leave it,' I said. 'You're well enough fed, buster.' But he'd already vanished into the undergrowth.

In the back corner of the grounds beside the garden shed, which was drowning in waves of honeysuckle, I came upon a ladder, a barrow and an assortment of clippers and hedgers sheeted over with a plastic tarp. Beside it was a respectable pile of cuttings from a partly trimmed hedge that formed a screen around a bed of lilies struggling in the heat. I wondered how Jake planned to get rid of the prunings. And whether the barrow and other implements were his, or had come from the garden shed. (Must I empty that too?) Gazing around at the undisciplined wilderness, I thought that if he played his cards right, he could land a permanent job here. Unless whoever wound up buying the Reach had three strapping sons all keen on manual labour.

Exploring further, I saw that Jake had dug over a portion of the rose bed, leaving a tidy heap of weeds on the path. I hadn't got that far yesterday with the hose, but the bed had also been watered, and some dead wood removed from the bushes. The scent of the roses and the wisteria behind it wafted over me and I drew in a deep breath, leaning back against the pergola post. It gave a little with my weight and I saw that the upright was crusted with lichen that had eaten into it in a form of rot.

Further investigation showed a sag in the rafters supporting the vine. Well, the structure could have been standing for the better part of sixty years. Grandmother had probably married young – girls did back in her day, as young as fifteen sometimes – and she had, or so I believed, been brought here as a bride. It wasn't going to fall down tomorrow, so repairs could be left in the hands of the new owners, whoever they turned out to be.

Back indoors I turned on the old-fashioned wireless on the kitchen bench and peeled vegetables for my tea, one ear listening for the phone. Phillip didn't have the number of the Reach, of course, but Kevin Knott would have passed it on – if Phillip had been in contact yet. I listened in vain then and later while I watched TV with the sound lowered so as not to miss the call that didn't come.

The following morning, Jake arrived in the middle of my breakfast. He gave a cursory bang on the kitchen door before thrusting his head in to announce his arrival. Before he could withdraw it, I asked him what plans he'd made for the removal of the garden trash.

'The tip,' he said briefly. 'I brought my trailer. I'll want reimbursing, mind, for the fees. It'll be more than one trip.'

'I realise that. Tell Mr Cabot. And get receipts for each load. How long do you think the job'll take, Jake?'

He shrugged. 'Depends. You just want a face-lift, maybe seven, eight days. A proper job, which'd mean resurfacing the court, new posts for the pergola, sortin' out the gravel – how long's a piece of string?'

'I doubt we need that much upheaval,' I demurred. 'The Reach is for sale. I guess the agent doesn't want to scare the horses by presenting it as surrounded by jungle.'

For the first time I saw the hint of a smile, just a brief upturning of the corner of his mouth really, there and gone in an instant. His lower front teeth were a little crooked. 'A fair enough description. Right, I'll get started.'

'Have a cuppa first,' I said impulsively and, as he hesitated, 'Oh, go on. You surely don't have to start before eight?'

'All right, thanks. I'm my own timekeeper.' He came in and pulled out a chair as I poured his tea. In the clear morning light I revised his age upwards. Without his hat, which he'd pulled off as he entered, grey streaks showed in his hair. Certainly in his upper forties then, rather than the thirties I'd initially pegged him at.

'Are you from round here, Jake?'

'I'm from all over. What about you?'

I shook my head. 'Just a visit. I came up from Hahndorf. A slice of toast?'

'I'm right, thanks.' He shook his head, then cocked it as if listening to the silent house. Faint bird calls sounded through the window and something creaked far back in the building as a joist or floorboard settled. 'You're ain't scared at night, staying here alone?'

'I hadn't thought about it.' I shrugged. 'I hated the place as a child but that's silly. It's just a house. And as far as I know there are no ghosts – though I daresay there will be when Grandmother dies. I can't imagine God or the devil wanting her, so she'll be back here for certain. Though I'll be long gone by then.'

'So you don't get on?' he asked dryly.

'You could say that. To be honest, I don't know anyone who does get on with her. She's lived here all her married life and I'm apparently the only person she could find to help out when she needed it, and that for a wage. And that shows she's neither lovable nor likeable, don't you think?'

He shrugged. 'But you came.'

'Yeah, well, I'd just lost my job and my partner's overseas. Believe me, I'm not here because I want to be.'

'What do you normally do?'

'Retail. I worked in a shop. What about you – have you always done gardening?'

He shook his head, drained his cup and stood. 'Nup. Whatever comes along. Jack of all trades, that's me, an' I better get back to this one. Thanks for the tea.' He clapped his hat back on and lurched to the door, Claude skittering in past him as it opened.

'Plainly a question too far.' I spoke into the silence, then eyed the cat, advancing a tentative hand to stroke him. He hissed and I snatched it back just in time to avoid the claws he slashed at me. 'You're a horrid thing, aren't you? I suppose you want breakfast. After that, how would you like to help me clean windows?' He ignored me, stalking to the corner where his food dish was, plainly waiting for his meal. 'Make a pal of him outdoors,' I suggested. 'You've got a lot in common.'

Betty turned up with a batch of scones and a jar of homemade jam in time for smoko. Jake was monosyllabic throughout, despite her best efforts. I washed the cups and plates, then suggested a run into town. 'If we're going to feed him, I really need more provisions. And I'm not having you slaving away in my absence. Come on, it won't take long.'

When we returned, there was still time for Betty to make a tuna bake for lunch while I got on with the windows. It was warm work and tiring, reaching up while balanced on the stepladder. I got a crick in my neck and, pausing to ease it, heard what sounded like a chainsaw start up behind the tennis court. The sprays were going again and earlier I had seen Jake unloading a lawnmower from the back of his ute. My morning inspection had shown the pile of prunings was still in situ but he probably wanted a full load for the tip. The chainsaw's snarling suggested that he'd soon have one.

I phoned Grandmother that evening with a progress report. She skipped a greeting, saying accusingly the moment she heard my voice, 'You didn't ring last night.'

'There was nothing to tell you beyond the fact that you now have a man for the garden. And I assumed Mr Cabot would have let you know that. Claude's fine. And I'll start emptying the cupboards tomorrow. I can pack all the stuff that's not on show. What do you want done with the rest of your clothes?' There was a wardrobe full, everything from winter coats to hats and even a fox-skin stole complete with head and tail, an obscene-looking object that I couldn't believe women once wore.

'Throw them away.'

'I can – but, Grandmother, what if I were to give the older ones to the local theatre group? Things like the hats and the fox skin and the evening gloves. I'm sure they'd appreciate getting their hands on the sort of garments you can't buy any more. Would that be all right?'

'When did you get to be so argumentative, Margaret? Time was you did as you were told.'

'I'm no longer a child, Grandmother,' I said carefully. 'What difference can it make to you – throwing them out or giving them away? I just think it's a shame; if they can be used . . .'

'Oh, please yourself,' she snapped. 'Have you been leaving the window open for Claude?'

'Yes. He comes and goes as he wants. He's there for his meals. The rest of the time I barely see him.'

'Make sure he gets his treats,' she said and hung up.

I waited until eight o'clock without hearing from Phillip, then turned disconsolately to television to fill the evening but could find nothing on the box to hold my attention. I poured myself a sherry and, carrying the glass, wandered through the house, pulling open drawers at random and pausing to stare at heavy-framed oil paintings. I had no idea whether they were any good. To me they all looked dull and old fashioned, insipid-faced women and idyllic country scenes. None of the books, leather bound and lined up like soldiers on the bookshelves, invited my interest. There didn't seem to be a modern paperback in the house.

In the end I settled at a small writing desk, an *escritoire* – I dredged up the word from some forgotten Regency novel – in my grandmother's bedroom and pulled open the drawers. If she had written letters, she must have done it here. Or maybe this was where, like some like ancient chatelaine, she had kept her housekeeping affairs in order? In 1990 did one still run accounts with the butcher and grocer? Surely not, but it was hard to imagine her pushing a trolley in the supermarket like everybody else's gran.

I had, I saw, been spot-on about the letter writing. There was a sheaf of expensive paper with the property name on the top, a fountain pen (dry) and a packet of discreetly monogrammed envelopes. An address book lay beneath them but many of the entries had been crossed out. Well, I realised, if they were her contemporaries, they had probably died. There was a packet of paperclips, a stapler, a small lidded box containing stamps, along with a dried-out stamp-pad and well-worn stamp that I eventually made out to read PAID backwards. So yes, housekeeping. She had a diary, but flipping through it I found very few entries. Things like *doctor* and *hair app.* and several *B. Meet.* Board meetings, I wondered? That wouldn't be surprising. Cabot's name appeared a few times and *Bank*, and the rest was blank.

I riffled through the last few pages and was about to put the book aside when a photograph fell out of the back. It had been tinted, a studio portrait of a wedding. Not Grandmother's; it was too modern for that. The wide-skirted gowns of lace and pearls placed it much later. There were eight figures altogether, three groomsmen and three bridesmaids grouped either side of the newlyweds, who, it had taken me a moment to realise, were my parents.

I don't know why I was shocked by the sight of them. The bridal couple looked very young – and they were. I knew my mother had married at nineteen and that my father had been two years older but, as I had no photographs of them, I carried no clear image of them in my head. The picture my grandmother had in her room at Woodfell was the only photo I'd ever seen of them.

I held the picture under the direct light of the standard lamp, examining it for a likeness. Both my parents were average sized, my father a trifle taller than his bride. Her hair looked darker than my own fair head, but it was hard to be sure given the faded tinting. She was very pretty – no, she was beautiful, I thought dispassionately – and even in this frozen moment caught nearly three decades before, you could see the blinding passion uniting them. They seemed completely unaware of anything but each other. Neither was looking at the camera, and my father wore that special little half smile he had given only to her. It cost me a pang to remember how hard and how often I had tried to win it for myself.

The bridesmaids were all of a height with the bride and just as pretty, but were wearing puff sleeves rather than the bare arms of their girlish companion, for none of them looked to be more than teenagers. There was a similarity to two of them – probably the dress and the hairstyle, which mimicked the bride's. One of the groomsmen had his chin tilted up and was grinning at the camera, stiff-backed as any soldier, and I wondered if he had been one. Perhaps Betty would know who he was. As a neighbour she should have rated an invitation, though with Grandmother, I reflected, slipping the photo back between the pages of the diary, you could never tell.

Chapter Six

When Betty arrived the following morning, she found me sorting and packing the contents of Grandmother's wardrobe: one box for the theatre and the other for Lifeline. 'She told me to throw them out,' I explained, 'so I'm throwing them at a charity. It seems sinful not to. The lingerie and nighties can go in the skip, but these dresses and skirts and jumpers are perfectly able to be worn again.'

'What Ellie doesn't know won't hurt her,' Betty agreed. 'What about the shoes? There must be dozens of pairs.'

'I'm thinking they'd do for dress-ups too. Her feet are average sized and she must've been vain about them. I mean, they're not your regular older-woman's shoes, are they?'

'Nothing I'd wear with my bunions,' Betty agreed. There were open-toed sandals with coloured straps, red shoes with high heels, black court shoes, half boots, slip-ons.

I picked up a pair of stilettos and shook my head. 'Good Lord! It's a wonder she didn't break her neck. But maybe they're an old pair, though they're not very worn.'

'I didn't see Jake's vehicle,' Betty said, folding a ruby-red coat into the theatre box. 'Has he quit?'

'Gone to the tip with a load. He's really done quite a bit in the garden. It looks awfully raw where he's been but at least it's tidy and being watered.'

'And it won't take long for new shoots to come through,' she agreed. 'I wonder where he's living?'

'I have no idea. All I know is he's not from round here. Which reminds me.' I jumped up and, retrieving the photo, showed it to her. 'It's my parents' wedding. Any idea who the attendants are?'

'Well, that's Iris,' she said, studying the picture and touching the figure of the bridesmaid closest to the bride. 'The other two, no idea. Some friends of Fleur's. The same with the young men, except that one'—she touched the groomsman with the stiff, soldierly stance—'that's young . . .' She frowned and tapped her teeth. 'Walter Sullivan!' she said triumphantly. 'He went into the army . . . His family farmed south of here. They've sold up since, of course. They only had Walter but he wasn't farming material.'

'He looks like a soldier,' I commented. 'It's the way he stands. Who's Iris – another local?'

The glance she gave me was odd. 'She's your aunt, Meg. Or she was. Your mother's twin. I'm surprised you didn't recognise her. There's quite a likeness, after all.'

I goggled at her. 'Mum had a twin? I didn't know – well, only that there was a sister. But didn't she die as a child? I always thought . . .' I frowned. 'I'm sure somebody said so.' At the edge of memory I seemed to hear a voice – my mother's? *She died a long time ago. Now run along, Margaret, do.* I took the photo back and stared at the image. 'Well, plainly not. So when did she die, and why?'

'I'm not totally convinced that she did,' Betty said slowly. 'Die, I mean. She left home, ran away really, sometime after the wedding. It caused quite a stir at the time, though Ellie tried to pretend she'd just gone visiting. She did come back once briefly, then left again and after a while – I'm not exactly sure when – the tale got around that she'd died. Just before Daniel Chapman's fatal heart attack, it was. Or that's how I remember it.' She frowned then, thinking back. 'I never heard the details of her death, whether it was an accident or she fell ill. I can't even remember being told – it was just something people picked up, you know, and passed on – *Oh, did you hear about the Chapman girl? Dreadful! So soon after her father, too, and her so young. You wouldn't wish it on anyone, not even the Chapmans.* Ellie wasn't real popular in some quarters, you know, pet. And as she never contradicted the rumour, it came to be accepted as true.'

'But why wouldn't it be?'

'Because there's no memorial stone in the cemetery, or even here, and old Pastor Burnside, who had the church back then, never held a service for her. Which was odd, really. It's made me wonder since, not that I've any real grounds to . . .'

'What?' I said, as she hesitated. 'What did you wonder?'

'Well, you know what she's like about respectability, your grandmother. Maybe it was a case of not actual death, but dead to Ellie. Daughters didn't leave home except to get married. Not in Daniel Chapman's world anyway. It pains me to say so, but your grandfather was a bully. No, he was more than that – he was a domestic tyrant when it came to his family.'

'You may say what you like,' I assured her. 'I don't remember him. Surely my mother must've known what happened – I mean, if Iris was her twin, they'd have kept in touch, wouldn't they?'

'Yes, perhaps.' Betty seemed doubtful. 'But they weren't identical, and I never thought they were particularly close. Not like some sisters.' She glanced at the clock above the fireplace. 'Gracious, is it that time? I'll put the kettle on. If Jake's back, he'll be looking for his tea.'

The man who came to appraise the furniture arrived shortly after lunch. Jake had just left with a second load for the tip when the car pulled up out front. Its occupant was an elderly man called Morris Peabody. He was wearing baggy shorts and a polo shirt with a monogrammed pocket. He carried a clipboard and made appreciative noises as he jotted down details and his estimation of what each piece might bring at sale.

'Very nice, Ms Morrisey,' he said when we'd completed the tour. 'I'll give you a copy of the list and a couple of names of reputable dealers. Ones who won't rip you off. Personally, I'd go for an auction, but that can be risky . . . Really it depends on the day and what people are willing to take a chance on. If you intend to clear the entire house, a secondhand dealer would take the rest. I'd reserve the Staffordshire porcelain though. And the crystal, and the Venetian ware. That's become a real collector's item. My advice would be to contact a specialist dealer about that. The rest'—he wrinkled his nose—'it's nice enough, but nothing special. Your secondhand dealer again.'

I shook his hand and thanked him for his trouble as he left.

Perusing the list he'd given me, I noticed that he'd written 'original' next to some of the pieces. No doubt that explained the (to me) astronomical prices listed beside them. Grandfather must've been rolling in the stuff, I reflected. The dining suite alone . . . Unless there were residents of Glenfield wealthier than I supposed, that was plainly headed for a city saleroom.

'He's gone?' Betty looked up from the sandwiches she was arranging on a plate. 'Pity,' she said with customary country hospitality, 'he could've had a cuppa with us. Do you mind if I leave straight after? I've a few errands to do in town.'

'Of course I don't mind! You must do as you please, when you please, Betty. I really appreciate your company and your help, but I've no claim on your time. I think I'll ring Thingummy – the agent . . .'

'Josh Latten,' she said helpfully.

'Yes, him, after smoko. The garden's not ready for photographs yet but I don't see why he can't send the man out to do the house pics, and come back for the garden just before they print the brochure.'

She absently ate a stray breadcrust. 'Or you could get Jake to trim back a few metres of gate hedge and he could take a pic of the gates and maybe the wisteria and a rose or two. They're looking splendid right now.'

'Yes. I could ask Jake before he leaves today. If he agrees, I'll tell Josh to send the camera along tomorrow. Then we can really start packing.'

'I expect you're keen to get finished and gone.'

I nodded. 'I miss Phillip. I mean, finishing up here won't bring him home, I know that, but it *seems* that way. I just wish he'd ring. There must be a phone somewhere in the wilds of New Guinea. He's rung me from Antarctica, for heaven's sake!'

'I'm sure he'll find a way,' she said soothingly. 'Not to sound like Ellie, but will you two get married?'

I shrugged. 'We might, one day. It doesn't seem all that important to us right now. I know your generation believed in it, but love, fidelity, happiness – it isn't guaranteed by a ceremony and a piece of paper.'

'That's very true,' she said. 'It's down to the couple concerned – always has been. Some are luckier, or'—she thought about it, the worn fingers that caressed her chin showing the thin band of her wedding ring—'cannier in their choosing, perhaps?'

'My mum and dad . . .' I said abruptly, 'were they lucky or clever, Betty? I was too young to know about adult stuff when they died, but I've never seen any couple since quite so . . . so besotted with each other.'

'I know what you mean.' She shook her head, frowning. 'I don't think I'd have liked that degree of oneness though. I mourned when I lost Ted, but I got through it, as you do. But those two – what if they hadn't died together? How would the one left have ever managed alone?'

Maybe by paying more attention to their child? I didn't say it. Never mind more attention – any would have been welcome. I shook the thought away. It was history now, and I didn't know why I let it continue to bother me.

Jake agreed to my request about the gates. 'Just prune enough to make a decent photograph,' I explained. 'The rest can wait a bit. Percentage-wise, how far are you from finishing the whole garden?'

He snorted. 'I'd say I've scarcely done a quarter. And I keep finding new jobs. Did you know the cover over the well's just about fallen in? I never noticed till I cut the plumbago back and got a look at it. The boards have rotted through. There's a couple of day's work there alone by the time I've cut and shaped new timber.'

'Does it matter?' I asked. 'It's not a real well.'

'Where'd you get that idea?' he demanded. 'Of course it is! Just drop a pebble down and listen for the splash.' He swallowed a mouthful of tea and selected a slice of Betty's fruitcake from the plate. 'At a guess,' he added, 'it was sunk about the time the house was built. The top bricks are newer, but I'd say they date from when the mesh grid was cemented over the well. That's bust now, rotted away – you can see bits through the broken boards, and I reckon that woulda been the reason the cover was added. It's law,' he added thickly. 'Like swimming pools being fenced.'

'He's right about that, pet.' Betty nodded. 'Health and Safety's very particular about farm tanks and wells, these days.'

'Well, fancy that,' I said inanely. 'I always thought of it as the wishing well. I never imagined it was real.' I had once tried to drop my wishes into it only to be foiled by the close-fitting timber top. Grandmother wouldn't have noticed the deterioration, I thought. It was entirely probable that she hadn't penetrated that far into the garden for some years. 'Um, well, I guess you'll have to tell Mr Cabot. He'll want to keep his client on the right side of the law.'

Betty stacked her cup and plate and reached for the milk. 'Everybody finished? I'll just clear up.'

I forestalled her. 'It's okay. I'll do it. You get off.'

When she'd gone, Jake said idly, 'So your gran's in a home. I gather from old Cabot she's a bit of a tartar. That right?'

'It's a fair description,' I admitted wryly.

'So why are you the one lumbered with this?' He waved his hand to take in the kitchen and rooms beyond.

'Because I'm the last of the family. My parents are dead. So is my grandfather. I don't even remember him, so it's down to me.'

'Ah.' He thought about that. 'Well, the place must be worth a bit. I guess you'll be sitting pretty when the old girl snuffs it.'

'I doubt it.'

He raised his brows. 'No? Why's that, then? There's someone else she favours over you? Why isn't he or she here then, doing the donkey work?'

I shook my head. 'I told you, there's nobody else. My mother had a twin but she died too. And my grandmother's what Betty calls a cross-grained old biddy, so I'm not expecting a cent beyond my wages. That's okay. I don't want it – we've never been close.'

He eyed me curiously. 'That's a lot of death in one family. What happened to your parents, and your aunt?'

'In my parents' case, a light plane crash. Dad was a pilot. Not professionally – he was actually an architect – but he had a plane and they often flew places. My aunt?' I shrugged. 'Until recently I thought she must've died as a child, but Betty said she was a young woman when she more or less vanished. As far as I can work out she was presumed dead because of it.'

'Just like that? Didn't they look for her?'

'I don't know. I was just a baby and it's a long time ago.' I rose to gather up the remaining cups. 'Anyway . . . If you can tidy up the entrance this afternoon I'll tell the agent he can send his photographer out tomorrow.' Claude stalked into the kitchen at that moment, stared hard at Jake, and then carried on to his water dish.

'Up yours too, mate,' the gardener muttered and got awkwardly to his feet.

I laughed. 'Turn him into an old lady and that's pretty much my grandmother.'

I phoned Josh Latten and then stood in thought, tapping the handpiece against my chin, before ringing Cabot and Hawley. It hadn't gone four yet so Mr Cabot should still be in the office. He was. I told him what the valuer had said, reading off the list I'd been given, adding, 'I don't think my grandmother could manage the fuss of a private sale – finding a buyer, arranging inspection and transport – and I won't be here. The stuff is too valuable to just be lumped in with the rest as a job lot, and I think that's probably what would happen if she has to deal with it. So . . .'

'Quite right, Ms Morrisey,' he said. 'I'll see her and arrange something. How are things shaping in the garden? That chap I hired is satisfactory?'

'Yes,' I said. 'He's made a big difference already; he really toils. Which reminds me – he says the cover over the well has rotted away and it'll have to be replaced. I told him to see you about the necessary materials. I hope that's okay?'

'Of course. And he's right. We don't want any blowback from a sale should an accident occur.' I could almost see his lawyerly shudder at the thought. 'I'll call on Mrs Chapman later today and set things in train with the furniture. And I'll organise an account for timber at Byland and Sons so John can collect what he needs for the well.'

'Jake,' I corrected.

'Jake. Quite so. Well, if that's everything?'

'Yes. Thank you.' I put the phone down and went off to deliver the message.

Chapter Seven

When Jake's vehicle drove off loaded with the latest lot of prunings, I walked down the drive to see how the entrance looked. Trimming back the growth had made quite a difference. The hedge looked raw from his efforts, but the gate swung easily now. The gravel was still studded with weeds but perhaps they wouldn't be so noticeable in a long vista shot? Phillip would know. I sighed on the thought and wandered back, detouring down the side to smell the roses and to notice that the lawns had been cut and were even greening up, now that the old grass had gone.

I inspected the well, peering curiously through the crumbling timber into the lightless depths I hadn't known existed. I hunted around until I found a pebble and, leaning above the opening, dropped it in, listening for long seconds before the splash of its landing sounded. Slats of age-darkened, rotten timber clung to the brick edges, the missing bits, I assumed, having taken the path of my pebble. The shingles were peeling on the cutesy little peaked roof covering the toy windlass. It must have been added after it ceased being used as a water source for the homestead.

I made a mental note to ask Jake where the present supply came from. We were surely too far out for it to be the town water.

I lingered by the front steps, not really wanting to enter the house. Presently I'd have to phone my grandmother and after that the evening stretched endlessly ahead. I could make my dinner, watch TV and wait for the phone to ring. Or I could drive into Glenfield – to do what? Visit my grandmother? God, no! Have a meal or a drink somewhere? But I knew nobody and didn't fancy sitting alone watching those with friends and partners to share their evening with enjoying themselves.

As if he'd got wind of my thoughts, Claude stalked into view along the verandah, eyes narrowed in disapproval. 'Yeah, yeah,' I muttered. 'You're sure you're not channelling Grandfather? He was a tyrant too, so I hear. He wouldn't have approved of young women out on the town alone, either.'

Claude hissed and at the same moment I heard the crunch of tyres on gravel. I looked up to see a taxi coasting towards me down the driveway.

It pulled up and I had time to stare and say, 'Who in the world . . .?' before the passenger door opened and Phillip's lanky body struggled slowly out, left arm hefting a grubby backpack, his right immobilised in a sling. The ever-present camera hung bulkily around his neck.

'Phillip!' After a second of shocked surprise I flew at him, arms out. 'God, what happened? How did you get here? When—?'

'All right, Elf.' He dropped the bag and leaned gingerly to return my hug with his left arm, wincing as I squeezed him, the camera hard against my body. He kissed me. 'Careful, I'm a bit bruised still. Thanks, mate,' he called and the cabbie rolled away. 'Kevin told me where you'd gone,' he said, glancing around. 'Talk about the back of beyond! I've spent a fortune on taxis. If you wanted to run away, couldn't you have picked a place with a train service?'

'I'm not running anywhere, you cretin. I lost my job. But don't stand there, come inside. You look whacked. Are you all right? What's happened to your arm?'

'It's broken – half a hill fell on our hut.' He swallowed, then said hoarsely, 'That was days ago. Brad was killed.'

I gasped in horror but he shook his head. 'I'll tell you later, Elf. It was a bloody disaster for us and the village . . . Right now I need to sit down somewhere. A stiff drink wouldn't go amiss either.'

'I'll see what I can find. There's sherry. Will that do?' I frowned, eyeing him. 'I've been waiting and waiting for your call. Kevin might have told me you'd been hurt,' I added indignantly, grabbing up his bag. 'No, let me, I've got it.'

'He didn't know. The place was a shambles after the quake – the one that got us, I mean, not the original. I got out on a RAAF plane, one of those flying in tucker and medical supplies.' He paused in the hall, swaying a little, and I grabbed his arm. 'Well, this is a bit posh! A rellie's house, Kevin said?'

'My grandmother's. She's in a nursing home so it's being sold. Here, this way. God, you look terrible, Phillip.' Alarmed, I steered him to the right. 'Come through to the kitchen – or would you rather lie down?'

'A chair'll be fine, Elf. And I wouldn't say no to a feed.'

'Coming up. But first I'll get you a glass of sherry. I doubt Grandmother kept anything stronger. If she did, I haven't found it.'

I grabbed the filled decanter from the sideboard in the dining room and flew back to pour him a generous glassful, watching anxiously as he sipped it. His face was drawn and pale, and every movement seemed made with effort. Whenever his left hand was free, he used it to support his right elbow, though I couldn't see a cast within the sling.

'Where exactly is your arm broken?'

'Just below the shoulder joint. A roof beam did it. They couldn't plaster it, they said. ''S'okay if I keep it still. I was lucky,' he said, his face twisting. 'Even the camera gear made it. Unlike Brad.'

I sat down, my hand going to my mouth. In my shock at Phillip's appearance, that part of his story had barely registered before. Brad was the journalist who accompanied him on his trips. They'd worked together for years. 'That's terrible! What happened to him? Hasn't his wife just had another baby?'

'Yeah. He didn't make it out when the hut collapsed.'

'Oh, God! Poor Jenny! I'm sorry, love.' I had met Jennifer at a welcome-home party after the Antarctic trip, and had run into her again once or twice since. 'We'll have to visit her.'

'I've already been.' His face was haggard and I cupped it between my hands, caressing it with my thumbs.

'It must've been awful. Two children . . . what will she do? Poor Brad. And I didn't even know! It might have been you.'

'It wasn't though.' He took my hand and kissed it. 'I'm fine, Elf; a few bruises, and this arm'll keep me sidelined for a bit.' He looked past me. 'Hello, where'd you come from, old fellow?'

I glanced behind me and scowled at the cat. 'That's Claude.

I expect he wants his dinner. Well, his lordship can just wait till I've made yours. What about an omelette? Or I've some cooked mince – I could do pasta with it?'

'The omelette will do, thanks.' He clicked his fingers at Claude, who ignored him to sit down and begin washing his hind leg. 'So, tell me how you came to be here. Kevin was a bit short on detail – not that you can blame him given the circumstances.'

I explained while I beat eggs and put bread in the toaster. 'I'd have refused if I could,' I said, 'but it's a job, and I wasn't sure of finding another in Hahndorf.'

He raised his brows. 'Why would you refuse? She's your grandmother, and in a home, you said.'

'You haven't met her,' I retorted grimly. 'I hate the old bat. And don't try to talk me round. Even her neighbours didn't like her. If she'd had a single friend to ask for favours, I wouldn't be here.'

'That's very sad.' He reached to set his sherry glass down, gasping involuntarily as he did so.

I said accusingly, 'That's not your bad arm. Let me see.' Despite his protest, I pulled the neck of his shirt wide, then, numb with shock, rolled the hem up to disclose his ribcage, which was black and blue. 'Oh, my God!' His back was similarly patterned. 'Are you sure your arm's the only thing broken?'

'Let be,' he said testily. 'It's just bruising. They delivered me to the hospital in Moresby and I've been X-rayed and prodded by experts both there and in Darwin. I told you, a hill fell on us – well, part of a bloody mountain, really. It collapsed the hut and everything in it. I'm fine, Elf. Don't fuss.'

'You're going to eat,' I said firmly, 'and then you're going to bed. The hospital had no business letting you out in this state.'

My bed was a single, so while he ate I raided the linen chest and made up the double one in Grandmother's room. It looked like something birthed in Queen Victoria's day when bulk equalled quality, the four corner posts like young trees, while the headboard, almost a handspan through, could have doubled for a table. But the mattress was firm and deep, and long enough to accommodate Phillip's height. I found an extra pillow to cushion his broken arm and, once he was sitting on the bed, crouched to remove his trainers.

'I can do it, Elf,' he protested. 'I should have a shower.'

'In the morning. Lie back and undo your jeans.' I pulled them off, gasping afresh at the bruises across his thighs. The shirt took longer with the need to ease the sleeve under his sling and off the broken arm, and I felt the prick of tears at the sight of what it uncovered.

'Oh, God, Phillip! You poor thing. Isn't there something I can get you?'

'Yeah.' Grimacing, he gripped the top of the headboard to pull himself up. 'Painkillers, in my bag. A couple of them and a glass of water'd be great.'

'I'll get it.' I hurried from the room and when I returned, it was to find him twisted awkwardly about, examining a hollow in the bedhead and the items he'd taken from it.

He looked up at me. 'There must've been a hidden spring. When I grabbed it, the panel just slid open. Whose room was this?'

'My grandparents'. The bed's an antique, the valuer said. What did you find?'

'A pipe and a gold bracelet. The chain's broken on it.' He held it up to show me. Putting the tumbler and pills within his reach on the bedside cabinet, I took it from him.

'That was my mother's. She always wore it. I remember it well, because I wanted one like it. It must've broken in two places because there should be a little golden padlock – I remember I used to wonder how there could be a key tiny enough to open it. Her name's on the little plate. See, it's engraved right here . . .' I turned the narrow plate to show him and was disconcerted to find it wasn't so. 'Oh, it says Iris!'

'Who's she?'

'Mum's twin sister. She passed away – or at least she vanished – about the same time my grandfather died. According to Betty, anyway.'

'Betty?' he repeated.

'A neighbour who's been helping me. I didn't even know, before she told me, that Mum and Iris were twins.'

'Well,' he said, 'if they were, I expect they were both given the same things. How come I've never heard you mention her?'

'Because neither Grandmother nor my parents ever did. I mean, I knew in a vague sort of way that she'd been born, but I thought she'd died as a child. It was Betty who told me otherwise when I found . . . Hang on.'

I rifled through the desk to locate the diary and carried the wedding photo back to show him. 'Look, this is Iris, and see – she's wearing the bracelet.' I stared at my mother's right wrist, which was just visible over my father's clasping hand, for they stood arm in arm, she on his left with his right hand across his body holding both hers. 'And Mum is too. You can just see a bit of the chain on her arm. So you're right, they both had one. Iris must've lost hers before she cleared out.'

'Is that what she did?'

'So Betty says.'

'It's overexposed,' he murmured, examining the print. 'Pity they had no colour back then. I can see the likeness.' He glanced from the photo to me and back. 'There's a likeness there to your mum, something about the eyes, and the shape of your brow. He was a good-looking bloke, your dad. I've never seen a pic of your parents before.'

'That's because I don't have any. I might keep this one though. Grandmother has a studio portrait of them, and I suppose it's possible there's a family album somewhere. I haven't had a proper look yet. So, what exactly did you do to open that?' I nodded at the bedhead.

He swallowed the pills and lay down with a sigh of relief. 'Just grabbed it. I'll have a look tomorrow, find out how it works.' His eyes closed and he lay rigid, waiting for the pills to work.

I worked the folded-down sheet from beneath his feet and pulled it up over him then patted his closest leg. 'I'll clear up in the kitchen and ring Grandmother, then I'll come to bed. I'm so sorry about Brad, love. And so glad you're safely home,' I said, brushing a kiss onto his forehead. 'Rest now.'

I fed Claude, tidied the kitchen and went to the phone. Grandmother answered on the first ring as usual, and I pictured her sitting there in her wheelchair, hand raised to snatch up the receiver.

'Yes, Margaret, what have you to say?'

'How's your day been, Grandmother? I hope you're well?' But she just brushed the pleasantries aside so I got on with my report: that the valuer had been, and what he'd said. I read her the list of antiques: the dining suite and sideboard, the Queen Anne chairs, and longcase clock; and in her bedroom, the bed itself, the little desk and the cabriolet armchair. 'And the Staffordshire items and crystal and the better china . . . stuff like that. He said they should go to auction or private sale too. The photographer is coming tomorrow, so I imagine the sale brochure will be ready in a few days. And'—I took a breath, wondering how she was going to react—'my partner has come to visit. He's been hurt. There was a second earthquake in New Guinea, and the RAAF flew him home. The man with him was killed. So he'll be staying at the Reach with me. I trust that's all right, because he needs caring for.' She was, I thought, astute enough to grasp that I intended to do so, even if it meant leaving her employ.

She sniffed disparagingly. 'What's wrong with him?'

'His right arm's broken and he's so bruised he can hardly stand.'

'He won't be a great deal of help to you then. If that's all and Claude's well, you may ring me tomorrow, Margaret. Don't forget.' She hung up then without a goodbye.

Fuming, I put out fresh water for the cat, checked that his window was open and went back to Phillip, who was asleep, his long fair hair (in need of a wash) screening half his face. His jaw was stubbled with shadow from a missed shave, and he lay lax in sleep, the mottled bruising that covered most of his body shocking against the whiteness of his torso. I shivered, realising how lucky I was to have him here alive in my bed, unlike poor Jennifer . . . Half a hill had fallen on them, he'd said. It looked more like a full mountain range. Moving the lock of hair aside from his mouth, I kissed him and eased gently in beside him, taking care not to bump his arm. He would grieve for his friend and workmate and probably suffer from nightmares for a while, but I had him back, and for now that was all that mattered.

Chapter Eight

I woke the next morning with a lightness of heart directly attributable to the presence of Phillip beside me. He'd had a restless night, thrashing about and crying out at one stage, the pain of jolting the broken bone awakening him. He'd sworn, holding his arm, face dewed with sweat in the light of the bedside lamp I snapped on.

'Bad dream,' he gasped. 'I'm fine, Elf. Go back to sleep.'

Instead, I'd checked the time and risen to fetch a glass of water and more painkillers. 'Do you want the fan on?' I'd also brought a towel to wipe his face.

He dragged it brusquely over the sweat and shook his head. 'No, it's fine. I'm fine, really – it was just a dream. But when we heard that roar . . . it was bloody terrifying, you know?'

'I can imagine.' I snapped off the light and, lying beside him, I took his hand, rubbing my thumb across his knuckles. 'Do you want to talk about it? How did you even get there? Kevin said the roads were all wiped out by the first quake.'

'They were. We hitched as far as we could and then trekked. Brad'—he swallowed and I heard his voice shake in the darkness—'Brad said it was hopeless. I should've listened to him, but I said, I *insisted*, we could make it. There was a village on a river, upstream of the epicentre. When we got there the water was rising and the people were scared. They said the quake had woken the river, and the spirits were angry. They wouldn't take us, so I hired a canoe. Oh, God, Elf! I wish I'd learn to mind my own bloody business. I should've listened to them, or to Brad when he wanted to turn back.'

'But it was your business,' I said, trying to soothe him. 'You know you always get your shots. Of course you had to get there however you could.'

'Yeah, well I did,' he said bitterly, 'and Brad's dead because of it. The river was rising because the first quake had blocked the gorge downstream. We paddled a couple of kay, saw what the problem was and hiked up and over the mountain. The same one that fell on our hut and broke the gorge open again so all that dammed-up water drowned what was left of the village.'

His face wore a tortured look as he said despairingly, 'I hope to God the rock and earth killed Brad, Elf, I really do. Because otherwise he must've smothered in silt. The water was coming, roaring up the slope while I was clawing myself out. I could feel the earth slipping beneath me. There was no time to look, to go back to see if I could dig—'

'It's not your fault, Phillip. Hush.' I cradled his head. 'You were doing your job, that's all. Try to sleep now – it's ages yet till morning.'

'Tell that to Jenny,' he said morosely, and then, 'I'm sorry, love. Not fair burdening you with it. Go to sleep.'

I didn't immediately and neither, I knew, did he. He didn't

speak again or move, but there was nothing restful in the way he lay, and was still lying, when my eyelids closed again.

And now morning had come, and the feline horror would be wanting his breakfast, and Jake would be arriving, and I needed to head into town to buy food – but not before Betty arrived. Otherwise the photographer was bound to turn up the moment I left. Yesterday we had decided I should put a vase of roses on the side table in the hall, and one or two more in the lounge and dining room.

'Give the place a gracious air,' Betty had said seriously. 'You never know. That Josh – you said he spoke of it maybe becoming a restaurant, so it needs to look welcoming and expensive. I'd use the crystal vases, and maybe have the Waterford set on a tray on the sideboard.'

I had agreed it couldn't hurt and after breakfast, which I had delivered to Phillip in bed with strict instructions to stay there, I took the secateurs out to the rose beds and cut a bucketful, placing each flower straight into water as I had often seen my grandmother do. Jake, with a rag pulled over the lower part of his face, was spraying weeds from a heavy-looking tank on his back. He stopped when I approached, pulling the cloth down to say, 'Mornin', Meg. Something you want?'

'No, only to say the photographer will be along today. I thought if you showed him the rose beds – they do look wonderful now you've weeded and mulched them – and maybe the pergola, it'd help the sale. Oh, and the gates.' I jumped as water hissed suddenly behind me and a spray came on in the shrubbery. 'Who did that?'

'Timer,' he said succinctly. 'Needed settin', that's all.'

'Oh.' It explained how Grandmother had managed to keep the garden alive at least. Reminded by the action, I asked, 'Where's our water coming from, Jake? If they used the well once . . . What's the go now?'

'Bore, in what used to be the Backstrap paddock over there.' He waved an arm behind him beyond the garden's boundary. 'Hear that faint hum? It's the electric pump. Turns on automatically when a tap's opened.'

'Oh,' I repeated, recalling that I had frequently heard and dismissed the sound as coming from the machinery of our distant neighbour. 'So it doesn't matter how much we use? There's plenty?' With tanks in mind I had been feeling vaguely guilty about the way I had previously let the water run on the lawns.

'Nope. Good supply. Shallow too. Bit over a hundred-footer, she is.'

'Is that good?' I did a mental conversion. Call it thirty metres then. 'How do you know that?'

'Worked on it, didn't I? Offsiding for the driller.'

I gaped at him. 'Then you do come from round here, Jake?'

'Once,' he said uninformatively and pulled the cloth up once more across his nose.

'Then you knew my grandfather. I mean, if you worked for him—'

'Oh, yeah.' The words were muffled but there was no mistaking the dislike in his tone. 'Mean as a brown snake, the old bastard. I'd've bought his coffin myself to see him underground.' He lurched away and began systematically poisoning every weed he passed.

Mulling over his words, I returned to arrange the flowers and run a duster over the furniture. The timber floors shone in the early light streaming in from the windows and the elusive fragrance of the roses filled the rooms. Claude arranged himself under the piano stool, then reared up to claw at its legs.

'Hey!' I shook the duster at him and he hissed at me and fled, just as Betty arrived bearing her usual offerings for smoko.

'Very nice.' She glanced at the hall flowers. 'Ellie always had the most beautiful roses. I don't know how many prizes she won with them in the show.'

'Really? I didn't know that. At Glenfield, you mean?'

'Yes. The annual agricultural show. You'd have been at school because it's held in August. It's still quite an affair. Top quality in everything. So, when's the photographer turning up – did anybody say?'

'No.' I thought of something. 'Betty, did you know Jake originally came from round here?'

'Does he? Well, everybody comes from somewhere.'

'Yes, but he worked for my grandfather. On the bore actually. I didn't know there was a bore.'

She shook her head. 'Of course there are bores, or dams, on every farm. How do you think the properties work, Meg? Everything has to drink – gardens, livestock, people.' She thought a moment. 'What's his surname? I might know the family.'

'Um, I think Mr Cabot mentioned it once – Lark or Lake. Something with an L . . .'

'Could it be Lynch?' she asked.

I nodded. 'That was it! Jake Lynch. Mr Cabot called him John by mistake,' I remembered, and saw her face alter at the words. 'You do remember him, then?'

'Of course! JJ. John Jacob Lynch. Well, he's changed! I certainly didn't recognise him.' She frowned, seemed to hesitate, then shook her head. 'You might as well know. He was gaoled as a young man for stealing from here, from the Reach. Your grandfather accused him of the theft and he got two years for it. It was just after your parents married. Apparently the police recovered some of the stolen stuff in a pawnshop in Adelaide. The owner was the one who identified Jake as the man who'd sold it to him. I wonder why he's dropped the John? Everyone called him that, or JJ.'

'Wow!' My brows shot up. 'Do you think Cabot knows? But he must, given what he does.'

Betty nodded. 'I imagine so. The thing is, it was a highly contentious affair. Not everybody thought he'd done it. He had an alibi, you see – but in the end the jury didn't believe him.' She hesitated again. 'There was some talk – it was only that, mind – of undue influence.'

'With the jury? From whom?'

She shrugged. 'Your grandfather. That was the word at the time. He was a popular young man, JJ – a noted footballer. He captained the Glenfield team. Nobody wanted to believe he was guilty. His father was a cabinet maker, had a shop in town. He made fine furniture, but he sold up and moved away after the trial.'

A footballer. Somebody young and fit. I thought of Jake's present lurching gait and felt a stab of pity. 'I see. Well,

Mr Cabot must think him trustworthy, or he wouldn't have given him the job, would he?'

'Unless he couldn't find anyone else. Or he thinks him reformed. It was all a long time ago.' She cocked her head. 'I hear something – maybe that's your photographer now, Meg.'

Chapter Nine

It was. The photographer was a young man with an acne-scarred face, and clad in those camo pants with a million pockets down the legs. He nodded impatiently as I explained about the garden.

'Yeah, yeah, I got it. Done hundreds of these jobs, you know. Always the same. Make the rooms look bigger, the garden fancier than it is.' He eyed the ceiling as I led him inside, then fiddled with his gear, plucking the light meter from its hook on his belt and changing a lens. 'Piece of cake.' He dismissed me with a nod. 'I'll get on then.'

I went to see how Phillip was and found him dressing, grimacing as he bent for his shoes.

'Sit – I'll get them.' I held them for his feet. 'How do you feel? How's the arm?'

He sighed. 'It's fine. Look, I know you worry but you don't have to. A broken arm won't kill me, Elf. What are you doing?'

'Well, the photographer's come.' He stood up and I went hastily around the bed, pulling it straight and picking up his discarded items from the floor. 'I expect he'll be in here shortly, though if you'd wanted to stay in bed I'd have kept him out, but seeing you're up . . .' I plumped the pillows and smoothed the coverlet. 'Come to the kitchen. I could make you a cuppa. Or do you feel strong enough to see the garden? It's really something – or it used to be.' He was looking at me with a funny little smile, his head on one side. 'What?'

'Nothing. Just, I love you. You're like a little wren, Elf, flitting here and there. Such anxious little birds, always busy, but I'm only bruised you know, not dying.'

'I know.' I suddenly had to swallow. My voice shook as I said fiercely, 'But you could have been. If I lost you . . .' I hugged him, mindful of his arm, and felt him drop a kiss on my head.

'You won't. Now, supposing you give me the tour. How long are you likely to be here, anyway?'

'Only until I can get away. If the agent doesn't make an immediate sale, then Grandmother can just hire a caretaker. I'm sure Betty could keep an eye on the place and see that the garden gets knocked into shape. She's just on the next farm, after all. Come and meet her. I've known her forever.'

Betty was in the kitchen, cutting up meat for the casserole I'd planned on having that evening.

'So you're Phillip,' she said, when I made the introductions. 'Meg's told me all about you.'

'Well, she's never mentioned you,' Phillip responded, 'but then I didn't know she even had a grandmother, much less one living within a day's drive of us.'

'I can understand that,' Betty said. 'Ellie Chapman is nobody's favourite person. So when did you get here?'

As they chatted away, I reflected fondly that everybody got on with Phillip. It was one of the things that had attracted me to him in the first place. His gawky frame and shambling gait held a great well of kindness, partly expressed in the interest he took in people, which one and all responded to. I thought it helped explain the success he had with his portraits: Phillip genuinely cared for others' opinions, their differences and likings, with the result that they unfailingly warmed to him, as I could see Betty was now doing. She had urged him into a chair and was busy reaching the cups down from their shelf.

'Because it's near enough smoko time. Did you say you were going into town, Meg?'

'Yes. Can you keep an eye on things? I want Phillip to rest but as long as he's not actually tossing the caber I'll be satisfied.'

'Hey, I'm not five years old,' my love interjected. 'Will you be seeing your grandmother while you're in town?'

'Heavens, no! It's just groceries. Why?'

'Only if she's giving me house room, I ought really to visit her.'

'No,' I said immediately, and Betty also vetoed the idea.

'I wouldn't do that. She can be very unpleasant, Ellie. Tongue like a razor. Now'—she gave him a practised up-and-down glance—'you could do with some more weight on your frame. Eat up, there's a good lad.'

I took my list out to my car and trundled down the driveway, pausing at the gates to again view Jake's work there. The now neatly clipped hedges to either side gave quite a different impression of the Reach to the one I had gained on my arrival. Weeds still marred the gravel, but if you ignored the ground and lifted your gaze to the house, the garden appeared far more kempt than it actually was. I wondered how long Jake's employment would run: whether he'd been hired for a specific term, or just until the main pruning and tidying of the place had been completed.

I also wondered about his criminal record. Of course, he hadn't set foot in the house apart from the kitchen, where there was nothing of intrinsic value to steal, anyway. And a man could change, I reminded myself. Betty seemed unconvinced of his guilt. As, I had to assume, was Cabot, or surely he wouldn't have employed him. Still, I was responsible for my grandmother's goods, I reasoned, getting out of the car again to shut the gates, so I shouldn't be too trusting.

I returned from shopping to find the photographer gone and Phillip in the garden, sitting on a moss-grown seat in the dappled shade of a pepper tree by the tennis court.

'Just thinking,' he said when I asked what he was doing there. 'It's so quiet and peaceful. This place must've been lovely in its heyday. Why have you never mentioned it, Elf?'

'Because I hated it. Looking back now, it seems I was either at school in the city or dumped here with my grandmother. My parents farmed me off to her whenever they wanted to take a trip or just spend time alone. I can't remember a school holiday I didn't spend here, trying to keep out of Grandmother's way. I used to dread the thought of school break-ups.'

He frowned, his blue eyes concerned. 'Did she abuse you, Elf?'

'Only with her tongue. I was dull, and unwanted, and a burden on her. Nothing I did was ever right.' I sighed unhappily. 'She might as well have physically tortured me because she took away my confidence, made me doubt my own worth. She's old and helpless now, and you know what? I'm still afraid of her. It's pathetic, but you don't know what she's like, Phillip! Each time I ring her I have to force myself not to agree with every demand she makes.'

'Oh, Elf. But how . . . I know your parents died, but before that, why did they leave you with her? They must've known what she was like.'

For the first time I spoke aloud the truth I had long known. 'They didn't care. They never wanted me.' It was a shameful admission. I dropped my gaze and didn't see him surge to his feet, but I heard the groan the movement elicited and felt his undamaged arm wrap about me.

'Elf,' he murmured. 'No wonder your heart is sad.' His hand rose to stroke my hair. 'I hope there's a special hell waiting for people who torment helpless kids.'

I rested my head on his chest, feeling the strong beat within it. 'She's a bitter old woman – she always was. Maybe nobody loved her either? But she had daughters, a husband – though according to Betty he was a nasty piece of work too.' I pulled myself away to look up at him. 'It's all in the past, anyway. But you can see, can't you, why I never talk about it? I just want to forget.'

'You're too nice, Elf. Too forgiving, but I love you for it. Come on.' He dropped his hand and gestured with his chin. 'I noticed there were apricots going to waste over yonder. Let's go pick some. Nothing like 'em for the flavour of summer.'

'Probably full of fruit fly,' I protested, but I followed him anyway, assessing him as we went. 'You look awfully sore still. How are the muscles today?'

'It takes time,' was all he said. 'You should have seen me when I flew home. There's some small improvement each day. By the end of the week the aches and pains should all be gone.'

That was true enough for bruises but, remembering him thrashing about last night in the grip of the nightmare and the tortured self-blame that had followed, I doubted that his inner healing would be so rapid. The mind scarred more easily and took longer to mend than the body.

Later that day, pulling the filled garbage bags from Grandmother's emptied closet into the hall, I remembered the cubbyhole that Phillip had found in the bedhead. He was in the kitchen when I joined him, helping Betty stack cake tins and jugs of assorted sizes into cartons destined, like the clothes, for a charity shop. Stepping around the clutter, I said, 'Stop a bit. Before we pack any more we should work out how to get rid of it, or we won't be able to move. The hall's just about blocked with the wardrobe's contents. It would take me a dozen trips in the car just to shift what's already packed.'

'The charities will send a truck if you ring them,' Betty said. 'The Salvos do, so I should think they all would. I know someone who works at Lifeline. Shall I phone her, Meg?'

'Please. It's that or just keep filling boxes until we run out of space to put them.' I flung up my hands. 'There must be fifty years' worth of stuff in this house. D'you know I even found an old separator stashed in a cupboard in the laundry?'

'A what?' Phillip asked.

'Separator. Dairy farms used them to split the cream from the milk. They consist of about a thousand spinning funnel-shaped thingies with two spouts. Cream comes out of one and skim milk from the other.'

'A thousand?' my love queried. 'Really? And you know this how?'

'Well, two dozen anyway. And I learned it on a school trip.' I remembered the pretty dished faces of the jerseys with their black muzzles and large brown eyes, and the aromatic smell of the feed in their mangers. 'We were doing Rural Industries or something that term. Melanie Peters,' I said with reminiscent pleasure, recalling a particular girl who had frequently teased me about my lack of height and whom I had disliked intensely, 'stepped in a cow pat and practically had kittens.' I glanced at the clock. 'Look at the time. Jake'll be needing his afternoon cuppa. And after that I want you to show me how the bedhead thing works.'

'Your wish and so forth, Elf.' Using his left hand to push against the cupboard, Phillip got to his feet. 'But why? It's empty now.'

'Yes, but wouldn't it be odd to have only the one cache in the bedhead? It's . . .' I sought the word '. . . unsymmetrical. There was a pipe with the bracelet, so presumably that was my grandfather's side of the bed. I'm just a bit curious to see what my grandmother might have kept in such a private place.'

I didn't say it, but my mind had played with the possibility that she might have kept a diary. Wasn't it supposed to be a favourite pastime for women of her generation? If she had, and if she hadn't destroyed it, wouldn't the cubbyhole be the perfect place to keep such a thing? From earliest childhood, the question I had never dared ask had lurked at the back of my mind: *Why do you hate me so?* If it wasn't actual hatred, then it was the strongest dislike. I wasn't vain enough to expect automatic affection from everyone, and grandmothers didn't invariably dote – I knew that. They could be indifferent, or uncaring, but to display actual malice to a child? There had to be a reason for it. And if there was a diary, it might contain an explanation.

But I wasn't about to get an answer that afternoon for, when it came to it, Phillip couldn't reopen the hidden compartment, much less find its companion, if it existed, on the other side of the bed.

'But you just pulled on it,' I protested. 'Look, lie down, just as you were before. Now reach up and grab the headboard.' He obeyed but nothing happened. He shifted his position and his hand half-a-dozen times with the same result. When he finally sat up, defeated, he was holding his opposite elbow and hissing gently through his teeth.

'You've hurt your arm,' I said remorsefully. 'Leave it. I just wish you hadn't closed it because then we might have seen how it worked.'

'That's why I did it, trying to see . . . But hidden drawers and cubbyholes were meant to stay hidden, Elf. I expect they'd have predated safes, so my finding it was the sheerest fluke. What you really need is an antique furniture expert.'

'Oh sure, and there'd be two to a street in Glenfield. Never mind. It's probably empty – if it even exists.'

'There's another way, you know. You could always ask your grandmother.'

I looked at him and shook my head emphatically. 'No.'

He raised his left hand. 'Okay. It was just a suggestion. Oh, hello, old fellow.' He was addressing Claude, who'd chosen that moment to stroll into the bedroom. And to my utter amazement, the cat lifted his head and made a beeline for

Phillip, where he proceeded to rub his head against Phillip's ankle. Phillip dropped a casual hand onto Claude's back, stroking his body from head to tail until the tabby fur crackled with static electricity and the sound of purring filled the room.

'When did you get so pally with that monster? He does nothing but snarl at me.'

'He doesn't mean it, do you? What a handsome boy you are,' Phillip crooned. He rubbed a knuckle beneath the cat's chin while the purring intensified.

'I give up!' I gave the bedhead a slap of frustration and marched off, blowing on my stinging fingers as I went. 'If you want a drink I'll be in the kitchen. And seeing he likes you so much, you can earn your keep and give the rotten beast his tea.'

Chapter Ten

Breakfast the following day saw a little improvement in Phillip's condition. The bruising on his body was still an angry black and purple, but a yellowish cast had appeared around the edges and some of his stiffness had gone. He was still careful of his arm, but was becoming bored with inactivity – mainly, I thought, because he needed both hands to use his camera. Give Phillip a lens and he'd be happy in any condition, no matter where he found himself.

'Maybe I can help Jake,' he said. 'Give us a yell if you need me.'

'Okay. Don't overdo it. I'm going to ring round the charity shops, see who'll come out and collect.'

'I thought Betty had arranged it?'

'No, the woman she knew was away from home. I have to do a quick tidy in here too. You never know, Josh might fetch a client out at any time.'

'Josh being?'

'The real estate man.'

'Oh, right.' He went off and I picked up the phone book

as Betty came cycling up the drive. Later, while she continued to empty cupboards, I grabbed the broom and a duster and gave the rooms a quick once-over. In our bedroom Phillip had, as usual, left a mini-storm of untidiness. I emptied his collapsed bag onto the bed before tossing it into the now-empty wardrobe and sorted his camera gear into the bedside chests. A spare lens cap rolled away from me and, feeling blindly beneath the coverlet for it, I overbalanced and fell, saved only by the solidness of the bed. By the sheerest fluke, as I slapped a hand down to grab at anything to stop my fall, I encountered the bedhead and, next moment, the secret cavity silently opened, just as its mate had for Phillip on the opposite side.

It was disappointingly empty. Or so I thought until a second glance revealed that the dark panel at the rear was actually the cover of a book. An album, I saw, as I withdrew it with some difficulty from the narrow opening. It had been stashed upright, being far too tall to lie flat on the narrow shelf. Taking care not to touch or joggle the bedhead, I carried the album across to the chair by the dresser, sat down and opened it.

Scrapbooking plainly hadn't been invented back when it was begun. The first pictures were sepia prints of figures in old-fashioned clothes, mounted in little gilt corners that allowed for the photos' removal. I couldn't tell whether they represented a young Ellie Chapman or her parents. I flipped the pages looking for something recognisable and paused at a cluttered shot of a half-built house standing in a morass of mud and building supplies. Hunters Reach – sans verandah, chimneys, roof and garden. The next page proved my guess correct, for here was another shot with the walls up and then the finished building with one or two stripling trees looking spindly beside its bulk. There were photos of farm industry – men in braces and shirtsleeves digging, men building a haystack and the like. Then a wedding party: my grandmother in a calf-length dress with a veil and my unknown grandfather very stiff and solid beside her, sporting enough facial hair to stuff a small pillow. Like all photos of that era, the women's faces seemed smooth and ageless. Grandmother could have been fifteen or twenty-five within the shrouding veil. Girls had married earlier at the beginning of the century, I reminded myself, so either age was possible – or anything in between.

A blocky, old-fashioned car with high mudguards and a vertical windscreen was parked to one side of the shot. So my grandfather must've been wealthy even then – new house, new bride and a motor vehicle. Not bad going for the, what, early thirties or even the late twenties? I checked but there was no date on the back. Had my grandmother been happy that day, I wondered? Now I came to think of it, she had never appeared that way to me. Perhaps – this was a new and arresting thought – she didn't know what happiness was? If that were the case, it might explain but not in any way excuse her behaviour towards me and the rest of the planet.

The following pages showed brief vignettes of her life as a Chapman. Country picnics with women in hats and veils and men in collared shirts; motoring trips depicted by the loaded car, petrol cans lashed to the running boards. The arrival of the twins – chubby little faces in sunbonnets and later stiff portraits of them side by side, wearing dresses with Peter Pan collars and puffed sleeves. You could see the likeness between them but it wasn't striking. I stared hard but couldn't decide which sister was my mother. There were few family shots, one or two taken at Christmas with a tree in the background and the chandelier in the top corner identifying the lounge. Grandfather stood with his hand on his wife's shoulder and the girls seated before them, very *pater familias*. One year both daughters had plaits tied with large bows, but in the next their hair had been cut.

I flipped on through increasing numbers of photos taken of the now well-developed garden. Here was the tennis court under construction, there a picture of the obviously newly installed fountain, interspersed with a photo showing a winner's sash around the neck of a show bull, and – perhaps the first of Grandfather's real estate ventures? – the Grange Hotel in Glenfield's main street. Images of the twins over the years – in jodhpurs, holding tennis racquets, dressed up for dances or parties – a shot of the Reach, the front garlanded with lights and a marquee on the lawn; and then, jumping out at me, a picture of my father, smiling his crinkle-eyed smile at the photographer.

The whole of the next page was taken up with wedding photos, the ones Grandmother hadn't chosen to enlarge. It had been, by the looks of it, a lavish affair. The same three bridesmaids, including Aunt Iris, and the matching number of groomsmen. My mother's gorgeous dress: lace beaded with pearls and a tiara to hold the veil; a huge bouquet. Pictures of the cake, informal shots of the bride and bridesmaids with their friends . . . my eyes skipped over the unknown faces, snagged a moment, went on and then returned to one of a young man grinning and standing very close to Iris, their entwined hands all but hidden in the folds of her skirt. I stared, thinking myself mistaken, but no, it was him. Jake Lynch. Well, there was a surprise. He'd said he hated my grandfather, yet here he was, a guest at his daughter's wedding. Whom, I remembered, he'd never mentioned knowing, yet he was holding her hand. He looked young and very happy, but had the occasion just been an opportunity for him? Was this, in fact, the day that he'd committed the robbery that had landed him in gaol?

After the wedding, Grandmother's interest in photography seemed to wane. There were a few more pictures taken around the garden and the farm – I recognised a tractor I had climbed on as a child – and one or two snaps of my father's plane and one of an early model Holden car with my mother at the wheel. I flipped impatiently, looking for baby photos of me but there were none. The last image was a close-up of a rosebush in flower and then nothing but empty pages.

I removed the photo of Jake and stuck the album in a now-empty dressing table drawer. Slipping the picture into my pocket, I gathered another armful of the flatpack boxes and took them through to the kitchen to be assembled as needed.

Betty nodded at my action. 'Right on time. I've just filled the last one. The good news is the cupboards are finally empty.'

'I hope you kept enough back so we can cook and eat?'

'Well, of course. It's only the extra that got packed.' She eyed the photo I pulled out of my pocket. 'What have you found?'

'This. Comes from Mum's wedding pics. Isn't that Jake there with her sister?'

Betty pushed her glasses up her nose and studied the snap. 'So it is. My, he's changed. Well, so have we all. She was a lovely bride, your mum.'

'He and my aunt look pretty close,' I observed. 'Were they, do you know?'

She nodded. 'Mmm. Ellie didn't approve, of course, because he was just a trainee carpenter at the time working in his dad's shop – even if he *was* the darling of the football team – but Iris was always wilful. Went her own way. She and Jake seemed joined at the hip that summer, though Daniel Chapman made his opinion of the lad clear to any who'd listen.' She smiled reminiscently. 'His mistake. Jake's mother, Maeve, was an Irish redhead and fierce as a lion about her brood. I remember her bailing Daniel up in the main street and giving him a piece of her mind about his jumped-up notions of gentility. At the top of her voice and pretty earthy language. I reckon half of Glenfield enjoyed the show. He was a successful man, your grandad, but he wasn't much liked.'

'So why didn't Iris and Jake just clear out together? Wasn't she old enough?'

'She'd have been nineteen. Old enough these days, but not in Daniel's eyes. The set-to with Maeve happened before the wedding, then right after it the break-in occurred at the Reach and Jake was arrested. Iris left soon after he was sentenced. So,' she added meditatively, 'if Daniel framed young Jake, as I've sometimes thought, that backfired on him too. Because it cost him his daughter.'

'I see.' I stared blankly at the frozen images and the transient happiness they portrayed. 'God! Life's a gamble, isn't it? You fall for the wrong man, get born to the wrong parents, maybe even yield to an angry impulse and your whole life is screwed up.'

Betty sighed. 'Isn't it the truth, pet? Now, before we start filling any more cartons, did you find somebody to come and collect them?'

'The Salvos will. After lunch, they said. So I was thinking we could maybe clean the linen chest out by then and pack the spare blankets? We could use garbage bags for them, save on the cartons.'

'Good idea.' She glanced at the clock. 'Smoko first? The boys will be ready for their cuppa.'

'Why not – though Jake's hardly a boy. Neither's Phillip. He's thirty-one, five years older than me.'

'So?' Betty made a sound, part derisive, part amused. 'You get to my age, you're all just children.'

'It must be nice to be so – so confident and sure of yourself,' I said wistfully. 'Is it just experience or were you always like that, Betty? I was terrified of my grandmother but I never remember you being scared of her.'

'Why would I be? I never liked Ellie – she was mean-spirited and plain nasty. Plus, she gave herself lady-of-the-manor airs because I worked for her. Though to be fair, that was a family failing.' Her eyes twinkled at me. 'Except for you, thank goodness. Still, I could've found other work if I'd wanted to.'

'So you stayed for my sake? Thank you.'

'Well,' she said as she shrugged and got up, 'you had no one else. Now, if you get the cups out, I'll put the kettle on.'

Phillip came in with Jake, sleeving sweat from his brow with his good arm. 'We've got a load for the tip,' he said. 'Thought I'd go along for the ride. Nothing you want in town, Elf? We go right through, Jake said.'

'No, I'm good, thanks.' I eyed his sling. 'Don't overdo it, will you?'

'Swear to God,' he said solemnly, and I flicked a finger against his good arm.

'See you mean it then.' I was glad he was busy. It wouldn't stop him grieving, I knew, but, however momentary the distraction of work proved, I hoped that it might prevent him from constantly dwelling on the death of his friend. And tiredness might give him the dream-free nights that, so far, he had lacked.

The Salvos truck with its distinctive logo appeared before the men returned from their trip. I wondered what they could possibly be doing. Perhaps they had stopped for a bite of lunch in town? In the meantime, the two volunteers with the truck carted the filled cartons out and loaded them. I showed the driver the scrawled list of contents on the side of each box.

'I hope it helps whoever unpacks them.'

'That's fine, love.' He eyed his load before pulling the door shut. 'Emptying the house, are you? Has the old lady died?'

'She's moved into a home and the place is on the market.'

'Ah, well, I expect we'll be back, then,' he said cheerfully. 'Ta for calling. See you next time.'

'Have they gone?' Betty's head popped out of the kitchen.

'Just this minute.'

'Let's eat and not wait, in that case. I can't think where those boys have got to.'

Chapter Eleven

It was after two before our own men returned.

'Where on earth have you been?' I demanded of Phillip. 'Have you eaten?'

'Yep. We picked up a pie and a Coke from the bakery. I wouldn't say no to a cuppa though; Jake too, I reckon.'

I looked beyond him. 'Where is he?'

'Unloading the timber. We had to wait for it to be cut. The bloke who did it was out.'

'What timber?'

'For the well cover,' Jake said, stepping through the door. 'Supposed to be all arranged but of course the dozy bugger hadn't got round to measurin' the planks.' To Betty he added gruffly, 'Sorry if we put you out with lunch.'

'It was only sandwiches. Have a couple now with your tea. What sort of meal is a pie for growing boys?' she asked with obvious disdain, and Jake's dour expression was lightened by a sudden grin.

'Growing? Twenty years back maybe, but thanks. I will.'

Impulsively, I said, 'I found a picture of you, Jake, in my

grandmother's album. Wait, I'll show you.' I'd moved the book to a drawer in the dining room and now carried it back to the kitchen, flipping the pages as I went to find the right image. 'There. You're with my aunt.'

'Right.' He stared at the photograph, sandwich in one hand, then glanced away.

'It must've been taken here because there's the rose garden behind you, only I can't place that bit of trellis. Has it been taken down?'

'No idea,' he said brusquely. 'Looks like a party. But I went to a few back in the day.'

'It's your mum's wedding.' Phillip was turning pages. 'Right here, at the Reach. A good-looking couple, weren't they? How old would they have been, Elf?'

'She was nineteen. Dad was twenty-one.'

'Mmm.' He turned and scrutinised my face. 'You took after your mum more than him.'

'Grandmother said once that I had my mother's eyes,' I offered.

'Well, you certainly haven't got hers,' he replied. 'I've never seen anything so cold – like a lake just before it freezes. It wasn't only the timber yard that held us up. I dropped in on the old girl at the home. It was'—I could see him thinking about it—'an illuminating experience, let's say.'

'I told you not to!' I said heatedly. 'Was she horrible to you? What did she say?'

He raised a placatory hand. 'It's okay, Elf. Words are her only weapon and you ought to know they just roll off me.'

'And what is that supposed to mean?' I demanded.

'Huh?' He looked surprised. 'Oh, only that I'm untidy as you frequently tell me, but you haven't managed to organise it out of me yet. Anyway, we came to an understanding of sorts. She'll probably never be a fan of mine'—a hint of a grin showed—'but I pointed out she was hardly in a position to call the shots.'

'You threatened her,' I said, not a little awed.

'No, I just told her she was through bullying you. And if I thought it was happening I'd be taking you away. She said a few uncomplimentary things about our domestic arrangements and unprincipled men in general, and I promised to visit her again.'

My mouth literally fell open. 'You didn't, Phillip! You surely don't mean to?'

'Of course I shall. She's your family. Whatever has made her the way she is, a bit of kindness can't hurt.'

'You're wasting your time, lad,' Betty said.

I opened my mouth to agree with her and the phone rang. 'I'll get it.' It was a blessing. If we were going to argue, it shouldn't be in front of the others.

The caller was Josh Latten. He'd had a nibble, he announced buoyantly. Would it be all right to bring the clients out this afternoon – say in about an hour? He apologised for the short notice but they seemed keen, and in his experience it was all about keeping your irons hot and in play, as it were.

'Don't let opportunity slip, you mean? Yes, by all means.' My mind darted through a checklist, but everything was in order. Yesterday's flowers wouldn't have drooped and, thanks to the Salvos, the clutter in the entrance had gone. 'That will be fine. We'll see you later then.'

I went back to inform Betty and found her alone, placidly washing cups and plates.

'I'll get off before they arrive,' she said when I told her. 'If he should report back to Ellie, we don't want her learning I'm here.'

'She should be grateful,' I said roundly. 'You didn't have to look out for Claude, or help me pack up.'

She shook her head. 'When did gratitude and Ellie ever meet? I'll see you tomorrow, pet.'

When the prospective clients, a man and a woman in their forties who were dressed in business clothing, followed Josh's vehicle up the drive, I opened the door to them then stepped out myself, leaving the agent a clear field. I remembered then that I hadn't closed the secret compartment in the bedhead, but it was empty and if the couple took the house, they wouldn't be buying the furniture so it hardly mattered.

I wandered across the lawn, passing the rosemary hedge (now trimmed and aromatic in the heat) that separated the still-untouched kitchen garden area from the rose beds, noticing the new stack of timber by the well. Jake would have to get that done before a contract was signed, but didn't property sales have a cooling-off period between purchase and signature? There should certainly be time enough for him to complete the job for the garden already looked a hundred per cent better than when I'd arrived.

I found Phillip seated once again on the bench behind the tennis court in a brown study. Grieving, most likely. I shivered. He would probably never forget the manner of his mate's death, or cease blaming himself for it, absurd though that was. Claude was sitting at Phillip's feet, the cat's front paws tucked beneath his chest and his eyes mere slits as Phillip's foot rubbed gently against his ribs.

'You've hynotised that beast,' I said. 'Maybe you should start a career of lion taming. You could include nasty old women as an extra.'

'Elf.' He smiled a greeting and patted the timber beside him. Claude rose, arched his back in a stretch, then stalked off.

'See? He hates me.' I sat down and blurted, 'Why on earth did you visit the home today? I told you what she'd be like.'

He picked up my hand. 'We've been together for two years now, Elf, and in all that time I haven't met a soul from your past, so I was curious. Which is natural enough, I think. You've hardly said a word about your life before we met. I knew you were orphaned and, really, when I think back, that's about all you've ever told me. Oh, and that you went to boarding school. It's okay,' he said when I would have interrupted. 'If you don't want to talk about it, that's fine. But when I see the unhappiness in you – well, you can't blame me for looking for ways to fix it.'

'I'm not unhappy with you,' I said quickly. 'I love you, Phillip, more than you could possibly imagine. You're the first person that ever counted in my life, apart from Betty and her husband. Her being at the Reach meant the world to me when I was a kid. But there was nobody else . . . I wasn't good at making friends. Didn't know how, I suppose. I was paralysingly shy growing up and I guess,' I admitted with difficulty, 'if you know you were never wanted, it makes it hard to believe anyone *could* care about you – enough to want you for a friend, I mean. I had to work hard enough to convince myself that *you* did. I don't know if Grandmother was nasty or just thoughtless, but she seemed to delight in tearing me down. It scars you when that happens, and if it goes on for years . . .'

He kissed my hand as I trailed off. 'I know, sweet. I've seen what it does.' He looked around, taking in the garden, tennis court and house. 'I've been trying to understand . . . They had so much, your family. Couldn't they have spared just a spoonful of love for a child? It doesn't make sense.'

'Tell me about it. I think if I'd known why, it wouldn't have hurt so much. Or I could maybe have figured out a way to reverse it. Stop whatever it was that made me unlovable in their eyes. Make myself over to something more pleasing. That's what I thought, anyway.'

'It wasn't up to you,' he said violently, then took a deep breath and visibly relaxed. Phillip's ability to control his emotions had always amazed me. It took a lot to upset him and I think that the air of calm he generated was what had first attracted me to him. After a lifetime of implied, expected or actual criticism, his easy acceptance of whatever I said or did had been balm to my soul.

I changed the subject. 'You know that photo I showed Jake – of him and my aunt? I know he pretended not to remember the occasion but I'm pretty sure he was in love with her.'

Phillip's brows rose as he eyed me. 'Really? And you can tell this how?'

'The body language in the photo. They were holding hands and leaning into each other. They were happy, Phillip. You could see it.'

'It was a wedding,' he reminded me. 'They were probably

both a bit pissed. Drinking loosens inhibitions. Maybe he fancied her and she was just mellow enough to flirt.'

'It was more than that. Betty said they were close but my grandparents didn't approve. And they were right, it seems, because he went to gaol for robbing the place. Maybe he wasn't there that day for the wedding so much as to get the layout of the Reach? See where the valuables were kept. I don't suppose that in the general to-do of such an occasion you'd even notice if someone was casing the joint. You might remember later, after the goods were gone, who it was among the guests that didn't really fit. I mean, he was a blue-collar worker and my grandparents were nothing if not snobs – what was he even doing there? I can't believe he had an invitation, unless it was from Aunt Iris. So he'd be an obvious suspect, wouldn't he? If my aunt *did* love him, it's probably why she ran away. She might've felt as though he'd just used her to get into the house.'

'Yeah?' He frowned. 'If that's so, what's he doing working for the old girl now?'

'I suspect she doesn't know that he is. And maybe he was the only man available. Her solicitor, Cabot, hired him. He must've known about Jake's past, so not telling her who he'd hired was probably the easiest way. And maybe, like Betty, he doesn't believe Jake was guilty?'

'The courts obviously did.'

'Well, who knows?' I shrugged. 'Juries have been known to make mistakes, and Betty said he had an alibi, even if it wasn't believed. Anyway'—I suddenly remembered—'I found that pic in an album in the bedhead. I got the secret compartment open, purely by chance, just the way you did. I wonder if Grandmother forgot it was there? You'd think she'd want to keep her photos. Though they stop soon after the wedding.'

'Is the cubbyhole still open?' He stood as I nodded, and said, 'Good. I'm going to find out how that thing works. There's got to be a spring or a rod somewhere. It's been bugging me, you know?'

'Have at it then. And if you do, show me. I don't think I could fluke it again.' I cocked an ear as a vehicle purred to life. 'Sounds like the viewers are leaving. If he hangs around long enough, I'll see what Josh thinks about them.'

The agent was heading for his car when I caught up with him. He pursed his lips and oscillated a palm when I asked about the clients. 'Hard to say. On the one hand they loved the place – went on about the space and what the rooms could be used for. But they showed no interest in the grounds.' He shrugged. 'Six of one, half-a-dozen of the other. Still, we've got time. Plenty more fish in the sea.'

Which was fine for him but I had no wish to be stuck here for months waiting on a sale. Phillip's arm would mend and he would be off again with his camera, and I had no intention of being left behind, dancing still on my grandmother's string. Sighing, I went back inside to see how Phillip was getting on with the bed and was alarmed to see him on his back on the floor, half under it.

'What happened? Are you okay?' I rushed to his aid only to find that his position was intentional.

'Look at this, Elf.' He pointed at something above his head. I folded to my knees and wriggled in alongside him.

'What am I looking at?'

'The rod. Easier to feel it, just proud of the baseboard here – got it?'

'Yes.'

'Push it in and it closes the compartment. Not all the way 'cause I've shoved something in the opening. It works from a catch or button up top. Haven't found that yet. But I will.' He swivelled around until he could sit up. 'They were pretty smart, those old joiners. This is the eighteenth century's answer to the wall safe.'

'Except there was nothing valuable in it,' I pointed out. 'I mean a pipe, a broken bracelet and an old album? Given their money, I'd have expected diamonds at the very least.'

'If she's got any, they're probably in the bank,' Phillip said. 'Your gran's not the sort to miss a trick. Particularly if the place has been burgled once already.' Reclining again, he scooched himself across under the bed, his voice becoming disembodied. 'Ah, I can see the other one. Easy to spot when you know what you're looking for. This one's a lot stiffer though. It'll have to be done from the top.'

I sat on my heels on the rug, watching him work his way across the top of the bedhead just as he'd done before, but this time he fluked it again.

'Clever.' Scooping the pipe out of the drawer where I'd placed both it and the chain, he used it to block the entrance, easing the panel back and forth, while checking occasionally beneath the bed until he was satisfied the rod was moving easily. Then he reached a hand in to explore the second cavity prior to closing it. 'Just checking. You don't want stuff rattling when they take it out, do you? Somebody might try to force the panel and wreck it, just out of curiosity. Hello – thought you said this one was empty?"

'What have you got?'

He looked at the small volume he held, then passed it over. 'A book of flowers, homemade by the looks. It was lying flat, which was how you missed it.'

I examined it curiously. It was smaller than a paperback, and the pages had been cleverly stitched and bound in a hard cover that was painted over with pansies. *The Language of Flowers*, the title read in flowing script, hand-drawn, for I could see the slight variations in the letters. There was a flyleaf but no printing history. The book's contents, I saw, were alphabetically arranged in two columns, the left being the name of the flower and the right what it stood for. *Abatina*, which was first, was listed as *fickleness*. The pages, browned with age at the edges, were each ornamented with a spray of flowers. The writing was print, done in a clear and precise hand that, I noticed as I paged through the little book, occasionally wavered and dipped and had one or two neat corrections inked in.

A faded inscription, in the same Indian ink as the book's contents, was written on the flyleaf of the volume: *To my dear fiancée, the loveliest flower in the garden, with all my love. M.*

I held it out for Phillip to see. 'Look at this.'

'Fiancée,' he said. 'Your grandad's gift?'

'His name was Daniel. This is from somebody else – M. She must've been married twice!'

'Or she changed her mind, or he died, and she met Daniel. Lot of work anyway.' He flipped through the pages and returned to the first entry. 'Abatina. That's a flower?'

'How should I know? I can tell a pansy from a rose and that's about it.' I glanced at the pipe he'd picked up. 'Look, will you please chuck that thing?'

'You don't want it kept?' He cradled the object in his hands, teasingly holding the stem just short of his lips.

I wrinkled my nose. 'Hardly. How hygienic is a disgusting old pipe somebody's been sucking on? Definitely not a recyclable item, mate.'

'True.' He put it down and picked up the broken bracelet instead. 'Not this though. If the old dragon's agreeable, I'll get it mended for you, Elf. You deserve one keepsake at least from your family.'

'It's a nice thought.' I got up and, tucking the little book into the bedside drawer, felt for the concealed button in the bedhead and saw the panel glide smoothly shut. 'I wouldn't bet on her agreeing to it though.'

Chapter Twelve

The following day, when Jake came in for smoko, he had a bloodstained handkerchief knotted about his left wrist.

'What happened?' I sprang up from my seat. 'Do you need a bandage?'

'Bloody bougainvillea,' he grunted. 'Oughta be outlawed. Tear the hide of a rhino. It's fine,' he said irritably when I went to remove the makeshift cover. 'I'll get worse yet. The stuff ain't been cut back since God was a boy.'

'It was always pretty sprawly,' I agreed.

'Yeah, well, it's killed whatever was growing in the planter. Swarmed all over it. *And* it's halfway up the maple. I'll finish it later.' He helped himself to a buttered scone. 'I've already got a load for the tip, so I'll dump that and pick up some welding gear from town. Oxy'll do it. You wanna clear it with old Cabot?'

'What do you need it for?' It seemed an odd request.

'To cut the weldmesh outta the top of the well. It's already bust, but it's been concreted in. Cuttin's the quickest way to clear it.'

'If you say so.' I was doubtful. 'Couldn't you just put the timber over the top?'

He lowered his brows. 'No. Job's worth doin', it's worth doin' right. You shift the chairs when you sweep?'

'What?' I couldn't immediately see the point of the question. 'Well, of course I do.'

'Same thing.' He returned to his scone.

'Mind if I catch a lift with you?' Phillip patted his pockets, then dug at them one-handed to unearth a notebook, handkerchief, a stub of pencil and the broken chain. 'Where did I put my wallet, Elf?'

'I don't know. Beside the bed?' I hazarded a guess. 'It's—' but I got no further, for Jake reached suddenly across to pick up the bracelet.

'Where did you get this?' His thumb and forefinger slid over the nameplate as he turned his gaze on Phillip.

'It was in a hidden compartment in Mrs Chapman's bed.' Phillip shrugged. 'Her daughter's, apparently. I want to ask the old girl about mending it for Meg. So is it okay if I get a lift? You could drop me at Woodfell on your way through, pick me up coming back.'

'Yeah.' Jake laid the bracelet down and used a finger to push it back. 'My mum had one like it. Dad always said he had it made for her, so seeing it gave me a bit of a shock. When can you be ready then? Plenty of time. I gotta load the trailer first. Pick you up straight after?' Without waiting for a reply, he got up and lurched out the door, leaving his half-drunk tea on the table.

The screen banged shut and I looked at Betty, who'd sat silent throughout the exchange. 'What was that about?'

'Search me. It's plain he did recognise the bracelet. It certainly upset him – he's left his tea. It does rather contradict what he said about that photo though, doesn't it?'

'Mmm. He can't recognise the venue it was taken at, he says, but he has no trouble identifying a bit of jewellery a girl wore what – twenty-some years ago? You're right, Betty. He really was in love with Aunt Iris.' I looked at Phillip, who appeared a little shell-shocked at my conclusion. I poked him. 'Best find your wallet, buster. I don't think Jake'll be in the mood for hanging around.'

'And that's no wonder. You'll have him married off before he's out the gate.'

'Men!' I said. 'You might as well all be blind. Well, I suppose I'd better ring Mr Cabot about the welder. You think the story of shifting chairs will work for him?'

'Try it and see, Elf.' He kissed my cheek. 'Back for lunch, probably.'

Cabot demurred a little on hearing Jake's request for cutting gear, but was eventually brought to agree. I assumed his reluctance arose from typical lawyerly caution, a conscientious regard for conserving a client's money, and to my own surprise I found myself defending Jake.

'You should come out and visit, Mr Cabot. See what a difference he's already made to the place. Honestly, the garden was a jungle when I arrived. It was hard to even open the gates. Now there are paths and proper beds and you can see over the hedges. It must be five years since some of the shrubbery was last pruned, and the volume of stuff he's already cleared away is enormous.'

'Well, if you're happy with the progress he's making, Ms Morrisey. I'm sure you have your grandmother's best interests at heart . . . Very well, then, I'll leave word at Saunders' Machinery. It sounds like a small job, so he should return the gear tomorrow. Let him know, will you? Any prospective buyers yet?'

'One couple came,' I said. 'The agent thought they were a bit ambivalent and I haven't heard from him again yet. I'm sure there'll be more though. Thank you for that. Saunders' Machinery,' I repeated. 'Which street is that?' He told me. 'Okay, I'll tell Jake.'

I'd scarcely made it back to the kitchen when the phone trilled behind me. It was Josh with another client. We fixed on two o'clock for a viewing and I made a mental note to check the flowers. Then, the men leaving, Betty and I resumed packing.

We chose the back bedroom for our next task. It had plainly served as a sort of boxroom, because the large wardrobe had been used to store things like fans and heaters and unused lamps, as well as a handsome set of monogrammed luggage, all leather, its corners reinforced and padded handles folding flat.

'They belong in a museum,' Betty said. 'I suppose they'll do to pack stuff in. They'll never sell though – everyone's got wheels on their bags these days.'

'Maybe the theatrical group would like them? They'd go nicely with the fox stole and the weird hats.'

'It's an idea. They might take those china ducks from the snug, and the set of bamboo pictures in the office too. To dress sets with, you know. Lord knows they're old-fashioned enough.'

'I remember the ducks,' I said. 'I had names for them. Quacky and Honky and . . .' I searched my memory. 'Waddle! That's it. Because he was last, and a bit lower on the wall. Like he couldn't keep up.'

'Everyone had a set of them back in the fifties,' Betty said. 'Flavour of the month, they were. Of the decade really. What's in the tallboy?'

'It's empty, I hope.' I opened the top drawer. 'Oh no, more clothes, and yet more.' I pulled open lower drawers as I spoke. 'And good grief'—I had reached the cupboard at the bottom—'hat boxes!'

Betty chuckled. 'Ellie's generation didn't get by on t-shirts and thongs, Meg. They dressed. At least we haven't found any stays yet.'

The clothes in the top drawer were packed in paper that exuded the scent of mothballs. Just below a silk jacket, circa 1930, I found Grandmother's tissue-wrapped wedding dress: a straight-skirted design that had reached to below mid-calf. When I held it against my body it fell to my ankles. The underskirt of silk was overlaid with lace and had a double ring of pearls stitched around the neckline, and was accompanied, in separate tissue, by a very fine veil, a little yellowed by age.

'It's a period piece.' I held it up. 'She must have been about my size, only taller.' I delved deeper. 'The whole trousseau seems to be here. It's beautiful quality, Betty. Look at this robe – it's got little ribbon roses all the way down the front instead of buttons. Somebody must've stitched for a week!'

'You can't dump that in a charity bin – not any of it.' Betty ran the silk through her fingers. 'I never owned anything half so grand. Of course, Ted and mine's was a war wedding. Lace and silk couldn't be had in '42, even if my parents could've afforded it. Well, if it was me, I'd dump it back in Ellie's lap, Meg. Go and see her. Find out what she wants to do with it, and then your conscience is clear – even if she says to burn it. What else is in there?'

'Heaps,' I said. There were shawls, scarves, evening bags, old-fashioned step-ins with perished elastic, suede gloves and, when I reached the lower drawers, the equivalent in men's clothing: jackets, cravats, braces, frilled evening shirts. The hat boxes contained shoes – ankle boots really, with buttoned sides and solid heels in white suede ('Wedding shoes,' Betty said knowledgeably) and two pairs of shiny black patent-leather court shoes with ugly block heels.

'It seems like she's kept all Grandfather's formal clothes. And the trousseau looks brand new. You'd think she'd have worn it. Let's just pack all her stuff into the big port until I've spoken to her.' I glanced at my watch. 'I want to change the flowers and get lunch over with before Josh gets here.' I cocked an ear. 'That might be the boys coming back now.'

Betty heaved herself up. 'Gracious! Where has the time gone? I'll get the meal on the table. I have to pop into town this arvo. There's a bus at half two I can catch from the main road, so I'll leave after the washing-up's done.'

'I'll drive you,' I said. 'Seriously, Betty – you live out here and don't drive?'

'I've got my trike,' she said, 'and the bus is reliable. I haven't bothered keeping the car registered. It's just an added expense when I'd only use it to shop. After Ted went . . .' She shrugged. 'I never really liked driving. He always did it, you see.'

'Well, you're being driven today,' I said firmly. 'We'll wait to let Josh in, then we'll go.'

And, I thought glumly, I would visit Grandmother. I just hoped she wouldn't think I was behind Phillip's idea of having Iris's bracelet repaired and given to me. I didn't want it and would tell her so if she raised the subject. I couldn't ever remember receiving a gift from her. My birthday was in February, so it and Christmases had come and gone largely unregarded once my parents had died, save for gifts from Betty and Ted. There had been new clothes and shoes each year from my grandmother, who was, after all, my guardian, but no personal presents. Christmas festivities for me had been lunch at the Robertses' house, for Ellie Chapman had always dined out alone on that day at a fancy restaurant in Glenfield.

I said suddenly, 'Do you remember the Christmas when you and Ted took me to that fair and I got to ride the pony? And the fairy floss that blew all over his mane and turned it pink? It was such a wonderful day! I've never forgotten it.'

'Fancy you remembering that,' Betty exclaimed. 'It was on Boxing Day, actually – the local fair – and just after your parents died. Such a sad little scrap you were, and we wanted to cheer you up. But you cried all the way home, as if your little heart would break. We didn't know what to do. I thought the pony must've frightened you.'

'No,' I said. 'Not the pony or the day. I loved them both. It was because I had to come back and couldn't stay with you forever.'

'Oh, Meg,' she said. 'If we could've kept you we would've. Ted adored you, you know. You were like the grandchild he never had.'

I felt my eyes moisten. 'I loved him too,' I said huskily. 'Life's not very fair, is it?'

Betty sighed. 'No, pet. It just is, and we have to make of it what we can.'

Phillip was back, clumsily pouring himself a cup of chilled tea in the kitchen. I took the jug from him before it spilled.

'Oh, so you escaped in one piece?' I said. 'Here, let me do that. Do you want lemon in it?'

'Please.'

I cut a slice from one in the fruit bowl and slipped it into the glass. 'Did you mention that Claude has taken a liking to you?'

He grinned. 'Didn't think of it. Actually, she was pretty silent after I showed her the bracelet. She was full of ginger before that but I just sympathised. Told her I knew old age was a sea of aches and pains, which must have an effect on people's moods and was therefore entirely forgivable. Then, while she was still wondering how to annihilate me, I produced the chain. Honestly, Elf, she just went white. I'm not exaggerating. I was afraid she'd pass out and was heading for the call button when she spoke.'

I stopped with my hands full of cutlery, arrested in my task of laying the table. 'What did she say?'

'Croak, you mean? It was like she'd been shocked to her toenails. "That was Iris's," she finally said. "Where did you find it?" I told her it had been in the bedhead and that I'd like to have it mended and replace the name with yours.'

'And?' I prompted.

'She stared at me for the longest time. I didn't think she was going to answer, until she said, "As a gift you mean?"

'Only with your permission, I told her. Then she pushed the bell and said, "Very well. But her name is Margaret. Not that stupid Elf you call her. You can go now. Don't bother coming back."'

I grimaced. 'Well, there's a surprise – and not. That she would agree, I mean, and then toss you out. What happened to smiling old age?'

'Mmm. What *I* wonder is what happened to her?' Phillip, gazing into space, sipped his tea. 'The way she hits out automatically, I mean. Like she always has to get in the first strike. People are usually combative for a reason.'

'And some are just born nasty. Do you mind moving? I've got to get to that end. Lunch in five, okay?'

Josh turned up on the dot of two. The client drove himself in his own vehicle, a middle-aged man in an expensive-looking car, who wandered away from the agent to stand and assess the front of the house, giving it a slow once-over from chimneys to verandah railings. When Josh started to introduce me, the client spoke across him. 'Acre and a half, you said – the grounds?'

'Yes. You'll be able to see them after—'

'Hmm.' He scowled. 'Not much. Three would've been better.' Catching my eye then, he nodded brusquely. 'Morris Langley. No need for you. The agent can show me around.' The last words came over his shoulder as he walked towards the steps. Josh threw me an apologetic look and followed.

I was still fuming when I picked up Betty. 'Ill-mannered pig! I'd hate to be working for him. I should've warned Phillip and Jake,' I realised, reaching automatically for my sunglasses.

'I wouldn't worry.' Betty tried to soothe me. 'I've a feeling your man can look after himself. And Jake certainly can. I see you've brought the clothes?'

'Yes. If Grandmother doesn't have any specific instructions, I'll take them to the theatrical place, or maybe even the Heritage Hall. And tell them not to use them until after her death,' I added hastily. I could just imagine her fury at the very notion of having her garments on display. Perspiration prickled my upper lip and I turned the air conditioning up. 'It needs re-gassing,' I apologised. 'You're probably better off just opening your window. It's hot enough to fry an egg out there.'

The cattle we passed were clustered in shade, dark humps beneath the trees, and no birds flew. The crops, so vividly green when I first came, hung head-heavy, already browning, their growth weighing them down as much as the heat. The leaves of the gums dangled limply against the strident light, and even above the car engine I caught the high shrill of cicadas. Memories surfaced of other summers when I'd travelled this road, heavy-hearted and squirmy-stomached, and I pushed them away. Betty had been the only good thing waiting for me back then. I stole a fond glance at her face, where the once-firm flesh was slackened by the years, and spoke impulsively.

'Don't let's lose each other again. When this is over, I mean. I should have kept in touch before, only . . .'

She nodded. 'You wanted to put it all behind you, didn't you? But it works both ways, Meg. I could've made the effort too. But I let it all slip when Ted—'

'I know.' I touched her hand. 'Somebody dies and it changes your world. Everything else seems so trivial, and what mattered before suddenly doesn't. Phillip's friend who died in New Guinea – his wife will be feeling that now.'

'Poor lass. And with a baby on the way, you said?'

'Oh, it's already born. I can't imagine . . .'

'You never really can when it's another's pain. What, by the way, did Ellie tell your young man about Iris's bangle?'

'She agreed to me having it.' I caught her sideways look and nodded. 'Yes, it surprised me too. I don't actually want it,' I confessed. 'I don't want anything from her, but Phillip seems set on it. I'd just rather he junked the idea, only it would hurt him if I told him that. He's . . . very protective of me. Though I don't need him to be,' I added forcefully. 'I can look out for myself.'

'Ah, let him do it,' Betty said comfortably. 'A woman's never the worse for a bit of coddling, Meg. Besides, it makes a man feel good. Ted got a real kick out of opening jars for me.'

I could have pointed out that facing down my grandmother required a different kind of strength, but let it go for we'd reached the outskirts of town. 'Where would you like to be dropped?'

'The bus stop will do, thanks. The supermarket's right across the road. There's a bench just inside so I'll wait for you there, okay?'

'I won't be long,' I promised, nosing into a parking spot to let her out. 'Half an hour tops. But you take as long as you want.'

Woodfell drowsed in the afternoon heat, the gardens deserted, doors and windows firmly shut to keep in the air conditioning. Bypassing Susan Pickering's office, I went straight to my grandmother's door, waiting until I heard her voice reply to my knock before opening it. Bracing myself, with the photo album clutched tightly against my ribs, I entered. My heart was hammering and for a cowardly moment I wished that I'd asked Phillip to accompany me, despite having just told Betty that I could look out for myself. Well, maybe now was the time to prove it.

Chapter Thirteen

'Margaret,' Grandmother said. She was in her chair again but today, I noticed, there was a tall wheeled walker standing in the corner next to the cupboard. 'What are you doing here, girl?' I saw sudden alarm in her face. 'There's nothing wrong with Claude, is there?'

'Not unless his taking a shine to Phillip worries you. How are you, Grandmother?' I asked dutifully. 'The garden's progressing nicely, Claude is fine and no doubt Josh told you he had another party wanting to come out today to view the Reach?'

'I know,' she said. 'So why are you here? Shouldn't you be back there showing the buyer around? It's what I'm paying you for, after all.'

'That's Josh's job. And you're getting your pound of flesh, don't worry. Ask him for the pics he had taken if you don't believe me. I came to bring you this, to see if you wanted to keep it.' Without relinquishing it, I showed her the album. 'It occurred to me,' I said untruthfully, 'that whoever buys the place might like some history to go with it. Shots of the house being built, and the early garden. Or you could give it to the local historical society. I'm sure they'd love to have these photos. They're part of the social history of the district – the different fashions, the early vehicles, even the men working the farms. Every one of them's a record of changing times.'

She looked at me suspiciously. 'So you don't want it for yourself?'

I steeled myself to return her gaze. 'No. I want nothing from you beyond my wages.'

She said waspishly, 'And an eighteen-carat gold bracelet, it seems.'

'That,' I said, 'was Phillip's idea, not mine. If I'd thought for a moment that you'd agree I'd have stopped him asking you for it. But,' I added, remembering my purpose and adapting my tone, 'I would like a photo of my parents. This one.' Riffling hastily through the pages, I found the wedding picture showing my father, his bride and her twin. Hoping to gentle the old woman into agreement, I touched the tinted bouquet. 'The flowers she carried look wonderful. Were they from the garden?'

'Of course.' Was it my imagination or had her voice actually softened? She leaned forward to pass arthritic fingers over the image. 'Carnations for scent, pink roses for a bride and blue delphiniums to match her eyes. It was beautiful. I made it up myself with ferns and baby's breath to set off the colours.'

'You have a real gift,' I said sincerely. 'So, may I have it?'

'I suppose so.'

'And the album? What do you want done with that, Grandmother? There are the clothes too. I have them in a bag in my car. If you could decide what—'

'I told you already.' The momentary thaw had snapped back to chilly impatience. 'Throw them out, burn them. I don't care.'

'But it's your trousseau and your bridal gown!' I protested, appalled. 'Beautiful fabrics – silks and lace and all that embroidery! You just can't burn them.' I was aghast. 'They were your wedding clothes! Surely they must represent happy memories and you'd want them saved. Half of them look as though they've never been worn.'

She drew an audible breath, and I waited to be annihilated, only to see an expression of such pain cross her features that I almost gasped in astonishment. Her face seemed to crumple and, for a horrible instant as I caught a shine in her eyes, I thought she was about to cry. Utter panic seized me, but then she stiffened, resuming her customary hard mask as if the moment's weakness had never occurred.

'They haven't been,' she said coldly. 'It was a period of my life I had no wish to celebrate. Tell me, Margaret, does this man of yours, this Phillip, ever intend to make an honest woman of you?'

'An honest . . .? Oh.' The penny dropped. 'If we both decide it's what we want, I suppose we'll marry some day. It's our decision and at present we're happy as we are.'

'You're fortunate then. In my day we had no such freedom, before or after marriage. Do what you wish with the clothes, though if you send them to a charity shop, I should pity any young woman ill-advised enough to take them for her own nuptials. No good will come of it.'

I said blankly, 'But that's . . . you can't truly mean that! Look, I'm sorry your marriage was so unhappy, Grandmother. But if Grandfather was – was unpleasant, or not your first choice . . .' What if, I thought wildly, she'd had a lover she'd been forced to leave? The mysterious M of the little book? Or was it a case of a stern papa out of a period novel marrying her off for family gain? 'But you had your family. Didn't that count – having daughters to love?' And a grandchild, I forbore to add.

She gave a sharp crack of laughter that held no amusement whatever. 'Unpleasant? He was a monster.' I gaped at the revelation and she shook her head tiredly. 'Go away, child. I need to rest.' Most of the snap had gone from her voice, but it wasn't that that got me out the door; it was her suddenly scary vulnerability, as if a lioness had lain down and offered her throat to me. In that moment, and for the first time ever, I saw my grandmother as just an ordinary person with all the fears and regrets that everybody has. I exited swiftly and stood for a few moments outside the closed door, my mind a whirl of conjecture. Straightening up and drawing a long breath, I found myself on the receiving end of a commiserating glance from a passing aide, and smiled feebly in return.

In the end I delivered the clothing and luggage to the theatrical group. The office was shut but the occupant of the house next door, who proved to be the group's secretary, received my offering as if it were manna from heaven.

'The luggage too?' She drew an ecstatic breath. 'Wonderful! And it couldn't have come at a better time. We're doing *The Importance of Being Earnest* next season. Do you mind if I look? The woman who takes care of our wardrobe is on holiday at the moment, so—'

'Knock yourself out,' I said cheerfully, and left her *ooh*ing in delight over the contents of the larger case.

I collected Betty and her bits of shopping, dropped her off and drove back to the Reach with the photo album riding still on the rear seat. I would remove the family photos and offer the rest to whoever bought the house. If they declined, I decided, it could find a home with Glenfield's historical society.

Back at the Reach, I wandered through the garden, my thoughts on my grandmother. So fearsome had her presence been in my young life that never once had I considered her state of mind, whether or not she herself was unhappy or upset. She had always appeared the same: hard, unbending, with a subliminal anger that had seemed aimed at my unwanted presence. That something other than myself might have been at the root of her unpleasantness had never occurred to me.

According to Betty, Grandfather had been a domestic tyrant, 'a bit of a bully'. Had he simply had a hectoring tongue, or mean ways with the housekeeping money, or was it worse than that – had his fists been involved? Battered wives who successfully hid the results of their beatings were hardly news. Had my grandmother been among that secretive sisterhood? Was that why she had poured her life into the garden – because it was something, unlike her home life, that she could control and unstintingly love?

I couldn't even guess at her relationship with her daughters, both of whom had apparently escaped her, and their home situation, at the earliest opportunity. I remembered how infrequently my parents had visited the Reach, even after my grandfather's death. And Aunt Iris had simply fled. Would my mother have done likewise if Simon Morrisey had not happened onto the scene? I thought it likely. In her own way, she had been as ruthless as my grandmother.

There was no sign of Jake among the garden beds. The sprays were going; I had come to recognise the soft, almost inaudible hum of the electric motor, and rainbow colours shimmered above the roses where the sun caught the falling droplets. A huge white bowl on its stained pedestal, uncovered when the bougainvillea was cut back, was under the spray, which highlighted the loose magenta bracts that had drifted into the bowl. It had probably once held bulbs, I thought. They would have been a pretty sight when in bloom, with the arc of the bright bougainvillea hedge behind them. Grandmother had, in her own way, been an artist. Her garden, even in its present state, bore witness to that.

Jake would, I realised, be in town, picking up the oxy-welding gear and Phillip had probably gone with him. I had wanted to share the new discoveries I had made at Woodfell, but it would have to wait. Sighing, I headed back indoors. Time to be thinking about preparing something for the evening meal.

Later, just as I put the new potatoes on to steam, Phillip came in from the garden, letting the door swing shut on his heel.

'There you are,' I said. 'Jake gone, has he?'

'Yep. Returning the welder before he knocks off.' He rumpled my hair on his way to the fridge. 'Want a drink? It only took him ten minutes with the oxy to cut the weldmesh free. The damp rising from the well had just about rusted it through.' He waggled a carton of fruit juice at me. 'Yes? No?'

'Just a small one then. So he can get the cover made and over it before the next prospective buyer? If that lout today doesn't make an offer, that is.'

'That bad, was he? Ah well, won't matter to us who gets it in the end.' He handed me a glass and sipped from his own. 'Incidentally, I know how your aunt broke her bangle. How's that for sleuthing?' He looked smug enough to smack.

'I can see you're dying to tell me,' I said dryly, 'so how, Mastermind?'

'You can sneer, but I have the evidence right here.' He fished awkwardly in his pocket to unearth a few stretched links of gold chain attached to the tiny padlock I had so vividly remembered. 'There. It was caught on a broken bit of weldmesh. She must've been messing about at the well and pulled her hand back without realising the link was caught on the mesh.'

'It would take a pretty strong pull to break the chain,' I objected.

He shrugged. 'Gold's soft, and the link that broke may have been worn. Anyway, I'll take it to the jeweller tomorrow. You may as well have the whole works, and at least it'll all match.'

'Why wouldn't it? Gold's gold,' I said and he grinned and flipped a finger under my chin.

'No, my little Elf, it isn't. Gold comes all colours. Depends where you find it. Did you know that a good assayer can actually tell not only which country, but in which mine in that country a nugget was dug from?'

'Oh, yes?' I said skeptically. 'And where did you garner this factoid?'

'South Africa. When I photographed the mine workers.'

'Oh. True then.' The most memorable picture of the series,

taken for *National Geographic*, had been of a black mine-worker deep underground, bare shoulders and the planes of his face beneath the yellow helmet shining with sweat, as he worked some sort of pneumatic drill. The shot had encapsulated both the man's strength and his weariness as he neared the end of his shift deep in the bowels of the gold-rich earth. It had made the magazine cover, the drama and energy of it fairly leaping at the viewer – but that was Phillip's particular gift. The word photography, he had explained to me soon after we met, literally meant 'writing with light'. So, in a sense, his pictures were poetry, saying much with little, as if he squeezed into each frame the very essence of the thing portrayed.

Which reminded me of the album and the conversation with my grandmother. I relayed the gist. 'She called him a monster, Phillip. She really seemed to hate him! I almost felt sorry for her – which I never thought to do.'

'Ah well, to know all is to forgive all,' he murmured somewhat sententiously.

'I wouldn't go *that* far. But it might help explain her general attitude. So, anyway, if you're going to visit the jeweller tomorrow, maybe you could drop a photo off at the camera shop for me? There's one in Benson Street where the courthouse is. Get them to enlarge and frame it. It's my parents' wedding pic. Not as good as your work,' I said honestly, 'but it's all I've got.'

'Well, every era had its style, Elf. I guess that a barefoot bride on a beach would've been a bit shocking back then. Put it with my wallet so I don't forget. Now, I'm starving. When do we eat?'

Chapter Fourteen

The dawn broke still and breathless, a sign of the heatwave to come. I knew that by midmorning the trees would be hanging listless in the hot air, the flowers drooping on their stalks. I wished it would rain but it seemed unlikely. The skies had been cloudless for days, brassy with heat and tinged with dust from the land further west. It was probably good for the grapes, but the stone fruit would burn and rot. I made a mental note to ask Phillip to pick the last of the apricots. Fewer leaves on espaliered growth meant the trees gave very little shelter to their fruit.

We had barely sat down to breakfast when Jake appeared at the door, rumpled and unshaven, and at least an hour before his usual starting time. He nodded a brief greeting to us both. 'Meg, Phillip. Can I have a word?'

'Good morning, Jake.' I swallowed my surprise. 'Come in.' Although in fact he already was. 'Have a seat. Is something wrong? You look . . . do you want a cuppa?'

He rubbed a hand over his face and tried to smooth his hair. 'Well, yeah, thanks. I didn't sleep much, I—' He looked at me, hesitated, then said, 'This might sound a bit odd, but I wanted to ask a favour of you.'

I passed him the tea, shooting a quick glance at Phillip, who wordlessly pushed the sugar bowl to the other man. 'What is it?'

'I want you to go—' He seemed to reconsider and shook his head. 'That's no good, first you have to understand . . . Look, the other day – that photo you had with me in it? I lied about it. Of course I remember that night, and Iris Chapman. I was going to marry her. I loved her. Head over heels as they say. And she loved me. That photo was taken on the last day we spent together, at her sister's weddin'. We were going to elope that night, only old man Chapman caught us together in the summerhouse. My own fault – we shouldn't've risked it.' His eyes went blank and he fiddled with the mug I'd given him. Then he sighed deeply and continued.

'He said some pretty unforgivable things to his daughter, then threw me off the place. Swore he'd have the police on me if I came back. Then he locked Iris up. Literally. I couldn't go near the house, so the next day I got a mate to come out with a message, but your grandmother told him her daughter wasn't there – that she'd been sent away. Only it was a lie, of course. My mate saw Iris at her bedroom window. As for me, I never set eyes on her again except in the courtroom weeks later, because two days after the wedding I was arrested. The old bastard went and fitted me up with a burglary charge.' A dull remembered rage smouldered briefly in his eyes and he sighed again. 'She didn't write while I was in prison and the letters I sent to her came back to me unopened, so I gave up on that. And I never expected her to visit. Like Chapman would've let her! I looked for her when I came out but what mates I had left in Glenfield told me she was long gone. Run away soon after my sentence was handed down. Like her feelings for me weren't enough to overcome the shame of prison, though she must've known I was innocent. Hell, I hadn't set foot on the place since that night, let alone got inside to rob it!'

His hands fisted briefly then relaxed again, his customary glower replacing the flare of anger. 'I tried to forget her,' he resumed, 'told myself if she couldn't stick, then she weren't worth lovin'. And I had other worries – like work and feedin' myself.

'My folks had shut down the business and were long gone. I heard that while I was inside, Chapman drove 'em out. The shop had been set on fire once an' he made sure any man doing business with or workin' for him boycotted the place. So if I'd ever doubted, I learned just what Chapman's influence could do round these parts. Same went for me when I got out. There was no work for an ex-con. None. Course he owned half the businesses in town, so no surprise there. But breaking us up wasn't enough for him, he wanted me out of the district, out of his sight.' He scowled. 'So I went. I guess I was tired of fightin' an' without Iris, what was I even fightin' for? I drifted off an' joined the army. Then after my discharge I got into the fire service until the accident—' He slapped his bad leg, then shrugged. 'That put an end to that so it's been odd jobs, nothin' permanent since . . .'

He waved the words away abruptly. 'Water down the creek, none of it matters now. Man draws the short straw he can't do nothin' but get on with it. Only yesterday, when I seen that bit of bracelet dangling over the well, it just came over me an' I knew.' He thumped the table, grey eyes flashing with conviction. 'She never left. Not me, not the district. She wouldn't've. I went to gaol and that vicious old bastard killed her and dumped her body in the well. It would've been 'im who sent the letters back too. So what I want,' he finished in a rush, 'is for the cops to investigate. But only you can get that started.'

If he'd placed a live grenade on my toast I couldn't have been more astonished. My mouth opened uselessly then closed again and, taking it for the first sign of a refusal, he crowded forward, elbows on the table, one of them nudging the sugar bowl aside.

'Don't you see?' he said urgently. 'I wouldn't ask if I could do it meself. I mean you owe me nothin' but it has to be a family member that asks. The cops aren't gonna search for a body without a good reason. They won't listen to just anyone. God knows the world's full of cranks, so you can't blame 'em. And as for me – an ex-con? Forget it. But they have to listen to a relative and at least consider the request.'

'But wait, Jake,' I said, speaking slowly to calm him. 'Listen, you've got it all wrong. Maybe she is dead but her body can't be in the well, because Betty told me that Iris came back, after she ran off. She came back, oh long after the court case and sentencing – maybe a year? I don't remember exactly. Did nobody tell you? Well, I don't suppose they would,' I added, my thoughts catching up with my tongue. 'But Betty said she was here, so she must've seen her or,' I amended, 'at least heard it from somebody who had. It was only later, after my grandfather's funeral, that word seemed to have got around about her having died. Though there was never a memorial service for her. Betty told me that too. I sort of gathered that she believed Grandmother was still angry.' I shrugged. 'Ergo, no service.'

He was doggedly unconvinced. 'So how did her bracelet get there? And why was the weldmesh torn apart, come to that?'

'I suppose it rotted. Phillip'—I looked to him for support—'said the rising damp had rusted the mesh?' He nodded and I spread my hands. 'Maybe she was leaning over, dropping something in and the chain snagged. It's sort of irresistible, isn't it? Looking and tossing a pebble down any deep hole to test its depth.'

'How?' he said bluntly. 'The bore was in use months before the wedding, so the well had already been capped. The timbers were screwed to a frame fitted around the wellhead. You can still see it there today. A proper job.' Even in the midst of presenting his argument I caught the approval in his voice. 'And leavin' aside why Iris would do it, supposing she had somehow taken the cover off, weldmesh don't rust, let alone rot away, in a matter of months. It's taken twenty-odd years to get the way it was.'

Troubled, I said, 'I don't know. What do you think, Phillip?'

'It sounds far-fetched,' he admitted, 'but Jake's got a point. She's wearing the bangle at the wedding, we have photographic proof of that. So if the well was already boarded over, the only way the chain could get there was with the removal of the cover. But it doesn't mean it had to be then. What if the chain was broken, and the weldmesh cut – because that's what you're implying, Jake – at a later date? When, for instance, Iris came back.'

'But – but why? Why then? If Jake's already been removed from the scene, isn't the problem solved? Why would

Grandfather feel the need to kill his own daughter when the relationship was already over?'

Phillip exhaled, shaking his head and lifting his good hand. 'I don't know. You did say he was known to have a temper. Maybe it was an accident? He lost it and lashed out and the deed was done? The more I learn about your family, Elf, the screwier they become. But facts are facts. The bit of bracelet was caught on the weldmesh; that's one fact. And it didn't get there by itself – that's either a pretty sound guess or another fact. I'm not for a moment suggesting that your gran knew anything about it, but maybe, before we contact the police, we should try talking to her. Get her take on the matter?'

Jake's brow contracted. 'That'll get you nowhere. The old trout's an expert at stonewalling. Besides, the moment she hears my name and learns I'm involved, she'll order you off the place and that'll end any chance we have of getting the police on side. They'll figure out I'm behind it and reckon it's just spite.'

We mulled this over for a moment. 'He's got a point.' Phillip looked at me. 'And if the old girl did sack you, well, it just bolsters Jake's argument. You're making trouble for her because you lost your job.'

'We need legal advice,' I offered. 'Supposing we were to ask Mr Cabot? Then it's up to him. I mean, aren't you liable for prosecution if you suspect a crime's been committed and don't report it?'

Phillip grinned. 'That's my careful little Elf. But what if you do, and it hasn't? Then you could find yourself being charged with wasting police time. That happens too in what they term vexatious cases. Your aunt wasn't ever actually reported missing, was she?'

I raised my hands in a don't know gesture but Jake shook his head. 'I never heard nothin' to that end. Course, I was inside, but local issues were still talked about.' His shoulders slumped. 'Makes it harder. If the cops don't believe she went missing – if they were never asked to look for her . . .' He trailed off. 'But I think Cabot's a good idea,' he said, nodding, plainly taking heart again. 'If he's involved, the cops are less likely to dismiss the idea. Christ!' he said roughly. 'All it'd take would be one frogman lowered down the bloody well. It's not like we're asking them to search a lake.'

'Do you think Cabot would listen to us?' I asked. 'Grandmother's his client. I daresay she's been worth a fair bit to him in the past. Is he likely to go behind her back?'

'He wouldn't be.' Phillip patted my hand. 'He'd be checking out something that came up and getting a handle on it before consulting her. That's just part of his job, to assess and advise.'

'So, shall we go and see him – all of us?' I asked.

'Better if he came out here,' Phillip said, cocking an eye at Jake, 'don't you think? Show him the crime scene – if that's what it is. The mesh is still there if not in situ, and I've the bit of bracelet to show what we found.' He thought about it while gently massaging his bad arm. 'We can't ask him not to tell your grandmother, but we could suggest he sees the police first, if of course he's willing to do so. That way, if they agree it's worth looking at, it'll be out of her hands if she does object. What do you think?'

Jake's face had lightened and he produced a smile of satisfaction. 'Any chance you're a lawyer yourself? I gotta say you think like one.'

Phillip shrugged. 'Just common sense, mate.'

I glanced at the wall clock. 'He won't be in his office before nine, and maybe not till ten. I'll ring him then. Where's the cat, by the way? He should be here.'

'He is.' Phillip tilted his chair back and I saw that the brute was actually sitting on his lap, tail neatly curled about his body and his eyes closed. 'Apparently he likes this chair. I tipped him off and he jumped straight back up again when I sat down.'

'He likes you,' I grumped, and he smirked.

'Can't blame him for his good taste. Come on, old fellow, down you get. Breakfast.' Claude perked up at the word and jumped off, almost as if he understood Phillip.

Jake heaved himself up. 'I'd better get started too. I was gonna burn the rest of the hedge trimmings today, save on trips to the tip, but maybe not. It's real bushfire weather.'

I waited until ten before making the call to the solicitor, wondering how best to ask him to make the trip out without actually telling him why. In the end I said that my partner and I had stumbled across something while clearing the house and would value his professional advice. I feared, I said, picking my words carefully, that if there was any substance to it (keeping the *it* carefully vague), my grandmother might be held responsible. I waffled and hesitated so artfully until he agreed to come immediately that Phillip, propped against the wall listening, shook his head.

'What a performance. I had no idea you could be so creative, Elf. You almost sounded as if you were worried about your gran.'

'Well'—I looked at him—'in a funny way, I am. Yesterday, when she told me that my grandfather was a monster, she looked so *old* and beaten it scared me. It's weird. Before she was just like a . . . a . . . I don't know, a nasty, irresistible force. I'd never associated her with fragility or weakness. She was like some bad-tempered immortal god, always glaring and disapproving and then I suddenly saw she was just an old, old woman, thin and weak and – and done with life. Almost, anyway. Too tired to bother being horrible any more. And I don't know why, considering everything, but I felt sorry for her.'

'That's because you're a poor hater.' He cupped my cheek with his good hand. 'You're always ready to give someone a second chance. It's what I love about you. That and your strength.'

'You think I'm strong?' His words amazed me. I had always despised my inability to stand up to my grandmother, my readiness to wilt before criticism.

'Of course you are! If you were weak or petty-minded you'd have ignored it when she sent for you. Only the strong answer a challenge. So, when will the legal bloke get here?'

'Half an hour, maybe? Depends how fast he drives.'

In fact it took him until ten forty-five. I had opened the gates for him and Betty had arrived by the time he drove slowly up the drive, obviously assessing progress on the garden as he came. I had put Betty in the picture by then. She heard me out and then nodded slowly as if weighing up both sides of an argument.

'It never would've occurred to me,' she said slowly, 'but you know, if it should turn out to be true, I wouldn't be all that surprised.'

That staggered me more than Jake's impassioned accusation against my grandfather. 'So you think he really could have done that? Murdered his own daughter?'

There was compassion in her brown eyes as she shook her head. 'Course it's not something anyone wants to hear about their own kin, pet, but he was a piece of work, your grandad. I never saw a man with a nastier temper. He'd just go raging mad if he was crossed. Oh, he was good at hiding it, and Ellie that proud that she never let on about his brutality, but he came pretty close to gaol a couple of times. Would've ended up in court if he hadn't greased a few palms. The local cops knew which side their bread was buttered. He was rich and powerful and had the ear of them further up the pecking order, you see. But Ted knew of at least one man he crippled. Your mum, she was the smart one – apple of his eye – she knew it and never put a foot wrong. But Iris . . .' She shook her head.

I shivered. 'Well, I'm glad I have no memory of him. He did me a favour dying when he did.'

'And Ellie,' she reminded me. 'She was a hard woman, but she still didn't deserve him.'

Then we both heard the car tyres crunch on the gravel and I went out to greet Mr Cabot.

Chapter Fifteen

Cabot was a short, solid-looking man whom on first meeting I had placed in his fifties. He had receding hair touched with grey and shrewd eyes behind rimless spectacles. He asked how I was, shook hands with Phillip and allowed himself to be ushered indoors. I noticed him noticing his surroundings and judged that not much got past him.

'You've got it looking nice, Ms Morrisey. Your grandmother would be pleased. I see the garden is coming along well too. Now, what seems to be the problem?'

'Would you like a drink first?' I asked. 'Coffee or something cold? I've some iced tea.'

'That would be lovely, thank you.'

While I served him, Phillip slipped out to fetch Jake and we were soon settled about the table, Betty hovering unobtrusively in the background. Cabot had greeted her, obviously knowing who she was, only nodding when she explained her presence.

'I'm just giving Meg a hand. No need to mention it to Ellie.'

'Quite. I understand.' Explanation was plainly superfluous.

'She can be a trifle'—he gave a little cough—'difficult. Won't you sit, though?'

So she did and without more ado Phillip began his exposition. Earlier Jake had agreed that he should lay the story out. 'Old Lyle's a straight shooter,' he'd said. 'He knew – well, he suspected all along that the robbery was a con job. Come to see me an' told me so after I was sentenced. But it'll sound better comin' from you. You ain't involved an' you've got a good head for argument. Me, I'm likely to thump the table an' do me block.'

Cabot listened to it all, his head cocked a little and a tiny frown between his brows. Phillip tabled the wedding photo showing the bracelet on Iris's wrist, and produced the broken bit of chain with its tiny padlock and stretched links. 'We found the rest of it in a secret drawer in a bedhead on old man Chapman's side of the room,' he explained. 'And before you ask, there was a pipe in with it, so we're assuming it's the side he slept on. The chain is presently in town with Haddock the jeweller – the old lady gave me permission to have it repaired for Meg.'

The solicitor fingered the scrap of chain, then knitted his brows. 'Just a moment. You believe this caught on the mesh and the weight of the body broke it?'

'That's correct,' Phillip said, 'so—'

'That being so,' Cabot persisted, 'shouldn't the rest of the chain have fallen also? But you say you have it – how do you explain that?'

Phillip paused and it was Jake who answered. Eyes bright with anger, he growled, 'I reckon when the bastard realised it'd caught he probably grabbed it an' yanked, an' never noticed it broke in two pieces.'

Cabot nodded slowly. 'Possible, yes. Hmm. Is that all you've got? So far you have a broken bracelet, which I have to point out, could have happened anytime after that photograph was taken. Perhaps she removed it after the ceremony. Or—'

'She never,' Jake broke in. 'She was wearing it that evening. Fact is it was damn near the only thing she *was* wearing when Chapman found us in the summerhouse.' He reddened.

'So he caught you in the act, as it were?' I said.

'Yeah. It's why he locked her up, framed me. A nobody like me daring to lay a hand on his daughter? He'd've killed me if he could've.'

'All the same, it doesn't prove—' Cabot began.

'You haven't heard the rest yet. Come outside, there's something you need to see.' Phillip pushed his chair back and we all trooped out behind him, feeling the sudden belt of the sun like a blow on our shoulders as we followed him to the well.

The weldmesh Jake had cut free lay on the browned grass beside the well coping. It was a rough circle of mesh, rusted and thin in the centre, where a body-sized hole gaped, and sturdier about the edges. Phillip leaned down to hook the bit of bracelet over a rotted spike of mesh. ''Bout there?' he asked and Jake nodded grimly.

'I reckon.'

'You have to remember the well was boarded over on top of the mesh. So there's no way that'—Phillip indicated the scrap of jewellery—'got there by accident. Somebody had first to remove and then replace the covering.'

Cabot blinked, then raised his eyes and gazed around him. We were out of sight of the house, the view of it blocked by shrubbery and the expanse of the kitchen garden that still awaited Jake's attention. 'I can see it's physically possible,' he said somewhat reluctantly. 'Daniel was a strong man and would only have been in his sixties when he died. A slip of a girl . . . yes. So, does your theory – because it is only a theory so far,' he stressed, 'does it have a time frame?'

Betty spoke up for the first time. 'It must've been at least a year after the wedding. Because Iris came home then. She wasn't around long, but I saw her, just the once. We were driving into town, Ted and me, and she was at the gates of the Reach when we got to the turn-off – standing there still wearing her coat like she'd just come out or was about to go in. I looked across – it's not much more than a hundred yards – and said, *That's Iris! What's she doing back?* But Ted, he said, *It's Fleur, girl. Thought I heard a plane come over.* Simon used to land on the Cowans' strip,' she explained, waving a hand towards the neighbouring place to the east, 'when they visited.

'But later,' she resumed, 'in town when I was in the chemist I was talking to young Flo Beames, and *she* said she'd spoken to her. To Iris. Said she'd got off the bus and was standing on the pavement with a bag waiting for a taxi when Flo walked by on her way to work. They chatted a bit, just the normal chit-chat, you know – Cold enough for you? What are you doing these days? – but she could back me up. They weren't identical, the twins, but they were pretty similar, which was why Ted, who didn't see as much of them as I did, mistook her for her sister.'

'So'—Cabot had listened patiently to her involved tale—'you would swear that it was in fact Iris Chapman at the gate that morning?'

'Yes,' Betty said stoutly. 'We weren't on the best terms with the Chapmans at the time so I hadn't a chance to see her again. Not that I needed to,' she added. 'Daniel wanted our top paddock you see, and Ted turned down his offer. So on account of that, I wasn't on what you'd describe as a calling footing with Ellie. He took refusals personally, Daniel did. When Ted told him no, he got abusive. Said he'd see Ted regretted his decision, and when Ted changed his mind, which he would, the offer would be half what he was putting up now.' She shrugged. 'That was his style. But back to the girls – I was at the Reach often enough helping out in the kitchen while the twins were growing up. I knew which one was Iris, right enough.'

We were all watching Cabot. For myself I hardly knew what to hope for – that he would declare it a mare's nest of groundless suspicion based on Jake's grudge against my grandfather, or that there was substance enough in the story to alert the police to a possible crime. Grandmother, I realised, would be furious with me in the latter case, and a secondary consideration was that if the authorities decided to investigate, the sale of the Reach would be placed on hold. Which meant a further delay in getting my life back.

I think we were all holding our breath until Cabot looked across at Jake and nodded. 'My opinion? It needs investigating. If there's a body down there . . . How deep would it be, by the way?'

Jake rubbed his jaw, considering. 'Water table here's about ten metres, an' they'd've gone a bit deeper so she didn't pump dry. Mighta silted up a bit over the years, I suppose. Call it eleven – twelve, maybe.'

'Right. Well, as I was saying, *if* there's a body, it doesn't prove Daniel Chapman put it there.' He sighed. 'You realise it's going to cause an unholy mess? And Mrs Chapman . . .' He trailed off with an eloquent grimace.

I said swiftly, 'The police might dismiss it, so don't tell her unless they decide to investigate.'

His smile was wry. 'Oh quite, I'd got there too, Ms Morrisey. It might be instructive to find out – if you can – the facts of her daughter's fate. What *she* believes happened to her.'

'I'll try,' I said, 'but you know Grandmother's not . . . I mean, you can ask, but if she doesn't want to tell you, well . . .'

Cabot nodded soberly. 'She won't have that luxury if it comes to an official investigation.' He removed the scrap of gold and stood weighing it in his hand. 'I think I'll take this to the police, but you should leave the weldmesh there. And the well as it is.' He gazed at the dismantled roof and windlass disposed tidily on the grass. 'Maybe pull a rope around it for protection? And it might be an idea to get the work on the rest of the bracelet stopped, if it's not too late. Just until we see what the police have to say.'

'Right.' Phillip turned towards the house. 'I'll give them a call now. He said he'd have to match the gold so maybe he hasn't started work on it yet.'

Cabot left, Jake hammered stakes in around the well and looped a nylon cord about it while Betty and I returned to the kitchen.

'Well,' I said, sinking into a chair, 'God knows where this is going to end now. Grandmother will flay me for not stopping it, though I don't see how I could have. I wonder how long it will take for the cops to decide? Maybe,' I added hopefully, 'Mr Cabot will call this arvo and say they wouldn't listen.'

'Don't get your hopes up, Meg. After all, it'll be fairly simple to check. I mean it's not like they have to dig up foundations or search a paddock for a burial site – and they've done that before with runaways they suspected were murdered.' Betty sat down opposite me.

'But Iris was never reported missing, was she? She purportedly just left and, from what you've said about her, that's quite in character. And if she was nineteen – well, twenty if she returned twelve months after – she was entitled to do what she liked, go where she wanted. Even if Grandfather didn't think so. She sounds like she was quite the rebel.'

Betty nodded. 'I'm not saying that your mother wasn't spirited too, but Iris was always the more independent and adventurous of the two. Fleur would obey, even if it was plain she didn't want to, but Iris would stick out her chin and demand "Why?" She was like that even as a toddler – once she decided some rule was silly or unfair she'd carry on like a pork chop, no matter what you said. It drove Ellie mad. She was always stricter with Iris. And when it came to her early teens, the two were like Kilkenny cats.'

'But Mum toed the line? I wonder,' I mused, 'what she'd have done if they'd tried to break up her and Dad?'

'Luckily they approved of him, but I've a fair idea. Like I said, your mum didn't lack spirit. It was just that she was canny enough to see she got more by falling into line. And she was afraid of her father – well, Iris was too, but she was braver, or perhaps she just felt a greater need to be free. The young are so ardent; they take what seem like stupid risks to us older folk, but maybe that's because we become more prudent with age. Your mum was prudent. Iris'—she sighed—'was the wild card. They should've been proud of her,' she said, suddenly fierce, 'but Ellie feared scandal more than anything and Daniel was just a plain brute.'

Phillip came back at this point. 'Any luck?' I asked.

'Yeah. Apparently the bloke I saw has been away. The chain's still as it was, so I told him to hold off doing anything until he heard from me. I expect,' he said, sitting down and clicking his fingers at Claude, who immediately sidled over to rub against his chair leg, 'that if the cops make a move, the first thing they'll do is confiscate it. It'll become Exhibit A in their case.'

I shook my head in dismay. 'It's all galloping out of our control, isn't it? Where's it going to end?'

'With lunch?' my beloved suggested. 'Talking seems to make me hungry.'

'Well, I don't wonder!' Betty said, eyeing the clock. 'Is that the time?' She seized her apron from behind the door. 'I'll get lunch on. What have we got, Meg?'

'Salad things, cold meat. And I'll fetch what apricots I can salvage. The heat's about done for them.'

'Wear a hat,' she said absently, as if I was still ten. 'And could you grab a handful of mint while you're at it? Those lemons will juice into a nice refreshing drink. Why are you smiling?'

'It's nothing,' I said lightly. 'Dear Betty, I don't believe you've changed one iota since I was ten. I hope you never do.'

I went out into the searing light leaving her flushed with pleasure behind me.

Chapter Sixteen

The day passed slowly but Cabot didn't ring. I hovered around the phone, not leaving the house for fear of missing his call, though common sense insisted that of course he would try again. But the instrument remained obstinately silent. Jake had returned to his hedging. By now he had built an impressive pile of cut branches on the open ground beyond the tennis court, the twiggy branches poking skywards like skeletal fingers where the browning leaves had already dropped.

'Be a regular bonfire when he lights it up,' Phillip commented. He'd been helping pile up the last load before Jake left for the day. Betty had long gone, leaving her apron hanging on the hook behind the door like a flowered ghost of her presence. 'We could toast marshmallows, Elf.'

'Not in this weather,' I replied. Phillip was a Taswegian by birth and had been in Africa the last time South Australia had suffered from wild fires. 'The country's like a tinderbox. I wish it would rain.'

'I expect it will, eventually,' he said comfortably. 'It's no good fretting, love. The phone will ring or it won't, there's nothing you can do about it.'

I sighed. 'I know. But the more time I have to think about it . . . Don't you find it odd that she'—I meant my grandmother—'would just accept what was basically a rumour that her daughter was dead, and not do anything about it? I mean, wouldn't she make enquiries, demand an inquest, whatever?'

'We don't know that she didn't. There could have been an inquest.'

'So why does nobody seem to know how she died, or where she's buried? I thought Jake was crazy to suspect something, but I'm no longer so certain. It does make a weird sort of sense. People don't just disappear.'

Phillip fetched two glasses and a bottle of sparkling wine and, when I put my hand out to open it for him, shook his head and jammed it between his knees, using his left hand for the office.

'Not quite useless,' he murmured, pouring, 'and you'd be surprised, my love. Apparently busloads of people vanish in this country every single year. And only about one per cent of them are murdered. The rest want to drop out of sight for whatever reason. Australia's a big place.'

The phone hadn't rung by the time we went to bed. I locked the front and back doors, checked that the kitchen window was open for Claude and then found the cat sitting at Phillip's feet in the bedroom, claws tightening rhythmically in the carpet as he received a back massage from Phillip's big toe.

I switched on the ceiling fan and sniffed. 'Do we have to have that animal in our room?'

'You're just jealous he likes me best. Come here.' He reached a long arm to encircle my waist. 'What did the old girl have to say?'

'Nothing. I didn't ring her tonight. I was afraid she'd know somehow what I've done.'

'You haven't done anything. It was Jake's idea and Cabot's decision. How does that make you responsible?'

'I don't know,' I admitted, 'but in her eyes I will be – I can guarantee it. If the police do come out, that's when I'll tell her. She'll be mad enough when she learns that Jake is working for her, never mind that Grandfather's become a murder suspect. You heard what Betty said about her hatred of scandal. I'm sure the only thing that she'd consider a worse crime would be adultery.'

His lips moved under my jawline, nibbling at the tender skin there. 'Maybe she should've tried it sometime – might've found she enjoyed it as a change from her husband. Forget the old killjoy, love. Come to bed.'

The following morning, the phone rang as I was clearing away the breakfast dishes. I picked it up carefully, my mind divided between Grandmother and the solicitor. He wouldn't be in his office yet, I thought, and braced myself for an angry tirade, only to find it was him after all. Calling from home, obviously. I felt a little sick.

'Mr Cabot. Good morning.'

'Ms Morrisey,' he responded. 'I thought I had better inform

you at once. The police have just rung to let me know they have the go-ahead from Adelaide to check out your well. They'll be coming out to the Reach sometime this morning. Apparently it was a case of getting the equipment brought up – from Mt Gambier as it happens – which accounts for the delay. Not too much call for underwater gear around here, you see.'

'I wouldn't call it much of a delay. They've only known since yesterday.'

'Quite so. You'll keep me informed if they find anything?'

'You're not coming out then?' I felt a spurt of panic. I had counted on him taking charge of the matter.

'No need. The police will do what's necessary. Then it will be time enough to inform my client. Have a good day, Ms Morrisey.'

He hung up on that incongruous sentiment, leaving me wondering what shape a bad one might take. I relayed the news separately to Phillip and to Jake. The latter, up a ladder with a saw on a pole, swearing to himself as he wrestled with runaway bougainvillea limbs that had colonised a tree, was grimly pleased. Phillip, collecting rotting stone fruits into a bucket, wiped his messy hand and shot me a concerned look.

'So. Well, at least we'll know. Maybe it's all a pipe dream, Elf. Just because Jake *wants* it to be true, doesn't have to mean it is. In which case there's no need to tell your gran anything.'

'No.' I had made my decision last night after our lovemaking, lying in the dark, watching the moonlight on the curtains and listening to Phillip's steady breathing beside me. 'I'm going to see her today, tell her what's going on. It will only be worse if I wait till they find the body. Iris is down there, Phillip. There's no other way to explain the bracelet. And she's her daughter. Grandmother has a right to know. Just because she's old—' I broke off, tears threatening. 'It's so horrible! To think all these years . . . They fought, Betty said, but she must've loved her. She *must've*!' I don't know why it was so important to believe that, but I found I had to. 'And think of the horrible shock it would be to have some copper bursting in on her to break the news. No. I have to do it.'

'All right, love. I see that. I'll come with you. Just let me get cleaned up.'

'No,' I said. 'Thank you, but she'd hate it, having a stranger there. It's family business and in her eyes you're not that.' I drew a deep steadying breath. 'I'll manage.'

'Of course you will.' He kissed me and for a moment I stood within the shelter of his strong arm with the buzz of insects in my ears, smelling his sweat and sunshine, and the sweet tang of rotting fruit. It was going to be another scorcher. The morning sun already had a bite to it and the cloudless sky was faintly tinged with haze that could have been dust or distant smoke. 'I'd back you against a charging rhino any day, Elf,' he said.

I mustered a weak smile. 'I'd best get my safari gear on then. See you later. Tell Betty where I've gone. She'll see to your smoko.'

Chapter Seventeen

It was barely nine when I reached Woodfell. Grandmother called, 'Come,' at my knock and I entered the pretty room with my heart beating so fast I felt faintly ill.

'Well,' she said from her chair, laying down the magazine she held, 'you didn't ring last night to report. Why are you here?'

'I've come to talk to you, Grandmother.' Nervously I cleared my throat. 'I don't think I've ever talked to you properly – or you to me. Perhaps it's time we started. I have something to tell you, and I would like you to answer some questions. We're kin, after all. I might not be your favourite relative but I am your only one. So, can we please just talk for a while?'

Her eyes narrowed at me. 'Why? I've never found words much use.' A sudden look of alarm crossed her face. 'Has something happened to Claude? If you've been careless with him! He's hurt, or lost, or—'

'Claude is fine,' I said hastily. 'He's palled up with Phillip, sits on his lap, curls himself round his feet . . . He was purring like a dynamo last night while Phillip rubbed his back. It's nothing to do with Claude. I'd really like you to tell me about my Aunt Iris. Like, for instance, what happened to her? I think I remember hearing that she died. Is that right?'

She stiffened in her chair, and one knee, which had been moving agitatedly in her alarm, stilled. 'What's brought this on, miss? What possible interest could you have in a stranger, even if she was your aunt, who, you are quite correct, has been dead these twenty-odd years?'

I pounced at once. 'That's what interests me,' I said. 'Are you quite sure that she's dead? Because there's no grave in the cemetery.' The implied lie was, I felt, justified. She couldn't know I hadn't looked and it kept Betty out of it. 'Where did she die, and what from?'

Grandmother gave me a look of intense dislike. 'You are exactly like your mother. Irritating, single-minded and without consideration for others. If you must know, she killed herself.' My mouth dropped open in surprise. 'In Smitherton,' she continued bitterly, 'some backwater little town in Victoria.' She spat the words out, as if the destination was an opium den in Turkey. Shaking her head, she pointed at the wardrobe. 'Yes, I can see you're even going to argue about that! Top shelf. The briefcase. Bring it to me.'

Obediently I did so, wondering if she was stalling. I watched her snap the catch on the worn leather case and remove a handful of papers, which she proceeded to search through. I couldn't get more than a glimpse but they seemed to be mostly legal matters to do with leases and deeds; I recognised the Cabot and Hawley letterhead on several, and that of the bank she dealt with, before she found what she was after.

It was a piece of newsprint, cut from a larger page, the paper yellowed by age, some of the black typing faded across the top of the letters.

'See for yourself, miss.'

It was a short enough account. An obituary from the death notices for Iris Eileen Chapman. A life tragically cut short. Missed and remembered by her friends. The date some fifteen months after my parents' wedding.

Without waiting for permission, I sat on the bed and reread the small print. 'This doesn't mention suicide.'

'It wasn't a word one bandied around in the sixties, let alone publicly discussed the way it is now,' she said waspishly. 'Derelicts suicided, and the deranged. Not girls from decent homes.'

'So how do you know she did? Is that where she's buried? In, where did you say, Smitherton? Did you attend her funeral?' I pressed.

'Your grandfather went. Afterwards we told a few people it was pneumonia. We couldn't—'

'Couldn't admit that you'd driven her to it?' I flared.

She sniffed, arms folded defensively. 'It was an act of unmitigated selfishness! But there was always something a little wrong with Iris. Unstable, always wanting her own way against all advice. She was fated for a bad end right from the start.'

'Grandfather told you that, did he? So he what – went off for a few days, then came back with a report on the funeral? And you believed him? You didn't even check for yourself?' I felt anger swell inside me. Believing her own daughter dead, she had let her fear of scandal keep her from even seeing the body.

Only there hadn't been one, I was positive of it now. Not in Smitherton, Victoria, anyway. Daniel Chapman had been responsible for inserting that notice to cover her murder. He'd chosen suicide because nothing would more surely deter his wife from associating herself with the death.

'I'll bet he told you that the police had rung with the news – but you didn't speak to them yourself, did you? Was there an inquest? Because, you know, there has to be for every suicide. But there couldn't have been if it never happened. And you only have his version of events to say it did. At least I really hope that's how it was, because otherwise you are in a world of trouble, Grandmother.'

She blinked at me, sitting bolt upright in her chair with rage gathering in her features. 'What are you talking about, Margaret? Are you actually threatening me? Iris died in another state. I never saw her again after she left. Ran away,' she added bitterly, 'and all because we wouldn't countenance her marriage to that – that gaolbird.'

'But in fact, she came back to the Reach about the time that obituary was published. You didn't see her?'

Her eyes narrowed. 'What are you saying? She did no such thing! I told you, she killed herself in Victoria.'

I sighed. 'I'm not disputing her death, Grandmother. Only the manner of it. There's no easy way to tell you this, but probably right about now the police are at the Reach. They'll be searching the old well for my aunt's body.'

Her eyes bulged alarmingly. 'What? How dare . . . Why?'

'Because Jake Lynch is convinced that Grandfather murdered her and that the well is where he hid her body. He was working on re-capping it when he realised—'

Her face went crimson, then white with passion, as she broke in, all else forgotten. 'Lynch? What's that criminal got to do with it? What have you been up to, miss? How dare you allow him onto my property?'

In for a penny, I thought, patting the air with my palms in the vain hope of soothing her wrath. 'I didn't. Mr Cabot engaged him to work in the garden. Like I said, he was mending the well cover. The timber had rotted away, you see, and he found the missing bit of her bracelet hanging under the wood. It had caught on the broken edges of the weldmesh. Jake and Iris were in love – but you know that. He said you stopped her from seeing him, and that your husband framed him for a crime he didn't commit. He asked me to report his suspicion to the police, because I was family and they'd listen to me, but not to him.'

'And you were fool enough to do so, you stupid girl!' she blazed. 'This is the gratitude I get for raising you, for all I've done—'

My hands clenched until the nails bit into my palms. I was shaking but I lifted my voice to drown hers. 'No,' I said, 'I called Mr Cabot, and *he* came out to see the evidence for himself. *He* called in the police. He had to, because if there's reasonable suspicion that a crime has been committed, then you have to report it. Particularly if you're a solicitor. He could be struck off or debarred, or whatever you call it, for not doing so.'

'And by this evening it will be all over town,' Grandmother said bitterly. 'Seventy years I've lived here without a hint of scandal and now this! Gossip and innuendo! You're your mother all over again! I might have known you'd cause nothing but grief.'

'Actually,' I said, wondering at my daring even as I spoke, 'I understood that my mother was the obedient one. And as for no scandal, did you really not know what was said about Grandfather? That he crippled a man; that he regularly bashed you up; that he bribed a witness at Jake Lynch's trial? From all I've heard since coming back, he was either hated or feared by most of his neighbours. And if he had any friends, nobody's mentioned them to me yet.'

'It's a lie.' Her face was the colour of old bone and she was shaking with passion. 'Get out! Go!' Grandmother pointed dramatically at the door. 'And as soon as I find a replacement you can leave my home and take your fancy man with you. And you are wrong, miss! Wrong! My daughter killed herself in Smitherton. If the police want proof, let them look at her grave there.'

She smacked her hand down on the arm of her chair for emphasis and a spasm of pain crossed her features but did nothing to mitigate her glare. I got out of the room, then stood for a moment leaning against the door for support. My legs were trembling, and I could feel my heart hammering a panicked rhythm in my chest.

A nurse came by pushing a trolley. She cocked a sapient eye at the chalked name on the board, then clicked her tongue and grinned sympathetically. 'Trouble?'

'Just a bit of a row,' I said shakily. 'I'll be off now. My grandmother may be out of sorts for a while.'

'When isn't she?' she said cheerfully. 'Don't worry, we'll cope.'

*

Phillip was waiting on the verandah with Claude settled comfortably at his feet when I pulled in before the Reach. The cat arched his back and stretched as Phillip rose and came down the steps towards me.

'You okay?' His eyes searched my face. 'How did it go?'

'She's as mad as fire, and I've been sacked,' I said baldly. 'But, typically, when it suits her. I can leave when she's found my replacement and you, as my "fancy man", get the heave-ho too. Honestly, I thought she'd have a stroke when she found out that Jake was working here. I expect Mr Cabot – if he survives the phone call she's probably already made – will be out shortly to give him his marching orders. Is that the police?' I indicated the car pulled off to one side of the sweep of gravel.

'Yeah. A Sergeant Grimstead and his offsider. They're talking to Jake, giving him a hard time. They indicated that my presence wasn't needed. Did you manage to get your gran's version of what happened to your aunt?'

'She believes Iris suicided. She's got a death notice from some paper, but naturally the shame of it kept her from attending the funeral. Plus a bit of nudging from my grandfather, I would think. She wasn't even aware that Iris had come back – so she says. The thing is, she really believes it, Phillip, and I'm kind of glad because it would be too horrible to have both of them murderers.'

'So you do believe Jake's version?'

'Yes,' I said. 'It's just too easy. Grandfather told her the police had rung with the news, then afterwards at the proper time he produced the notice, which is a bit convenient, don't you think? I mean, if she killed herself in some little town in

Victoria, how did he just happen across the paper carrying it? Unless he'd paid for it and had a copy sent to him. Then she doesn't see her daughter's body, doesn't see the grave. He absents himself for a time to attend to it all and afterwards they put it about, very discreetly, that she died of pneumonia. Gossip, and people's natural inclination not to intrude upon grief by raising the matter with her, does the rest.'

I pondered for a bit while he waited patiently. 'Grandmother was never the sort to encourage questions, particularly of a personal nature. And what about the inquest? If she had killed herself there must've been one, but she knew nothing about it. Probably didn't even realise that one would be held. Also,' I remembered, 'the notice had no date on it and because it was cut from the full page, it doesn't show which paper it came from.'

'And if it was a really small town,' Phillip mused, 'it was probably a regional rag covering the whole area, so it mightn't even have been based in – where did you say?'

'I didn't, but it was Smitherton. I've never heard of it.'

'Um.' He thought, frowning a little. 'There's a place in South Africa called that, or maybe it's Smithtown. It could exist here, I suppose. Not every little hamlet is on the map.'

At that moment the two police officers, a man and a younger woman, appeared around the corner of the house. The older of the two, the sergeant, veered towards us, nodding at me. 'Ah, Ms Morrisey? The site has been cordoned off. Please don't let anyone interfere with it before we return.'

'There's nobody here but we three – and Mrs Roberts,' I remembered. If he hadn't already met her, Betty must be in the house. 'So . . . you are going to investigate, Sergeant?'

'Alan Grimstead.' He shook hands, a hard-faced man with a nose like a blade and flat, cop eyes. 'And Constable Vickers. What can you tell me about the family history? Our records don't show Iris Chapman was ever listed as missing.'

'She wasn't. Her mother, who is in Woodfell, the aged care home, believes she committed suicide and was buried in Smitherton in Victoria,' I volunteered. 'I'm afraid that's all I know, and I only learned that today. I didn't get a date but as far as I can gather it happened about the time I was born. Or a bit before, maybe. Sometime in the early sixties, anyway.'

'Smitherton.' He filed the name away. 'We'll look into it. Meanwhile I've told Lynch not to leave town without informing us.'

'You must be perfectly aware that he was in gaol when my aunt vanished,' I said more tartly than I intended. 'Probably on a charge my grandfather manufactured. And, remember, it was Jake Lynch who first raised the possibility of Iris's murder.'

He shrugged. 'Juries mostly get it right, Ms Morrisey. And if he believes he was framed, then plainly he has an axe to grind with the late Mr Chapman.' He nodded to us and with the constable following headed for his vehicle.

'Huh!' I exploded as we watched the car back around and accelerate smoothly away down the drive. 'Mr Chapman. Money makes an impression, it seems, even when you're dead.'

In the kitchen Betty was preparing our morning smoko. 'Lyle Cabot rang,' she said, setting down the kettle. 'He said to tell you that he'd instructed the agent not to bring anyone out to view the house until the police have finished.'

'It makes sense, I suppose. Not that they can keep it quiet. Word will leak out and that won't do much for the sale price. Josh'll be lucky to shift it at all. Did he say anything about Jake?'

'Like what?' She tipped biscuits onto a plate – homemade I saw – and added slices of fruitcake.

'He's getting the sack,' I said unhappily. 'Grandmother hit the roof when I told her what was happening with the well. I'll bet she was on the phone to Mr Cabot the moment I was out the door, telling him to give Jake his marching orders. It's not fair, of course, but when was she ever that?'

The door opened on the man himself, who had plainly heard our exchange. He raised his brows, not looking very upset. 'So the old vixen knows I'm here, eh?'

'I'm sorry, Jake. But she was bound to find out.'

He shrugged. 'She'll soon have more to worry about than me. You're getting the boot, too?'

'But not until she finds a replacement,' I said dryly. 'Serve her right if we packed up today – only I want to see this thing through.' We sat down and Betty poured. 'The thing is, Jake, I do believe she's unaware of it all. If my grandfather did kill my aunt, I'm pretty sure that she knew nothing about it. She's quite convinced that her daughter suicided – very mortified over it too. Apparently it wasn't something that girls from good families did. So if there is a body down there, it's without her knowledge or connivance.'

'Well, we'll soon know.' He bit into a slice of cake. 'The cops need to organise some sort of hoist for their man, but that won't take 'em long to sort out. Chances are we'll know by evenin', tomorrow at the latest.' Amazingly, he winked at me. 'Man's gotta work out his notice, so I oughta still be around.'

'Look on the bright side,' Phillip affirmed. 'We might've got our marching orders, but yours have been delayed.'

Chapter Eighteen

It was four o'clock before the police returned with a hoist on the back of a small truck and a black Toyota Camry containing three men, one of whom was Sergeant Grimstead. Why did anybody, I asked myself, drive a black car in South Australia's searing summer heat? The truck was a sensible white that could have done with a wash, the hoist on the back an industrial orange, a large steel hook swinging gently below its extendable arm.

Standing in the lee of the rosemary hedge near the kitchen garden, I shivered despite the heat. All my silent comments and criticism couldn't disguise the horror of the task. If Jake was right, if there was no other explanation for the bracelet and the broken wire, I couldn't begin to imagine the furore that would be released. Hunters Reach would become notorious and I the granddaughter of a murderer. The knowledge might very easily kill my grandmother. It would be a nine-day wonder and in years to come I could imagine neighbours pointing out the (now) derelict house and grounds as the place where old man Chapman killed his own daughter and immured her in the well . . .

'No word from Lyle Cabot yet?' Jake asked beside my shoulder and I jumped, not having heard him approach.

'Not unless he's rung in the last five minutes.'

He grunted. 'Looks like I've still got a job then.'

Distressed, I said, 'I'm sorry I ever mentioned you to her, Jake. If she could just see the miracle you've wrought here . . . My family's treated you very badly, and I do apologise. Though I know that's not much help.'

'Ah, there's plenty of odd jobs knockin' around. I'll find somethin' else.'

'What did you do before – when you were young? Did you train for anything? Football apart,' I said, remembering.

'Worked in the business with my dad. He was a joiner. A good one too. Wouldn't be surprised if there ain't a cabinet or a cupboard or two in the house'—he jerked his head backward—'of my makin'. They knew quality, the Chapmans, I'll give 'em that, even if they were a right lot of snooty bas—' He broke off. 'Sorry, Meg. Not you and not Iris. The rest of 'em – not worth spit.'

'Did you even know my parents?' I asked coolly. They might've broken my heart, but I still felt the need to defend them.

'Fleur, a bit.' He ignored or didn't notice the change in my tone. 'Enough to know she hadn't much time for the likes of me. Sweaty workin' class, you know. So not well. Simon – I only met him at the weddin' – never had the chance after that. Clever, they said, only remaining son, came from money.'

'Really?' I had never met my paternal grandparents. One, though I couldn't now remember which, had died before I was born and the other sometime since. I wondered if they had attended their son's wedding, but of course I wouldn't have recognised them if they were among those photographed. My father would've inherited if there had been money, but I had never heard mention of it. I must ask Mr Cabot about that sometime. Dad had owned his own plane and he and my mother had spent a lot of time travelling. It had never previously occurred to me how costly that must've been, so perhaps that was where it had gone – if it had existed in the first place. It couldn't just have vanished and I certainly hadn't benefitted.

Phillip joined us, and then Betty. 'I thought I'd just wait until . . .' She paused. 'I couldn't go home, not knowing.' She stared at the bustle about the well where a sinister-looking figure cloaked head to toe in black with a mask over his face was being hooked onto the hoist's arm. 'Iris was such a little scrapper as a kid. I used to say to Ted that *Won't* was her middle name. Truth is, pet, I shouldn't say it, but I preferred her to your mum.'

'I wish I had known her,' I murmured. 'Look, there he goes.' The winch hummed as the diver's body slowly disappeared into the well. I felt Jake stiffen beside me and Phillip's left hand come to rest on my shoulder. It seemed we waited an age as the winch hummed and the men conferred, their backs a solid wall cutting off whatever was happening. On the back of the truck the winch hum stopped as the man squatting beside it did something. He joined the huddle around the well, then leapt lithely up into the truck bed again and the hum recommenced. The cable continued to unspool and finally, at some hidden signal, abruptly stopped.

'He's gotta be at the bottom,' Jake muttered. He was leaning forward tensely, his hands unconsciously clutching at the hedge so that the scent of the bruised rosemary was suddenly chokingly strong. A bee buzzed past my ear, then another and I realised somewhat belatedly that the plant was in flower, the whole length of the hedge starred with tiny blue blossoms. We stood frozen, breathing in the heavy perfume, then the sergeant raised his hand and the winch began to hum again, the cable winding back up.

The frogman's head and shoulders appeared in his harness at the wellhead, the oxygen cylinders on his back gleaming wetly in the strong sunlight. There was a brief halt in events while the men spoke, but the diver wasn't raised any further. One of the police handed him some sort of bag, then the man replaced his face mask, raised a circled finger and thumb and the hoist hummed into life as the diver slowly vanished from sight.

'They've found her then,' Jake said hoarsely. He was sweating, his face pale and damp as he dragged a trembling hand down over his mouth and chin. 'Jesus Christ! All these years and I never guessed. Poor girl,' he whispered like a benediction. 'My poor little love.'

'Jake, I'm so sorry.' I put a tentative hand on his arm, but he shook it off and lurched away, the smell of his sweat mingling with the overpowering scent of rosemary.

We remaining three stood waiting for the diver to re-emerge but, before he did so, Sergeant Grimstead came across to tell us what we already knew.

'We have human bones,' he said. 'Whose, it remains to be ascertained.'

'It has to be Iris,' I said, and felt his hard gaze upon me.

'Maybe so. However, the area has become a crime scene. It'll be cordoned off. I must caution you about trespassing upon it. Or allowing anyone else to do so. There'll be a man left here overnight. He'll take statements from you all.'

'He had better start with Betty then,' I suggested, 'before she goes home, which she usually does about now.'

'Very well.' He turned back to his companions.

Feeling slightly sick, I said, 'Let's go in. If they want us they can come and find us.'

They duly did, first corralling Jake, who was packing up for the day. We gave our statements and signed them, then Betty and Jake left.

'Should we ring Cabot?' I wondered. 'Or do you think the police will already have done so?'

Phillip lifted his good shoulder in a shrug. 'He won't be in the office now. It's too late.'

'No, but he'll be in the book.' I let my fingers do the walking and came up with a home address, saying as I dialled, 'It would be better if he broke the news to Grandmother. Preferably before the sergeant gets to her.'

'You're right. If she truly believes the story she told you, it'll be one helluva shock to the old girl.' He hesitated. 'Do you think we should go in ourselves?'

'I do not. She sacked me, remember? I'm the last person she'll want to see. Particularly as I'm now proved to be right.'

'Well,' he said, 'on the bright side, Jake's still employed.' The wind had picked up and the back door, which had come unlatched, was creaking to and fro. He secured it and I held up my hand as the ringing tone stopped and Mr Cabot's clipped voice spoke in my ear. 'Hello. Lyle Cabot speaking.'

When I'd replaced the receiver, Phillip said, 'I take it you're not ringing the old girl tonight?'

'I don't think so.'

'How 'bout a stroll before dinner then? It's cooler out and there's a full moon. We can surreptitiously check on what the copper's doing. I wish I could use the camera. With the light as it is, I could get some great silhouette shots.'

'Never mind. There'll be other nights, other moons.' I sniffed the wind as I stepped outside. 'That's not smoke, is it?' It was just the briefest whiff. I sniffed again, but the elusive scent had vanished. I slipped my hand through the crook of his good arm. 'I must've imagined it. Oh, smell that – it must be the lemon tree! I noticed that new blossoms were coming even though it's still bearing. Let's go down through the gates and I'll show you my favourite old tree. The one I used to climb. I'd pretend it was the Magic Faraway Tree, you know the one in Enid Blyton's books? You climbed it and there were all these wonderful places it could take you to.'

'And bring you back in time for tea?'

'That too.' I sighed. 'I wasn't much of a Walter Mitty, I'm afraid. I couldn't dream big enough to escape reality.'

It was a beautiful night, the newly risen moon hanging like a great golden orb in the sky. It would silver as it rose, I knew, but at present it was like a benignant sun, flooding the world with cool light, the topmost branches of the maple shivering dark leaves in silhouette against its face as the wind stirred again. There was no sign of the policeman and I wondered if he was napping in his car, though it was surely a little early for that.

'What will he do for dinner?' I wondered. 'Should we ask him in?'

'They'll have worked out something to feed him,' Phillip said. He peered at the gates, which we had reached. 'Is there some way to lock these?'

'Whatever for?'

'Journalists. It's only a matter of time before the press hear about the body in the well. God, the headlines write 'emselves, don't they? They'll be swarming all over when they learn it's filicide.'

'What?'

'The murder of a child by its parent. We had better warn them at Woodfell when the news breaks. You don't want your gran being bothered.'

I snorted. 'I think Grandmother would be more than a match for any journalist. Still, you're right. I hadn't thought that far ahead. I wonder if Cabot's told her yet?'

'He'll probably wait till the morning.' I had stopped beyond the gates to climb through the fence and Phillip now paused beside me to look up at the towering red gum with its wide trunk-dividing crotch. The untidy litter of shed bark crunched underfoot as he went forward to pat it. It had a massive trunk, streaked with darker patches and marked by trails of weeping resin as though the tree had bled. Its moon-dappled skin was wrinkled about the knobbly protuberances erupting from it and its branches were broad and smooth. Cockies and possums had regularly nested in the tall hollows below the crown and I had often seen the rounded hump of a koala sleeping in its topmost branches. The moon hung, huge and lucent between the boughs, making the tree look both stately and mysterious in the cool light as my eyes traced the route I had once taken out along its smooth limbs.

'So this is your magic tree?'

'Uh huh. See the second branch up with the burl, and the fork going off there to the right? That was my possie. There's a bit of a stub above the burl where a branch broke off. A little hollow too small for birds or possums to use. I used to keep my treasures in there.'

He said gently, 'Oh yes? What sort of treasures?'

'Just things I valued. Nothing much.' I thought back. 'There was a little shell spoon – so tiny I called it my fairy spoon, but I think now that it must've been for a mustard pot. I found it in the kitchen garden one day when I was pulling a carrot. I wonder what became of it?' In the way of children, I had simply stopped visiting the tree. It had become meaningless all at once as all childhood pastimes eventually do.

'There was usually a favourite book so I could read up there. And a little wooden dog Ted Roberts carved for me. Scotty, its name was. A secret pet, Ted called it when he gave it to me, because Grandmother wouldn't hear of letting me have one. He was a dear man, Ted. I used to pretend he and Betty were my real parents, you know, even though they were old. They took me to a fair one Christmas time. Betty and I were just talking about it the other day, and the pony I got to ride.' I laughed a little sadly. 'I suppose I was just desperate for affection.'

Phillip squeezed my hand. 'And you kept your treasures here because . . .?'

'I didn't want them touched – well, contaminated really, though I don't suppose I thought in those terms back then – by the house. It was never a welcoming place, the Reach. It still isn't. There's been too much . . . well, I would've said unhappiness before, but really it's hatred, isn't it? When I told Grandmother I'd give her trousseau to a charity shop, she said she'd pity any girl who bought it. She must've really loathed my grandfather, Phillip. And it seems with good reason now that we know he's a murderer.'

'Alleged,' my love corrected. 'I doubt, after this long, it can be proved he's responsible.'

'Unless the paper that printed Iris's death notice kept records,' I reminded him. 'If he paid for that, then he must've killed her.'

'You have a point.' He studied the tree. 'You know that's a pretty high perch for a little kid. However did you get up there?'

'It was easy enough. See how the trunk is wrinkled in places? That's as good as steps for bare feet. I loved being up high, hidden in the leaves. Like a chick in a nest. It felt safe.'

'Maybe you're a wood nymph,' he teased, 'not an elf at all.' His good arm went around my shoulders. 'Come on, let's head back.'

Chapter Nineteen

The call from Woodfell came just before noon the following morning. I was deadheading roses when Phillip hallooed from the back door, 'It's the home, Elf. You're wanted on the phone.'

I hurried indoors, my heart thumping. So Grandmother had got the news. I wondered if Cabot had beaten the police to it – I hoped so, he had promised he would. But it was Susan Pickering who answered my tentative 'Hello?'

'Ah, Ms Morrisey, I'm sorry to have to tell you that your grandmother has been taken to hospital. A sudden collapse. Fortunately one of our staff was passing her door. She heard a clatter and naturally entered to check that Mrs Chapman was okay. We immediately rang for the ambulance and they took her off about, oh, twenty minutes ago?' Her voice rose on the final words as if they were a question rather than a statement. 'I thought you'd want to know. She seems to have bumped her head when she fell so we're unsure what caused her collapse – a dizzy spell perhaps? Or a teeny stroke. They can occur out of the blue, as it were. They're not necessarily life threatening, so don't worry too much.'

'Yes,' I said numbly. 'Thank you for calling – had she had a visitor this morning?'

'Oh yes. Her legal man came by with a policeman, but that was much earlier. Around eight o'clock, I believe. They were with her for half an hour or so.' She sunk her voice conspiratorially. 'I think they may have *had words*, but there's no reason to suppose that had any connection . . . I mean,' she finished frankly, 'Mrs Chapman lost her temper with someone most days.'

'Yes. So – the Base Hospital? I'll give them a call. Thank you for letting me know.' I hung up.

Phillip, who had been listening said, 'Problem with your gran?'

'She collapsed. They whisked her off to the Base. Sounds like a shouting match ensued earlier with Cabot and some policeman who was with him. The copper must've insisted on being there when she was told, because I'm sure it wouldn't have been Cabot's idea. It looks like the shock of it all has caught up with her.' I frowned. 'I wonder what state her heart's in? I never thought to ask.' Reluctantly I added, 'I suppose I'll have to go and see her.'

He said instantly, 'We'll go together.'

'Well, thank you, I could do with the support, but I think I should see her alone – at first, anyway. She'll find it bad enough, me knowing the truth, without having an outsider . . . if you see what I mean?'

He said impatiently, 'She's got to know the whole world will be party to the news when the media get hold of it.'

'Yes, but they won't be at her bedside, judging her. I know you wouldn't, but if you're there too, that's how she'll see it. Anyway, I mightn't even get in depending on how bad she is.'

'So ring and find out.'

I inhaled audibly. 'Well, give me a chance! I'm about to.'

At first the hospital couldn't find any patient by the name of Chapman, but when I explained, the voice in my ear said brightly, 'Oh, she'll be with Admissions still, and a doctor may not even have seen her yet. Why don't you call back in an hour? She'll be settled in by then and we'll have a better handle on things.'

I thanked her and hung up, glancing at the clock. 'We'll go after lunch then. Maybe I'll take her some flowers.'

Phillip, pushing himself off the wall, raised an eyebrow, saying dryly, 'You haven't forgotten she sacked you?'

'She probably regrets it, but there's method to my madness, mate. Flowers seem to work on her the way music's supposed to soothe savage animals. When she was getting narky once before about things, I praised the bouquet she'd made for my mum's wedding and it was like talking to a different woman. She even explained what the flowers were for – why she'd chosen them. I fancy she would've made a great florist. So you never know – a bunch of roses might soften her to the point of talking to me. Because,' I said, 'I really want to try and save Jake's job. I feel responsible for getting him thrown off the place.'

'But he hasn't been – yet.'

'No, but I'm sure when she catches her breath . . . That might even be what the argument with Cabot was about, rather than the bones in the well, in which case she'll take a bit of convincing, but I have to try.'

'Seems a bit unlikely,' Phillip demurred. 'Sacking can't trump murder. Anyway, I'm sure he can look after himself. You just feel sorry for him because of his leg.'

'There's that.' I didn't bother to deny it. 'And he's been very badly treated by my family. He fell in love, Phillip, and they ruined his life. How is that right? Besides, I like him.'

He nodded. 'I know, I'm only teasing. He seems a decent enough bloke. One who's been stuck with the shitty end of the stick through no fault of his own. And murder – Jesus!' He shook his head. 'It's unforgivable. You can hate that accidents happen,' he said slowly and I knew that he was thinking of Brad, 'but not the actual cause. I mean, a mountain falls on you and if it's not natural, it *is* nature, so it's no use hating the mountain. But to cold-bloodedly kill – let alone your own child . . . If I were to lose you that way to some maniac, I don't know what I'd do.'

'Well, you aren't going to. And speaking of death, should you ring Jenny to see if they've recovered Brad's body yet? Surely there's been time by now.'

His face tightened. 'They won't have. They weren't going to try. There must've been a thousand tonne of rock and scree and mud on top of the village. I wouldn't be surprised if the quake hasn't altered the course of the river, so it could all be under water now. The villagers who survived knew long before the rescue effort got there that nothing could be done about their dead. And there was no way of getting heavy machinery in. It was a pretty remote valley.'

'Oh God, Phillip.' It was the only time since that first night that he had spoken about his experience. His stark description made it hideously real, underlining the narrowness of his escape and the brutal finality of Jenny's loss.

'Hey, hey, you're trembling, Elf. It's okay. *I'm* okay.' He put his arm around me and I clutched him tightly. I had come so close to losing him and at the time I hadn't even known. It was how it must have been for Jake too, for what else could he believe in the face of Iris's silence and disappearance, other than that her love had been too feeble a thing to endure the disgrace of his prison sentence? The desolation he must have felt at her supposed betrayal of their love swamped me with sudden grief for my lost aunt. Death was one thing, but to die as she had, misjudged and unmourned, would be as unbearable as the anger and remorse Jake must now feel.

Following the midday meal, we left Betty to get smoko for Jake, who had turned up as usual, and headed for Glenfield. I had picked a large bunch of roses, choosing the fragrant pinks and reds from those on offer, and a few sprays of baby's breath to set them off.

'She's not moved against Jake yet,' Phillip observed.

'Where he's living may not have a phone,' I pointed out. 'And you know, I have a feeling that she'll probably issue instructions to Cabot rather than speak to Jake herself. Seeing that he employed the man, he mightn't be so willing to jump to obey.' We were running into the outskirts of town by then, and I halted at a traffic light. 'There's a nice little cafe near the post office. What if I drop you off there? You don't want to be waiting in the carpark. It might take me ages to see her if the doctor's still doing tests.'

'You sure you don't want me to come in with you? I could count flies in a waiting room.'

'Yuck! I should hope there aren't any! I'll be all right. She can only yell at me, after all.'

'It's on green, Elf.'

'Oh.' I changed down as the vehicle behind me bipped impatiently. 'All right. Keep your hair on!'

'You know,' he said with a little smile as we moved off, 'you're getting quite assertive. Whatever happened to the timid little thing I used to know?'

'Am I?' I flashed a quick glance his way. 'I think,' I said slowly, 'that coming back, facing her, has been a sort of catalyst for me. Grandmother was always this huge ogre who terrified me and I couldn't get past that. But really, I can see now that she's not half as scary as I built her up to be. She's just a bitter old woman with a nasty tongue. She still makes my heart pound and my knees go weak, but now it's like I can see she's helpless and just lashing out at whoever's closest. Maybe she always felt that way, Phillip. Trapped in a marriage she couldn't escape and so desperately unhappy that she didn't care what she did.'

'Except that she's been widowed for years,' he pointed out.

'True. But maybe it was habit by then and she saw no need to change. She'd already driven her daughters away. I spent all the school holidays here, but my parents rarely visited, and if Iris was already dead . . .'

'Then she'd lost out again.' Phillip nodded. 'Could be. And if she'd ever had friends, surely they'd be in evidence now, but we haven't met a single one. Is this it?' he asked as I pulled into a side street to park.

'Just round the corner. Mind your arm,' I cautioned as he bent sideways to ease his tall frame out of the little car. Then the door clunked shut and I pulled away, heading for the hospital.

*

I found Grandmother in bed in a private room next to the nursing station. I thought she was sleeping, but her eyes opened as if she had sensed my presence.

'Margaret.'

'How are you feeling, Grandmother?' Her tone had sounded more martyred than welcoming. 'What happened?'

She raised her left hand as if brushing the question off, the plastic tag around her wrist accentuating the thinness of the limb. 'A lot of fuss. I'm fine.' She didn't look it. There was a new gauntness to her features. 'I had a fall. At my age anyone's likely to trip. Why have you come?'

I sat down on the only chair. 'To see you. And the nurse I spoke to said that actually you'd had a little stroke. No lasting damage apparently, so you'll be fine and able to go home in a day or so.' I paused, hoping I wasn't going to cause her another. 'So they told you about it – Mr Cabot and the policeman? The skeleton they found in the well?'

Her lids closed and she said in a defeated voice, 'It doesn't prove it was Iris. Or that Daniel—'

I interrupted gently, 'It won't take them long to confirm it, Grandmother. They've only to check the cemetery in Smitherton. If there's no grave marker for her . . . And there's this new DNA science they've recently discovered. I don't know if it works on bones, but apparently it can identify people just from their saliva or blood.'

'If it is her, anybody could have done it,' she said, but without the heat I would have expected. I knew then that she had accepted the truth of her husband's guilt and was simply refusing to admit it. Ruled as always by her stupid pride, I thought crossly.

'And how could anyone else have got her bracelet into your bedhead? Something that must've been done after her death, remember?' I demanded tartly. I was tired of her games. 'It's time for the truth, Grandmother. Don't you think your daughter deserves that?'

She moved restlessly in the bed, an expression of extreme dislike on her face. 'You're such a gadfly, Margaret. I see you've brought flowers, so why don't you get them into water before they die? Roses shouldn't be let dry out.'

I was startled to find myself still holding the blooms. I had forgotten all about them. In some confusion I laid them on the bed for lack of any other surface, for the bedside trolley top was cluttered with a water jug and glass, a tissue box and a towel, and left the room in search of a vase. An aide loitering by the desk provided one and when I returned Grandmother was sitting up, propped against her pillows, sorting through the bouquet. She shook her head irritably when I would have taken them and proceeded to arrange them herself.

'Don't put them there where I can't see them, girl! The windowsill,' she directed me. 'Flowers need light.'

'You do know that the police have stopped the agent from bringing buyers out until they've finished at the Reach?' I said. 'So the sale is going to be delayed. You need to be finding someone to replace me. I'll be leaving soon. Jake too, if you're going to sack him. Which is a shame, because he's doing wonders with the garden. I hope at least you'll admit you and Grandfather did him a terrible disservice. And I'm not even talking about framing him for a crime I'm certain he didn't commit. He truly loved Aunt Iris, you know. Why couldn't you have let them marry, if she was happy with him? He's a decent man.

Nothing like the monster *you* said you married. I just don't get it, Grandmother.'

Instantly furious, she jerked erect with snapping eyes, letting the banked pillows fall behind her. 'You can leave the room, Margaret. And the Reach, whenever you wish. You were always an ungrateful child. I—' She seemed to jerk and her eyes went momentarily blank, then she made a little *uhhn* sound and fell back in the bed, her eyes closing.

'Oh my God!' I lunged for the bright red button on the wall beside the bed and pressed it. 'Grandmother!' I shook her and to my great relief her lids fluttered up again, though her eyes were vague and blank looking.

'What's happened?' A nurse rushed into the room, took in the scene at a glance and went immediately into action, lowering the bedhead as she took her patient's pulse.

'She just collapsed,' I said guiltily. 'She was telling me off. It was my fault, I shouldn't have . . . What's happened?'

'Possibly another little stroke.' She wheeled the sphygmomanometer across and nodded at me. 'Ask the nurse at the desk to come in, please. Then stay outside.'

Poor Phillip had been waiting for the best part of an hour by the time I returned to pick him up. I had paced the corridor for ages counting the seconds, first for the doctor to appear, and then for him to emerge from Grandmother's room. His eventual diagnosis had confirmed the nurse's guess. They would do a scan, he said, but it seemed pretty clear-cut and it wasn't uncommon for multiple little strokes to occur in a patient after the first one. Occasionally, he had warned me, they were a precursor to a potentially more damaging, and sometimes fatal one. But she was a good age after all, and for the present, once her initial confusion passed, she would be as she was with no loss of speech or mental acuity.

Chastened, I left the hospital, knowing that my spurt of temper had cost me. Because of it, I was now condemned to sticking it out at the Reach until the place had found a buyer.

Chapter Twenty

The following morning Jake failed to turn up for work. Ordinarily he arrived as we were finishing breakfast, but I had cleared away the dishes and swept the floor and there was still no sign of him. Later, when Betty appeared, I asked if she had seen his vehicle, thinking that he might have gone straight to work without a kitchen visit, but she shook her head.

'There's nothing but my trike out front. It's not like him to be late.'

'No. I wonder if he's ill? It's ridiculous, but I don't even know where he's living. Otherwise I'd ring. Surely wherever it is must have a phone?'

'You would expect so. Maybe he had to do some shopping?' Betty suggested. 'I hadn't thought before, but with the hours he spends here, he must be buying his food from a corner shop that's open twenty-four-seven. He might just have decided to visit a supermarket instead. I expect he'll turn up,' she said, unworried as she pulled the apron over her head. 'So, any news?'

I told her about my hospital visit. 'She was all set to annihilate me, Betty, and instead she just collapsed. The doctor's thinking a second little stroke. They're doing tests to confirm it. I felt dreadful! I should have known better, but I got so wound up about Jake . . . She told me to leave – there, and here. And, of course, I can't now. She's helpless and I'd feel even worse if I abandoned her.'

'You always did have a very tender conscience, pet. There's plenty who would be packing their bags this minute, stroke or not. The woman's her own worst enemy.'

'Maybe,' I said, reverting to Jake's absence, 'she has sacked him, though he said nothing about it last night. I wonder if his gear's still here?'

I went to check the area behind the tennis court and found a neatly covered pile of equipment – barrow, chainsaw and a selection of secateurs and loppers. So, he would be returning at some stage if only to collect his tools. Perhaps he was sick, or just taking a day off? He set his own hours, after all, and might intend to make up the lost time over the weekend. I thought briefly about ringing Cabot to get Jake's address but shrank from the notion, unable to find justification for such a request.

It was peaceful in the early morning with the soft cooing of courting doves in the shrubbery and the scent of flowers mingling with the odour of damp earth. The sprays must have been running late yesterday, for the intricate lace of a spiderweb stretched between two shrubs was spangled with droplets that flashed with colours borne of the sun's rays. Late blooming jonquils had pushed through the soil near Phillip's favourite seat, brought on, I thought, by the daily watering. I bent to gather a handful to brighten the kitchen and was turning back to the house when Phillip appeared.

'There you are, Elf,' he said. 'Kevin rang. I've just got off the phone.'

'Oh, yes? I hope you told him you're not fit for work yet. The doctor said six weeks, didn't he?'

'Yes, but it wasn't about that. The paper's organising a memorial service for Brad. Day after tomorrow. I told him I'd be there. Jenny's attending, and her mother and sister, and everyone on staff. I couldn't not agree, Elf. Besides I need to be there. Turning up is the last thing I can do for him.'

'Yes, of course you must go.' I thought rapidly. 'You can't drive, but there's a bus service from Glenfield. I'll drop you off first thing tomorrow. It used to leave at eight – we'll check. Where will you stay when you get there?'

'You won't come with me?' He sounded disappointed.

I shook my head regretfully. 'I would if I could, but I can't. You must see that, love. Grandmother might have another stroke at any time and if she sent for me . . . Oh, I know it's unlikely – the sending part,' I added quickly, 'but I feel bad enough now, and then not to be here . . .'

He sighed, 'Yes, of course. You're right.'

'How long will you be gone?'

He considered. 'Two – three days? I'll drop in at the paper before I come back, get a handle on what's happening. Maybe pick up another lens from home. It wouldn't hurt to check out the house either. We've been gone for a while now.'

He was restless, I could see, wanting to get back to work. Missing the travel and the excitement of his latest assignment. 'Just remember your arm's not ready for anything yet.'

'I will, Elf.' He glanced around. 'Jake still not here?'

'No. I hope he's okay.' I looked at my flowers. 'I have to get these into water. And you'd best find yourself a decent shirt somewhere, or make time to buy one. You can't turn up for a service dressed like that.'

I drove into town early the following day and saw Phillip off. He had his battered travelling pack with him but had left his camera gear behind. It was odd to be waving off his lanky form without seeing the customary padded bag slung from his shoulder, and I sighed as I turned back to the car. The time would drag without him, especially with the agent still banned from showing the house. I supposed I could help Jake, or if he really had been sacked, take over operating the sprays and continue a bit of weeding while I waited upon events.

These events, however, caught up with me the moment I got back; the phone was ringing as I opened the front door. I snatched it up before it could stop.

'Hunters Reach, Meg speaking. Oh, Mr Cabot, good morning.'

'Ah,' his pedantic voice came dryly over the line. 'There you are. I tried earlier. Just to let you know that the police have said we can carry on with selling the property. Apparently they're satisfied there's nothing more they can do out there.'

'Does that mean we can pull the tape down and Josh can bring future buyers out?'

'Quite so. I've left a message to that effect at the hospital as I wasn't able to speak to your grandmother.'

Alarmed, I said, 'Why? What's happened?'

'Nothing I'm aware of. She was sleeping when I rang.'

'Oh. Do you happen to know where Jake Lynch is, Mr Cabot? He didn't turn up for work yesterday and I haven't seen him this morning – though I left the Reach quite early so he may have come since.'

'Ah, if he hasn't arrived yet I'm sure he'll be there soon. I understand he had business in town yesterday.'

'I see. Well, will I ring the real estate people to tell them or—'

'That's all right. I've already done so. Well, if there's nothing else?' He said goodbye and hung up just as Betty came cycling up the drive, her bike pannier full as usual with the fruits of her labour. This time it was apricot jam and scones for smoko. I had made her take the excess fruit home and she had promptly turned it into jam, so there were two bottles for the house and a third for Jake, who, it seemed, had finally arrived: she'd glimpsed his ute parked down the side next to the spiky prunings of the bougainvillea.

'Morning, Betty. That looks wonderful. Apricot's my favourite jam. I hope you kept some for yourself too?'

'I did, but there's more than I can manage. So Phillip got off okay? Did you know the press have been calling? I met a journalist who was heading back into town. You must have just beaten him here. He stopped me to ask if I knew whether the owner of the big place up the way was at home. I told him she was in intensive care following a heart attack, and the house was locked up. He'd already tried the gate, so it's a good thing you had the chain on.' Phillip had insisted on it after the bones were removed, issuing both Jake and Betty with keys.

I gave her a hug. 'Thank you! Well, it had to happen. Maybe that'll hold the media off for a bit – we can hope. Anyway,

Phillip's left for the city and we're back in business with Josh.' I told her what Cabot had said. 'I'll just get rid of the police tape and, when I see Jake, tell him he can go ahead with the well cover. Do you know how many packing boxes we have left?'

Betty pursed her lips in thought as she carried the jam inside, then automatically reached for her apron. I watched her busy hands tie the strings, reflecting that she seldom seemed to stop. Perhaps it was her way of staving off the loneliness of Ted's absence. They had been a devoted couple. 'Maybe a dozen? What did you have in mind?'

'We might use them for the crystal and other stuff that's going to auction. There's not much else we can do now, except the garden shed. I thought it should be cleared while Jake's still here because half of it's bound to be only good for the tip and that way he can take it. Maybe we should tackle that first, because I should probably get some bubble wrap for the other stuff. I mean, it's quite a chance trusting the Waterford crystal to a few sheets of newspaper, don't you think?'

'It's a thought,' she agreed. 'There's the Crown Derby service too. It should probably all go into wooden crates, particularly for a road trip.'

'Or,' I said slowly, 'what if I rang some of those addresses the valuer gave me – I wonder if they'd send a buyer up? They would probably offer less than it might make at auction, but the packing and removal would be at their expense. I suppose I should check with Cabot first, though I'm sure Grandmother wouldn't care one way or another.'

'Good idea.' Betty's attention had wandered to the fridge's contents and the next meal. 'What have we got in the meat line?'

Chapter Twenty-one

When I went looking for him, I found Jake loading up the tangle of bougainvillea cuttings, wearing heavy leather gloves and wielding a long-handled fork.

'Morning,' I called. 'I thought you were going to burn that lot?'

He wiped an arm across his forehead to dry the sweat and grunted. 'You seen the news? 'Nough bushfires burnin' already, not to mention a total fire ban for the whole area. Tip'll just have to take it, an' anymore I cut.'

'I was speaking to the solicitor,' I said. 'The police have finished here so you can get on with the well cover anytime you like. Oh, and my grandmother's in hospital, so sacking you has probably slipped her mind for the moment.'

'I know.' He'd stopped work and was leaning on the fork. He contemplated the tangle of thorny branches for a moment, then said abruptly, 'I seen her yesterdee. She sent word through Cabot to get me up there. 'S'why I wasn't on the job.'

'And?' I prompted when he said nothing more.

He seemed to drag his mind back to the present, gave a

little shrug and dug the fork back into the mess before him. 'She apologised.' His lip curled. 'Dead easy for some, eh? Wreck a man's life, then tell him you're sorry when it's too damn late to fix it.' He spat aside, then continued without a change of inflection, the subject obviously closed. 'I'll get onto the well cover when I've finished here. I'm gunna chuck that folderol from it on top of this lot – the roof and winch thing. Timber's all rotten anyhow.'

'Okay. It's always been a bit pointless seeing the well was covered over.' I was too amazed by my grandmother's action to even express astonishment at it. When, I wondered as I returned to the house, had she ever admitted regretting anything she had done? It was only as I was opening the back door that I remembered I had meant to tell Jake about the garden shed. Well, smoko time would be soon enough for that.

Later, lunch over, I phoned two of the contacts the antiques man had given me. The first expressed no interest in travelling to view old china and crystal, but would give me a decision if I brought it into the shop. The second, who sounded younger, told me he could promise nothing, but he'd be willing to come out to the Reach and take a look. I gave him directions from Hahndorf, which anybody could find, and hung up, feeling hopeful.

'Fingers crossed,' I said to Betty, who was humming along with the old-fashioned radio upon the kitchen bench. 'He sounded interested. It's too late to come today, but he said he could make it Wednesday. He can stay overnight in Glenfield. Any sale would have to go through Cabot and Hawley anyway, so two birds with one stone. I'll be down in the shed if anybody rings.'

She glanced at the oven, which was on. 'Do you want a hand, Meg?'

'It's all right,' I said. 'No point both of us getting filthy. I had a peek earlier and I doubt anyone's seen the back wall since well before Grandfather died.'

'Wear gloves then, and watch out for snakes.'

'Oh, thanks very much! Now you've put that in my head, I'll be imagining them everywhere.'

'Better than stepping on one!'

She was right about that. I equipped myself with a torch for dark corners and went on my way.

The garden shed had a roller door, and at some stage the key had been broken off in the lock. It creaked upwards, disclosing a dark interior, its walls and floors hung and piled with junk. It was plainly the place where every worn-out or unwanted article at the Reach had come to die. A small amount of light struggled through the dirty louvres of a tiny window in the back wall but did little to lessen the gloom. Cobwebs and hanks of old rope dangled from the rafters and everything was layered thickly in dust that had lain undisturbed for years.

Hands on hips, I wondered where to start, but there was really only one place and that was to shift the stuff blocking the way in. I grabbed the handles of an antiquated lawnmower, its engine covered with rust, and pulled it out. It looked like it hadn't run in twenty years. Definitely tip material. There were stacks of plastic garden pots, rotting potato sacks, old hoses with ragged reinforcing showing through peeling plastic, a wooden ladder with a broken rung, a chair minus its seat, and a plethora of rakes with missing teeth, a broken-handled spade and several garden forks. What looked like a composting bin was perched atop a round table whose timber veneer was peeling, while beneath it was some sort of roller, studded with spikes and half-covered in several metres of rusted chain. I found a rotting tennis net, old gas bottles from a barbecue – the barbecue itself nestled alongside a metal doll's pram – and a giant glazed ceramic pot, too heavy for me to lift.

I had forgotten about snakes and nearly died when, shifting a collapsing carton of junk – dibbers, trowels, leftover tiles and jars of old seeds – a lizard darted from under it across my foot. When my heart calmed down I dragged the box out into daylight and returned more cautiously for the next object, a heavy old tarpaulin with frayed rope ends affixed to the eyelets studding its edges. A cover for something agricultural, or had my grandparents had camping holidays? With the lizard in mind, I prodded the mass with a fork, then slipped the end of its long handle beneath the tarp to lever the dusty heap a little way off the floor. Nothing was lurking there so, seizing a couple of ropes, I towed it out, only to have the folds flip open behind me to disclose a battered portmanteau rolled within it.

I think it was its age and obvious quality that brought the word to mind: this was no cheap or ordinary travel bag. Hand stitched, I judged, and made from leather, it was well up the luxury list. The bold brass buckles, now sadly tarnished, the very heft of the padded leather handle, proved that. It came from an age when a set of matched luggage lasted a lifetime and plastic zips were unknown. And, I realised, it was a match for the two I had given to the theatrical society. Had my mother also owned one, then? I couldn't remember. I brushed off the dust with my gloves, clapping them together to get rid of the excess, then knelt to pull the stiffened straps through the buckles.

The weight of it made a mockery of my assumption of emptiness. Lifting the lid, I saw an array of neatly folded clothing topped with a yellowed nylon nightie and a toilet bag. Then the name printed on a card and slotted into place on the inner lid of the bag caught my eye. *Iris Chapman, Hunters Reach, Glenfield, S.A.* I sat back on my heels, staring. So! Iris's bag. Undoubtedly the one the woman from the Glenfield chemist had noticed with Iris when she was waiting for the taxi.

Grandfather, I reasoned, must have hidden it away after he killed her. And it had lain forgotten in the shed ever since. The taxi had carried my aunt and this bag out to the Reach and to her death, only to coincidentally come to light now shortly after her skeleton had. Of course, the police had not yet declared the poor remains in the well to be hers, but there could be little doubt of it.

And here, I realised, was the proof.

Should I hand it over to the police? But what could they do? The murderer was dead, so there was no trial to prepare for. I would tell Cabot, I decided, but I'd have a sticky into the contents first; she had been my aunt, after all. Rebuckling the straps, I hoisted the bag and carried it back to the house, pausing at the door to remove the rest of the dust with a rag before dumping it on the kitchen table.

'What have you got there?' Betty asked, wiping her hands on her apron.

'Aunt Iris's bag. I found it in the shed. Right at the back, wrapped in an old tarp. You would not *believe* the junk in that shed, Betty.'

'Oh, I would. Men are natural hoarders, and farmers most of all. How do you know it's hers?'

I gave her a tight smile with nothing of amusement in it. 'Having her name in it's a clue. And the girl who saw her said she had a bag with her. You know Grandmother denied that she ever visited? If that's what she believes, it lends more credence to Grandfather's tale of her having committed suicide, doesn't it? If Grandmother had seen her, talked to her and she was okay, but a week or a month later she kills herself . . . well, is she going to find that credible?'

'But,' Betty objected, 'that would mean Daniel Chapman had to kill her between us seeing her at the gate and her reaching the house. Surely he didn't throw her body down the well in broad daylight!'

'No-o. That's unlikely, I grant you. For one thing he'd have had to get the lid off the well, and I noticed the other day it was screwed on, so it would have taken him a while. But there're plenty of places he could've stashed her corpse until dark. You said he had a temper. If he lashed out in a rage . . . It might have even been an accident?' I said dubiously. 'He hit her but didn't actually intend to kill her? Or maybe she fell against something . . . Either way, he's got to get rid of the body and the evidence. This'—I indicated my find—'is the only tangible proof that she was here. He wasn't to know that you and Ted had already seen her, or that anybody in town would remember or mention it if they had. The bus runs early before the shops open – not too many people in the streets at that hour.'

'It's possible,' Betty agreed. She nodded at the bag. 'Are you going to open it?'

'Yes. I daresay the police will want it, but I'm having a look first,' I said, and then the phone rang.

It was Sergeant Grimstead. Cabot, he said, had asked that I be kept informed on developments re the deceased from the well. It sounded so stiff, he might have been reading the words from a notebook. I said, 'Oh, yes?' and waited.

First off, he announced, there was no actual clear-cut proof of murder. The evidence of that was circumstantial to say the least. The pathologist's report showed death had probably resulted either from the broken neck or the cracked skull he had found, but either injury could equally well have come from the body's falling headfirst into the well.

'Is that likely?' I interrupted. 'There was surely more than a metre of water! And what about the well cover? How did she remove that and then replace it again after she accidentally, or purposely, fell to her death?'

'Look, Ms Morrisey,' he said, his voice sharper. He no longer sounded as if he was reading from a script. 'There will be an inquest in due course to thrash out these matters. For now, with her identity uncertain and the party accused already deceased, the position of this office is that there's nothing further we can achieve. We're hoping her dental records – the skeleton is female, by the way – will give us an identity. Until then, there's nothing more we can do. If the woman *is* Iris Chapman and her father did kill her, then proceeding with the investigation would be a waste of police resources. As things stand, with the knowledge of the wellhead being secured again, the inquest will most likely find her death to be murder by persons unknown. You'll be informed when the inquest is due. Now, I'll not keep you longer. Good day.' And he hung up.

'Was that the police?' Betty demanded. 'You didn't tell them about the bag.'

'I didn't get a chance, and anyway they're letting it go,' I said blankly. 'He's dead so there's no one to charge. Besides, she could have jumped into the well herself, apparently. *As if!* There'll be an inquest and I bet the findings will be just that – all down to persons or reasons unknown. Grandmother's obviously been on the phone, scotching scandal.'

Betty's face reddened. 'That woman!' she exploded. 'If you're right, she won't even seek justice for her own daughter. How can she do that?'

'She probably owns the sergeant's house,' I said waspishly. 'Well, one thing's certain. They wouldn't take Iris's bag now even if I took it into them.'

'No,' she agreed, and then said practically, 'Well, let's see what's in it then.'

I don't know what I'd expected to find. A diary was too much to hope for, but letters would have been nice. Anything that gave a glimpse into her life: where she had lived, how she had lived. She must, I supposed, have supported herself. Was she trained in anything? As far as I knew my mother hadn't been, save for domestic duties in that she could cook and keep house. Daniel Chapman's daughters would not have been expected to earn their own living.

The clothing the bag contained was modest, serviceable stuff, nothing fancy – no evening clothes or gloves, no jewellery. Cotton underwear, two pairs of seamed stockings, step-ins, several jumpers (it had been winter when she came, Betty had said), a carefully folded jacket, skirts and tops, several dresses, an opened packet of Modess, a set of winter pyjamas, socks, handkerchiefs . . . Disappointed, I laid the items out on the table. There was nothing personal – no make-up or address book – but those items, I realised, would have been in her handbag. There was nothing to tell me about the woman herself or what her plan to return had entailed. Was she penniless and desperate, or had she hoped to mend the situation with her parents?

And then, right at the bottom of the bag, under a layer of yellowed tissue that I had taken to be nothing more than a liner, was a layette and, wrapped in a separate piece of the fragile paper, a silver-handled baby rattle with the name Elvira etched into the tarnished grip.

I was still goggling at it when Betty's gasp brought my head round to see her stricken face and the hand pressed to her mouth. 'Merciful heavens – she had a child!'

'We didn't think of that,' I agreed slowly, 'but is it so unexpected? She was young, in love. Might it not have been the reason she went in the first place? Because she was pregnant? I wonder if Jake knew?'

Betty shook her head. 'Not that. I meant what happened to it – to her? Elvira, is it?' She turned the handle, squinting at the etched characters. 'It looks expensive – a gift, do you think? So, what happened? Did she leave her with someone for the day? And if so, what did that person do when Iris didn't return? Unless . . . Oh, no, he wouldn't have killed the baby too?!'

I considered that. 'It's not likely. The diver would have found her skeleton as well. Anyway, she didn't have a baby when you and Ted saw her – or the woman from the chemist either. Of course'—I fingered the soft wool of the layette—'this and the rattle might have just been keepsakes. Maybe the little girl died. It doesn't look very used, does it?'

'They weren't though,' Betty objected. 'Something like that was for special occasions only, and babies grow so quickly.' She smoothed the grosgrain ribbon on the tiny bonnet. 'If she was born in summer, she'd probably only have worn it for her christening.' Brow furrowed, she looked at me. 'Are you going to tell Jake?'

'Of course. He must have been the father, so he has a right to know. Unless . . . Betty, can you pin down exactly when Iris returned? Not that it helps much, because we don't know how old little Elvira would've been then. But the baby would've had to have been his.'

Betty thought, then shook her head. 'Other than it being winter, no. She had a coat on . . . I can still see her standing there in it. But the date – I've no idea. I think it might have been before Jake's release, because I know I didn't immediately assume, *Oh, she's come back to him*. It was more like, *What's she doing here?* I'm sorry, pet, but it's a long time ago.'

I chewed my lip. 'So he had a two-year sentence. Long enough for Iris to have carried a child and given birth to it. But a bit too soon, wouldn't you think, for her to have found somebody else to have fathered it? If they were as madly in love as Jake claimed. But I think Elvira died, because otherwise there must have been a terrific fuss made by whoever was looking after her, when Iris didn't return, supposing she *had* left her with a friend, that is. And you'd be bound to remember that – it would've been all over the news.'

'Yes,' Betty agreed. 'Only if she'd come from the city – or interstate even – the baby could've been swallowed up by the welfare system in just a matter of hours from it being reported. So maybe not. Women *do* abandon babies, Meg. It would have been state but not necessarily national news. So is it kind to tell Jake? He'd never find her now.'

'He still has a right to know,' I argued and she sighed.

'Well, you must do what you think best, pet.'

Chapter Twenty-two

I thought about it long and hard, for I knew that Betty's point was a good one. It was common knowledge that tracing adoptions verged from difficult to downright impossible, especially when the adoptee was a baby too young to remember anything. If Elvira had lived and was unaware of her situation, there was no way in the world that Jake would find her. I spent time wishing that I could talk it over with Phillip but then abruptly decided that it was a family matter and I should make up my own mind. Elvira either was or would've been my cousin, so it was up to me to decide. I just hoped I wouldn't be adding grief to Jake's already traumatised existence.

I waited until afternoon smoko was over and finally, still unsure that I was doing the right thing, I stopped Jake as he made to rise from the table.

'Could I speak with you for a minute? There's something I want to show you.'

'Yeah, sure, Meg.' He turned to the back door but with a jerk of my head I said, 'No, this way.'

I had thrown a spare sheet over the dining room table onto which I had laid out the contents of the case. The clothes in a neat pile with the shoes, toiletries and jacket to one side and the layette and rattle front and centre.

'I found it wrapped up in a tarp at the back of the shed,' I said simply, indicating the bag. 'Iris's name is in the lid. Did you know that she was pregnant?'

'What?' He looked thunderstruck. He hadn't, I thought, taken in the import of my arrangement, his gaze still fixated on the bag itself. 'It was hers?'

'Yes. And this'—I indicated the layette—'was packed right at the bottom, wrapped in tissue, like something precious.'

'She had my baby and I never knew?' His face seemed to crumple and I looked away from the naked pain on it. He reached to stroke the complicated pattern of the little jacket, the delicate wool catching on the roughened skin of his fingers before he closed them over the rattle.

'A girl,' I said. 'Her name was Elvira. The name's engraved on the handle, see? I think she must have died, Jake. I'm sorry. But I thought you should know.'

I went through my reasons to believe that the items were no more than beloved keepsakes, adding, 'And apart from that, there was nothing else, just women's clothing. If the child had lived, there surely should be something – a bib, a nappy. I was going to give it to the police but'—I took a breath and told him—'they've given up on Iris. They're not even admitting it's murder. Not really. She could've fallen, or thrown herself down the well, they're saying, and they're waiting on the inquest. Victim and suspect are both dead so it's easier to go for misadventure, I suppose. The sergeant rang to tell me so.

I challenged him on it but I suspect my grandmother's behind his reluctance, though she'd never admit it.'

Jake accepted it dumbly, just nodding. I suppose he'd got used to injustice. 'Tidier, I reckon. An' like I said, the Chapman name. I ain't surprised. Well, that old bastard Daniel framed me, but he had some help fittin' the frame, didn't he? There might be honest cops, but I don't trust none of 'em.'

'Then,' I continued, indicating the bag, 'would you like to have this? I mean, if things had been different we'd be family. You'd be my uncle. And if little Elvira had lived, she'd have been my cousin.' I smiled wistfully. 'I'd have liked that.'

'I'll take it,' he said, scrubbing roughly at his jaw. 'Jesus! A baby . . . it never occurred to me. Of course, I never saw her again after the night of the weddin'. It was our first time together like that.' He turned the rattle, smoothing his palm over the inscription. 'Elvira,' he said as if testing the sound of it. 'My sister was called that. She died young too. Iris must've remembered me tellin' her.'

'You could write to the Registrar in Adelaide, get her birth date and full name,' I suggested. 'It's not much, but it's something. Or, if she wasn't registered there, you could try Melbourne, if Iris really was living in Victoria.'

'Yeah,' he agreed. 'Yeah, I'll do that. I'll come back for the bag before I leave today, okay?'

'I'll pack it up for you.'

'Thanks, Meg.' His voice sounded strange. He laid the rattle down on the layette and limped from the room without speaking again.

*

That evening, after Jake had gone, I rang Phillip and told him about the sergeant's call, my discovery in the shed, and the conclusion that Betty and I had drawn.

'Poor bloke,' he said of Jake. 'He's had a helluva life, hasn't he? Fiancée's murder as good as ignored, baby dead, gaol time, and his injury . . . What else is happening, Elf?'

'The agent rang this afternoon. He's bringing another buyer out tomorrow. And I've contacted an antiques dealer about the furniture. He's coming in a day or two. Also, I believe that Claude's missing you. He's been pacing around the place yowling his head off. I think he's feeling deprived of pats. Have you seen Jenny yet?'

'Tomorrow. The ceremony's at St Mary's – Kevin's picking me up at eleven. And there's a lunch afterwards at some hotel. Brad's people are putting it on. I gather they'll be mounting a plaque in the church when it's all over.'

'Give her my love,' I said, speaking of Jenny. 'How's your arm?'

'I will, and it's fine. What about your gran?'

'The hospital hasn't contacted me but if she is behind the cops' decision, I guess she's okay. Maybe I'll visit tomorrow – if I've calmed down enough. I don't want to trigger another stroke.'

'No. Well, take care. Love you, Elf.'

'Love you too,' I echoed, suddenly feeling the weight of the distance between us. 'How long before you're back?'

'Couple of days. Be good.'

'You too,' I said, hanging up.

*

Josh came early the following day. Betty had barely wheeled her trike into its customary resting place when his car came sweeping up the drive, stopping at a little distance to allow his passengers to take in the vista, then pulling slowly forward to park near the steps.

'Ah, Meg,' he said expansively. 'I'd like you to meet Harvey and Linda Telford. They're on the hunt for a country home with a bit of space, right in this area. I've been telling them they've come to the right spot. Secluded, quiet, but still close to civilisation . . . I have a feeling that Hunters Reach is the perfect match for them.'

'How do you do?' I shook their hands, mentally cataloguing them as likely buyers. In their late forties, perhaps, Linda blonde and attractive, toned and tanned. Golf, maybe, or gardening? Harvey was tall and slender, with a riotous mop of hair and an easygoing manner. Lawyer, banker – something professional. They looked prosperous and eager. 'Come in.' I gestured at the door. 'Josh will show you around. He will have told you the Reach is my grandmother's property, but I'm happy to answer any questions that he can't.'

'Thank you.' Harvey spoke for them both. 'It's a fine-looking place. These old houses – they built them to last and they understood form.' He swept an appreciative eye over the exterior with its columned verandah and symmetrical row of chimneys.

'And the garden,' Linda said. 'Whoever designed that, it's plain he knew what he was doing. And I've only just glimpsed the front.'

'It was actually my grandmother's doing. She loved her garden. I believe her roses won ribbons every year at the local show. It's great rose country, this.'

'I'm already sold,' Linda said. She smiled warmly at me and, linking her arm through her husband's, followed Josh up the steps.

Betty and I waited in the kitchen, listening to their footsteps and the sound of Josh's voice, muffled or clear as he moved about, extolling the virtues of the property. Doors opened and closed and we heard them on the verandah, and then the crunch of gravel as they moved into the garden. Linda's clear laugh floated back to us just as Claude, tail up and fur ruffled, shot in through the kitchen window, obviously not pleased at finding strangers in his domain.

'Honestly!' I rose to clean up the spilt tea leaves from the canister he'd knocked over on arrival. 'Why on earth wouldn't Grandmother have a cat flap like anybody else? Oh, stop that!' I added crossly as the cat began howling. 'He's not here. Other people would pat you, you know, if you let them.' He hissed at me and padded into the hallway, still caterwauling, and I shrugged. 'Suit yourself, buster.'

'You and that cat.' Betty laughed, then sobered. 'I haven't had the chance to ask – did you speak to Jake?'

'Yes, just after you left yesterday. He was absolutely stunned, as you can imagine. I gave him the bag and suggested that he contact the Registrar in Adelaide. They'd have the baby's birth record if she was born in this state. So at least he'd know his daughter's birthday and middle name – if she had one.'

'And when she died,' Betty said.

'Mmm, yes, that's a thought. Unless she was stillborn.' I stared at her. 'We didn't think of that. Do they register stillbirths? What if Elvira was a stillborn baby? It would explain the unused look of the layette, the lack of other baby stuff.'

'That's true.' She reached for the kettle. 'I guess we'll never know, now.'

But I would make it my business to find out, I thought. What I had told Jake held good – we were almost family, and it was through no fault of his that the union wasn't official. I would write to the Registrar myself for proof of Elvira's brief existence and, if possible, the cause and date of her death. I reached automatically for the cups as the kettle boiled and Betty made the tea, then hesitated. 'Do you think we should offer them one – Josh and his clients?'

'Why not?' she said placidly. Country hospitality came as naturally as breathing to Betty.

I had been almost right about Harvey; he was an accountant who was selling his business in the city. If they settled in the area, he explained, he would buy into a smaller agency as a partner and work part-time. Linda, who had studied design, had already given up her job running a successful interior decorating business.

'It was frenetic,' she said. 'Absolutely crazy trying to keep everything juggled. I scarcely saw my family. We've two, a boy in uni and a daughter – she's just qualified for the law. Life was one mad scramble with no time to draw breath. But this,' she said, letting her gaze wander about the room, over the six of us seated around the homely scrubbed pine of the table with the mismatched cups that were all we had left, and cocking her head to the sound of a willy-wagtail scolding outside the window, 'this is heaven. Harvey, the garden is pure magic. Such peace and beauty . . .' She shook her head, unable to put it into words.

'It's not at its best at the moment,' Josh put in eagerly, and I could almost see him totting up his commission on the sale. 'The owner hasn't been up to the work in recent years.'

'My grandmother is eighty-eight,' I said. 'But Jake here has been getting it all back under control. He's doing a great job.' And he might, I thought, even keep the work if they bought the place. This woman with her elegant nails and fashionable hair-do could well find the huge area beyond her strength and experience too.

'Even so, I still love it. The space, the layout, the birds . . . If you don't mind, Harvey, I think I'll just have another little walk through it. You're not in a hurry, are you, Josh?'

'No, no. All the time in the world. Suit yourself, Linda, whatever you want.'

If his own home was on fire, I reflected cynically, there was no way he'd mention it if it meant perhaps jeopardising the sale. I remembered the photo album then. 'If you're interested,' I said to Harvey, 'I have a pictorial history of the Reach. I could show you that while you're waiting?'

'Sure thing,' he said. Betty began to stack the cups and Jake nodded at us and limped out the door, though not unobserved.

'Good worker?' Harvey asked. 'He has an injury, I see.'

'Very,' I said firmly. 'You wouldn't believe the difference he's made to the place since he started. The garden hadn't really been tended for at least five years. And he doesn't let his disability slow him down with the heavy work.'

'Good attitude.' He nodded approvingly, then turned his attention to the album as I brought it to him, while Josh surreptitiously checked his watch. Perhaps time wasn't all that elastic after all. I pointed a finger at myself and then the door, mouthing, 'I'll go see,' and he nodded as I slipped out.

I found Linda on Phillip's seat, her hands clasped over one knee and Claude crouched at her feet, rubbing his foot against her ankle.

'Good heavens!' I said. 'What is it with that cat? Don't tell me he's let you stroke him?'

She smiled. 'Yours? He's a handsome boy, isn't he?'

'No. My grandmother's. He can't stand me. I think the others are waiting, if you're ready?'

'Yes.' She rose reluctantly. 'It's so peaceful here, and the roses are divine. I always wanted a rose garden, only I'd have a climber too. What was in the planter on the pedestal? I've never seen one that big before.'

'No. Enormous, isn't it?' It had to be more than a metre across. 'I'm afraid I've no idea. It was buried under the bougainvillea and I didn't even know it existed. I don't live here, you see. I've only come back to pack up for my grandmother.'

'I'd plant it with bulbs,' she said dreamily. 'Or maybe salvia, with pansies around the edge. Are you a gardener, Meg?'

'I'm afraid not. But,' I added reluctantly, 'I remember it from when I was a child. The Reach garden was really spectacular then. And it could be again if somebody cared enough.'

'Why Hunters Reach – the name, I mean?'

'I have no idea.' We were walking back, and she pointed at Jake, cordless drill in hand, as he fitted a board in the well cover.

'What's he doing there?'

'It's the old well. The top was rotten and he's making a new one. Safety regulations, you know.' I wondered if Josh had mentioned the skeleton to them. There had been a snippet on the news the day before, but thankfully no pictures and no further visits from the press. And if he had not, did I have a duty of disclosure? If the police were letting the case die, there'd be no further developments to fuel the media . . . Before I could decide, she was offering me her hand and calling, 'Coming,' to her husband, whom we could see waiting with Josh by the car.

'Thank you, Meg. For your hospitality and letting us see your beautiful home. I have a feeling we'll be back.' Then she was gone, pausing only to run her hand through the rosemary hedge as she hurried towards the vehicle.

Chapter Twenty-three

'Well,' Betty said, listening to the departing engine. 'They seemed really keen.'

'*She* certainly is. But I wonder . . . do they know about the body in the well? There was only that one brief mention on the news and, unless that reporter has been trying his luck at Woodfell or the hospital, nothing more from the media. I suppose decades-old bones haven't that much news value. I mean, no suspect, no ongoing investigation. Would you buy a property where there'd been a murder?'

Betty considered, pursing her lips. 'I suppose it would depend. On how gruesome and how long ago it was committed,' she explained as I raised my brows. 'And, I guess, how much imagination I suffered from. It's not like the place is notorious, or likely to be. There'll be no hunt for the killer, no press speculation and horror stories. So, I suppose I might.'

'I don't think they know,' I admitted. 'She mentioned the well, but just to ask what Jake was doing there. I think,' I added, 'if they're planning to make an offer they should be told.'

Betty shrugged. 'It's Cabot's job to instruct the agent, not yours. Now, what do you fancy for lunch?'

We had scarcely finished eating when Jake cocked an ear. 'Car coming?'

'They surely can't be back already?' I said, but when I opened the door it was Sergeant Grimstead standing there. I stared at him, nonplussed.

'Afternoon, Miss Chapman. Hot enough for you?'

'It's certainly that, Sergeant. Something I can do for you?'

'Bit of news for you and Jacob Lynch – him mainly, but I thought you should know as well. Being his employer, like.'

'I'm not that,' I protested. 'Have you heard from Mrs Chapman lately, Sergeant?'

'Why would I?' he asked blandly. 'No, it's Lynch I need to speak to.'

'He's inside.' I led the way to the kitchen. 'We've just finished lunch.' Unwillingly I added, 'Would you like a cold drink?'

'Wouldn't say no.' He nodded to Betty, 'Mrs Roberts,' and to Jake, murmuring, 'JJ,' and it occurred to me for the first time that the two men were of an age and had possibly known each other back in the day. The sergeant might even have been a constable when Jake had been arrested.

'Grimstead,' Jake said, without rising, sounding anything but friendly. 'What do you want?'

The policeman accepted the glass I gave him with a word of thanks and drank a little. 'Two things. Dental records show that your well victim was Iris Chapman. Also, to let you know that we picked up Roger Flint a few days back. Wasn't hard – he's still in the same business. Anyway, we leaned on him a bit, talked about making him an accessory to a little job that went down last month involving grievous bodily harm, and he couldn't wait to retract his original statement about you. It's on record now. The gear was never stolen. Chapman delivered it to Flint himself.' Noting Jake's lack of reaction, he said, 'You're in the clear, man. Seems the old man slung Flint a thousand quid to frame you. Ellie Chapman knows it too now, but I understand she's had a stroke or something, so I thought I'd better make sure you'd heard.'

'Right.' There was a shade of bitterness in Jake's tone. 'So now you believe me. That's supposed to fix everything, is it? It won't bring Iris back though. If I hadn't been locked up, she'd never have been killed, so don't expect any thanks from me.'

Grimstead drank off the rest of the glass. He said, 'The jury convicted you, JJ, not the police. And it's not clear yet that Iris was murdered. Could've been suicide.'

Jake's lip curled. 'My arse,' he said rudely. 'But I get it. I'm cleared as long as she's forgotten. Jesus! Cops. You couldn't lie straight in bed.' Grimstead flushed but made no answer as Jake asked contemptuously, 'How long's Flint been fencing stolen gear, hey? And all of a sudden you catch him out. Bloody convenient.'

I said reproachfully, 'The least you could do, Sergeant, is make a public statement to the effect that Jake was wrongly arrested and imprisoned. It's the rest of the world that needs to hear it, not him.'

'That'll be up to my superiors,' Grimstead replied stiffly. 'I'll be off then.' He hesitated. 'I am sorry, JJ.' He made to offer his hand but a glance at Jake's hard visage had him changing his mind.

'I'll see you out,' I said. We walked silently down the hall to the door, where he paused to sniff at the air.

'Smoke,' he said. 'Fire must be closer.'

'A fire?' I hadn't seen the news the evening before or today. 'There was a faint sort of glow to the east last night, but I thought it was just the moon rising.'

'Bushfire in the nature reserve near Clennan,' Grimstead replied. 'They'll be evacuating the town if the brigade doesn't get on top of it soon.'

'As bad as that?' Still, Clennan was a fair distance away, so there was no cause for worry. 'Goodbye, Sergeant.'

He sketched me a wave and left, jingling his vehicle keys as he went.

Back in the kitchen, Jake was hauling himself to his feet. Obviously continuing a train of thought, he said abruptly, 'Huh, I guess that explains why the old harridan apologised. You reckon she could've arranged the deal? 'Cause for a bloody cert that's what it is.'

'Grandmother didn't tell you the police know you were innocent?'

'Never said a word about it. I was expecting her to sack me, then she just came out with the apology: *It seems I was wrong about you. I'm sorry.*'

'And that was it?' I was incredulous.

'Yep.' He frowned, scratching his jaw where several days' bristles showed in patches of grey and black. 'I assumed she was talkin' about Iris. That her daughter and me making a match of it was fractionally better, in her view, than Chapman killing her. Though seein' I was banged up at the time, I didn't exactly follow her reasoning. Truth is I thought her wits must be wandering a bit.'

'If that doesn't take the cake!' I exploded. 'She knew what Grandfather had done and that's the best she can do? I—' Words failed me.

'Ah, it's not your fault. Water down the creek.' He waved a dismissive hand. 'And speaking of water, I'd better finish the cap on that well. They seemed right taken with the place, that couple today.'

'I thought so too. She really loved the garden, so maybe they'll be the ones,' I said hopefully.

I told Phillip as much that evening on the phone, describing Linda's raptures over the place. And I mentioned the fire outside Clennan. It had led today's news. The townspeople had been told to evacuate and there were images of smoke-laden skies and fire trucks roaring along narrow roads that cut through the nature reserve, where the whole landscape seemed painted red.

'I watched it too,' he said. 'You can see the smoke lying over the hills from here.'

'I can imagine. Phillip, Betty was right about Jake being fitted up. Grimstead came out today.' I told him what the sergeant had said. 'Jake says it's a trade-off and thinks Grandmother may have organised it. They get a pardon for Jake and drop Iris's case. And,' I said wrathfully, 'can you believe Grimstead had already told my grandmother and she didn't say a word about it to Jake?'

'So he's still got a job?'

'Yes, he was capping the well today. Oh, and Claude seemed to take quite a fancy to Linda Telford. He was actually rubbing himself against her ankles, if you please.'

I heard him chuckle. 'What's so strange about that, Elf?'

'Huh!' I didn't dignify that with an answer, asking instead how the service had gone. We talked a little longer, and then I went to lock up, pausing on the verandah to gaze in the direction of the bushfire. There was no mistaking it tonight. The horizon glowed red and pale columns of smoke rose up towards the faint powdering of stars. I felt the wind on my face and pitied those in its path. South Australia's summers were littered with the ashes of past bushfires. The news had said the fire was now among the vineyards, tearing through the softer country south and east of Glenfield. But well south still. We should be all right at the Reach.

The following morning, out in the garden picking roses, I heard the phone. It was too early for Betty to have arrived and I ran for the door, wondering if it was the hospital. I had talked to Grandmother last night, only for a minute, as she'd hung up on me when I began to question her as to whether she'd spoken to Grimstead. Or, my heart leapt at the thought, it could be Phillip. I wasn't expecting him back so soon but if he'd changed his mind, he could be phoning with his arrival time at the depot . . . Of course the ringing stopped before I reached it and I was left wondering. Well, if it was important, whoever it was would call back.

Nobody did but, a little after the morning smoko table was

cleared, a car pulled up before the house and a dapper-looking man wearing a tie over his blue shirt got out.

'Thomas Greenfleet.' He offered a firm hand for me to shake. He was of average height with a darkish complexion and a strong-boned face with heavy eyebrows and dark eyes. He looked Mediterranean in origin, although his name certainly wasn't. 'I did ring,' he said apologetically. 'Chances were there was no one home but I thought I'd take a punt as I was in the area. It's a long drive from the city.' Seeing my palpable bewilderment, he laughed. 'Oh, I'm sorry. Greenfleet and Sons? You contacted us about some furniture.'

'Oh, of course!' The antiques man. I'd forgotten the name. 'I'm sorry, I heard your call but wasn't in time to take it. Come in. It's good timing actually, because I think we may have a buyer for the house. And I'd prefer not to have to store the pieces.'

Greenfleet chatted to me as I showed him the dining table, Grandmother's bed and other bits that the valuer had made notes on. He was the son in the business's title and did the legwork, touring auctions and house sales for what he could find. It was an interesting job, he told me.

'People very often don't know what they've got. To them it's just granny's old chair, or a cabinet that has stood in the kitchen since they were kids, and they see no value in it.'

'Well, I have to tell you that isn't the case here,' I said firmly. 'I've had a valuer look at the pieces and price them, so don't expect bargain basement deals, Mr Greenfleet. I should also tell you that any sale will actually be done through my grandmother's solicitor. I can only show it to you.'

He smiled. 'That's fine, and I like what I see. The longcase clock, maybe not. They're rather plentiful and don't command great prices at present. But the dining table, yes, and the bed, the escritoire and that sweet little chair. Maybe the dining room dresser. If I can come to an agreement with your solicitor, I'll certainly take them.'

'Good. I'll let him know. When were you planning on heading back to Adelaide?'

'I'd thought this afternoon, but—'

'I'll give him a ring then, find out if he can fit you in today, shall I? When could you collect them, do you think?'

'Oh, I'd arrange it before I left,' he assured me, 'so if we do the deal, maybe tomorrow, if I find a suitable carrier?'

Phillip and I, it seemed, would be needing another bed. Well, there were plenty of other bedrooms at the Reach. I let the thought go. 'That would be great. Now, seeing you're here, would you like a quick look through the rest of the house before you leave?'

'If we could make that call to the solicitor first?' he suggested.

'Of course. What am I thinking? I'll give you his address too.'

Cabot's receptionist answered on the first ring and a time was fixed for three that afternoon. I repeated the hour for Greenfleet's benefit, raising a questioning eyebrow at him. He nodded.

'Fine. I'll stay in town overnight. It'll give me plenty of time to organise the packing and delivery.'

He meant to buy then. I suddenly remembered the other items we had set aside for auction. Perhaps he also dealt in them? It was worth a try. 'There's a few smaller things, not furniture, if you'd like to see them? Silverware, crystal – stuff like that. We had intended to find a specialist auction but if you'd care to take a look?'

'I'm here, so why not?' He smiled suddenly. 'You know, I love this job. I guess it's the thrill of the hunt. These old places – they're often full of real treasures, hiding away like secrets waiting to be uncovered.'

'Yes,' I said ironically. 'The Reach has its share of those. This way, they're in the dresser in the dining room.'

Chapter Twenty-four

Thomas Greenfleet browsed the house like a reader let loose in a library. He was pleased with the silver, sorted unerringly through the crystal to set the best aside, but shook his head at the Staffordshire pieces.

'We've rather too much of this, I'm afraid. I'll give you the number of someone who could be interested though.'

'Thanks,' I said, but he'd already turned his attention to the polished gramophone case. 'Bless me!' His dark face lit up with pleasure as he raised the lid. 'I don't suppose there are records to go with this?'

I laughed. 'Dozens. Maybe even a hundred or so. I doubt if they've been played in twenty years. I was going to toss them. Who has LPs these days?'

'Me, for one. It's a hobby of mine.' I showed him the cupboard where they were stored, packed upright in their sleeves awaiting disposal, and he crouched happily above them, examining each piece as if it were jewelled. 'What do you want for them?' he asked at length. 'I'll take the lot.'

I reminded him that Cabot handled the money and he nodded. 'Of course. I'll make him an offer for that and the player.' He glanced about, raising his eyes to the ceiling. 'You don't have an attic, do you? Amazing what you can find in them.'

'No, thank God.' I gazed around the lounge with its still filled bookcases, its multiple little side tables and pouffes and the breakfront cupboard still crammed with knick-knacks. 'I've enough on my plate here. Do you fancy any of that?'

He shook his head. 'Too modern, I'm afraid. Unless'—he eyed the long bookcase—'there are any first editions. Would you know?'

'Haven't a clue. But check if you want. I'll be back shortly.' I left him, heading into the kitchen to tell Betty we would likely have an extra for lunch and finding her glued to the wireless.

'Oh, Meg.' She looked distressed. 'It was just on the news. The fire's gone through Clennan. There are whole streets of houses burned.'

'My God! Really?' I said numbly. 'That's awful! How could it get into the town?'

'There was a gale driving it, apparently. At least nobody was killed but still . . . to lose everything. Those poor people – what will they do?'

'I can't imagine,' I said. 'It would be so awful! Look, can we manage another for lunch? He's going through the bookcases at present and he's already said he'll take the record collection. I think he'll be here for a while yet.'

'Yes, of course. I—' The phone rang and she waved her hand. 'Never mind. I'll let you get that.'

It was the hospital. I caught my breath as the woman

introduced herself but she was only calling to tell me that Mrs Ellie Chapman had been sent back to Woodfell in an ambulance.

'Oh, right. How is she?' I asked dutifully. I hadn't visited her again, deeming it wisest to stay away.

'Quite well, considering everything,' the woman replied. 'Her mind is still very sharp; it's just her body having the occasional little failure. But one must expect that at her age.'

'Yes, well, thanks for letting me know.' I sighed as I hung up. I should go in this afternoon and see her. Best get it over with, and news of the Telfords' interest in the Reach might sweeten her mood enough for me to escape unblasted.

Once Greenfleet had gone, Betty and I spent an hour boxing up the contents of the bookshelves.

'Though I doubt anyone still buys encyclopedias,' I said. 'You can get it all on a CD these days. But we can't just burn them.'

'Not with a fire ban on,' Betty agreed. 'So it's the op shop or the tip.'

'We'll load the boot of my car, and I'll drop them off after I've been to Woodfell.'

Betty tsked. 'You're too forgiving for your own good.'

'Probably.' I sighed. 'I thought I'd take her that flower book, maybe find out who M is. Besides, just because she's horrible, I don't have to be. Betty, it would be awful to think that nobody on earth cared about you. I don't, but it seems kinder to pretend. She is very old.'

'Huh! She'll last another ten years. The woman's pickled in

bile,' Betty said with unaccustomed bitterness, 'and I'm not up to pretending otherwise.'

Later, driving into town with the hot gusts of wind battering at me through the partly opened windows (the air conditioning seemed finally to have failed), I wondered what Grandmother had done, or said, to have earned such dislike. It probably concerned Ted, I thought. Betty would forgive anything except damage done to the man she had loved.

The gardens about Woodfell drooped in the punishing wind, the formerly bright sky glary with heat and what could have been dust. I hurried inside, flower book in hand, grateful for the cool stillness as the door closed behind me. The receptionist looked up from her task to smile at me. 'Hot out?'

'Dreadful,' I said. 'The wind's like a furnace. I'm visiting Mrs Chapman. The same room?'

'Yes.' She flicked her hair back and gave a little grimace. 'Good luck then.'

I was probably going to need it. I knocked, waited for her voice and went in to be greeted with, 'Whatever is it now? Oh, Margaret. What are you doing here?'

She was propped up in bed, holding a magazine in one veined hand, on which what looked like a large emerald ring glittered. 'I came to see how you were, Grandmother. And to tell you that we have a buyer for your best furniture. He's also taking the silver and the crystal.' I took a quick breath, having decided on the way in that attack was the best way of surprising an answer from her. 'Why didn't you tell Jake he'd finally been found innocent of the crime Grandfather framed him for?'

She lowered the publication to the bedclothes and fixed me with an annihilating gaze over the top of her glasses. 'I should think that my discussions with my employees were my own business, Margaret. It was enough that I apologised to the man.'

'Or was it that you couldn't bear to admit you'd done him a terrible injustice?' It was amazing how indignation could conquer my better intentions. I wanted to learn about the mysterious M and instead I was annoying her. 'And while we're at it, couldn't you have told him about the baby? Even if little Elvira died, don't you think he had a right to know? He was her father! You've had children, Grandmother. Can't you see how cruel that was?' Her eyes flashed daggers at me. 'If you'd cared more for your daughter's happiness and less about his status, or lack of it . . . You judged him unfit, didn't you, to be your son-in-law? And Grandfather did the rest.'

'He was a common labourer,' she said coldly. 'And how, might I ask, do you know about the baby?'

'I found Iris's suitcase in the shed. Oh, yes,' I said as her eyes widened. 'Grandfather stashed it there after he killed her. There was a rattle with the baby's name on it, and a layette packed in tissue paper.'

'I see.' She stared at me, lips pressed into a thin line. 'And what leads you to suppose that Lynch was the father anyway?'

'The fact that they loved each other? That they'd slept together? He told me that. When I get Elvira's birthdate I'll prove it, if you like. Because thanks to that monster you married, I know when they were together last.'

Her unnerving stare pierced me. 'You'll do no such thing, Margaret! I am warning you – leave it alone. No good ever comes of stirring the past. I will not have it known that my daughter bore a child out of wedlock!'

'And whose fault was it that she was unmarried? Not Iris's, and certainly not Jake's. Besides,' I added, 'Jake's already contacted the Registrar'—well, he was going to, I excused myself—'so you're a bit late with the warning. And why would he take any notice of you?' I was still standing near the door, having taken only a couple of steps into the room. In as reasonable a tone as I could manage, I said, 'And you know, when it comes to the inquest, nobody will accept that Iris's death was an accident. Not with the well cover being replaced and her suitcase hidden in the shed. No matter what your tame policeman says.' Giddy with self-righteousness, I drew a calming breath. 'Now, seeing I'm here, is there anything you want before I go?'

Apparently there wasn't. Grandmother lay back into the pillows, no longer looking at me, dismayed, I thought triumphantly, to have found a situation that she couldn't control. The magazine had slipped off the bed and I stepped forward magnanimously to retrieve it for her. 'I'll be off then,' I said, laying it within her reach. My fingers were trembling as I reached for the doorhandle to exit the room, but I felt somehow lighter as if, in finally standing up to her, I had shed the weight of fear that I had carried far too long. Back at the car I realised that I still had the little flower book clutched in my hand and, tutting, put it in the glovebox. I'd been foolish to bring it. She wouldn't have told me who M was anyway.

The wind continued all day and by late afternoon we could see the smoke of the bushfire.

'It's getting closer.' I looked worriedly at Betty. We were on the verandah and the smell of burning, driven to us on the wind, made my heart race and my fingers twitch restlessly. Flight, the urge to flee from danger, was probably the most sensible instinct we humans possessed and mine was screaming at me to act, to remove myself from the scene before it was too late. 'What about your place? You haven't planted lots of trees around it, have you?'

'Only the one,' Betty said absently, 'and Robert keeps the firebreaks graded.'

'Who?'

'The man who leases the land – Robert Cox. And the paddock closest to the cottage is fallow at present. I'll be fine, Meg. Maybe you should come and stay for a bit, though,' she said, eyeing the loom of the distant plantation that lay beyond the farm, a solid mass of fuel visible in the far distance behind the trees that fringed the Reach's garden. '*That* will certainly carry a fire.'

'But it's way off,' I protested. 'I'm just panicking. Of course it won't come near us. But I'll ask Jake to check the gutters, and maybe we could rig a sprinkler on the roof? Fire might've been an issue before the place was cleaned up – all that rampant growth and dead stuff – but it'll be fine now. Still, I wish Phillip was here.'

And then, shortly after Betty had cycled off, Phillip arrived. He hadn't rung so I wasn't expecting to see him that day, but here he was climbing out of a serviceable-looking twin cab HiLux driven by a shortish, curly-haired man somewhere, I judged, in his forties.

'Joe Habble,' Phillip said by way of introduction, 'this is Meg. How are you, Elf? Everything okay here? How's the old girl?'

'I'm fine,' I said. 'So's she. How do you do, Joe? How do you come to be bringing him home?'

'He's a journo, love,' Phillip said. 'We'll be working together once I'm back.'

'I'm covering the bushfire, Meg. Pleased to meet you, by the way. It was in the right direction so I just gave your bloke a lift.' He had a nice smile and his gaze didn't seem to miss much as he took in his surroundings. 'Fine old place. Hope the blaze doesn't get this far. It burnt a dozen homes in Clennan, you know. But the word is they're expecting a water bomber to arrive tomorrow, so they should get things under control. It's a whopping blaze, though.'

'I hope you're right about controlling it.' The heat and the smell of smoke still prickled my skin in atavistic warning. 'Won't you come in, have a cuppa or a cold drink?'

'Thanks all the same but I'd best get on. I'll catch up with you when your wing's mended, Phil.'

'Look forward to it. Thanks for the lift, mate.' Phillip waved, then stooped for his bag as the car made a slow turn on the gravel and drove off. He bent to kiss me. 'Good to be back, Elf. You look a bit hunted. So how're things really?'

'I've lots to tell you,' I said, linking my arm through his. 'Come inside and prepare to be astonished.'

Chapter Twenty-five

Thomas Greenfleet didn't waste any time. He returned the following morning, leading a removalist truck, and personally packed for transport the smaller items he had bought. The furniture was draped and padded with heavy blankets, while the vinyl collection went into the boot of his own vehicle. The dining room, bereft of its large table and sideboard, rang hollowly with his footsteps as he followed the removalists out and shook hands with me on the verandah.

'It was very nice to meet you,' he said, 'and to see the house. I hope whoever buys the place appreciates what they're getting.' And, with a last lingering look around at the garden, he left.

I walked back through partially emptied rooms, echoing now with the strangeness of their missing furniture. The long-case clock looked lonely facing the empty wall opposite, and I missed the sparkle of the Waterford decanter and glasses where the dresser had stood. Well, they hadn't been mine, and their disposal put me one step closer to getting back to my life in Hahndorf.

Betty arrived then, calling a greeting as she entered. 'I saw the truck. He bought it all then?'

'Well, I hope so!' I said, suddenly struck by the knowledge that I only had Greenstreet's word for it that Cabot had agreed a price on every item. Still, a reputable firm wouldn't last long if they went around fleecing their customers. 'I never expected anyone would pay for all those old records, so that's a bonus. Have you seen Jake yet?'

'I just arrived,' she pointed out. 'Why?'

'Oh, I was just wondering if he'd heard back from the Registrar.'

'A bit soon, isn't it?'

'Depends. He was going to ring them and have them fax a copy of the birth certificate through to the post office, then mail the real thing. It costs a bit more but they will do it apparently. Oh, and Phillip's back.'

'Ah, that explains it. You look happier,' she amplified. Glancing at the gloves on my hands and the box I was holding, she asked, 'What're you up to today?'

'Garden shed. I didn't get any further than Iris's case before. There's more to come out and I thought anything salvageable could be packed up'—I patted the box—'for disposal where it'll be useful. Local gardening club, maybe?'

'It's an idea.' She repeated her earlier warning. 'Watch out for snakes.'

'That's what Phillip'll be doing,' I said.

Jake had left for the tip with a combination of green waste and the broken and outdated refuse from the shed, so it was lunch time before I set eyes on him. When I asked what he'd learned from the register, he handed me a much-creased facsimile sheet that looked as if it had been folded, then unfolded again, more than once.

It was the first time I had seen such a document and I studied it with interest. Elvira Rose had been born in the Emergency Maternity Hospital Mile End, on the 22nd of December, 1965 in the district of Hindmarsh. ('Adelaide,' I noted aloud.) Her sex was denoted as F and she was the daughter of John Jacob Lynch, aged 23, of Glenfield, South Australia, and of Iris Eileen Chapman, aged 20, also of Glenfield. The father's profession was entered as 'Labourer' and the information was provided and testified to be correct by Iris on the 3rd of January, 1966. The whole was certified to be a true copy of an entry in the register, and the declaration was signed with the Registrar's illegible scrawl.

I said gently, 'You didn't think to ask for the death certificate too? Because, you know, you could probably find her grave if you knew where she had died.'

Jake shook his head. 'No. Because I don't know she *is* dead.'

The dogged look on his face showed that he didn't want to believe it. It was natural, I supposed, however unrealistic. Would Iris have left her baby behind to come home? Surely, if she'd sought a reconciliation with her parents, a grandchild would be a powerful bargaining point? Well, possibly not with my grandfather – unless, of course, it had been a boy. I hadn't known Daniel Chapman but, by all accounts, he seemed the sort of man to place a higher value on a male grandchild than a female one.

'If she lived,' I said hesitantly, 'then she'd have been taken into care. In which case, I don't think you'll find her, Jake.

It's just about impossible to trace adoptees, and she'd be well into her twenties now, married maybe, with a different name.'

'It won't stop me lookin',' he said roughly. 'I've wasted years already. But you're right. I oughta check for sure that she's living. An' if she is, I *will* find her.'

'He means it too, poor bugger,' Phillip said later when we were alone. He shook his head. 'I can see now why you wanted nothing to do with your grandparents. If ever there was a toxic pair . . . Fancy never letting him know he was a father, however briefly.'

'So you think she's dead too?'

'Realistically? She may as well be. Brad did a story, years back, that got a very vocal response from readers. About a single mother who'd given up her baby for adoption and was trying to trace the child, years later. It wound up costing her everything. She'd kept the baby a secret from her husband and other kids. He threw her out when he found out and the kids sided with him; she spent everything she had in the search, made herself ill and was no closer to finding the baby she'd lost. Even the law was against her. The whole thing sucked. All she wanted was to see her child again, but it never happened. Jake'll face the same battle, I'm afraid.'

'So how did the reading public react?'

'Something like sixty per cent wanted the law changed to allow parents to trace their kids. The rest, of course, were for having the mothers gaoled for giving up their babies in the first place, apart from the usual point two per cent of the lunatic fringe who thought they should be sterilised so they couldn't repeat their mistake.'

I said dryly, 'But not the men who fathered the babies?'

'Nobody suggested that,' he agreed. 'So what next?'

'I guess we can put the ladder and the gardening tools back in the shed. Let the Telfords have them if they buy the place. The pots and other bits we can maybe offload onto a gardening club. Then we can start on the laundry. The separator can be junked and I'm pretty sure there's a meat grinder in there as well. I expect somebody made sausages and other smallgoods back when the Reach was a farm.'

'Really?' Phillip sounded surprised.

'Not Grandmother, but she must've had help in the house. Apart from Betty, I mean – who could only have worked here occasionally, anyhow, because she and her husband had their own place to run.'

'Well, let's get to it. And I've been thinking we're about due for a break. What do you say to dinner out somewhere tonight, Elf? Know any good restaurants in town?'

I looked at him. 'There's a cafe or two I know of, but do you really think I was allowed to go on dates at seventeen? And I certainly didn't have the money to shout myself. I'd saved up what turned out to be a week's rent by the time I left. If I hadn't lucked straight into a job, I don't know what I'd have done. Starved, I suppose.'

He threaded the fingers of his left hand through mine, squeezing with gentle pressure. 'Never mind. We'll remedy that tonight. A trial run for next week.'

'Next week? Oh.' I smiled and squeezed back. 'My birthday. Do I get a cake?'

'We'll see.' He leaned in to peck a kiss onto my forehead. 'Meanwhile, cupboards, was it?'

Despite Joe Habble's assurances that the water bomber would soon have the bushfire under control, the evidence in the sky suggested otherwise. The day's heat seemed only intensified by the heavy smears of smoke across the blue. Cicadas drummed incessantly and the leaves hung in limp protest on the trees. Jake knocked off soon after Betty left at four, his cotton shirt a sodden rag.

'Too bloody hot to think,' he said, mopping his face. He nodded at Phillip. 'I was you, I'd be gettin' a plan in place. That fire don't look like stopping any time soon.'

'You think we could be in danger here?' Phillip sounded startled. 'I heard they were getting aerial assistance.'

'Well, that don't always stop blazes. All I'm saying, wouldn't hurt to have your vehicle packed. See you tomorrow.' And he was gone, his uneven step loud in the gravel.

I said worriedly, 'He was a firey. So he knows what he's talking about. We haven't much with us – we could pack it all into the boot, just in case.'

'What about the house?'

'If it comes to a choice, let it burn,' I said sharply. 'For heaven's sake, Phillip! You've just missed out on dying in an earthquake. I know you're addicted to danger, but there's a time for common sense too!'

'All right, love,' he said pacifically. 'The first sign of risk and we're off. In fact, I'll go pack the camera gear this minute.

And I'd best find a box for Claude. Did we toss out that crate from the shed? That'd do.'

'It's on the rubbish pile. And if you wanted the brute, he wouldn't be around, you can bet on that. And supposing he was, how would you close the top in?'

'Oh, tack some boards over it. I'll find some,' he called back from where he'd paused at the door, 'and keep the hammer handy to close it up once he's in. Just a matter of moments.' The screen closed behind him and I let myself relax now that he was taking the situation seriously. If push came to shove, I thought, I'd leave the damn cat to look after himself, but I supposed it wouldn't do. Then, as if aware of my thoughts, Claude slunk into the kitchen, fleering his lip at me as he went to lap from his water dish.

'Just make sure you're here, buster, if we need to leave.' I had a sudden nightmare vision of hunting for him through the shrubbery when every minute counted, then gave myself a mental shake. It wouldn't come to that. Meanwhile, what did I have that would be suitable wear for a smart restaurant? I was on my way to inspect my wardrobe when I heard a car door slam out front. I sighed. It was too hot for surprises or visitors. 'What now?'

It was Harvey and Linda Telford, the latter smiling a little anxiously as she came around the car to meet me. 'I do hope you don't mind, we just – well, we wanted another look. Oh, not inside, don't worry. But I wondered if I could show Harvey the garden? He didn't really see it last time. We won't interfere with your day, I promise, but it's so important to the place and I want him to feel . . .'

'Yes, of course,' I said hastily. 'Feel free to wander where you like. I'm afraid Jake's already gone and I don't know much about plants, but—'

'Oh, that's okay, neither does Harvey,' Linda said. 'I just want him to experience it the way I did. If we're going to live here . . .'

'Then you are thinking of buying?'

Harvey spoke for the first time. 'Maybe. My wife is very taken with the place, as you can see.' He gave her a fond smile. 'Very into feelings, Linda is, and she says there are good vibes here.' The word was obviously intended to be set in quotation marks. 'I'm a plain man myself, don't go in for that sort of thing, but happiness makes a home and if she's happy . . .'

Happiness was the last thing I would ever have thought of as a feature of the Reach, but it was their experiences that counted, not mine. 'Wander where you will,' I said. 'And if you do end up buying, I hope you'll be very happy here. My grandmother put her whole life into the garden, so I'm sure she'd appreciate having someone who really cares taking it over.'

And that would be about right, I thought resentfully, as Linda led her husband past the rosemary hedge to where the summer flowerbeds flourished now that Jake had removed the weeds that had been strangling them. Grandmother would have her happy ending with an ardent gardener to cherish her legacy after she herself had gone. Even the damn cat had taken to the woman. It seemed intensely unfair that things should always go as Ellie Chapman wished. One more example of the wicked flourishing at the expense of the rest of us.

I had the unworthy thought then that Linda's positive 'vibes' had overlooked the murder that had been committed in this very garden. She'd feel very differently about the peace and magic she'd spoken of if she knew that, I thought vindictively, and was then ashamed of myself for envying the woman's happiness. As it wasn't up to me to ruin it by disclosing the fact, I went indoors instead to shower and change.

Chapter Twenty-six

Phillip had browsed the yellow pages, so we wound up dining at the Golden Grape, a restaurant off Rose Street with an uncrowded space I found pleasant, even if the service was a little slow.

'This is quite nice.' As we waited, I glanced around at the timbered walls turned to a mellow amber by the domed lights. 'As long as you're not in a hurry. I wonder if they do lunches?'

'We can ask,' Phillip said, 'but why?'

'Is it very expensive? I was thinking we should take Betty out to lunch as a thank you for all the time and effort she's put in at the Reach. Not to mention the baking she's supplied. I get it that she's lonely and enjoys the company, but still – it's a lot of work.'

'Good idea. Though I think this joint's a bit too swanky for the lunch trade. We can find somewhere nice. Now, fish or meat before I order the wine?'

I settled on fish, which proved to be, like the service, disappointing. We lingered over our wine, holding hands across the cloth like new lovers. When the bill was presented in a discreet leather folder, Phillip's eyebrows rose a trifle. 'Ouch,' he murmured. 'They know how to charge. Be with you in a moment, Elf.'

'So,' I said as he held the door for me, 'not a lunch spot then?'

'Not at those prices,' he agreed. 'Flaming hell! Look at that sky.'

Startled by his tone, I looked to the south. In the restaurant we had sat in an alcove that shielded us from the street and I now saw that the expanse of sky beyond the town, which should have been in darkness slightly diluted by Glenfield's street lights, was coloured an angry orange.

'Dear Lord! How far off do you think that is?'

'A good way still, but the aerial bombing certainly hasn't stopped it. And this wind isn't going to help.' Even sheltered by the buildings, there was a noticeable surge in the air, lifting my hair and tugging at our clothes. Not yet a gale, but pretty strong.

'Jake was right,' I said soberly. 'Let's get back. We should check the alerts. The radio station might be broadcasting warnings. A good thing the car's packed. If we have to leave, it's just a matter of grabbing the cat and going.'

Phillip was fumbling one-handed with the key, his eyes on the sky. 'It'd have to be forty or fifty kay away, but you're right. We'd better keep an ear out. Maybe check up on Betty, too?'

'I'll ring her first thing.' I took the keys from him. 'Hop in. I'll drive.'

The phone was ringing as we entered the Reach. Phillip leaned past me in the hall for the handpiece and spoke into it. 'Hello. Yes, she's here. Who's calling please? Ah, of course.' He handed me the phone. 'It's Woodfell.'

'Hello?' I glanced at the longcase clock in the corner. It was after ten so it couldn't be good news.

'Ms Morrisey? It's Carla Renshaw, night nurse. I'm ringing to let you know that your grandmother has suffered a heart attack. The paramedics revived her and she's been rushed to the Base hospital. She's stabilised now but I thought you'd want to know.'

'I see,' I said slowly. 'Thank you for calling. I don't suppose there's anything I can do?'

'Well, no. She's in the best place she can be and they'll take good care of her. It was to be expected,' she said carefully. 'Those couple of little strokes she had previously? They're often a forerunner to something more serious. She'll be in intensive care, so I think that the morning would be soon enough to try seeing her. I made sure the hospital has your phone number there if they need to contact you.'

'Very well. Thank you for letting me know. Goodnight, then.' I hung up and lifted my shoulders at Phillip's enquiring look. 'She's had a heart attack.'

'You want to go back in?'

'There's no point. We'd sit around for hours and even if they did let me into ICU at this hour of the night, she's probably in a drugged sleep. I'll go tomorrow.'

'Okay. Bed then. I'll get the radio from the kitchen. If there are warnings out, we'll hear 'em while we're cleaning our teeth.'

In the morning the smoke was so thick you drew it in with every breath. It hung like a miasma of approaching doom, its ominous presence stirring prickles on my nape. The wind had died down overnight but the stillness only added to my unease. It was like being blind and deaf, I thought, knowing there was a monster somewhere close but having no sense other than smell with which to locate it.

When the phone rang shortly after breakfast I rushed to answer, already certain it would be Jake cancelling for the day, but instead found myself speaking to Josh Latten. The Telfords had just rung him to say they were buying, he reported jubilantly. They would be in the office in an hour to sign the contract.

'Well, that's great,' I said. 'Congratulations. I just hope the house will still be here for them. That bushfire seems to be getting much closer. It's very smoky out this way.'

'Oh, I doubt it'll get that far. The CFS is out in force, lots of fire trucks, and they've got a water bomber up. Besides, it's still way the other side of Hepton. It'll be right, Meg. I wouldn't worry. I tried to ring Ellie with the news but they tell me she's in hospital?' His voice rose, making it a query.

'She had a heart attack last night,' I said shortly, annoyed by his insouciant attitude. 'Maybe it'd be best if you just told Mr Cabot. I'll be seeing her this morning. I'll tell her then, should it be appropriate.'

'Ah, sorry to hear it,' he said. 'Well, thanks, Meg. Give her my best.' He rang off and I stood for a moment taking in the news. It was over, then. I supposed we'd have to stay a little longer. The Telfords wouldn't be ready to move in tomorrow, so Jake's job should last at least until that occurred. But we could send the rest of the furniture off over the next few days and ready the remaining stuff for the op shops or the tip.

Of course, I thought belatedly, all that planning would depend on Grandmother pulling through her present crisis. If she should die, it would put a stop to everything, including the sale if the contract hadn't already been settled. I went to find Phillip and Jake, if he'd arrived, to tell them the news.

At the hospital I was directed to the doors of the Intensive Care Unit, where I was shown to an uncomfortable seat and told that Mrs Chapman's doctor would see me shortly. When he appeared, a tubby, balding man in a white coat, he shook hands and perched a bent knee on the chair beside me, obviously not intending to stay very long.

'Ah, Ms Morrisey, is it? Yes. Well, I'm afraid your grandmother's condition is'—he rocked a pale, stubby hand from side to side—'good, and not so good.' The stethoscope around his neck gleamed and his eyes were keen and kind.

'Yes? What does that mean exactly, Doctor?'

'Well, it's good that she survived the heart attack last night. That's a start. But I'm afraid it did quite a bit of damage. She's not young, well into her eighties, I understand?'

'Eighty-nine next month.'

'Just so.' He smiled self-deprecatingly; he would be used to delivering such news. 'I think that worthy phrase *she's as well as can be expected* just about covers it. She could have another attack today, tomorrow or next week. You notice I'm not saying next month? It's that likely, I'm afraid. She'll not be leaving hospital again.'

I swallowed. 'I see. Is she conscious?'

'Oh, yes. Her body is tired, Ms Morrisey. She's old and her heart's worn out. I should bring the family in, just one at a time and soonest, if I were you. Let them say their goodbyes.'

'I am her family, Doctor. There's no one else. She might want to see her man of business, though. I'll ask. I can see her?'

He lowered his leg to the floor. 'Yes, of course. Just a few minutes. She'll probably fall asleep. Don't wake her if she does. Second bed on the right.'

'Thank you, Doctor.' We parted and I went in through the heavy swing doors, wide enough to manoeuvre beds through, and found my grandmother in a curtained cubicle, hooked up to a beeping machine flashing incomprehensible figures at me. She was awake, pale and drawn looking, propped up on pillows with various leads vanishing into the neckline of the hospital gown she wore.

'Grandmother,' I said tentatively. 'They told me you were here. How are you?'

'I'm tired,' she said flatly. 'What do you want, Margaret?'

'Nothing. I've never wanted anything from you. Nothing you didn't want to give, anyway. I came to tell you that Hunters Reach has a buyer. They'll be signing the contract this morning. Is there anything you need? Anyone you want to see?'

Her eyes closed and for a moment I stood frozen, gaze glued to her chest, fearing that its faint rise and fall had stopped. I had never witnessed death and nor did I then, for the machine beeped on, the green numbers continuing to flash on its screen.

She said coldly in a thread of her normal tone, 'Nobody. There's nobody. Just go away. I said I'm tired. Tired of your accusing eyes. Your mother looked at me like that. I don't regret a thing I've done, and,' she muttered in a weary tone, 'smarming around me now won't change that.'

I swallowed my indignation along with the blaze of fury her words aroused. She was dying, I reminded myself. And a good thing too, my baser self muttered. I forced the thought away; she was past hurting me now. Her actions were more pathetic than vengeful. I said, 'Very well. We'll vacate the day before the Telfords move in. So this is goodbye, Grandmother. I won't be back.'

Her low 'Good!' was waspish and faint, following me from the cubicle just as the nurse approached to throw me out.

Chapter Twenty-seven

Back at the Reach, I phoned Cabot's office to tell him that his client was in hospital and not expected to survive the next heart attack, which her doctor believed was imminent.

'He seems to think it's just a matter of days,' I reported. 'Did Josh, the real estate chap, tell you that the Reach has been sold? He said the contract would be signed today.'

'Indeed, Ms Morrisey. The clients are meeting here in half an hour. So what are your plans now?'

'It will depend on when the buyers want to move in. We could leave tomorrow, but they're a nice couple, and we've still a bit of clearing to do to ready the house for them. I don't mind staying for that. If you could organise a truck from one of the secondhand places, we'll clear out the rest of the furniture for them before we go.'

'Yes, I'll see to that. Most likely tomorrow – would that suit?'

'Anytime.' I hesitated. 'I don't know if you have any need to see Grandmother, Mr Cabot, but if you do, I shouldn't delay a visit. I asked if I could send for anyone, but she said no.

It's up to you. I mean, if nothing else, won't they need her signature on the contract?'

'My office is authorised for that,' he said. 'I believe all other matters are up to date too. Perhaps I'll just pop in this evening.'

'That would be kind,' I said, while wondering why I bothered. The old besom had made it perfectly plain that she wanted nobody near her, but it seemed pitiable to think of her dying ignored and alone.

Finishing the call, I wandered outside to view the smoke-covered horizon, dark enough now to serve as a backdrop for the faint orange glow rising from the distant fire. Betty joined me, pursing her lips as she studied the skyline.

'It looks bad, doesn't it? But it's a long way off, pet. I pity those in its path though.'

'Mmm. I hope to God they can stop it. The Telfords will be worried. Imagine parting with your money, then losing the place to a fire before you even move in.'

'Oh, it won't come to that,' she said. 'Robert has good protection in his boom sprays and it has to get past the farm to reach here.'

'I hope you're right.' I turned back indoors. 'Will you be okay in your cottage?'

'Of course I will. We've had fires before, Meg. And, if push comes to shove, there's always the old underground tank at the farm. It had water in it the last time we sheltered there, back in the fifties. Halfway to my waist, it was. We lost the hayshed and the back wall of the house, and all the hens – we had three hundred back then and sold to the Egg Board. Now that *was* a bad fire. It's dry now though – the tank. If need be, we'd all just pop down there and wait it out.'

Stupefied, I said, 'You have an underground tank?'

'Well, the farm does. It was the house supply back in Ted's dad's day. There weren't many bores in the early days, you know, and not every place was suitable for dams. It's not used now because I have a house tank at the cottage, and the farmhouse is on the bore – the one Daniel Chapman sank in the days when he owned that paddock. But it's part of the farm now because Ted bought the ground, though he gave the Reach the right to draw from it.' She followed me inside and glanced at the clock, saying inconsequentially, 'I wonder if the contract's signed yet?'

'It should be. I think you'll like Linda, Betty. I don't know about Harvey – he seems a real city type. She's the one more into the country stuff, like gardens and jam making and recipes.'

She brightened. 'Well, maybe I can get to know her, and visit? It'd be good to have a friend that close. Robert's wife is nice, but with three young kids she hasn't much time for socialising.'

'I suppose not.' I smiled at her. 'I'm going to miss you, Betty. I'm glad we've had this time together. We'll be off soon, I expect, but I want you to know you'll always be welcome at ours. Seriously, you could hop on a bus anytime and come down. We're only a day away.'

'I know, pet.' She opened the fridge. 'Salad? There's no meat . . . What if we boil some eggs instead?'

'I'll do it.' I got the saucepan and the eggs as she began to assemble vegetables.

'It'll be odd not to have Ellie here,' she mused. 'Not that I ever saw her these last few years. You're sure it's the end for her?'

I shrugged. 'The doctor thinks so. He said she wouldn't be leaving hospital. Why? Did you want to see her?'

'No.' Betty's lips thinned. 'The cat I don't mind. It's not a dumb animal's fault who owns it, but I vowed I'd never speak to her again and I won't.'

'What did she do, Betty?'

'I don't want to talk about it. Did she say anything to you? Like thanking you for coming back, by any chance?'

'Nope. Just stated that she regretted nothing she'd done. And she was tired – tired of me looking at her. I think she could be feeling guilty and accused, though it's never been my intention. But at least I'm no longer afraid of her. Oh,' I remembered with a flicker of indignation, 'and she asked me what I wanted from her. Like she thought I only came back in the hope of landing her money.'

'That's Ellie.' Betty chopped a cucumber with unnecessary force. 'Always judged people by her own standards. Well, it's her loss, Meg. I just wish she knew what she'd thrown away with you.'

'Oh, Betty.' I gave her a hug. 'I don't know how I'd have managed without you.' I ran my eye over the table. 'We just need the bread now, then I'll call the men.'

The removal truck duly turned up the following day to collect the furniture. Jake had volunteered his services to disassemble the spare beds and help separate the cabinets, which came in two parts and locked together. Phillip helped where he could, but it still took most of the afternoon before everything, except the bare essentials, like our bed, and the kitchen table and chairs, had been carted out. Only the built-in cupboards were left.

The fire was much closer that afternoon, the smoke denser and screening the sun, which had become a diffused yellow ball in the sky. The driver, handing over a receipt for the goods, cast a wary glance south. 'You mighta saved this lot from burning,' he observed. 'I hope you're plannin' on leavin' before it gets here?'

'If need be,' I said. 'Where is it exactly, do you know?'

'Approaching Southby, last I heard. People were quittin' the town. We seen 'em headin' for Glenfield back where the roads join. Horse floats, trucks loaded up, kids, dogs – all gettin' out.'

'Okay. Maybe we should too.' Rubbing my arms, feeling the hairs rise and prickle in the dry heat, I watched the truck leave. The wind was gusting, carrying the smell of the fire. The tree foliage tossed restlessly and I watched a trio of galahs shriek and circle, settling on branches, then immediately taking flight again. The wild creatures sensed the danger too. We could start the sprays, I supposed, and just let them run till the fire passed or the electricity gave out, if the poles went down. Then, once Betty was safely home and Jake on his way, it would be high time to grab Claude and make tracks. We could get a room in Glenfield and await events. If the Reach burned, that was that. If it survived the fire, we could return and wait until the Telfords arrived.

We laid our plans over a late smoko. Betty protested that there was no need for us to travel to Glenfield. We could have the couch at her place. It folded out to a double bed, she said, and we were more than welcome, with the haven of the underground tank to retreat to if the worst happened. Hearing the invitation, it occurred to me that she might not wish to be alone.

'Why don't you come with us?' I said, forgetting that there were only two seats in the runabout.

'Riding on the roof? I'll be fine, pet.'

'Ah. Well, I'm sure Jake would give you a lift into town.'

'If you want,' he agreed. 'But you'll have to wait a bit. I've just remembered there's a gizmo on the roof. Chapman set it up years ago and I'll have to check if it's workin'. Might take a bit of time, but after that, sure. Happy to run you in.'

'No, I'll be fine,' Betty said firmly, just as I spoke.

'What sort of gizmo are you talking about, Jake?'

'Fire prevention unit. Big water cannon thing, like a fire hose, only it's sprays. It's hooked up to an electric pump in the roof. Prob'ly wouldn't've been turned on since he died. If it still works, you could drive off an' leave it runnin'. Better'n the fire brigade for prevention.'

'How long?' I asked uneasily. 'I don't want the place to burn, but if it comes to our lives . . . It's only a house.'

'You go, Elf,' Phillip said. 'I'll give Jake a hand with it and follow on with him.'

'No way, buster.' I put my hands on my hips. 'You are not climbing around on any roof with only one useable arm. If he needs help, I'll do it and we'll leave together, and that's flat.'

Phillip rolled his eyes. 'Right, we'll all wait then. In the meantime, we'd better find the cat. Anybody seen him today?'

'At breakfast,' I remembered. 'Not since.'

Of course, the wretched animal was nowhere to be found. Phillip and Betty looked for him while Jake dragged the ladder out of the shed and propped it against the roof. I steadied it as he made a halting ascent, favouring his bad leg until I could stand it no longer.

'Look,' I said, 'why don't you let me do it? Just tell me what I'm looking at and what to do. I'm scared you'll fall, Jake.'

His refusal was immediate and firm. 'No! Hang on to the damn ladder, see it don't slip. Anyroad, I can't tell you what needs doin' till I know myself, and for that I gotta see it.'

'That's all very well, but—'

He stopped climbing and turned his face down. It was strained and beaded with sweat. 'Jesus!' he said roughly. 'Will you just quit arguin', girl, and let a man get on with it?'

Chastened, but in no way convinced that he should be climbing, I bit my lip. As if regretting his outburst, he offered gruffly, 'I'm fine. By the way, I checked, and she ain't listed among the deaths.'

'What?'

'Elvira – my daughter. She's not in the death register.'

'Oh. Well, I'm glad.' But that only meant that she'd been adopted. She might be married. She could be living, or even have died, come to that, under any name. Doubtfully, I called up to his back, 'Grandmother thought she'd died, you know. At least she didn't contradict me when I said it.'

A sound like a snort drifted down. 'And I should believe anythin' Ellie Chapman says? She wouldn't tell the truth on her deathbed.' He'd reached the roof. 'Get a good grip now,' he called and the metal shuddered in my hands as he heaved himself up, bad leg dragging heavily.

I waited anxiously, feeling the wind gust against my back. The trees rattled and moaned and Betty's voice came fitfully to me from the shrubbery calling, 'Puss, puss. Here pussy . . .'

I stifled a sigh. It would be Claude all over to go missing at the eleventh hour. The smoke was closer, darkening the sky, and for the first time I noticed ash being carried on the wind. A flake hit my hand and I stared at it, as bemused as a rookie soldier seeing the first spot of blood. Southby was twenty kay distant! The fire couldn't possibly be closer than that.

The roof creaked as Jake, now out of sight, made his way up it. I waited impatiently and finally climbed up half-a-dozen rungs to call, 'What's happening, Jake?'

'Not a bloody lot.' He sounded frustrated. 'I need a wrench. Can you find one in my toolbox and heave it up to me?'

'Hang on.' I looked about in vain for Phillip, then hurried across to where Jake's ute was parked. The toolbox was a huge metal thing and I rooted among its contents, coming up with three separate wrenches. Or Stillsons. Were they the same thing? The largest looked too big, so I took both the others and panted up the ladder to slide them over the gutter before climbing onto the roof myself. 'Here. Is this what you want?'

Jake was standing using a chimney for support, looking out over the country to the south. I followed his gaze and gasped.

'Yeah,' he agreed. 'We don't want to bugger round none. Give us the smaller one, and get yourself back on the ground. Soon as I've cleaned the head, I'm comin' down.'

So shocked was I by the sight of the flames in the timberline behind Robert Cox's place that I obeyed without demur. It seemed ages, but it could only have been ten minutes or so before Jake dropped the wrenches over the roof's edge and lowered himself laboriously onto the ladder. It shook in my hands beneath his weight as he descended. I heard him swear once when his bad leg slipped, and a groan escaped him but after a moment he made his way steadily down, almost falling as he stepped off the final rung.

'All fixed?' I asked.

'Maybe.' He grunted. 'Needs testin''. There must be a switch somewhere inside. Where's the board?'

'I don't . . . oh, wait – there's something with a lot of fuse-boxes on it in the hall. Is that what you mean?'

'Prob'ly,' he said. 'Show us.'

'I think we should hurry. That fire looks awfully close, Jake.'

'I'm goin' as fast as I can, girl.' He followed me into the house, ran a rapid eye over the conglomeration of switches and thumbed one on. 'Oughta be it.' He cocked his head and a few moments later something heavy pounded on the roof. 'She's workin''.' He nodded. When we hurried outside, the house was already running with water from the heavy spray shooting out on all sides from the centreline of the roof.

'I'll get the others.' I slipped past him just as Betty came around the corner. 'We're ready to go. Have you found Claude?'

'Phillip's just bringing him.' I heard hammering as she spoke. He was closing the box.

'Okay,' I said. 'Get in, Betty. The fire's almost here. We have to go.'

'My bike—'

'I'll chuck it on the back,' Jake said, as Phillip appeared, lugging a crate one-handed. 'Give us that. It can go on too.'

Claude yowled as he was unceremoniously dumped beside the toolbox, then the men grabbed Betty's trike between them and threw it up as well. 'Follow me,' Jake called, yanking the cab door open. 'We should stick together.'

I hesitated by the car door. 'Should I run and start the garden sprays?'

'No time,' he yelled, 'besides it'd halve the flow to the house. Just get movin'.'

'I'll drive.' Phillip was already behind the wheel.

'You should let me.' But he had no intention of yielding the seat so I scrambled in and we took off after Jake. The wind was buffeting the vehicle and the sun had completely vanished behind inky layers of smoke. I closed my window, panting in the heated air. It could have been evening for all the natural light that was left. The sight of the dark, crimson-shot sky made me cower in my seat, overawed by its fury and might.

'How did the fire get here so quick?' Phillip sped through the open gates. 'No, leave 'em. We're not stopping,' he said as I automatically reached for the door handle. 'God almighty! I can see the actual flames.'

He was right. Orange and scarlet, two metres high or more, they formed a line a kilometre or so in front of us, charging forward on both sides of the road, embers blowing like sparklers through the heated air. I cried, 'Look out! He's braking,' as Jake's taillights flared in the gloom. Then the ute fishtailed into a spin and he was racing back through the smoke towards us. Phillip jammed the brakes on and jerked his window down as the ute slid to a stop beside us.

'We'll have to go back. Get to the farm,' Jake yelled. Betty, clutching her side door, had paled, and even over the noise of the engines I heard Claude's indignant protest.

'If we hit the gas we could get through it,' Phillip began just as the fire reached the far end of the blue gum plantation.

There was an unearthly roar and flames shot into the sky, a background to Jake's urgent shout.

'Like bloody hell! Christ! It's crowning, man. Move! The fireys are comin'. Don't block their way.' He roared past us and, swearing, Phillip spun the wheel and we shot over the verge and round to follow him. Behind us, emerging out of the smoke, I saw the flashing lights of a fire truck. I couldn't drag my horrified gaze from the inferno chasing us. The tops of the eucalypts whirled in a strange, fiery dance as the great mass of flames, a solid wall really, surged from tree to tree, spurting embers like spiteful spawn to ignite the writhing foliage ahead of them. Around us the world had darkened to night and we drove by the hellish glare of the approaching monster.

I bitterly regretted the time spent protecting the house. What did it matter compared to our lives? The runabout cornered badly onto the narrower farm track and Phillip swore as his bad arm jerked with the movement. The road was unfamiliar, with sudden dips and tight turns. We flashed past a fallow paddock with Betty's cottage beside it, then roared up to the collection of once familiar farm buildings, but there was no time to remember or take in the changes made during the last decade. The taillights flared as Jake stopped and then he was out, lurching around the ute to grab Claude's box. Phillip pulled up behind him and we piled out too, and a few moments later the first fire truck came to a halt behind us.

A man came running out of the dimness surrounding the farmhouse. He beckoned us, greeting Betty by name. 'You okay, Bets? Good thing you came. Get 'em into the tank. Rose and the kids are already there.' To the first fireman out of the truck, he called, 'Water? Follow me,' and set off at a jog with the orange-coated figure shambling beside him.

'This way.' Betty bustled off, Jake following with the crated cat but Phillip broke back to the car to grab something from the boot he must've unlatched when he got out.

'Phillip!' I cried. 'What? Come on!'

'Camera.' He grabbed my hand, pulling me after the others. 'Let's go, Elf.'

Chapter Twenty-eight

The underground water tank at the farm was a huge concrete cube sunk into the ground and covered with a layer of earth, upon which stuff was growing. It had once, I assumed, as we made our way down the wide-runged ladder bolted to the wall below the manhole, been connected via pipes to the farmhouse and possibly shed roofs, which had channelled rainwater into it. Now it was dry, its gloom lit by a pressure lamp. One end was stacked with hay bales, two of which served as seats for Rose Cox and her children.

We introduced ourselves and Jake, his limp more pronounced than ever, dragged a few more bales out of the pile for us to sit on. Rose had drinking water and snacks for the children, who had all brought a favourite toy along. They weren't playing with them though. The youngest, a little girl, was grizzling for her daddy and the other two, an older boy and his sister, stuck close to their mother, silent and fearful looking.

I remembered the cat then. 'Where's Claude?'

'Robert said he'd bring him down,' Jake muttered and I realised that neither he nor Phillip could have managed crate and ladder together. Then, as if the creature had heard us, there came an earsplitting caterwaul and the wooden box containing the cat swung into view on the end of a rope. I darted across to grab it, looking up into the farmer's face as he stood above the manhole.

'Got him, thanks. Are you coming down?'

'Not just yet.' He vanished and Rose momentarily closed her eyes.

'He'll be okay.' Betty patted her hand. 'He knows what he's doing.' She fished about in her pocket and withdrew a length of wool. 'Well, look at that!' she exclaimed to the children. 'Who wants to learn to play cat's cradle?'

The middle girl was looking at Claude's container, where its occupant was still raising an unholy fuss. 'Can we play with the kitty instead?'

'I don't think so, sweetie,' I said swiftly. 'His claws are very sharp. He scratches, and he bites. Show *me*, Betty. I'd like to learn a new game.' It convinced the two older children and they were soon happily engaged, pinching the wool between their fingers and pulling it where directed.

'I'm Meg.' I had left them to it to introduce myself to Rose. 'My partner and I have been packing up Hunters Reach for my grandmother. We were heading into town but we left it too late. We met the fire on the road and had to come back. Is this the first time you've had to shelter down here?'

'Yes.' She glanced around. 'As you can see, Rob keeps hay in it.'

'How does he get it out?' I wondered. It would be an awkward job taking it up, a bale at a time, through the manhole.

Rose pointed to the roof. 'There's a big hinged section. He uses a hoist. Both for it and the hay. How close is the fire?'

I shivered. 'In the plantation, so quite close. I've never seen anything like it! We were trying to get through to Glenfield but we had no chance. Luckily the firetrucks were right behind us. I don't see them stopping it though – not the way it was roaring along.'

'What about the Reach? Will it be safe? We heard the old lady was selling.' She looked suddenly struck, leaning towards me, one hand automatically soothing the grizzling child. 'She's not still there?'

'No, she moved into town a month or more ago. As for the house . . .' I shrugged. 'It's anybody's guess. But, yes, it's been sold. I just hope it survives for its new owners. We set the roof sprinkler going before we left, but honestly? The way the fire is, it'd be like fighting it with buckets.'

Rose nodded, rocking the child in her arms. 'Rob thinks we'll be all right. The nearest paddocks are dry but they're grazed down too. And with the brigade to help—' Her lips tightened. 'I wish he'd come back though.'

'I expect they know what they're doing,' I said soothingly and was suddenly fiercely glad of Phillip's broken arm. If it wasn't for that, he'd be up there now with his camera, running God knows what risks for the perfect shot. I looked towards him and saw that he actually was snapping shots right that moment with the camera propped on hay bales and him crouched, squinting, behind it. To change the direction of my thoughts, I said abruptly, 'Do you know my grandmother, Rose?'

Her eyes were suddenly wary. 'That's right, you said she was . . . I'm so worried I'd already forgotten. And we'd assumed, Rob and I, that you were just working there. We've seen you driving past, you see.'

'Both are true,' I said. 'I know she wasn't much for socialising. Had you met her?'

'Once,' she admitted, looking away. Her cheeks pinkened. 'Mrs Chapman wasn't very nice – in fact, she was really rude about the children. I left them in the garden while I called on her – just being neighbourly – and Bobby picked some flowers. He didn't mean any harm . . . they're allowed to pick them at home. She might be old,' she said feelingly, 'but she was scary.'

'Tell me about it. She's dying, according to the doctor. That's why the place was on the market. I think you'll like your new neighbours. They seem quite a nice couple. Are you locals, you and Robert?'

She shook her head. 'Rob's from Victoria and I grew up in Adelaide. We met at summer school during uni. Why?'

I shrugged. 'Just wondered if you'd known my mother, but you're too young anyway. You'd have been a child when she married.'

She shook her head. 'Sorry, and about your gran. I mean I didn't like her, but—'

'Don't be. I don't care for her myself, but there was nobody else for her to commandeer. She's my only blood relative.'

'I see.' She hesitated. 'There was a bit on the news about finding a body at the Reach. Do you mind my asking . . .?'

'The skeleton in the well? It's perfectly true,' I said. 'What wasn't published was that my grandfather was the one who killed the young woman. Allegedly, of course. Nobody can prove it and he's long dead, so the police aren't investigating any further. It happened when I was a baby, and nobody ever guessed because the woman wasn't known to be missing.'

'God, how awful!' Rose swallowed and, glancing over at Betty, whose ear was bent attentively to something the little girl was saying, shook her head. 'It's just unbelievable! We've heard a few things about old man Chapman from Betty, but murder!'

'I know,' I said flatly. 'The only good thing is that he's dead. From what I could learn, he seems to have been a real tyrant with an ungovernable temper, who indulged in a lot of sharp practices. Probably how he made his money. I'm glad I never knew him.'

She seemed unable to find an answer to my words, and after a moment I got up and went over to the men, who were now perched in desultory conversation on another bale. Smoke had seeped into the tank and hung, mist-like, above our heads. It tickled my throat and I wondered uneasily if it would fill the container and smother us all. There was a distant background roar of sound and I cocked my head. 'Good Lord, what's that awful racket?'

''S'what a bad fire sounds like,' Jake said. He shifted on the bale, easing his leg.

'What are the fireys doing?'

'Defending the farmhouse,' he said. 'They can't tackle a crowner. But she'll slow when she hits the paddocks and they'll meet 'er there. Good chance they'll do it.'

I thought of the heat and terrible storm of flames I had witnessed. 'You really think so?'

'Yeah. 'Specially if they get a bomber in to dump on the paddock.'

'I wish I could do something,' I said restlessly.

'You can,' he said. 'You stay safe. Lives and property.

That's what those blokes out there are fightin' for, so we stop here till they say diff'rent.'

It was a hot, slow wait. Every now and then I climbed up the ladder but there was nothing to see but smoke and the glare of the crimson sky. The heated, smoke-filled air brought on a coughing fit, causing me to retreat quickly downwards. Once I heard a plane, but it was hard to pinpoint amid all the noise going on – trucks moving, the throb of an engine, the howl of the wind and the steady background roar of the flames consuming everything in their path. Eventually that died down. We were drinking tea by then, from the thermos that Rose had brought into the tank with her, and Jake was entertaining the two older children with the tale of an epic fight he had once witnessed (he said) between two dingoes and a big old roo they had cornered in a dam.

'Listen,' Rose interrupted. 'Hear that? Something's changed.'

'Wind's dropped.' Jake cocked an ear. 'I reckon she'll be outta the timber by this. They'll get a handle on her now.'

'Go on, Jake,' Bobby urged. 'What happened then? Did the dogs kill him?'

'No way! That old roo just grabbed the first dingo in his arms – them little arms are mighty strong, you know – an' he held him under the water till he drowned.'

'Serve him right,' Bobby said with satisfaction.

'But that's cruel!' his sister objected.

'Yeah, well, he was gonna eat the roo, remember. Then he gave the other dog a good squeezin' till it didn't know if its insides were in or out. That fixed him. It cleared off an' the roo just hopped away.'

'Good,' Bobby said, just as his sister started to her feet with a glad cry.

'Daddy!'

Robert Cox, grimed and weary, his face reddened from the fire's radiant heat, turned from the ladder and smiled tiredly at his daughter. 'Okay, pumpkin?'

'Rob.' Rose surged to her feet to join him, the child still in her arms. 'Are you all right? Is it out?'

'Not quite.' He patted her back. 'They stopped it in the paddock. We've lost a bit of fencing and the crop's gone but we've been damn lucky.'

'So it's still a danger?' I asked. 'Sorry, I'm Meg Morrisey from the Reach. This is my partner, Phillip, and Jake Lynch.'

'Robert Cox.' We all shook hands and I repeated my question.

'Not desperate. And the captain reckons they might get on top of it tonight. They've been fighting it for days. You can all come out now and I was thinking, love'—he turned to his wife—'if you could make the men a meal? They must be buggered. I know I am.'

'Of course.' She handed him the baby. 'You bring Jenna. They've all been so good, no squabbles at all.'

'Good kids,' he said abstractedly, and to me, 'You're quite welcome to join us. In any event, you shouldn't leave just yet. There could be trees down across the road.'

'Good advice,' Jake said gruffly. 'A fire ain't over till she's out.'

'Thank you.' I looked at Phillip, who nodded.

'We'll hang around, thanks, but we don't need feeding. Wouldn't say no to a cuppa though. Elf?'

'That would be lovely.' I turned to Rose. 'Only you must let me help.'

'We both will,' Betty said. 'And you'll both stay with me tonight, Meg. The fire's not out yet but it can't burn back over where it's been.'

So that's what we did. Phillip wanted to return to the Reach to check on the house, but that plan was vetoed by the captain of the brigade, a weary veteran who had come, sweat-marked and blackened, straight from the battle.

'Time enough for that tomorrow,' he ruled. 'After we've taken a dekko first.'

The following day, we retraced our steps over the road we had hurtled along in such terror the day before. The country was drowned in ash, layers of it, soft and grey, lifting in little tendrils as the breeze stirred, its expanse dotted with the blackened shapes of trees. Even my old red gum had burned and still was, the heart wood smouldering with a dull red glow where a branch had come down and given the flames access to the trunk. But the tree also marked the limit of the fire's reach. Beyond it the gates of Hunters Reach stood untouched, as if the pruned and now-shooting hedge had acted as a fire-proof barrier to the flames.

'Looks like it's okay.' I could see the chimneys and as we drove through the gates, the sharp outline of the roof. 'My Lord! Let's hope that roof's sound. If the sprinkler's still going the place will be swamped.'

The garden was at any rate. Water still hosed from the valve above and I hastened in through the unlocked door to find the switchboard and managed, after a couple of attempts, to flick the correct switch. The noise on the roof died and Phillip, removing muddy boots at the door, called, 'It's stopped.'

'I can hear.' The phone began to ring and, leaving a string of muddy footprints behind, I went to answer it. 'Hunters Reach. Hello.'

'Oh, you're there,' the caller gasped. 'I'm so glad! We've been worried sick! But we can't get out there; the police have closed the road. But if you're there, the house is okay, right?'

'Linda. Yes, yes, everything's fine. We've just this minute got back from the neighbouring farm where we overnighted. The fire didn't quite make it to the gates, so there's no need to come out. I haven't looked properly yet – as I say, we've just arrived – but the garden doesn't even appear to be singed.'

'Oh, thank you, thank you. The thought of—' Her voice faded and I heard her call, 'They're there, Harv. It didn't burn,' and then she was back, saying rapidly, 'We won't come out then. Can you bear to hang on just for another week? We've booked a truck to shift our stuff but the police have closed some roads, and there are a hundred little details besides . . .'

'Of course, Linda. No bother,' I assured her. 'We'll wait till you're ready to move in.'

Chapter Twenty-nine

Ash had fallen like snow over the grounds, speckling the growth of thistles and clover and soursobs in the still undug kitchen garden space, and dusting the verandah.

'It'll sweep off.' Phillip was freeing Claude, whom we'd brought back in his cage. 'There you go, old fellow,' he said as the cat shot away, his tail fluffed out to twice its normal size. Phillip glanced around at the green oasis surrounding us and said soberly, 'We've been bloody lucky. Well, us and the Telfords. Robert lost his crop and I expect there'll be a few worse off than that.' The sky above us had cleared but the fire still burned to the east, for smoke was smeared low across that horizon. 'I think,' he added, 'if you'd set up the tripod for me, I'll try for a few snaps.'

'I can,' I said doubtfully, 'but how will you manage?'

'Only takes one finger to press the button, Elf. I've been idle long enough. While you're doing that, I might try and get hold of Joe. See if he can pick me up. He'll be somewhere around, covering the fire.'

Joe, I remembered, was the writer, his new partner. 'How will he get here? Linda said the road was closed.'

Phillip laughed. 'He's a journo – they can get anywhere. Probably riding with the fireys and nobody'll stop them. What'll you do?'

'There isn't much left to do. Check our food supplies, I suppose. Take a walk around.' I sighed. 'I think it's going to be a long week, but I did tell Linda we'd stay.' And tomorrow, or whenever the road opened, I should drive in to see Grandmother. She might be worrying about damage to the Reach, not to mention Claude. Of course, stuck in ICU, there was a chance she didn't even know about the fire, and I couldn't imagine the medical staff telling her, so perhaps . . .? But, no. The stress of worrying, if she did learn of it, might actually kill her and I didn't want that on my conscience.

I made a sandwich lunch for us and shortly afterwards, Joe Habble's twin cab spun up the drive to collect Phillip. He had his camera gear and had packed a small bag, I saw, as he walked out onto the verandah to meet Joe.

'You're not planning on being back tonight, then?'

'Who knows, Elf?' He kissed me absentmindedly, raising a burdened arm to wave at Joe, who was getting out of the vehicle. 'Coming! See where the story goes. You're safe here. I'll call you.'

'Yes.' If the lines weren't down, or all the phones burnt where he was going. 'Please take care. Here, I'll carry that out.' I took the unwieldly tripod from him, squeezing the legs shut. 'Just don't make your arm worse. Ask Joe for help.' He wouldn't, of course. 'Get some great pics and remember to eat.'

'I will.' He sketched a grin. 'Love you, funny face.' He hurried to the vehicle, and I handed the tripod in through the window, receiving a careless wave from Joe, now back behind the wheel, as he swung the twin cab around and drove off.

'Well.' I stood for a moment listening to the fading hum of the vehicle and reflecting that the sound was symptomatic of my life with Phillip. He was always charging off somewhere and, realistically, I couldn't expect that to change. But I had never felt so abandoned as I did just then.

Of course, I had had a job before and my own life. So, when the week here was up, I would have to find another one – or a very absorbing hobby, I thought wryly. It would drive me insane to be idle. And with this thought in mind I went hunting among Jake's tools for the secateurs with the aim of filling a few vases. I had always loved flowers. Didn't most women? Or was it something – heaven forbid! – that I had inherited from my grandmother? I rather hoped not.

A rose I could recognise, and an ordinary daisy, but not much else. There were lilies and, among the rest, tall, bold-faced orange flowers, some bell-shaped ones and others with spreading heads consisting of multiple smaller blossoms. Lace something, I thought vaguely, or was that another name for baby's breath? There was lavender in the bed beside the roses, unmistakeable by its smell, and a growth of tall-stemmed, vivid blue flowers with fern-like foliage. Which were . . .? I shut my eyes, recalling the wedding photograph. What had Grandmother said about blue? 'Delphiniums!' I spoke the word triumphantly. To match my mother's eyes, she'd said. I snipped half-a-dozen stalks to add to the pile, then carried the lot inside, remembering only then that all the vases had been disposed of.

'Damn!' Well, there had to be something big enough to hold them; I couldn't just throw them out. I found the (empty) milk jug for the roses and, with the others temporarily stashed in the sink, went hunting through the rubbish bin to locate the pickle jar we had finished the previous day. Its utilitarian form did nothing to offset the arrangement but it couldn't be helped. I returned the secateurs and then, because that side of the house was in shade and the ground thoroughly soaked from its night-long sprinkling, set myself to weeding the kitchen garden beds.

When the phone rang that evening, I leapt to answer it, only to hear Betty's voice enquiring how things were.

'Oh, fine, thanks. No actual damage, just a lot of ash lying about. Linda rang soon after we got back – she was so relieved! She asked me if we'd stay on another week because of the road closure, though hopefully they'll open it sooner than that. Anyway, I said we would. Phillip has gone off with a journalist – his new workmate – to the fire. He can use his camera if it's on the tripod, so that's what he's doing.'

'And you're there all alone, Meg?'

'I was before,' I pointed out. 'I'll survive.'

'I'll come over tomorrow.'

'There's no need,' I protested. 'Everything's done.'

'All the same,' she said firmly before she hung up. 'I'll see you then, pet.'

*

She was as good as her word, cycling up the drive on the dot of nine. Jake had already turned up. I had found him standing, hands on hips, surveying the place just as the sun rose behind the blackened trunks of the forest now visible beyond the Cox's farm; the fire must have cleared everything before it, because I had never seen it before from this angle. The sky was brighter, and though the smell of burning still thickened the air, the smoke had mostly gone.

'Morning, Jake. Where'd you stay last night? You could've come back here, you know.'

'Yeah, thanks, but it was okay. I got a bed at the farm with the off-duty fireys. I see it worked out for 'er though. Mighta known it would.' His voice was somewhere between resigned and contemptuous. 'Old Chapman musta signed a pact with the devil and it's still holdin'.'

'It's no longer Grandmother's,' I reminded him. 'The new owners couldn't get out yesterday and I'm to hang on here for a week until their furniture comes. Phillip's gone off with his camera. So it's just you and me now. You haven't heard from Cabot?'

He shrugged. 'How?'

'Of course. You weren't home last night. Well, he hasn't rung here either, so presumably he knows the Reach isn't a pile of ashes.'

'Not his worry now, is it? Well, I'd better get on with it. See you been doin' a bit of weeding.'

'I was bored. And there's a week to go, so I'll probably be begging you for jobs before it's over,' I said lightly, and saw his saturnine grin flash as he lurched away.

*

Betty and I spent a gossipy morning that was broken by a visit from a uniformed policeman in a patrol car. He was checking up on the people who'd chosen not to evacuate, as well as the state of the roads, he said, as fallen trees could be as much a hazard as the actual fire. Betty gave him a cup of tea and asked about losses in the district, nodding gravely when we heard of a farmhouse and two sheds of machinery burned to the ground.

'But nobody was killed?' she asked.

'No.' The policeman was a youngish man with a dark moustache he probably considered ultra-cool, the way his fingers kept straying upwards to pet it. 'A couple of places lost their crops, and walnuts'll be going up in price seeing as how the Carmodys had three-quarters of their trees burned. Fairly ripped through 'em, the blaze did.' The company of Carmody Brothers produced most of the walnuts in South Australia. 'And,' he continued, 'they're shooting stock over towards Linton. Bunch got caught in the scrub when the fire came through. Vet reckons they're too bad to save. Sheep, and I heard there was a couple of horses too.'

'That's horrible.' Betty looked sick. 'Crops will grow again and sheds can be rebuilt, but the animals . . .'

'Yeah.' The constable, seeming to regret his frankness, stood up. 'Well, thanks for the cuppa. I better get going. That gum tree beyond your gate's still burning, but the limbs are clear of the road.'

'When will that be open again?' I asked.

'It already is. The SES boys were out early with their chainsaws. It's good to go right now.'

'That'll make life easier.' I waved him off, reflecting that although I had no burning desire to go to town, I no longer had any excuse to avoid visiting my grandmother.

Once he had gone I looked at Betty. 'Feel like coming for a drive? I have to go see Grandmother, but I could drop you off first. A cafe, or the library? And we can have a look at the fire damage on the way.'

'Mmm.' Betty thought for about two seconds and removed her apron. 'Could we pop into my place first? I could change my library books – save me humping them home on the bus.'

'Of course. I'll just grab my bag.'

The old red gum by the gate that I had climbed as a child was in a sad way. Denuded of branches, nothing but a couple of metres of its trunk remained, a smouldering wreck being slowly consumed by the embers within. Soon, despite its seeming immutability, it would be gone forever, passed into memory, like Hunters Reach itself would be to me. Even though I held no fondness for the latter, I felt a measure of sadness at the thought, with its reminder of the transience of all matter. The tree was immensely old; it might be two, or possibly three hundred years since its tiny seed had sprouted. Against that, my life and Phillip's were as the beat of an insect's wing. It was a sobering reflection. Barring further fires or other catastrophes, even the Reach itself would outlast us both.

Beyond the Robertses' farm, the landscape was blackened with just the skeletons of trees remaining. All the timber fences had burned, only the tangles of wire and the occasional steel gate or grid-post left to show where they had been. Twice we passed cattle roaming free, lipping at blown leaves along the road verges in their search for grazing, and once a little cluster of alpacas, bounding long-necked from the roadside. In the plantation, amid the black sticks of the trees, wisps of smoke showed where fallen trunks still burned. Even the enamel of the roadside signs had bubbled and melted in the passing inferno. The sight shook me, underlining how little I had comprehended, while it had actually raged, of the fire's ferocity. Proof that you had to experience some things before you could truly gauge their effect.

'God! We were lucky, Betty. Seeing this . . . I really don't know how firefighters survive.'

'No,' she agreed. 'Did you notice all the birds have gone?'

'No insects left, or seeds. I suppose that's why.'

'Or they perished in the fire.' We continued in silence then, both of us overwhelmed by the devastation.

In Glenfield, I dropped Betty off at the library before driving to the hospital. I asked at the desk and was told that Grandmother had been moved from intensive care to a private room just down the corridor.

'Does that mean she's improved?' I asked. 'Because the doctor said—'

'I'm afraid not. Her heart is really very weak. They moved her for privacy, and the quiet, of course. ICU's a very noisy place. You can go on up.'

I tapped lightly at the room door and let myself in past the half-drawn curtain that hid the bed's occupant from the hallway. 'Grandmother?' I spoke softly but got no reply. She was sleeping, her mouth slightly open and her hands folded over her spectacles, which rested on the white hospital coverlet. I seated myself quietly in the visitor's chair and studied her, my mind reverting as always to the enduring mystery of her dislike for me.

Sleep, or perhaps approaching death, had smoothed the hard lines from her face, leaving it wrinkled but serene. The iron-grey hair was thick still, though somewhat lank as if in need of a good shampoo, but her skin had the well-cared-for look of a woman who had never stinted herself on lotions and creams. As far as I knew she had enjoyed comfortable life-long wealth, dating, if not from her birth, then certainly from her marriage. She had always had the best in material things, a large expensive home, all the trappings of social position . . . but also a family she had driven from her side, and a husband who had resorted to murder. I sighed, and as if the sound had penetrated her sleep, she stirred, grey eyes looking at me in momentary bemusement.

'Iris?' She swallowed, worked her mouth, and I saw then that her false teeth had been removed, partly accounting for the sunken look of her cheeks. Her gaze, unaccustomedly cloudy, focused on me. 'Who . . . what?' Her voice was weak, more fractious than angry; she rolled her head tiredly and muttered. 'Sleep . . . I was sleeping.'

'Yes. Did I wake you? I didn't mean to. Why did you think I was Iris, Grandmother?'

'Eyes,' she mumbled, then, 'Water.'

There was a drinking cup with a straw on the bedside table. I held it to her lips and the liquid seemed to revive her. Her voice came more strongly, with something of its old snap. 'Margaret.' This time she knew me. 'Why have you come?'

I put the cup back and reseated myself. 'I thought you

might be worried about the fire, and I came to tell you that the Reach is safe. It didn't burn.'

'Fire?' She sounded querulous. 'Where is the fire?'

I explained but she stopped listening before I'd finished. Her eyes fluttered down, then opened again. 'Yes, yes. Burn it all,' she mumbled.

She was wandering. I said patiently, 'It's safe, Grandmother, I promise you. The fire didn't damage it. Hunters Reach is still there.'

'Pity.' The word came clearly, and this time I was sure that she had understood. 'Cold heart – needs fire. Only the garden . . . Want to sleep.'

She either fell into a doze then or pretended to, and after sitting for five minutes watching her chest rise and fall I tiptoed out, utterly flabbergasted. She hadn't even asked after Claude.

Chapter Thirty

Betty, books selected, was waiting for me in the library and agreed to my suggestion of a coffee before we started back.

'The Rose Garden is nice, and the coffee's good,' she suggested. 'You can usually get a park in the post office lane.'

She was right and we were soon settled beneath a broad umbrella on the pavement, she with a minuscule teapot and I with a cappuccino.

'So how did you find Ellie? Here,' she said, pushing the plate with the second scone upon it across to me. 'Have it. They make them far too big for one person.'

'I don't really need it,' I demurred.

'Neither do I.' She followed the plate with the jam and cream. 'So? Ellie.'

'Um, not really with it.' I broke the scone and layered jam on one half. 'I don't think she recognised me at first, called me Iris. But she had just woken up. Then she seemed to think that the Reach had burned and when I assured her it was fine she said it was a pity! That it had a cold heart. I don't know if she's delusional or actually telling the truth. And, before I could say anything, she'd dropped off again. She just seems to drift in and out. What really shocked me was that she never even mentioned the cat.'

'Well, the things you cared most for seem to matter very little at the end,' Betty observed. 'It was like that with Ted. It's as if everything just gets stripped away – all the hopes and fears and worries. It's probably a good thing, pet. Maybe young deaths are different, but a lot of the elderly seem almost ready to welcome it.'

'I suppose,' I said doubtfully. 'Anyway, I've done what I set out to do, even if it proved unnecessary. And I was right. She didn't know about the fire. Isn't that Mr Cabot?'

It was. Walking purposefully, he seemed headed for the bank only two buildings along, but he saw us and checked his stride to cross the pavement to our table and offer a greeting.

'Mrs Roberts, Ms Morrisey. This is a fortunate coincidence. I had planned on driving out to Hunters Reach later today, but as you're here, Ms Morrisey, I wonder if you could pop along to my office when you've finished?'

'Well, yes.' I was mystified. 'Why? Has something come up about the sale?'

'No, no, that's all smooth sailing. Signed and sealed, as they say. It's just that I've received a communication for you, and, as you're already in town perhaps you could collect it, thus saving me the trip?'

'Yes, of course.' I wondered if his old-fashioned delivery had anything to do with his profession. 'I'll be along shortly.'

'Good. Thank you. I've a brief transaction to make, then I'll head straight back.' He left us and I raised my brows at Betty.

'A communication – what does that mean?'

'A letter?' she hazarded. 'Can't just be a message, or he could have phoned.' She refilled her cup, saying, 'Amazing what these little pots hold. You pop on down and I'll wait for you. Take your time, it's nice here.'

I'd scarcely been seated five minutes in the solicitor's small waiting room with its squashy chairs and potplants before Mr Cabot entered and nodded to me. 'Ah, there you are. If you'd like to come through. No after-effects from the fire, I hope? I heard it reached as far as the Robertses' farm.'

'No. The Reach is fine, thanks, and so are we.' His room's decor, as I'd discovered during my initial visit, slipped a trifle backwards into the fifties, all dark wood with one wall covered in labelled pigeonholes in which papers rested. There was a shelf of lawyerly tomes and, incongruously resting below them on a plinth, an orrery fashioned from brass. His desk was broad and busy looking with two leather padded visitor's chairs opposite his own. He pulled one of the former back for me.

I felt strangely nervous, as if I was facing a doctor with a dubious diagnosis to impart. Sounding more confident than I was, I said, 'So – a communication? From whom, Mr Cabot? I mean, nobody even knows I'm in Glenfield. And if they did, why wouldn't they send whatever it is straight to the Reach?'

'It's from the firm of Greenfleet, the antiques dealers. They sent a covering letter with the package they discovered in a hidden drawer in the, erm—' he glanced down at a paper on the desk as if refreshing his memory—'ah, yes, the escritoire. So, as the purchase went through this office, they very properly returned the item to us.'

'I see.' I thought about it. 'Well, actually, I don't. That makes it estate business, doesn't it? Shouldn't you be handling that?'

'The letter states it to be of a personal nature. So I'm sure it's self-explanatory. Should it raise any issues, of course, you are at liberty to seek advice from us and I will be happy to offer whatever assistance I may,' he assured me in his stiff, old-fashioned way.

'Thank you.' I accepted the buff-coloured envelope securely sealed with tape as he handed it to me, and rose. 'If I need help with it, I'll let you know then. Um . . . the new owners have asked me to stay on at the Reach for another week, so I take it that my employment is over? Phillip's already gone back to work.'

'Quite.' He rose also and offered his hand and for a moment I could have sworn there was a twinkle in his eye. 'It has been a pleasure, Ms Morrisey, and I see no reason why your wages shouldn't run till the coming Saturday. We'll call it danger money, shall we? After all, you didn't sign up for bushfires.'

'Thanks.' I smiled at him. 'I visited my grandmother this morning. She's very tired and I fancy sinking fast. About the funeral when it comes – will I . . .?'

'It's all in hand,' he assured me. 'Mrs Chapman has left explicit instructions with me about that. A simple burial. No flowers, or mourners. She and her late husband have a double plot in the cemetery. Daniel Chapman organised that decades ago. So nothing will be expected of you.'

'Right.' I was relieved. 'Thank you.' I placed the envelope in my bag and was at the door when I suddenly thought of something else. 'And Aunt Iris? There will have to be a funeral eventually for her remains, won't there? Who . . .?'

'Quite,' he said. 'But that is also in hand. JJ has taken responsibility there, but of course nothing can happen until after the inquest.'

'I see.' I should have guessed that Jake would do it. I said, 'You called him JJ. You do like him then, Mr Cabot?' I don't know why it mattered that he should, but since learning of Iris's murder and witnessing his grief, I had really felt for the man.

He harrumphed, nodding curtly. 'I do. I'm sorry I couldn't do more for him back when he was arraigned. I've always felt that his was a very unsound verdict. Now, I really must get on, so if there's nothing else . . .?'

'Of course. Thanks again,' I said and left.

'All right?' Betty asked, getting up from her chair.

'Mmm. It's just some paper found in that fancy writing desk that the antiques dealer bought. I'll open it later. Cabot just told me the most astounding thing! Grandmother's organised her own funeral. Isn't that unreal? No flowers, and apparently nobody's to attend it either. Maybe she suspects that nobody would go. It's a sort of relief, but awfully sad too, don't you think?'

'And about what she deserves,' Betty said grimly. 'You reap what you sow, pet. Any farmer'll tell you that. And Ellie Chapman never sowed a kind thought in her life. I reckon fixing her own funeral just proves she knows it, too.'

'Whatever did she do to you, Betty?' I had never heard her speak so harshly of anyone. As long as I had known her, she had been the soul of forgiveness.

'Nothing actionable. But Ted's death is on her and she knows it. She wanted our farm, God knows why with the land she already owns, but she'd set her heart on having it. And, like any small farmer, we had debts. The sale of the place was going to clear them though, with enough left over for a little house by the beach.' Betty looked at me as our lagging steps reached the corner of the post office lane. 'A nice little cottage, that's what we'd planned, and an end to the work and the worry. We had no son for the land, so that's what we thought, Ted and I. The doctor had told him it was time to take it easy. Give up work, he said, no more stress and you've years in front of you.' She shook her head, expression bitter. 'Six months to the day, that's what he got.'

'But what did Grandmother do?' I frowned. 'And why that particular bit of land?'

'I don't know, Meg. There was some talk in town at the time that a consortium was looking into building a fancy retreat for the rich and were after somewhere rural in the hills. It might've been that. A property with room for its own golf course and riding stables and, I suppose, a swimming pool. It never happened. But what I do know is that she bought up our debts and tried to force Ted to sell to her. Maybe she hadn't known we were planning to sell anyway. I mean, all she had to do was come with an offer . . .' She trailed off, waiting while I unlocked the car, then settled herself beside me, reaching for the seatbelt. I sat there holding the key in my hand as she went on. 'Well, it was the wrong way to go about it. She got Ted's back up threatening him with the bailiffs, and he was one stubborn man. Mules had nothing on Ted once he made up his mind.' She shook her head, eyes sorrowful. 'Lord, he could be stubborn. There was no way he'd give her the satisfaction, he said. It was a terrible time, Meg. For him and me. He was that stressed and the angina attacks were getting worse, I was so worried about him . . . Then Robert Cox turned up. It was like an answer to a prayer. He couldn't afford to buy, but he was dead keen to lease the place.'

'It was a way out for us, just when I'd despaired of finding one. Ted agreed to a two-year lease with an option to buy after that. The contract helped with the debt and we took that to arbitration, arranged a schedule of payments. Ellie had to agree, the court saw to that. Of course, it was too late for Ted. He collapsed in the shed the day we learned it was going to be all right. The ambulance came, but even when they were loading him into it I think I knew it was over. He died three days later. A massive coronary that should never have happened.'

'I'm so sorry, Betty.'

She patted my arm. 'Not your doing, pet. But that's really why I'm still here. Not that I wanted to move with Ted gone, but without the sale I couldn't afford the cottage. And even if I could've, I had no heart for living in it alone. When the two years were up, I just renewed the contract with Robert. He knew by then that it'd take more like twenty good years before he could hope to buy the farm. But he's good for the land, a good tenant, and the lease gives me an income. And I've got my friends and my little house, so I'm comfortable enough,' she ended.

I said bitterly, 'To do that to a neighbour! How could she?'

She patted my hand. 'It's why I didn't want to tell you. I haven't spoken to Ellie since I lost him.'

'And yet,' I marvelled, 'you still fed her wretched cat!'

'Ah, you can't blame a dumb animal. Besides he'd have killed more birds if I hadn't.'

'I doubt that he's stopped, even so.'

'Probably,' she agreed. 'I'd have belled him if I could have caught him. Feeding just seemed the next best thing.'

'And I don't imagine he's even grateful,' I said, backing carefully out of my slot.

'Now there's a thought!' She gave a little chuckle. 'A grateful cat. He'd be in a museum.'

I smiled. 'Very likely. Nothing else to do while we're here? Right, next stop home.'

Back at the Reach, Betty busied herself preparing lunch. When Jake answered the summons he was carrying a watermelon, the long green shape filling his arms.

'See what I found behind the tennis court. Ripe, too. Looks like the cockies got the rest of 'em, only this 'un was back under a bush.'

'Very nice,' Betty approved. 'I'll cool it off. We can cut it later.'

'Jake,' I said when we were seated and helping ourselves to the meal of chicken and salad, 'I saw Mr Cabot this morning and he told me that you were going to organise Aunt Iris's funeral when it happens. Will you let me know when? I'd like to come back for it. I didn't know her but she is – was – family.'

'Yeah, I will. Might be a while, but. What did he want, Cabot? Not givin' us our marchin' orders?'

'Of course not. As a matter of fact, he agreed to pay my wages up to the end of the week. He's not obliged to but I'm not arguing. And I'm sure he'd tell you himself if you were being laid off. No, the reason for the visit was to give me a document sent to him by the man who bought that old desk of my grandmother's. Apparently he found it in a hidden drawer. There was a bit of that done in the old days. Cabot thinks it's my business and passed it on. God, I'd quite forgotten it.' I'd been too incensed by Betty's disclosure. I jumped up. 'I suppose I should see what it is.'

I fetched it from the bedroom, slitting the tough legal packaging with the breadknife. Inside was a smaller expensive-looking envelope with my name written on it in the round, flowing script that as schoolgirls we had known as the 'Sacred Heart hand', that being the convent school, one suburb over from mine, that invariably took the inter-school prizes for handwriting contests. The ink was slightly faded but the envelope, save for slightly rubbed corners, was as pristine as the day it had been addressed.

The glue on the flap had dried out and it opened at a touch. Inside was a letter folded within a stiff, official-looking sheet that proved to be a will. Seeing the name of the legatee, I said in surprise, 'But what . . .?' and then, absorbing its contents, was left no less puzzled.

'What is it?' Betty asked.

Ignoring the question, I looked at Jake. 'It's Iris's will! Elvira is the legatee. She's left her a diamond necklace, for heaven's sake! Here it is, look: *To my daughter Elvira Rose Chapman I bequeath the only thing of value I possess. The diamond necklace I received from my parents, presently in the custody of the Commonwealth Bank, 14 Bardle Street, Glenfield.*'

I held it out to him. 'It's one of those self-help wills – buy the document and fill it in yourself. They must still be legal though, even if it's not written in legalese. Look, it's been properly witnessed – by a justice of the peace, no less.'

'Lordy!' Betty exclaimed. 'I'd completely forgotten about the necklaces! They were birthday gifts on the girls' eighteenth. Fleur had one too.' She looked at me. 'Didn't it come to you when your mum died?'

'I didn't know she had it,' I said blankly.

'When's it dated?' Jake asked, ignoring the interruption.

I glanced at the will. 'January 1966.'

'A month after the child was born, then.'

'Yes.' I brushed the observation aside. 'But why address it to me? And why hide it? Only somebody with a knowledge of antiques was ever going to find it.'

'Unless it wasn't meant to be found?' Jake suggested.

'Then why not just burn it?'

'For heaven's sake!' Betty interposed, her voice rising above ours. 'If we're getting into the why of things, why not just read the note that came with it? Maybe it'll tell you.'

'Good idea,' I said and picked up the folded sheet.

Chapter Thirty-one

It wasn't a note but a letter. It began *Dear Margaret*, and a quick glance at the bottom showed the signature, *Fleur Morrisey*. I caught my breath and, catching Betty's eye, blurted, 'It's from my mother.'

'If it's private—' Jake started pushing himself to his feet but I stopped him, the breath coming hard in my throat.

'No, stay . . . It's . . . oh my God! I—'

'What?' Betty demanded. I hardly felt her hand on my arm as she shook it urgently. 'You're as white as a sheet, Meg. What is it?'

Eyes racing down the page, I had reached the end. Ignoring her, I read it again, incredulity growing, then pushed the letter at her with shaking hands. 'Read it. It says I'm not . . . they weren't . . . I will *never* forgive that woman! Why didn't somebody tell me? How can you just *do* that to a person?'

I heard Betty gasp then as she read and moved my gaze to Jake, staring at him so fixedly that he gave me a little embarrassed grin.

'What's up then? Have I grown another head?'

'You're my father,' I said baldly. 'That letter . . . It's a – a confession. She writes that I . . . that you—'

'Now, hang on a minute!' He was startled into roughness. 'That's utter bloody rubbish! Me an' Fleur Chapman? I hardly knew the woman. Why would she claim . . .?'

Betty had finished reading. She looked at me, shaking her head. 'The wickedness of it! Never to tell you. Not Fleur, Jake. *Iris*. Our Meg isn't Meg at all! She's Elvira Rose – Iris's daughter. And yours.'

'What?' The blood drained from his face. He said stupidly, 'How . . .?'

'Ellie arranged it.' Betty gave an unladylike snort. 'Who else? Seems Iris went to her sister and left the baby with her before she came home that last time.' Betty picked up the letter and read the words now engraved upon my brain: '*It was supposed to be just for the day, but that night my father rang. He said Iris had seen him and gone again, hadn't even stopped to visit her mother. She'd been in a wild mood and just taken off. He thought she'd come back when she cooled down. He knew about the baby and asked me to keep you for a bit, but when a week passed without a word from him, or her, I rang him again.*

'That's when he turned up to collect you. He told us Iris was suicidal and that you were at risk, so it was just as well that she'd left you. He said Mum would keep you for a bit. Then we heard that Iris had killed herself, so it was arranged for Stephen and I to raise you as our child. Nobody local knew about your existence, so we just left for Europe for twelve months and came back with you, and nobody was any the wiser. It was to save the family shame, Father said.

Mum agreed. And it couldn't have benefitted you to know the truth. I hope you will agree that Stephen and I have done our best for you.

'I will give this letter and my sister's will to a solicitor to be passed on to you after both our deaths.

'Your aunt, Fleur Morrisey.'

If I had been white faced, Jake looked as if he had been poleaxed. He said hoarsely, 'Christ on a camel!' His eyes devoured me. 'You're not . . . but you've got her eyes. I noticed them at once, that shade of green, like sunlight on grass. She was taller, and her hair was dark, but the eyes are the same.'

Feeling absurdly shy, I said dazedly, 'Grandmother told me that once; said I had my mother's sullen eyes. And naturally I thought she was talking about Fleur.' It seemed strange to speak of the woman I had called Mum by her Christian name. I remembered a remark then. 'And she – Grandmother – put blue in her bridal bouquet, to match her eyes. I should've realised then, but you never look at your parents, do you? Oh my God, it's no wonder she didn't love me. Her entire life turned upside down by a squalling brat, her sister's mistake—'

I saw Jake wince and said, 'I'm sorry. I didn't mean that.' Tears spilled down my cheeks. 'I always felt they didn't want me and I was right. And they took me because Fleur always obeyed her father in everything. Not like her sister.'

'No,' he said heavily, 'not like my girl.' Then, reverting to the letter, he said, 'How did it get in a . . . desk, was it? She wrote she'd give it to the lawyer.'

'They died, remember?' I palmed my face and sniffed. 'Obviously before she could do so. Then I suppose Grandmother found it, clearing up after the funeral. It had my name on it, so she probably guessed the contents – or maybe even read it. I mean, what mother writes to her supposed child when she could talk to her? Only my moth—Fleur never talked to me. So, she'd know it was something unusual. Reason enough to squirrel it away where it wouldn't be found.'

'It'd make more sense to burn it,' Betty observed, 'if she never intended you to know.'

'People put things off,' I said, 'and she could've forgotten at the end. And really, what were the chances of anyone finding it? Those secret compartments were made to be just that.'

'Well, on the bright side,' Betty said, beaming suddenly at Jake, 'you've found your daughter, and you, pet, have your dad. So something good has come out of it all.'

I think we were both embarrassed by her words. I know I was, and I had no idea what I felt at that moment, or even how I should feel. Glad? Welcoming? I could think of nothing to say. Jake was a casual stranger I barely knew. That I had liked him, once his gruff manner had worn off and I'd seen more of him, was beside the point. This man, according to Fleur Morrisey's letter, was my father. That I believed it didn't make him less a stranger.

He must have felt something similar for he rubbed a big hand over his face and mumbled, 'It's a lot to . . . I gotta think on it, girl.' Then he got up and left, lurching from the kitchen like a man intent upon putting distance behind him.

Betty watched him go with a slight frown creasing her brow. 'I thought he'd be pleased. Hasn't he been bound and determined to find you? And he goes off to *think!* What's there to think about? It's the grace of God that letter turned up at all, found by a man honest enough to send it back. Aren't you at least glad about it?'

I said honestly, 'I don't know what I am, Betty. It's not like I'm a little kid and desperate for a father. I learned to do without one, because I never really had one, only an authority figure. So I don't know how I'm supposed to feel. I think'—I searched within myself—'that I'm mostly furious at Grandmother for deceiving me. She had no right to do that! I would've accepted that I was adopted. It would have explained so much, but to lie and deny . . .' A tear splashed my face and I sniffed and dabbed furiously at it. 'She is a hateful, vindictive old woman! If I'd known—'

'There, there, pet.' Betty's arms enfolded me as she pulled me into a tight hug.

I let her hold and rock me, finding the depth of my pain to mourn. 'Don't you see? It was such a *wicked* waste of time! I could've met him years ago. We might've built a relationship together. And Jake – she took everything from him. Because she never intended him to know – or me. She's had plenty of opportunity these last weeks, *and* she knows she's dying. I've a good mind to—'

'No, no, pet. Don't go near her again. And it's not too late, you know. You've missed a few years but you can make that up. And it's not as if Jake's a stranger to you, which, if you hadn't come back and he hadn't been working here, he would have been. Nothing more than a name with a criminal record . . . You mightn't even have wanted to know him, if that had been the case. But it didn't happen that way.'

Pulling back from the embrace, I had to smile, however weakly, at her hopeful optimism. 'And if your aunt had been a man, she'd have been your uncle.' I sighed. 'But it's true enough, I suppose. Why are you always so *reasonable*, Betty?'

'Just let things settle,' she advised. 'It's been an awful shock, for you and for Jake. But he'll be glad when he's had time to think,' she added. 'And meanwhile'—she picked up the will—'you've got yourself a diamond necklace.'

'Oh, I'd forgotten that . . . I wonder if it's still there in the bank? I mean, if Grandmother had opened the letter and seen the will, she might have gone and claimed it. She *was* Iris's next of kin.' It felt too weird to call her 'mother'. I remembered the layette wrapped so carefully and the rattle that, with its silver handle, surely must have been a costly purchase. What had she worked at in order to feed and clothe me? And all that remained of that hope and love now (for surely the layette and rattle spoke of love) were the poor bones from the well, for I had no memory at all of the woman who had given me life.

I wanted Phillip beside me for the comfort his presence would bring, but that wasn't going to happen. I didn't, I thought aggrievedly, even know his whereabouts. But if he were here, what could he do? Then I wondered if Cabot should be informed. Wasn't the law always involved in matters of wills? My mind was a whirl of questions and half-formed emotions: fury and sadness, but mostly outrage. I said helplessly, 'I don't know what to do, Betty.'

'Then sit down, pet, and I'll make us a fresh pot of tea. A cuppa always helps calm a situation down. We'll just take a minute for ourselves. That never hurts.'

*

An hour later, I donned my hat and went looking for Jake. I found him down by the tennis court, sitting on Phillip's seat, head bent as he twiddled a few stems of lavender between his fingers. The scent, dizzying in its strength, wreathed him like smoke. He laid them aside and gave me a perfunctory smile as I sat beside him. Not a real smile, I thought, more a social grimace without meaning beyond an acknowledgement of my presence.

'It was your mother's favourite flower,' he said, smoothing his fingers over the grey leaves.

'I didn't know that.' I felt my anger stir again. 'In fact, I don't know anything about her. That old woman has seen to that. She has stolen so much of my life – and yours. We could have met years ago, got to know each other . . .' I trailed off, fearing to presume. Because, perhaps, faced with the reality of my existence as his daughter, he no longer wanted that. It was one thing to yearn for an unknown child, knowing there was little hope of ever finding her, and quite another to be faced with the finished product, as it were, in the person of someone totally unexpected.

He cleared his throat. 'So, I'm your dad it seems.' He sighed and ran his hands through his hair, not looking at me. 'Hard to believe. How do you feel about it, Meg?'

I said hesitantly, 'I'm still getting my head around it. It seems kind of inevitable when you have all the pieces. And I never felt any closeness, any real connection with my supposed father, Stephen Morrisey. But you . . . you said you wanted to find Elvira. And now by the sheerest chance you have, and we're here together. So, are you . . . Is it how you imagined . . .' I trailed off, then steeled myself to ask, 'Is it what you want?'

He huffed out a breath and, to have something to do with them, I thought, his big hands reached again for the lavender sprigs. 'Christ! Ask me an easy one. I never went into it, not properly, to imagine how it would be if I ever found her – what sorta person she'd have become. It was more like an idea of my own little girl, maybe somebody the spit of her mother . . .' He turned his hands up, the delicate fronds of the lavender lying across one grimed and calloused palm, and shook his head, as if at his own blindness. 'See, I never really thought – just bulled ahead with the idea of lookin'. You're all that's left of Iris. Of course I want . . . But it ain't that easy, is it? You're a woman grown, with your own life – you don't need me.'

'Maybe not in the sense of providing a home for me, but you're still my father, Jake. If I have children one day, they'll be your descendants. They'll share your blood.'

He laughed harshly. 'Yeah, that of a cripple with a police record.' He shook his head as if bemused. 'I musta been crazy. I was thinkin' you'd be a slip of a girl in need of protection an' care. Only the truth turns out to be somethin' different. What do you want with someone like me, without even a trade to his name? A man with nothin'. My tools and the old ute are all I own.'

I felt the inevitability of defeat and cried passionately, 'I don't care about that! I just want – I mean, I hoped – you would be my friend. Of course we can't just fall into each other's arms. You're a stranger to me and I to you. But our blood and genes link us, and you loved my mother . . . Only she's gone, everything's gone. Can't you see, without you I have nothing left to tell me who I am? I'm just what I always was – so unimportant that nobody could ever love me.'

Stung, he said, 'I'da loved you if I'd known! Jesus, I could murder that bitch of a woman! The damage she's done, and all for spite, for what's it gained her? But you are loved, Meg. Any fool can see that bloke of yours is crazy about you. And Iris musta – she was the most lovin' person you can imagine. She'd've treasured every hair on your head.'

'Then tell me about her,' I begged. 'Nobody else can. Betty says she was a rebel, and brave – that she wanted freedom from her father's rule.'

'Aye, she did that.' He grimaced. 'That old bastard! He wouldn't see the world had changed since the war. He was all about control. Those girls of his couldn't step outside the gate without him needing the whole story of where they was goin' and why, an' who they were meetin'. Iris wouldn't stand for that . . .'

Eyes on the ground as if the past were written there, he talked on, fumbling for words, painting a picture of the bright, rebellious girl with the shining green eyes whom he had loved. Her passions had been near the surface, I learned, unlike my own repressed nature. She had laughed easily and shed tears of fury over her parents' reaction to Jake; she had played pranks on him and loved surprises, and had once, on a dare, skinny-dipped with a friend in the river. Unknown to her he had glimpsed her coming out – something he didn't tell her until the night of her sister's wedding. She had been his sun and his moon, and his reason for living, he said, waxing suddenly poetic. They had walked together with their little fingers linked and that touch had meant more to him than a date with Rita Hayworth . . .

'Who?'

'Film star. Back in the fifties. You're too young.' He trailed off, then raised a hand suddenly and touched my ear. 'She had the same little points on hers, you know. Now I really look at you there's quite a bit of your mother in your face – well, it's more your expressions. Just every now and then, like. And the way you put your hands on your hips when you're tellin' your bloke . . . Iris did that with me.'

'Really?' I felt my eyes film over and sniffed. 'I'm glad. Thank you for telling me about her, Jake. And we can be friends, get to know each other properly? I really want that. When I leave next week, you won't just go on your way and forget me?'

He shook his head, eyes fixed on mine. 'No, I won't. I dunno what I expected when I learned she'd had a child, but I'm thinking she'd be pleased to know the way you've turned out. And proud of you, too. I'm not much of a one for speechifyin' but I reckon I'm proud too, to call you daughter.' He put his hand on mine.

I turned my palm under his to clasp its hardness and leaned momentarily against his shoulder. 'Thank you, Jake. I'm so glad we've found each other.'

'What d'you reckon your Phillip'll think about it?'

'He'll be happy,' I said simply. 'He likes you. I just wish he'd ring so I could tell him the news.'

Chapter Thirty-two

Later that evening, when both Betty and Jake had gone, Phillip did ring. The bushfire, which I hadn't paid any further attention to that day, was about done, he said, and he was getting a lift back to Glenfield that night. He'd find a hotel room, and did I think I could pick him up in the morning? Phillip had managed a few decent pics and he'd sent the film with Joe, who was heading back to the city. Ordinarily, I knew, he'd process it himself for publication, but not with one arm. I heard him yawn; he sounded weary but happy, finishing off his burst of information with a question. 'So how's it going with you, Elf? What's happening there?'

'Quite a lot, actually. Turns out that I'm Elvira.'

'What?' The question came in the middle of another yawn suddenly bitten off. 'What did you say, Meg?'

'I'm her,' I said baldly. 'Iris's lost daughter, Elvira Rose Chapman. There's nothing about me – the old me – that's real, Phillip. Not my surname, my birthday – nothing.' And then I was weeping, trying to strangle the tears, then giving up so that I was just bawling into the phone, while poor Phillip tried remotely to stem the flow and comfort me.

When I finally stopped, he said anxiously, 'Elf? Look, I know you're upset, but it's a good thing, isn't it? I mean, you weren't so fond of your mother – who you thought your mother was, I mean – and you like Jake, don't you? I do. He's a great bloke and a decent man. And it does explain why your parents seemed not to want you—'

'I know.' I sniffed, smearing my wrist across my top lip. 'I've already thought of that. And, yes, I do like Jake, and I think – I think we can be friends, and maybe even grow closer than that. We had a talk today, a good talk. He was as shocked as I was at first, but he says'—I smiled a little at the memory and sniffed again, wishing I had a tissue—'that he can see a bit of my mother in me.'

'Well, that's great,' Phillip said cautiously, 'isn't it? So, what's really the matter, Elf?'

'Everything,' I said tragically. 'All the wicked, wicked lies. All the years that have been wasted. Sixteen years, Phillip! That's how long she's had that letter and my mother's will. From the time of the plane crash. And I would never have known if Thomas hadn't bought the escritoire. She hid it there so I'd never learn the truth. My mother's will was with it and suppressing that, I'm pretty sure, is a criminal offence. And,' I added for good measure on a hiccup of self-pity, 'I don't want to be called Elvira. It's an awful name.'

He said mildly, 'I'm not that fond of Phillip either, but has Jake or anybody else asked you to change from Meg?'

'Of course not.' I was suddenly cross. 'I wouldn't anyway. And what's wrong with Phillip? I like it.'

'Really? I think it's a poncy sort of a name. I blame my mother. She was a deadset monarchist. That's why she's going to love you, Elf. Margaret, see? After the Queen's sister. We're going to visit her next month.'

'We are?' I was bewildered. 'To Tassie? Why? You've never mentioned it before.'

'Maybe the time's right,' he said. 'Are you okay if I ring off now? My lift's waiting. Tomorrow morning I'll wait for you at that cafe by the bus stop, okay? Love you, my little Elf. Bye.'

'Be careful. Bye.' Whether intentionally or not, his announcement had diverted my thoughts. There was a *meow* behind me as I hung up and I turned to find Claude regarding me with a fixed glare. I glared right back at him. 'Oh, you're here, are you? I suppose you want feeding? Your master will be back tomorrow. Make the most of it, buster, because we'll be gone come the weekend.' Why the sudden decision to visit Tasmania? Where had that come from, I wondered. I had never met Phillip's parents, or his sister Anne, who was five years older and married to an IT man in the UK. Phillip's father, retired now, had been some sort of a professor at the University of Tasmania and once Phillip and his sister were through high school, his mother had filled an administrative post at the hospital. Phillip saw little of his family, due more, I thought, to his job than any disinclination to do so. And he seemed, with typical male carelessness, to ring his parents only at Christmas and, if I remembered for him, on their birthdays.

I slept eventually in the empty house and dreamed that I was a child again, cocooned within the branches of the old gum, with my handful of treasures from the hidey-hole there in my lap. Foremost among these was the silver-handled rattle and a sprig of lavender, which I pinned into my hair. High among the clouds the bright streak of Stephen Morrisey's Piper Cherokee flew and then crumpled to the ground, but I held my rattle and didn't care. Then the fire roared up out of nowhere and, somehow, I was standing to one side watching my tree burn. The thin branches writhed as they vanished, and I cried for its agony as the heavier ones groaned and fell, scattering crimson coals amid the strips of fallen bark. My rattle was gone and the lavender had crisped up in the heat and lost its scent.

Then, in the way of dreams, the landscape changed and I was indoors in the Reach, lying wakeful in my room as I had often done, listening to the noises in the chimney. Only this time they were human sounds: a man's hectoring tones, the clack of my grandmother's heels, the gush of water and the click of scissors as she snipped stems and filled a vase. There were flowers in mounds and piles in every room, their mingled scents – of rosemary, lavender, rose and honeysuckle – overpowering, but all failing to mask the odour of death beneath. My mother's bones rose from the well, eyeless sockets staring, skeletal hands groping for me while the bony jaw moved to whisper, 'Elvira.' I bolted awake with a cry of terror, heart in overdrive, while Claude, who must have sneaked in to curl up on the foot of the bed, fled with a hiss of displeasure.

Phillip, unshaven and wearing the same jeans he'd left in, was waiting for me in the cafe, camera on the table beside his emptied plate and the legs of the tripod sticking out of the top of his bag.

'Elf.' He rose to peck my cheek, blue eyes scrutinising my face. 'How are you, love? Do you want a cuppa?'

'No, thanks. I'm okay. Where did you stay last night?'

'Motel down the road a bit. Dirt cheap. On the corner opposite a video shop? The Dog something – they don't do breakfast – why it's cheap, of course.'

I nodded. 'That would be the Dog Rose. Is the bushfire really out?'

'Yep,' he said, standing up and slinging the camera around his neck. 'They stopped it at Roseglen, some little farmstead east of Hepton. Poor bugger lost his nut trees and cooked his crop – cabbages, I think – but the fireys saved his house.' He cocked his head. 'There's a helluva lot of rose names round this burg.'

'That's because Herman Rose was Glenfield's founder. What's all this about going to Tassie?'

'Ah.' He held the door for me. 'My little surprise. I rang Kev,' he added, speaking of his boss. 'Told him I'd be fit for work in a couple more weeks, so seeing that you're now free with the place being sold, I thought we'd take a bit of a holiday. You'll love Tassie, Elf. Apart from anything else'—he squinted as the sun hit us, carrying a bite even at this hour—'it'll be a damn sight cooler.'

'That wouldn't be hard,' I said. 'And thank you! It sounds wonderful. I've always wanted to go.'

'And now you shall. So, what about this will you mentioned? Is it legal?'

'I imagine so. It's on the proper form, signed and witnessed. I'm taking it to Cabot's office before we head back. It'll have to go to probate so he can handle it.'

He slung his bag in the vehicle and raised his brows doubtfully. '*Had* she anything to leave you?'

'A diamond necklace, apparently. That's if it's still there. It's supposed to be in the bank's keeping.' I shrugged. 'That's if Grandmother didn't reclaim it. Anyway, Cabot can sort it out.'

'Hmm.' Phillip rasped a hand over the stubble on his jaw. 'It's a nice morning – what say we walk around there? It's not quite nine yet, so we'll be too early if we drive.'

'Why not?' I relocked the car and turned as he slipped his hand into mine. 'It's been a weird few weeks, hasn't it? I still feel sort of dislocated from myself. Maybe Tassie is a really good idea.'

Phillip had been right about walking. The door to Cabot and Hawley was open when we arrived, but only just, for Mr Cabot was in the act of stowing a plastic box in the small refrigerator behind the receptionist's desk. His lunch, presumably. He seemed the sort who would bring his own.

'Ah, Ms Morrisey and, erm, Phillip,' he greeted us. 'I was about to ring you, just as soon as I got settled. Come through, please. No calls,' he said to the receptionist, who had plainly also just arrived as she was putting her handbag away in a drawer. He ushered us into his office, indicated the leather-covered chairs and took his place behind the desk.

'Why?' I asked baldly. 'Has something happened? Good morning, by the way.'

'Yes, good morning to you both. I'm afraid I don't have your surname,' he added, turning to Phillip.

'Doesn't matter,' Phillip said. 'What's happened?'

'It's Mrs Chapman. The hospital rang me at home, said there was no reply from Hunters Reach – perfectly obvious why, as you're in town. I'm afraid she passed away early this morning. Not unexpected, of course, with her heart, but still . . . a shock I'm sure. You have my sincere condolences.'

'Yes, thank you,' I said. 'Well.' I couldn't seem to think. 'It doesn't make any difference.' I meant to my purpose, realising only belatedly that it sounded terribly offhand. Still, I was past worrying about others' perceptions when it came to my grandmother. 'But what I came about, Mr Cabot, is this.' I fished the envelope out of my bag and passed it to him. 'The letter from the little writing desk? I thought the best thing would be to let you handle it. I mean we're leaving Saturday and . . .'

'Ah.' He glanced at the inscription on the envelope. 'I did wonder about that. So, er . . . what—?'

'Read it,' I said and watched him do so, his eyes flicking quickly over the letter and then perusing the second, stiffer page.

'Well.' He set the papers down and rubbed at his nose, pushing his spectacles awry. 'That's quite a facer, if you don't mind me saying so, Ms Morrisey – er, Chapman, as apparently you are. You do recognise the writer's hand? I mean, there's no mistake about the provenance of this?' He flicked a nail against the yellowed sheet.

'No, that's my moth— my aunt's, I suppose I should say, writing. Not,' I added firmly, 'that I have any intention of changing my first name. I don't have to, do I?'

'No, you may call yourself what you wish.' A brief smile. 'Marilyn Monroe did, after all.'

'And the will – is that legal? Can you ascertain if the bequest is still in the bank?'

'Of course.' He bent a rather stern look my way. 'You have reason to doubt it?'

'If Grandmother opened the letter, she could have claimed it,' I pointed out. 'If the bank staff were unaware of the will, wouldn't they have handed it over without question? When the news of my mother's death got around, I mean.'

'I'll look into it,' he said briefly. 'Have you a description of the item?'

I shook my head. 'I didn't even know it existed. Perhaps Betty Roberts could give you one? She knew the Chapmans – she worked for Grandmother off and on for years. She said the necklaces – my aunt got one too, though I've no idea what happened to it – were gifts for their eighteenth birthday from their parents.' I stood up. 'Thank you for all your help, Mr Cabot. I expect I won't see you again, but you can always contact me here.' I passed him the prepared slip of paper on which I'd written down the Hahndorf street address, and offered my hand.

'I take it that you'll see to the old lady's funeral?' It was the first time that Phillip had spoken.

Cabot nodded. 'Quite. Ms Morr— Chapman is aware of her grandmother's decision on that. There will be no need for you or anyone to attend. In fact, it was her stipulation that you didn't.' He walked us to the main door and said, 'Well, goodbye then. It has been a pleasure being of service. And again, my condolences.'

'Thank you.' The heavy door sighed shut on the coolness within as we stepped into the brilliant light of the street.

Chapter Thirty-three

Driving home, I wondered that the world was so little changed. The same black skeletons and scorched-looking land, with which I was now familiar, hit the eye but beyond that the sleepy rural picture was unaltered. As it had been, I assumed, when my mother was killed and my father carried off to prison. Grandmother was dead and in four days – no, three, because it was Wednesday today – Hunters Reach would become nothing but a memory to forget.

'You're very quiet, Elf,' Phillip said out of the silence.

'Just thinking, that's all.'

'You're not upset about her dying?'

I slanted him a look. 'Hardly. Though, I suppose,' I said slowly, 'it's sad she could matter so little, but it's how she wanted it. It's been a strange time, hasn't it? Your accident, Brad's death, learning the truth about my parents. The fire . . . everything. We've had enough drama for the whole year.'

'Oh, not quite.' His blue eyes held a glint. 'Friday we celebrate, remember?' At my blank look, he exclaimed, 'Your birthday, Elf!'

'I'd forgotten. And, of course, it's not actually my birthday. Elvira was a Christmas baby. She was born on the twenty-second of December. Which means I'm nearly two months older than I thought I was.'

'Well, you shan't miss out,' he said determinedly. 'Change it next December if you want to, but get out your party frock for Friday night and we'll paint the town.'

'Um, Betty too, and Jake if he'll come?'

'Nope. What about we have them over for dinner Thursday? Because Friday, my love, is just for us.'

We were back at the Reach in time for smoko. Both Betty and Jake received the news of Grandmother's death with indifference.

Jake said, 'Ah, well, the devil'll have his work cut out now.'

Betty merely looked thoughtful. 'I wonder how her will reads? There's a lot of property in town still in the Chapman name. It must be worth a couple of million at least. Then there's the sale of this place.'

'Fortunately that's Cabot's headache,' I said. 'For all I care, Claude could be the beneficiary. Which reminds me – nobody's said what's to be done with him.'

'If it's in her will, it's also Cabot's problem.' Phillip grinned suddenly. 'Unless you fancy housing him, Elf?'

'He stays at the Reach,' I said firmly. 'He was actually being nice to Linda when she was here. Maybe the damned animal is psychic and knows she's his next meal ticket? Anyway'—I dismissed the monster's fate with a flick of my hand—'not our problem. Listen, tomorrow night we want you both to come to dinner. Please?' I looked at Jake. 'We have to celebrate finding each other, and it's a thank you to Betty too, for all the help she's given. Do say you'll come.'

'Course I will,' Jake said gruffly. 'What time?'

'Oh, sevenish, or earlier if you like. I mean you needn't leave at all – you could just stay on until dinner's ready.'

'Nah,' he decided. 'I'll go home, clean up. Pick you up on my way back?' he asked Betty. 'No call for you to be bikin' it in the dark.'

'Thank you, Jake. That would be great.' To me, she said, 'I could give you a hand, or bring something?'

'No,' I said firmly. 'All you'll be bringing is yourself. You're to have the night off, both of you. Enjoy yourselves.'

'Then I will, pet,' she said. 'It'll be a treat.'

The following day broke clear and blue, the sky without a trace of smoke though faint whiffs of the burn gusted occasionally on the breeze. The garden seemed to have put on a spurt from the flooding it had received from the roof sprinkler; everything sparkled in the morning light with new shoots thrusting out on the pruned areas and the flowers showing vividly against the damp soil. I was picking flowers when Jake's old ute rattled to a rest out front and I met him on my way inside.

'Morning, Jake. The garden is a credit to you. It looks beautiful this morning. Whatever is in that huge planter is coming up. I thought it must be dead, buried as it was under the bougainvillea but there's green spikes coming through.'

'Yeah?' He had a ladder balanced on his shoulder and let the end rest on the ground when he stopped. 'Bulbs, maybe?

Or could be seeds blown in. It got a regular soaking during the fire. That'll do it ev'ry time.'

'You think? How do you know so much about gardens? Did you ever have one?'

He grinned, showing a chipped front tooth. 'Nah – know a bit of ev'rything, me. Jack of all trades.'

'What about your real trade?' I asked curiously. 'Why don't you make furniture and fix things?'

'I do that too, if it comes along. Plenty of tradies about, but, and I ain't got the dough to set up my own workshop. I get by, Meg. Don't worry 'bout me.'

I pointed at the ladder. 'What's that for? I thought all the pruning was done.'

'Ah.' He rebalanced it and jerked his chin towards the back. 'It is. Thought I'd see about stabilisin' that wonky post in the pergola. The weight of that vine on it'll be fetching it down one day. 'Bout the last job left, so I'd better get on with it.'

'Okay.' I took my bouquet into the kitchen, reflecting that it was typical of Jake to need to have all he turned his hand to perfect. Perhaps because he'd had so little control over the life fate had dealt him? I would miss him. I had grown accustomed to his big-shouldered presence, his thoughtful utterances and practical values – everything a little girl could wish for in a father. I thought of Stephen Morrisey's aloofness and impatience, and my heart grieved for all that I could have had if not for my grandmother's spiteful intransigence.

Betty arrived in time to prepare lunch. When the washing up was done, she untied her pinny and folded it over her arm.

'I shall miss coming over every day,' she said. 'I've enjoyed these last weeks, having you back. You'll be off Saturday, pet?'

'Yes, the moving van will be here early – that's the plan anyway – and the Telfords right behind it. We'll wait for their arrival. I have to tell them about Claude, after all – so it won't be early when we go. You should pop over too – we could make them a cuppa perhaps? You'll be neighbours, and maybe they'd be glad to find a friendly face to welcome them to the district.'

She nodded thoughtfully. 'I could do that. Bring a cake perhaps – a sort of house-warming gift. Lord knows,' she added with a laugh, eyeing the large mixing bowl filled with blossoms, 'they won't need flowers.'

'Good idea. You're off now? Okay, see you tonight.'

Thursday evening went off well. Jake, freshly shaved and spruced up in town clothes, brought a bottle of wine. 'Least I could do,' he said with a wink. 'Don't recall that dinner was in the contract too.'

'Thank you, that's lovely.' A little unsure, I gave him a quick hug, then turned to Betty, smart in a sleeveless dress of deep blue with a ring of white embroidered daisies about the neckline. 'You look very nice tonight. That colour really suits you.'

She flushed a little with pleasure at the compliment; her hair, I saw, had been freshly washed and set. 'You like it? It was Ted's favourite. I doubt it's had an outing since he died.'

'Then I'm honoured you wore it. Phillip'—I signalled him with my eyes—'will get you a drink. Shame we haven't any place to sit, or anything else to sit on, come to that, other than what's here.'

'Nothin' wrong with a kitchen,' Jake said, 'not smellin' as good as this one does.'

I was quietly pleased with the meal; cooking was one of my pleasures and, after the plates had been stacked, we sat over our coffee while the moon rose above the garden and Claude came slinking indoors to sit at Phillip's feet.

'I wonder how he'll like the new people,' Phillip said, leaning over to rub the animal's head. He'd been speaking of his African trip and the creatures he'd photographed. Betty had told stories of her early days as a new wife on the farm and Jake, in a rare burst of loquacity, had recalled incidents from his time as a firefighter. They had all lived such interesting lives, whereas I felt I had little to contribute beyond a pressing invitation to my father.

'When you finish here, Jake, I want your promise that you will come and see us,' I said.

'Only not for the next week or two,' Phillip put in, 'because we'll be taking off for Tassie on Tuesday.'

'We will?' I stared at him. 'When did you arrange this?'

'I booked our seats this morning. Birthday surprise, remember?'

'Oh. Do your parents know we're coming?' I had never met them and wondered nervously what they'd think about our domestic arrangement. But surely most people weren't so hung up on marriage as my grandmother had been?

He read me instantly and leaned to touch my hand. 'I'll give 'em a ring tomorrow, Elf. It'll be fine. When we get back I'll be starting work again fairly soon, but you'll be welcome any time at ours, Jake, so don't be a stranger.'

'Nor you, Betty,' I added warmly.

'We'll keep in touch,' she promised, 'but for now you should let me help with the dishes before we go home. The night's getting on, pet.'

'Definitely not,' I said, rising to hug her. I kissed her plump cheek. 'You go. We'll see to the clearing up. Please come over Saturday, though, to say goodbye. You too, Jake.'

'Right.' He stood too. 'I'll have to pick up me tools, anyroad. Thanks for the meal, Meg. You're a great cook. I'll run Betty back and be off. See you both in the mornin'.'

When they had gone, I plugged the sink and turned on the hot water. 'So, this Tassie trip – why specifically now? I know I'll love it, but what's going on, Phillip?'

He put the condiments back on their shelf and lifted a brow. 'Why should anything be? We'll both be free – I can't work yet and you'll be jobless – so there's no better time for a break. A bit of a treat for us, Elf. It's been a helluva year till now.'

It made sense, and I stretched up to kiss his chin. 'And this is my big birthday surprise? Well, thank you, love. We won't actually be staying with your parents, will we?'

'A bit of the time, but relax – they'll love you. I thought we'd get a car, tour the island, make their place the jumping-off point. Must be five years since I was home.' He picked up the tea towel in his left hand, then put it back with a sigh. 'Damn, I can't.'

'No, leave it for me. You take the scraps out and feed the cat. I'll see to this.'

'Okay.' He picked up the bin and dropped a kiss on my neck as he passed. 'Then come to bed, sweet. It's late.'

The following day I took rueful stock of my wardrobe, wondering what I could possibly wear for a celebratory dinner. I had nothing suitable. However, I reminded myself, there were shops in Glenfield, and I had the car. I changed out of my house shoes, ran a brush through my hair and went to find Phillip, who was giving Jake the use of his one arm at the pergola.

'I'm off to town. Won't be long. Can you get your own smoko? There're biscuits in the tin by the tea caddy.'

'Yep.' Phillip spared a quick glance for me from the tape he was reading and called, 'I make that two point five. Neat. Take care on the road, Elf,' he added as the tape spooled back into its housing.

'Don't I always? Back by lunchtime then.'

There were two dress shops in town. I looked through Gina's, finding nothing I liked, then moved on to Summer Styles, new to me, a place with a mirrored back wall and a curved counter. I wondered if they changed the name with the season. There were racks of clothing ranging from casual to extremely formal, and among them I found a little sleeveless dress in a soft, spring-green crepe with lemon-coloured scallops at both hem and neckline, the latter showing off the straight bar of my collarbones.

'Perfect,' the salesgirl declared. 'You just need a nice glittery chain and some make-up.'

I paid, wincing a little at the price, refused her efforts to sell me a blingy necklace and drove back to the Reach, well satisfied with my sortie.

The expense was justified that evening when Phillip, emerging damp haired from the bathroom to ask for help with his tie, whistled appreciatively. 'New dress? You look amazing, Elf. Come here, I could eat you up where you stand.'

I backed off, laughing. 'No way, buster. You'll muss my hair.'

'Later then.' He took a box from his pocket and handed it to me. 'Happy birthday, love.'

It was my mother's bracelet, whole again, gleaming softly against the white satin background. I turned the tiny nameplate and saw that the name Iris had been replaced with Meg. The tiny padlock was back on the catch so the police must have returned it.

'It's beautiful, Phillip. You spoil me. This and a holiday too – thank you.'

'And if you're counting, don't forget tonight's dinner. You're an expensive wench, but worth every cent.'

I clasped the bracelet about my wrist and brushed a kiss onto his jaw. 'Glad to hear it, Money-bags. Now, stand still while I fix that tie.'

Phillip had booked a table at Bon Vivant, a fancy-looking restaurant in the main street that I vaguely remembered as being the poshest in town. It had a cluster of comfortable armchairs to one side of the dining area, where shaded wall sconces shed a soft light over napery starched to within an inch of its life. Our table had a crimson bud rose in a slender vase next to the ribboned menu and, glancing around, I saw that every table held a different flower.

'Very smart. I sort of remember it, but of course I never ate here.'

'I didn't think so.' Forestalling the waiter who had led us to the table, Phillip pulled out my chair. 'I asked at the post office: "What's the fanciest joint to eat at in town?" They said this place wouldn't disappoint, that it had "held that distinction for twenty years". I came in to book and met the owner. A grand old boy, must be ninety if he's a day, but on the ball. I told him it was a celebration and he promised it would be special.'

'My goodness,' I said mildly. 'You do go to lengths to please, Mr Finchman.'

'I try,' he agreed modestly, plucking a tiny envelope from his breast pocket. 'I forgot to give you your card. I left it in the glovebox. So here it is. And what's the book doing there? Are you going to keep it?'

'What book? Oh.' I remembered the handmade gift from Ellie Chapman's former sweetheart. 'I took it in to the hospital but she made me so mad I still had it in my hand when I left. Well, maybe I will. Such painstaking work shouldn't just be discarded. I love the card! Thank you.'

It was a typical Phillip gift. The stiff paper showed a tiny winged elf balancing in the heart of a flower, her cupped hands holding a glowing jewel in the shape of a heart. Inside he had written: *My heart beats only for you. Happy birthday. All my love, Phillip*. I sniffed and blinked back the tears that would ruin my make-up. 'It's beautiful.'

The meal was excellent, served deftly and with precision, the maître d' stopping by once to ask in hushed tones if everything was satisfactory. There was a small dais to one side of the discreet bar set back in the rear of the room where a woman harpist was playing dinner music, the notes tumbling gently through and over the subdued conversation from the half-dozen tables.

I watched her hands flow over the strings and sighed, my mouth full of the last spoonful of a chocolate concoction that had come dressed with strawberries. 'It must be wonderful to be so skilled.'

'Everyone is, in their own way.' Phillip, who had finished his dessert, took my hand in his, smoothing a finger over the gold of my bracelet. 'You too, Elf. You're uniquely skilled at bringing me joy, on every day, in every way.' He raised my hand to his lips and kissed it. 'Which is why,' he continued, his eyes on mine, 'I want to make you my wife. Will you marry me?'

The question, totally unexpected, caught me by surprise. He released my hand to reach beneath the table and produce a ring box, which he opened, repeating gently, 'Will you marry me, my love?'

I looked at his dear, clever face with its blue eyes and the bleached hair tied neatly back, and wanted to cry from happiness. 'Oh, Phillip! Of course I will!' I straightened my hand for him and, awkwardly, because he was using his left, he pushed the ring onto my finger. 'Oh, it's beautiful!'

'A ruby for love.' He leaned in and we kissed across the table. I tasted chocolate and strawberries and was vaguely aware that the three waiters and the barmen were clapping. The harpist had broken off her melody to begin 'Love Is in the Air' and some uninhibited soul at a nearby table let out a piercing whistle.

Phillip was smiling broadly. 'Witnesses,' he murmured. 'You can't back out now, my little Elf.'

'As if I'd want to.' I held my hand out, admiring the stone, then looked dazedly about. 'You planned all this,' I said, eyeing the grinning waiter who appeared to remove the dessert bowls. I smiled at the harpist. 'The rose too?'

'Ah, that'll be Pearson's doing. The old boy I was telling you about. Here he comes now. He said he'd drop by to congratulate us once the deed was done. You'll like him, love. He might be older than God, but he certainly knows how to do things with style.'

Chapter Thirty-four

The owner of Bon Vivant was everything that Phillip had said. A tall, extremely thin old man with snow-white hair, he had a friendly wrinkled face and beamed at us from clouded blue eyes.

'May I be the first to congratulate you, young man, on your good taste and charming choice of life companion? I hope you enjoyed your meal?'

Phillip rose to shake hands. 'Thank you, and we certainly did. It was fantastic. Mr Pearson, this is Margaret Chapman, my fiancée. Meg, meet the man who designed our evening.'

'How do you do?' I held out my hand. 'You have a beautiful establishment, Mr Pearson – and a wonderful chef. That was a delicious dinner.'

'I'm glad you approve.' He held on to my fingers. 'May I see your ring? And wish you both all happiness for the years ahead?'

'Thank you.' I displayed the ruby. 'Please, won't you sit down for a moment? Phillip will get you a seat.' But there was no need, for a waiter was approaching with a tray holding three champagne glasses. He placed them on the table and whisked an empty chair into position between us.

The old man sat without fuss as the waiter vanished again, then shakily distributed the glasses. 'To health and happiness,' he said, raising his own, and we drank, having echoed the toast. Turning to me, he observed, 'So, you're a Chapman? Phillip didn't say – from these parts?'

'Yes. Well, I'm visiting at the moment, but my family lived here. Perhaps you've heard of Hunters Reach? It's a farmhouse out of town – it's actually just been sold, but my grandmother owned it.'

He put down his glass. 'Then you're Ellie's granddaughter?'

I nodded. 'You knew her, then?'

The clouded eyes moved off my face and he sighed. 'Long ago, when we were both young.' A wry smile lit his features. 'And that was a very long time ago, my dear. Sometimes I forget how long, but I loved her. And, in her fashion, she loved me, or so I believed. But in the end she chose Daniel Chapman instead.'

I said gently, 'I'm sorry. We weren't close, my grandmother and I. She . . . she was a difficult woman. If it's any consolation, she wasn't happy with my grandfather. In fact, she seemed to have loathed him.' A sudden thought struck me. 'You do know that she died?'

I could see that the news was a shock to him. 'No,' he said. He pressed his hand to his chest as if he had received a blow.

'I'm sorry,' I said gently. 'I shouldn't have just blurted it out. She was quite frail, you know. It was her heart.'

'Recently?' he asked. 'But how stupid of me! Of course, you're here for the funeral. My condolences, then.'

'No.' I shook my head. 'It happened on Wednesday. We – Phillip and I – have been overseeing the clearing and the sale of the farmhouse. As for the funeral, Grandmother left instructions that no one was to attend. The Reach is sold now, the new owners will be moving in tomorrow and that's when we leave, so, you see, this is our last night here.'

He abandoned his champagne, pushing the glass aside with long fingers. His hands were veined and spotted and the top of one digit, I saw, was missing. 'I see. Look, could I ask you to have a cup of coffee with me? I'd like to spend a few moments with someone who knew Ellie. It's many years since we spoke.'

About to say that I probably knew her less well than he did, I bit my tongue. When he rose, pressing down hard on the table to do so, I saw how much the news of her death had affected him. I said, 'Of course. Phillip?'

'We're not in a rush,' he agreed, finishing his glass.

The old man paused at that as if suddenly remembering. 'But – how thoughtless! I'm interrupting your evening. You should—'

'No, really, it's fine. In fact, if you won't find it too painful, I'd like you to tell me how you met my grandmother and what she was like back then, because, you know, she turned into a very'—I hesitated, choosing my words—'bitter'—it seemed better than vindictive or malicious—'woman.'

The old man led us to the furthest nest of armchairs and a glance at the closest waiter seemed to convey his wishes. The coffee came in a silver pot with a sugar bowl and creamer, and I busied myself pouring for us.

'So,' Phillip said, stirring his coffee. 'Where did you meet Ellie, Mr Pearson? Were you both locals?'

'No need for formality, young man – it's Michael. And to answer your question, no. I left the city and came here to better myself.' His smile was wry. 'Of course, it wasn't as easy as I'd imagined – the young have such hopes and so very little experience. A room at the bakehouse and a job stoking fires, sweeping, and delivering bread around town – that was my start in life. Ellie's people had come from somewhere else too, I forget now – interstate, I think. Her mother was an invalid; she had tuberculosis, though they didn't call it that. Her father had a barbershop – one of those run-down little places on the edge of seedy. She worked there for the pittance her dad could pay her. They hadn't a bob to spare between 'em. Neither had most people in those days, me included. The Great Depression was just starting, so things were tough.'

'How did you meet?' I asked.

A smile pulled at his lips. 'The first time? I knocked her down. Came racing around a corner with the basket of bread deliveries leading, and knocked her clean off her feet.'

Phillip chuckled. 'That'll do it every time.'

I shot him a reproving look. 'What happened?'

'Well, she was furious, mainly because of the mud on her dress. But I kept running into her – not literally,' he added. 'Even so, it was a month before she'd speak to me.'

The smile played over his face again as he stared into the past, temporarily forgetful of our presence. 'I was absolutely smitten. She was the prettiest thing I'd ever seen and I fell for her from the first moment. I was ecstatic when she let me walk her home. She always left the shop half an hour before closing, you see, to tend to her mother. It was about the only time we could spend together except for the odd Sunday afternoon. Bakeries bake every day, and I hadn't the cash to be taking her out.'

'What was she like back then?' I asked curiously.

'Oh, beautiful, as I said. She was fair like you, my dear, but her hair was longer and she wore it in a mass of curls. She was taller than you, and very slender, with a skin like the bloom on a peach. Witty, determined and'—he sighed—'she had a will like steel. But she could be funny and loving, though she was very impatient of my dreams. Her father was a dreamer, she said, and look where it had got him. Ellie hated poverty and she blamed her father for the way they lived. We'd walk past the windows of the big emporiums in town and she'd point out to me the clothes she meant to have, one day – dresses it would take a month's salary to buy, fancy hats . . . Women wore hats in those days, you see, and beautiful gloves. "I mean never to be poor again," she told me.'

He sighed again. 'I should have seen it then, but my head was full of plans for the future. And, in the long run, she wasn't prepared to wait. We did become engaged. I'd moved up a pace in the world by then, had even gone from my single room to a little cottage. That's when she agreed to marry me; she'd turned twenty-five and that was old for a girl seeking a home of her own. I suppose she saw me as her best prospect. She was very practical, Ellie. I didn't want to disappoint her expectations, so I told her it could take years to achieve what she wanted, but we were young. It was the one thing we had plenty of, time.'

'And you made her a book of flowers,' I interjected, certain now in my mind as to his authorship of the volume. 'Phillip, it won't take a minute. Could you . . .?'

'Of course.' He got up and left.

Our host looked puzzled. 'How did you know?'

'Because I found it, *The Language of Flowers*. Grandmother kept it. She had a wonderful, extravagant garden you know. And I'm sure that every flower listed in that book grew in it. It must have taken you weeks to compile it.'

'Months.' His smile was fond. 'Heavens, that takes me back. I knew nothing of gardens; where I grew up the backyard was bricked over, but I could draw a little and I knew she loved flowers.' He laughed gently. 'Every old woman in the area contributed their bit to that work. Back then it was the sort of thing they knew as girls, because courting men would send messages in the flowers they gave.'

I remembered the rose on our table. 'Like a red rose for love?'

He nodded. 'Or if it had been a red bud rose, the subtext would be "pure and lovely". It was quite a comprehensive code. You could offer friendship, loyalty, accuse a girl of fickleness – I expect many a shy man found it quite helpful.'

Phillip returned then and handed me the little book, which I passed on to Michael.

'Dear me, after all this time.' He turned it in his hands, opened it, leafing slowly through the discoloured pages. 'So she kept it.' He shook his head and laid it aside. 'Thank you for showing me, my dear.'

'Keep it. It's yours, after all. But go on. So, she broke the engagement off – when my grandfather came to town?'

'Yes.' He sighed. 'I suppose it was inevitable. He was wealthy, assured, he owned a car – it mightn't have been the first vehicle in Glenfield, but it impressed Ellie. A week after she met him, she came to the bakery to tell me she'd changed her mind. She was wearing new gloves – a present from him. He waited out front in the car while she told me.' He contemplated his cup. 'She said she was sorry, but it was her life and she didn't intend to spend it waiting. Youth is always in such a hurry,' he observed sadly. 'You learn that when it's too late to savour the days.' He put his cup tidily on the tray. 'You young ones want to be sure to savour yours. A world of regret awaits those who don't.'

'I'm sorry,' I said again. 'But money or not, I think she came to rue her choice. Perhaps unhappiness made her bitter. She alienated everyone and, in the end, had nobody to love.'

'I'm sorry to hear it. Poor Ellie.' He shook his head. 'But it's old history and this is your night, after all. So when will the wedding be?'

I looked at Phillip. 'We haven't decided yet.'

'Soon,' he said, his eyes crinkling.

'And you never married?' I guessed.

The old man smiled at that. 'I'm not quite such a hopeless romantic! Ellie was my first love, but then I met Rosa. I lost her after only ten years – wonderful years, they were – but when she was gone too, my heart called it quits.'

'No,' I contradicted, 'you still care about things. About people . . . Look how kind you've been to us. And your work. This place, it's so perfect – the appointments, the service, the food – I'm sure it's all down to you. And I saw how my grandmother's death affected you. She was a fool to ever let you get away.'

His lids, thin and crepey, crinkled as he smiled. 'It's kind of you to say so. You were fond of her?'

'No, I'm afraid I wasn't,' I said honestly. 'Your paths didn't cross at all, then?' They couldn't have done if he really hadn't known what she was like.

He shook his head. 'I was gone for many years. I came back in the seventies, but it's a big town. I might glimpse her in the street, or driving by, but they never came to the restaurant.'

'Only her,' Phillip said. 'Chapman died in sixty-nine. They had two daughters but lost both young, and Meg here was the only offspring.'

'Then I am glad we have met, my dear.' He rose and took my hand, bowing over it with old-fashioned grace. 'An old, unhappy story. But now you have your own to make. I hope that tonight is just the start of a wonderful future.'

'Thank you,' I said, leaning to kiss his cheek. 'My grandmother was very foolish. I'd have chosen you any day.'

His eyes twinkled. 'I'm flattered. Now it grows late, so I'll wish you both goodnight.'

It was then that I noticed that the harpist had gone and the tables behind us had emptied. I thanked him again and collected my bag, while Phillip went to the bar to pay. Outside, the streets had quietened and the air was still and cool. Phillip took my hand as we walked to the car.

'It was a lovely evening,' I said. 'Thank you. And wasn't he an old sweetie? How different do you suppose Grandmother might have been if she had married him?'

'We'll never know, Elf. If she had, she mightn't have stuck around until he succeeded. It probably took a few years – longer with the Depression, and then the war. If she wanted money so badly, it could've been a real disaster for them both.'

'There's that,' I admitted. 'Life's awfully uncertain, isn't it?'

'It's an adventure, love. And it sounds like the old boy did find a partner to share his with, however briefly.'

'Yes, sad that he lost his wife. Did you organise the champagne?'

'No, that was his idea. Like the coffee. Neither was on the bill. I think he just liked the look of you.' He kissed me there in the street, a coffee-flavoured kiss that I returned with interest. 'And who wouldn't, my affianced love?'

I watched the streetlight flash on the ruby as I raised my hand to smooth his rumpled hair. 'I do adore you, Phillip. What next?'

'Well, I thought,' he said, opening the car door for me, 'that you'd meet the parents, then we'd have our holiday, which, by the by, will be our honeymoon. We can get married while we're down there. My mother – what?' he asked, for I was shaking my head.

'I can't,' I said. 'We can't. Jake has to be there too. I couldn't not ask him to my wedding.'

'Well, we will. Of course we will! Oh, you're thinking he couldn't afford it? I'll sub him, okay?'

'Would you? He might refuse.'

'We'll work something out,' he said patiently. 'He's not going to refuse to please you even at the cost of accepting a loan, if that's what it takes.'

'All right, then. I'll ask Betty too. The farm's leased, so she can probably afford it. She must be my oldest friend. And about your mother, Phillip – is she going to expect a big church wedding?' I asked with some trepidation. 'Because—'

He grinned and flicked my nose. 'It's us getting married, not her, Elf. You must choose, but I thought a celebrant in a garden somewhere? There's no shortage of lovely spots on the Apple Isle.'

'Yes,' I said, relaxing. 'That would be just right. I couldn't wish for a better idea. It's been a lovely, lovely evening. We should do what he said – Michael – and savour every moment.'

'That we will,' he agreed. 'It's a night for lovers. Let's go home.'

He didn't speak again until we had turned in at the opened gates, striped black and silver by the moonlight. Ahead, Hunters Reach was a solid block of shadow nestled into the dark sea of its garden. I could glimpse its chimneys outlined against the starry sky and, through the opened car window, smell the fragrance of the garden – damp earth mixed with the scents of lavender and lemon blossom. The tree seemed to be constantly in flower. As a child I had dreaded my arrival here but now I felt only a charged anticipation for the night ahead.

'I imagine,' Phillip's voice came softly from the dimness of the moon-striped vehicle, 'that we won't forget this place in a hurry. So much tragedy played out here . . . Did the Telfords ever learn about your mother's murder?'

'I don't know. I guess it was up to Josh Latten to tell them, or Cabot when he drew up the sale papers.' I shivered. 'I didn't feel that it was my place to do so.'

'Of course it wasn't. Are you cold?' His arm enclosed my shoulders.

'No, just a wandering ghost. I will be glad to leave tomorrow. Whatever the Telfords make of it, for me it's still an unhappy house. Do you know – in a way I'm glad Grandmother threw Michael over. He's such a nice old man and she wouldn't have made him happy. Not the way his Rosa apparently did.'

Phillip opened the car door. 'You're right there. Seeing your gran valued money and status so much, she'd probably have driven him to an early grave trying to match her expectations.'

'Well, luckily, I don't have any of you.' We'd reached the door of the house. He turned the key and felt left-handed for the light switch.

'What – none?' Phillip pulled a face, eyes widened in mock surprise. His hair had come free from its tie at the back and curled about the angle of his jaw, half obscuring his smile. 'And here I was looking forward to a night of unbridled passion.'

'Oh, yes,' I agreed, 'but beyond that. Once we're married, the most I want is that someday I may be able to train you into picking up your own clothes.'

Chapter Thirty-five

The following morning, the furniture truck arrived before the Telfords did. I suggested to the driver that they wait for the owners before unloading and provided tea to pass the time. Leaving Phillip with the removalists, chatting and making toast on demand, I wandered into the garden and encountered Jake, who had driven in behind the movers.

I told him about the wedding, showed him my ring and added my invitation. 'Will you come, Jake? I really want you to. It will only be a small affair. A civil ceremony in a garden somewhere. You could give me away – I'd like that, to have someone of my own there with me.'

'Course I will, Meg. Be proud to.' He swallowed and smiled. 'Never thought I'd have the chance to see my own daughter wed. So when's it gonna be?'

'It depends how long the arrangements take, but I'll let you know. And if the airfare's a problem—'

He stopped me. 'It won't be. I'll get there if I have to swim. So, what're you doing out here? I've come by to pick up my tools, an' say goodbye, of course.'

'Yes. Betty's coming over later for a farewell smoko. I'm just having a last look round. You've done a wonderful job.' I glanced at the repair work on the pergola. 'That was certainly above and beyond. Where did you get the post?'

'Reject, I reckon, from the power company. It was lyin' outside the fence under that mess of bougainvillea, so I just cut 'er to fit.' He looked about with complacent pride. 'Yeah, the old place looks a bit diff'rent now. Mind, that wreck of a garden shed oughta come down – got a proper lean on it an' there's borers in the rafters.'

'Tell the owners,' I suggested. 'Ten to one they'll hire you to do it. Do you know what those little white plants are in the bed over there? They're very pretty.'

'Where? Oh, that's Sweet Alice. Got some other name but that's the common 'un.'

I was impressed. 'You continually surprise me, Jake.'

He shrugged. 'Ah, you get around, pick stuff up. Couldn't really help it, hanging round the Chapman girls.'

'I suppose. Did they teach you the language of flowers too? The meaning behind the blossoms in a bouquet?'

'Only irises.' He smiled reminiscently. 'Thought I was so bloody smart nuttin' that one out. I got three of 'em an' a bit of fern from the florist an' gave 'em to your mother the day I asked her to marry me. Last of the great romantics, that's me.'

'And what do they mean – eternal love or something?'

'Nope. *I carry a message.* Of course, she knew what the message was.'

For a moment I saw the ageing man before me as the ardent, fit young footballer he had been and felt a pang of sorrow for all he had lost – well, never had really to lose, for the proverbial cup had been dashed from his lips following the first sip. It was so unfair! My heart ached for him and my attention was only recalled as he abruptly asked, 'He's good to you, that bloke of yours?'

'Phillip is wonderful,' I said simply. 'Untidy, but that's his worst failing. My love, my rock. You don't have to worry about me, Dad.' The word hung in the air between us. It had come almost unbidden to my lips, brought forth, I thought, by the question that any father might ask about a young man who proposed to marry his daughter. I heard him catch his breath before he smiled.

'Thank you, Meg.'

'You're my father,' I said simply, linking my arm with his. 'Come on, complete the tour with me.'

Betty arrived just ahead of the Telfords, who apologised for their lateness. The men with the truck were growing restive by then and immediately began hauling the furniture out and transferring it to the rooms. Only the grand piano, a large sideboard and the double bed were put into their permanent positions. Harvey, who I thought had correctly read the moving men's impatience over their enforced wait, told them just to put the rest wherever there was room.

'We'll sort it out from there,' he told them. Linda raised her brows at him but he said briefly, 'It'll be fine.' Then he took Jake aside and when I heard my father declare he had nothing in particular on for the rest of the day, I knew they had reached an agreement and who would be assisting Harvey. It would be ironic, I thought, if Jake were to find a permanent job at the place he had once been thrown off by my grandfather.

When smoko was over and Phillip and I had both received a misty hug from Betty, with a promise that wild horses wouldn't keep her from the wedding, I touched Linda on the arm. 'Can you spare a moment? I just want to show you something.'

'Of course.' She smiled, eyes gleaming in her tanned face. A faint fragrance clung about her, flower-like and pleasant. 'It's so exciting finally being here,' she said. 'I'm sorry we were so late arriving. Who does the cat belong to?'

'You.' I led her out through the garden and down to where the bougainvillea flowered. 'My grandmother died, so he stays with the Reach.'

'Oh.' She obviously hadn't heard. 'I'm so sorry, Meg. Of course we never met her but still—'

'It's okay.' I paused beside the huge planter. 'This is what I wanted to show you. Remember you said you'd grow pansies and whatever in this? Well, I don't know what they are, but something's beaten you to it.' Across the wide bowl of the planter, dozens of little green spears had thrust up through the soil.

She looked delighted, clapping her hands together and then squeezing them like an excited child. 'Oh, but that's wonderful! They're iris. I wonder what colour? Purple, yellow, white – they'd all be perfect with the magenta of the bougainvillea behind them. Oh, that's brilliant, Meg. Why – is something wrong?'

'No, of course not. I'm just'—I fumbled for an explanation—'amazed that you can take one look and instantly know . . . So you're sure they're iris? Those blue lily-looking things?'

'Well, quite different to lilies really – they have corms, not bulbs, and a different form – but, yes, they're certainly iris.

She was a real artist, your grandmother, only her canvas was earth and she painted with flowers.'

And maybe, I thought, grieved with them. For the daughter she had never mentioned and whose supposedly shameful death she wouldn't permit herself to openly mourn. My mother had had no grave or headstone; the police had established that. But lying forgotten by the world under the black well water, she had still had this secret memorial, here in the heart of Ellie Chapman's domain. I looked again but I hadn't previously noticed anything on the planter, and nor could I find an inscription now, just smooth, slightly stained plaster covering the cement casing.

I carry a message – of what? Remorse, forgiveness, sorrow? Linda was speaking, moving away, pausing to smell a rose and name it. I followed silently, lost in my thoughts. Who would have imagined that behind her iron facade Ellie Chapman was capable of anything so human as grief? Of sentiment of any kind? But if she had coldbloodedly thrown Michael over for a better financial prospect, she had still kept his gift of love. And while she may have grown a floral shrine to her dead daughter, she had also wickedly harmed my father, and ill-used me.

The others were waiting on us, grouped out the front on the gravel beside my car, all with the air of people running out of things to say. The truck had already gone and Betty's trike was vanishing down the driveway.

We were all responsible for our choices, I reminded myself, shaking hands with the Telfords, hugging Jake – Dad, I had to get used to calling him Dad – and we lived with the consequences. Phillip was holding the passenger door open for me, so he meant to drive.

'Come on, Elf,' he said good-humouredly.

'Sorry.' I grabbed for the seatbelt. 'I was just showing Linda the flowers in the planter, but I'm here now.'

'Right. Hahndorf tonight, Adelaide tomorrow. One day to organise everything and then we're off. Okay?'

'Whatever you say.' I smiled as the engine caught and leaned across to touch his cheek.

My choice, my responsibility. My love.

Acknowledgements

My thanks as always to the amazing crew at Penguin Random House: my publisher Ali Watts, editor Amanda Martin, cover designer Louisa Maggio and proofreader Sonja Heijn, all of whom contribute so much to my books.